The Past Master

The Past Master

Kenneth Cameron

FELONY & MAYHEM PRESS • NEW YORK

All the characters and events portrayed in this work are fictitious.

THE PAST MASTER

A Felony & Mayhem mystery

PRINTING HISTORY
First UK edition, ebook (Orion): 2013

Felony & Mayhem edition (First US edition): 2022

Copyright © 2013 by Kenneth Cameron

ISBN: 978-1-63194-265-5

Manufactured in the United States of America

Cataloging-in-Publication information for this book
is available from the Library of Congress.

About the Author

Kenneth Cameron was the author of seven novels featuring Denton, as well as of plays staged in Britain and the US, the award-winning *Africa on Film: Beyond Black and White*, and many other books, as well. He divided his time between northern New York State and the southern US, and he passed away in 2021.

Acknowledgements and Sources

As with the other of the Denton books, I owe much to the support and insight of Bill Massey, my editor at Orion.

Leon Edel's *Henry James, A Life* and Miranda Seymour's *A Ring of Conspirators, Henry James and His Literary Circle, 1895–1915* gave me most of the biographical information I needed. I read and enjoyed but did not pilfer from, I hope, Colm Tóibín's *The Master* and Joyce Carol Oates's 'The Master at St Bartholomew's Hospital, 1914–1916' (in *Wild Nights*). Ann Thwaite's *Edmund Gosse* was useful but was not responsible for my notion of Gosse. Frederick Porter Wensley's *Detective Days* gave me the details of the 'battle of Sidney Street', of which I give a fictionalised (and altered) version. I continue to use Hargrave L. Adam's multi-volume *Police Encyclopedia* and H. Childs's *'Police Duty' Catechism and Reports,* as well as such websites as those of the Metropolitan Police, Derelict London, the Booth Poverty Map, and MAPCO London and Environs. And, as always, the essential Baedeker's *Handbook of London* (several editions, 1894–1906) and John Ayto's *Oxford Dictionary of Slang*.

The icon above says you're holding a copy of a book in the Felony & Mayhem "Historical" category, which ranges from the ancient world up through the 1940s. If you enjoy this book, you may well like other "Historical" titles from Felony & Mayhem Press.

———

For more about these books, and other Felony & Mayhem titles, or to place an order, please visit our website at:

www.FelonyAndMayhem.com

Other "Historical" titles from

FELONY&MAYHEM

The Past Master

CHAPTER 1

'We look like a herd of penguins, waiting for Scott to discover us.'

Denton gave an obligatory smile. The other man, an editor whose name he couldn't remember at some firm he couldn't be sure of—was it Dent's? at least not the one that published Denton's own books—drifted away. They did look peculiar, he thought—a lot of mostly middle-aged men in evening clothes, standing around sweating in the cavernous ballroom of the Russell Square Hotel, waiting for a ceremonial dinner that he supposed none of them wanted to eat. It was summer, the air thick, a humid fug of tobacco and warm bodies. Denton, vulnerable to bouts of lassitude, felt like lying down on the floor.

'Aha.' A hand closed around his right elbow. The grip was firm. Henry James had hold of him.

'James. How are you?'

The bald head sagged. 'Only just back from our native shores, and not all, not much, not, um, significantly the wiser or the better or the more, um, feasted on the food of the soul than before I left. I am, however, now I am back in England, in the situation of the traveller in the desert who at last finds himself in an oasis.' The grip tightened; the arm was shaken slightly, as if it were a shoe in the teeth of a puppy. 'And you?'

Where James was shorter and stout and thoroughly English-looking, Denton was tall and lean and even in bespoke evening clothes looked American. The long moustache that hung down both sides of his mouth like Spanish moss only reinforced the idea of a Western cowboy somehow put into an English gent's clothes. He said, 'We were in Naples but we came home because there was cholera. I heard you were back. The States not your cup of tea?'

James shook the gloomy Roman head. '*Entre nous*, if not quite horrible, it was certainly something less than, mm, a delight. Our countrymen have chosen to live in a world of noise and constant, frenetic motion, busyness, comings and goings, whose goal, whose purport, whose destination, I must say, seemed to me hardly worthy of the effort. The women have the least pleasant voices I have heard outside the confines of the Regent's Park zoological gardens, the young ones the worst. If I say that the letter D has dropped from the middle of the collo-quial "didn't", you will understand me.' He sighed. 'They seem to believe that the nose exists to be spoken through.' He shuddered, surely done for effect; Denton saw that James was enjoying his own disgust. 'And the new buildings! I am making a book of it.'

Denton laughed. 'To make yourself popular in America?'

James shook his head again. 'Popularity has escaped me. It flees forever uncaught, like Keats's maiden, taking a good deal of one's hoped-for income with it.' His blackbird eyes peered into the crowd. 'Why, I wonder, are we giving George Meredith a dinner in the middle of July?'

'They thought he was dying, decided it was now or never. He wasn't, as it turned out.'

'I am surprised to see you at this sort of revel. I thought you a recluse. But just as well.' He caught Denton's elbow again and turned him slightly, moving closer and dropping his voice to a rumble. 'I wished to see you to plead that I be allowed to discuss a, mmm, somewhat sensitive, a, mmm, delicate, a potentially perhaps *distressing* matter—in your *other* capacity, I mean, not in any sense your literary one, but rather the, mm, other. Not your métier but your avocation?'

Denton of course knew what 'other' meant. Thirty years before, he had briefly been the marshal of a tiny Nebraska town. The legend dragged after him like Marley's cash boxes. Even in London, many people thought of him as a scourge of lawlessness first, an author second. He tried not to sound resigned as he said, 'Has something happened?'

James inhaled, the sound as quick and sharp as the passing of a bullet. 'One might say so. But not to be spoken of here. I wonder if I might impose, if I might intrude, if I might—'

'Call on me? I'd be honoured.' He wouldn't, but it was the sort of thing he thought he should say to Henry James. 'When?'

'Ah. Mmm.' James looked around, head lowered, a bull looking for something or somebody to gore. 'Later this evening?'

Denton started to frown, caught himself. He had hoped to go right home and get into bed with Janet Striker, if she were still awake. James sounded serious, however, and Denton always had trouble resisting an appeal to his 'other' self. He said, 'Well, if it's urgent—'

'I suppose this otiose affair will end by eleven. You live quite close, I believe; I shall come on foot. No, don't wait for me here; people will be tedious and want to talk. You go on; I shall follow.' James's head came up; his nostrils flared; his eyes narrowed and changed from the sharpness of a bird's to the hostility of a street cat's; he inhaled sharply again. 'There's that awful man Harris. Is he heading our way?'

Denton saw the somewhat notorious Frank Harris dodge between two black-suited men and, indeed, head towards them. James whispered, 'He is! I can't abide him!'

Denton didn't say that Harris was a kind of friend; he wasn't quite sure what kind.

'Here you, here you are!' Harris shouted. His shark's smile threatened to devour them both.

James looked over Harris's head. 'Oh, there's Percy! I absolutely *must* speak to him.' He went past Harris as if he weren't there, their shoulders almost touching.

Harris looked after him and turned his ferocious grin back on Denton. 'I'm the only man in London to whom Henry James regularly refuses to speak. Should I feel flattered?'

'Are you actually sober, Harris? What's wrong?'

Harris's usually inflamed eyes were clear; neither hand held a drink. He patted his abdomen. 'Quack's orders. Merely temporary.' Harris turned and looked where James had pulled up next to a much younger man. 'Aha, now I see—he passed me up for a tenderer cut of meat.'

'Who's that?'

'Somebody named Lubbock—one of James's young men. There are only two criteria: that they be very good-looking and that they call him *cher maître*. Beyond that, they can drop their H's and have unknown antecedents and smelly drawers and it won't matter.'

'Is that libel or slander?'

'Common gossip. You're such a prig, Denton. Ah, look there—it's Violet Hunt, the very last of the *very* last of the Pre-Raphaelites. Known to those who've seen the far side of her knickers as the Violent Cunt, although I've not had the pleasure. You? We must be the only two literary men in London who haven't. They say she has a new young man. Name of Raphael something—you suppose it's his real name? He's another of James's laddies.' He turned back. 'What're you doing at a dinner for a has-been like Meredith, anyway? No food at home?'

Denton muttered something about honouring Meredith's long career. 'He did the best he could, Harris.'

'That's the trouble with him.' Harris bounced on his toes, rubbed his fingers against his palms. 'You've been away. Italy again?' He made a face, something between disgust and resignation. 'I do hate being sober at this sort of do.' He ran a hand over his thick, wavy hair. 'Eddie Gas says you've got one foot in the abyss of vulgarity—you hear about that?'

By Eddie Gas, Denton knew he meant the critic Edmund Gosse. Gosse was in fact somewhere in the vast room. 'He said that to you just now?'

'No, no, wrote it in the *Review*. Warned you sternly that you are "pressurising Realism"—his word, pressurising, not mine—beyond the limits of good taste.'

'Makes good taste sound like the kitchen geyser.'

'Or my bladder. I really think I need a pee. Maybe a small whisky to go with it. Join me?'

'I think you'll enjoy both more alone.'

Harris sighed. 'One can't be said to enjoy a *small* whisky.'

A gong rang. The herd of London's literary best began to migrate towards the tables at the far end of the space. Harris said, 'Christ, now everybody will want to pee.'

Denton went up his own stairs and into his sitting room, trying to be quiet but nonetheless getting attention that produced a cry from the floor below. He shouted, 'It's me, Sergeant!'

The muffled voice came again. Denton thought it said, 'I didn't think it was Otto von Bismarck.' He dropped his silk hat and stick on a chair and strode the few steps to the top of his servant's stairs. 'Somebody's coming to see me in a few minutes. You don't need to do anything—this is business, not social.'

Atkins's head appeared at the bottom of the stair. Another, larger head appeared lower down, then a smaller one below it—two dogs, father and son. Atkins said, 'I suppose you think I don't have to answer the door if it isn't social.'

'I'll answer the door myself.'

'Who is it's coming?'

'Henry James. An author.'

'Oh, like I don't know who Henry James is. "An author," my hat. You think I'm going to have you answering the door to Mr Henry James? What would he think?'

'Who cares?'

'I care! This is a respectable house, General.'

Denton got called by a number of military titles, depending on Atkins's mood. They had both been in an army, Atkins in the

British for thirty years as a soldier servant, Denton as a Union infantryman in the American Civil War. It gave them a small common ground to bridge the gulf of class.

Denton mused on his curious relationship with Atkins for the thousandth time as he went out and along the side of his own house into the back garden, then through a door in the rear wall and so to the house behind. He let himself in, went up to the first floor and found Janet Striker in her study, as he'd expected. She was asleep, however, surrounded by three dogs, one very like the larger of the two that had appeared with Atkins. On the floor stood a pile of books: having finished University College at the age of thirty-nine, she was now an articled solicitor's clerk, so as to become a solicitor herself.

She opened her eyes. 'God, what time is it?' Her voice was husky, words slurred with sleep.

'After eleven. I've got a guest coming.'

She stared at him. 'Better you than me. I'm going to bed.'

'With me, I hope.'

She got up, rested briefly against him. 'It wouldn't do you much good. I'm exhausted.'

'You never know.'

She let him kiss her. He said, 'Sleep in my house, anyway.'

'Sleep is all I'd do.'

'Still.'

She said, 'I'll get some things.' She made her way out of the room as if she couldn't see, feeling for the doorway, then holding it as she rounded towards the stairs to her bedroom, the dogs padding behind.

He called, 'I'll be at home.'

She was gone. He went down again and into her garden and through the gate into his own. Light spilled from the open door to Atkins's quarters, Atkins partly silhouetted in it, watching the larger of his own dogs as he squatted.

Denton said, 'May I take the shortcut through your sitting room?'

'It's your house.'

'Dammit, Atkins...!'

'Sorry, General, sorry. Yes, of course, go right on through. Sit and have a cup of tea if you like.'

'Mrs Striker is coming through, too.'

'I could lay on some eatables, if you want.'

'Mrs Striker is going to sleep. Henry James was at the same beanfeast I was. No need.'

'Beanfeast? That's US, is it? You mean it's *British*? I'll have to remember that one. Good boy!' This last was to Rupert, the big dog. The smaller one trotted up out of the darkness and paused to sniff his father's leavings. 'Yesterday a beanfeast, today a pile of night soil. The story of life. All right, boys, inside.'

Denton, uncomfortable at best in evening dress, saw no reason to go on submitting to it; he climbed another storey and replaced the evening clothes with flannel trousers and an old shirt and a smoking jacket so threadbare at the cuffs that tendrils hung down around his wrists. Hating scarves, ascots, that sort of stuff, he put on a necktie for James's sake and went down in time to greet Janet, who drowsily kissed him and made her way upstairs. Denton was waiting in his armchair when the doorbell rang.

Henry James came into the sitting room rubbing his hands together as if he were cold and saying 'Ah' several times. With him came an odour of mature male—recently ironed wool, sweat, shaving soap, brandy. Behind him, Atkins followed with his hat and a coat that James surely hadn't worn in the heat. After murmuring 'Anything else, sir?' to Denton, Atkins actually gave a small bow before disappearing. All this was for James's benefit, perhaps in hope of a tip. James, after watching him go, said, 'You're quite comfortable here.' He seemed surprised.

'Whisky? Brandy?'

James shook his head. 'Those wines! How could they!'

'They went with the food.'

'Why is it that we honour people by eating badly, do you suppose? No, nothing for me, many thanks.' James sat in a chair opposite Denton's, seeming to understand which was Denton's and which the guest's, a man sensitive to small signs—in this case, perhaps, the deep dent in the more used of the chairs. Denton, too, sat; they now faced each other across the width of a small fireplace with a coal grate, now of course cold, fitted with some sort of paper fan that Atkins must have put there while Denton was changing. The rest of the wall was covered with books. James said, 'You read my brother's works, I see.'

'A lot of psychology, in fact. Yours are up there, too.'

James raised a hand, as if the idea would never occur to him. He seemed about to say something but stopped and looked down the room towards Atkins's stair. The electric light, far from flattering, put the lines of his face into shade, Denton thinking that he looked older and heavier than when they had last met a couple of years before. James had become imposing, perhaps senatorial (of Rome, not Washington); he seemed now in the shadows somewhat vulturish. The stare was intense. Suddenly he smiled, happily, handsomely. 'Goodness, it's a little doggy!'

Denton half turned. 'Oh, dammit.' The smaller of the two dogs had found his way upstairs. He was several months old, a mutt, yet peculiarly sure of himself; he would never be big but behaved as if he were. His body was a bit too long, his legs a bit too short; he had silky hair from his mother, apparently nothing from his father. He carried his head well up, his pointed ears even more so. He made for Henry James as if he'd heard of him.

'Well, doggy—well, well, well. Wha—'

The dog trotted down the room and without hesitating jumped into James's lap. Denton was snapping his fingers and making stern sounds.

James sounded delighted. 'Now, Nickie, now, now—Nickie, dear...!' He was leaning a little back from the dog, who had put his pointed nose very close to the great man's beak. 'Nickie—mustn't lick...!' He looked at Denton. 'Only listen to me! I called him Nickie. My dear little Nick—he passed away last year; I still grieve...'

'He's yours if you fancy him.' Denton had given up sounding stern, now sounded grumpy. 'We're having a time of it, getting rid of him.'

'Oh, no, no—down, little one, lie down—I couldn't; I'm at present at the Reform; they don't allow dogs. There.' The dog had curled neatly on James's thighs. 'Do you really mean to get rid of him? How could you?'

Denton explained the accidental, in fact unwanted, coupling that had produced the little dog—Atkins's Rupert and Janet's Sophie, cause of a lot of accusation and anger now past. 'His mother was one of those Neapolitan pups they throw into the gas of the Solfitara to show you how quickly it'll kill them. I grabbed her in time.'

'Oh, good, very good! How cruel people are. He has the look of a Welsh corgi.'

'He's a mutt on both sides, I'm afraid.'

'But some sheep-herding blood, don't you think? In Naples, the mother might have been entirely from a line of sheep dogs back to the era of the Greeks. Accidental breeding. One finds it in people, doesn't one.' James was slowly stroking the dog's head and back. It had fallen asleep. 'Does he bark awfully?'

'Never that I've heard.'

'I have always had dachshunds. They can be quite annoying in that way.'

Denton said nothing; dogs, he thought—hoped—had been exhausted as a subject. James was temporising, he was sure; if it hadn't been the little dog, it would have been something else. Books. He decided to let silence force James to whatever he had come to say.

James looked around the room. When their eyes met, he gave Denton a flickering smile. In the bad light, his face seemed to be suffering. He stroked the dog. At last he said, not looking at Denton but at his hands, 'I have encountered a difficulty.'

Denton waited. He thought of Janet in bed, the arousing comfort of her haunch.

James cleared his throat. 'This is rather embarrassing for me.' He looked at Denton again, got nothing, seemed to start over. 'We are mere acquaintances. I am imposing on you as if we had some long-standing friendship.' He stroked the dog, began yet again. 'You have made yourself expert in the ways of criminals, I believe.'

At last he had got to it. Denton allowed himself to make a sound, admitting nothing but denying nothing.

'I own a house, as you may know, in Rye. In Sussex. It is my particular treasure, my pleasure, I suppose my pride. Six days ago, it was burglarised. I was still at sea.' Again, he looked at Denton; again he got nothing. As if understanding that Denton hadn't heard of it and wanting to explain, James said, 'We managed to keep it out of the London newspapers. I was able to persuade, to cajole, to, mmm, cause the Sussex Chief Constable to call in New Scotland Yard. I learned that one can do so from my solicitor; I suppose you know all about such things.'

'Who did they send?' Something flickered across James's face—distaste, Denton thought, for his deliberate 'who', as if 'whom' had been cruelly treated.

'A Detective Inspector Wragge. A rough diamond, but *quite* a good man, I think. He seems to understand my situation, my preference for delicacy, my, mmm, *grippe* at public outcry. He visited the house with me and quite an extensive team of policemen—I was dumbfounded by their carefulness, their dedication, their, mmm, *passion* for detail. The consequence is that Wragge believes the burglary to have been done by a professional London gang.'

'Fingerprints?'

'Ah, you know about those, of course. Yes, talcum powder everywhere. My housekeeper was more than upset. Wragge is making inquiries in the Jewish East End, which is where these gangs seem to originate. You have heard of them?'

Denton grunted. Suburban houses had become easy marks for highly organised London criminals; some were said even to move about by motor-car. Advance scouts and watchers were thought to go back and forth by tramcar and underground trains like businessmen. Rye, however, seemed far to Denton—at least he had never heard of one of the London crews going so near the coast. He said, 'Your house was empty?'

'I had had tenants. I was in America for months and months, you know. But they had vacated at my request when I knew I was returning. So yes, the house was empty. I had told my housekeeper to use the time to visit her mother, who is very old and unwell. The maids, two very silly local girls, were supposed to be there, but it appears they were not. Wragge opined an "inside job".'

'And was it?'

'Wragge's decided that in fact the two girls seem blameless, if irresponsible. They're little more than children. Somebody invited them to ride in a motor-car, which they found irresistible.' He waited for Denton to say something, then added, 'The gardener lives elsewhere. Also the young man who serves me in a somewhat general capacity. However, all that's neither here nor there—it isn't the nature or the cause of the crime that concerns me. The police will deal capably with all that, I'm sure.'

Denton was sure, too: no point in James's having come to him unless there was something he particularly didn't want the police to know. Overhead, a footfall sounded—Janet in bare feet. James looked up, then wiped curiosity from his face. Denton said, 'And so?'

James's massive head was down. He seemed to be looking at the dog. He said, 'I have great difficulty in speaking of this.' He raised his eyes. 'I ask you to keep this in the most strict kind of confidence. As, as, as a fellow literary man.' He waited until Denton nodded, then said in the slow tempo that announces importance, 'Something is missing from my house that was very dear to me.' He met Denton's eyes. 'It was *very* dear to me.'

Running water sounded distantly, and the soft explosion of the WC. Neither man gave any sign he had heard.

'What?'

James sighed. 'A box. Wood, probably Florentine, possibly sixteenth century. The sort of thing of which they sell cheap copies all over today's Florence—gold and red, a heraldic design, and so on. Not of any great monetary value, so I don't know why a gang of thieves should have taken it!'

'The gold?'

'It was much worn. They took a number of things of real value, *objets de vertu*, my silver, a certain amount of jewellery, several smaller pieces of furniture that are what are called "antiques". Two paintings. A brass fender and the best fire set. My ormolu clock. Wragge has a list.'

Janet's footsteps moved, to Denton's surprise, towards the front of the house; was she so exhausted she was not able to sleep?

'They knew their business.'

'Wragge says they knew what would re-sell.' James's eyes went to the ceiling. Denton said, 'I have a house guest. Nothing can be heard upstairs that's said down here.' James looked pained. 'Did you tell Wragge about the box?'

James stroked the dog. 'No.'

'What was in it?'

The sharp eyes came up again; the dog, disturbed because James was disturbed, got up and turned around on James's thighs and, after sniffing at his neck, lay down again and put its head on its paws. Denton felt as if James's eyes were boring through to the back of his head. James said, 'I must trust you. I *must* trust you. You have that reputation—a man of law.' He bounced his fingers on the arms of his chair, made some kind of decision. 'Some papers. In the box.' He touched his forehead. 'This is *very* difficult for me, Denton!'

'It's why you came to see me, though, isn't it?'

'What I want is advice as to how to proceed.'

'Tell the police. That's my advice.'

'No!' James reached to a table beside him, opened a box of cigarettes, glanced at Denton for permission and took one. He sighed again. 'What I shall tell you next has been a secret all my adult life. You must promise me, Denton, on whatever God we trust, you and I, that you will keep it secret.'

Denton didn't hesitate. 'All right.' Before James could go on, he jumped in with a correction: 'Secret within the bounds of the law.'

James lit the cigarette with a match from the box that lay on the table, holding both match and cigarette where they couldn't fall on the little dog. He waved the match until it was out and placed it in the very centre of a glass-lined ashtray. 'When I first lived in Paris many years ago, I stayed in the house of a family friend. My family travelled constantly when I was a child; my father seemed to know everybody. When I decided to come to Europe on my own, this man was one of those to whom my father wrote letters for me. He—the friend—was very kind. He provided me with two rooms in his very large apartment in the *faubourg*.' James drew on the cigarette, exhaled; the smell of the tobacco had already reached Denton, enticed him. He started to reach for a cigarette, thought better of it—he was rowing on the river every day, distrusted the effect of smoking on what he called his 'wind'. Instead, he poured himself a whisky, offered James the bottle and was refused with a shake of the head.

'The Florentine box sat on a shelf in my friend's study—exactly as it was to sit on a shelf in mine. I hardly noticed it in the beginning. Then one day, he opened it and showed me the contents. I was reading a great deal of Balzac at the time, trying to write like Balzac—I'd made rather a deity of him, I think—and so I suppose I was bowled over to see that in the box was a *novelette* by the master. In manuscript. His own handwriting! Never published, my friend said, never known. And with it, five letters from Balzac. He was just the age when he wrote them that I was when I first read them.'

'Love letters?'

'Of course. How acute you are. To a young woman. In one, he asked her to marry him. In another, clearly she had refused him. In the last, he sent the *novelette*, telling her it was the best work of his life and that he gave it to her as an offering. A *cadeau d'amour*. He said the usual things that I suppose a romantic young man says—that she would never see him again, that he hoped she would sometimes take the manuscript out and think of him, that when he was old and famous she would know what they both had lost. Romantic, perhaps sentimental, but *profoundly felt*.' James drew on the cigarette very slowly and gently, then put his head back and exhaled in the same way. 'It had the effect on me of some great, some transcendental event. To touch something that Balzac had created and *given up*! I walked around for days with that moment in my head. I wanted... I desired...'

'You wanted it.'

'It went far beyond that feeble gerund *wanting*.'

'*The Aspern Papers*.'

James's mouth gave back that closed-lips smile that is a kind of wince. 'You *have* read my work.' He ground out the cigarette in the silver ashtray and reached for another. 'Yes, when I came to write *The Aspern Papers* of course it was in my mind; how could it not be? But there was no woman who demanded I marry her, nor was I a genteel cad. Or perhaps I was.' He lit the new cigarette.

'You stole the box?'

James's Roman mask was sombre, but he didn't flinch at the word *stole*. 'I fought with myself for a week. I had to leave the place for fear of what I might do. I made my excuses to my host and moved out. I came to London. I have never known a great deal of passion, Denton, only really the death of a young woman who seemed to me the very essence of youth and life, and what I felt at that death was horror, not romantic loss—is horror a passion? But my wanting the Balzac was a passion, I know.' He blew out smoke. 'Yes, I stole it.' He looked into Denton's eyes, a challenge. Denton nodded for him to go on.

'I went to Italy that winter. Going through Paris, it was as if I had planned it. I went to the *faubourg*, called, found that my friend was out—as I had thought he would be; he was a great maker of calls—and told the maid that I wished to return a book to his study. She knew me; she let me do it. I had bought a book on the *quai* for the purpose. I left him a note, as well. I took the box. Of course he knew who had done it.'

'But he let you get away with it.'

James smoked. Overhead, Janet's bare feet padded along the hall to the bedroom.

'He was a great aristocrat.'

Denton stared at him until James looked away. Denton said, 'What else was in the box when it was stolen from your house?'

Janet's footsteps returned to the front of the house. *What the hell was she doing?*

'Nothing. I took the Balzac and the letters and kept them all these years, but nothing else!'

'Not when *you* took it. When it was stolen *from* your house, I said.'

He saw that James was going to say there had been nothing else. That large, expressive mouth opened, the shrewd eyes narrowed; Henry James was going to tell a lie. He must have rehearsed the lie; he must have known how this tale would tell itself. Denton had actually read an essay that James had written about Balzac; in it, he had pointed out that what Balzac prized above all was deception, the ability to lie. He was about to be Balzacian.

And then he crumbled. 'You mustn't ask.' He actually shuddered. 'I'll have that brandy now.'

'If you won't tell me everything, then you mustn't ask for my help.'

'I can't!'

Denton shrugged. 'Let's talk about something else, then.' He got James his brandy and poured himself another whisky.

James struggled with himself. When he spoke at last, his voice was anguished. 'There were some other papers in the box. When it was stolen from me.'

'And they were...?'

'Denton, I can't, I can't...' His voice fell almost to a whisper. 'You don't need to know this to help me, you don't!'

'It's what it's all about. It's the only thing I *do* need to know.'

'No! The thieves couldn't have known what was in it and so there's no reason for you to know.'

'As I said, we might as well talk about something else.'

James put his head down so his nose was almost touching the dog's back. The dog's tail waved—pleasure? Gratitude? James said, 'They're such a comfort. Dogs.' With his face almost pressed into the dog's hairs, he muttered, 'There were some other letters.'

'To you?' Taking silence for the answer, Denton said, 'From him? The aristocrat?'

James raised his face. His eyes shone with the beginnings of tears. 'He gave me the Balzac. He turned my theft into a gift. He sounded hopeless. He loved me. I know how that must sound to you. But I'd done nothing.' He frowned. 'I was a very naïve young man. I knew everything from books, from gossip, from watching and listening, but I hadn't...done anything.' He straightened, drank off a good bit of his brandy. His eyes were still too bright; he seemed not to care. 'I have a particular aversion to the physical. I mean in its manifestation between, mm, between creatures. I used to be kept awake tormenting myself with the problem of the marriage night, teaching or showing or explaining to some young woman—all of that. I couldn't see then that it might be welcome even though I had such a horror of it myself. So you must believe me when I say that nothing had happened between this man and me. *Nothing happened!* Except...' He put his head back, his hands resting on the dog's back. 'Except I let him love me. As surely as a coquette lets, *makes* a man love her, I let him.' He shook his old, heavy head. 'That is how I knew I could steal the Balzac.' His voice was a whisper.

'That's in the letters?'

'I burned two of them when I got them. They were— unworthy. Literal. Offensive, in fact. But that he loved me, yes, that was in the letters.'

'Could you be blackmailed with them?'

'That isn't what concerns me.'

'Would you pay to get them back?'

'Of course—what do you think all this has been about?'

'So you *can* be blackmailed. Why?'

James stared at him. His eyes were dry now and hard as flints. 'Because I am so ashamed! Do you think that in my old age I want the world to know that I stole another man's property because I was a coquette? Do you think I want every greasy-handed newspaper reader knowing what he said about touching me and wanting to caress me? Do you think I want them reading into what he left vague, and inventing what isn't in his words? Because I am ashamed! Because it would all be true!' He thrust out his glass, now empty, the gesture demanding. Denton poured in more brandy. James, he thought, had already drunk enough at the dinner—Dutch courage?

Again James lowered his face to the dog. Denton felt as if the space around them had filled with a dense sadness, a darkness, a lowering of the heart. He could have told a different man that this sort of thing didn't matter; he could have told him to brazen it out; he could have told him to sue if the letters were ever made public. But he couldn't tell Henry James. James was a moralist. James was honest to a fault. James was a man for whom shame was permanent and hideous.

Denton leaned towards him. 'What do you want me to do?'

James raised his face. A few real tears were smeared on the pouchy cheeks. 'Get the box back.'

'The Balzac? Balzac's letters? Do you care about them?'

'No, no—I should have returned them years ago; they're merely a pleasant curiosity to me now; they're...*bibelots*. But *his* letters...' He made a sudden gesture with his head. The dog stood and then jumped down and trotted away. He paused at the head of the stairs and then plunged down; Denton heard him going down, front legs on the step below, then the rear, da-dump, da-dump, da-dump. James was looking after the dog, too; when he met Denton's eyes, he smiled. 'What an old fool I am.'

'No.' Denton was no good at saying wise things or comforting things. He got up and, on the excuse of emptying the ashtray, patted James's shoulder.

James said, 'I shall have just a whisper more of your brandy.'

Denton poured and put it down next to him, then sat. 'How did you leave it with the police?'

'They're to let me know if they recover my things. Wragge is working with somebody in the East End to try to find the gang. He believes that the detectives there know who the buyers of such stolen goods are.'

'*If* they try to sell the stuff. They may not for some time. The really organised gangs can afford to wait.' Denton poured himself another small whisky, thought of Harris, wondered how many small whiskies he'd managed by then. 'If you're lucky, your Wragge'll find the stuff and the box will be in it, unopened. Or they'll have forced the lock, seen the papers and closed it again. If, but it's unlikely, they're smarter than most criminals in fact are, one of them will see that the manuscript is old and take it to somebody who deals in such things. I'll ask around about that. Is your full name on the letters?'

'As "Henry James", do you mean? I think "Henry", perhaps even "Henri". I didn't keep the envelopes, I'm sure.'

'The sad fact is it's probably all in somebody's rubbish already. But...' Denton was running his fingers over the long moustache that hung down each side of his mouth.

'Yes?'

Denton shook his head. There was no point in making the man feel worse. 'I'll see if I can connect with your Inspector Wragge; everything may still be there if they actually find the stuff. Still, if the box turned out not to be with the rest of it...'

'Why wouldn't it be?'

Because maybe it was what they were really after and the rest was all theatricals. But Denton wasn't ready to say that, nor James, he knew, to hear it. 'I'd like to have the name of the man who wrote you the letters, also the names of the two housemaids who went out for a motor-car ride just when the burglars came. Plus the names of your tenants and anybody else who's been in your house in your absence. But that can wait a bit, if you like.'

Henry James was shaking his head. 'I'll not allow his name to become the subject of a vulgar inquiry.'

'All inquiries of this sort are vulgar. Also low and common. I want his name.'

'The man is dead!'

'Then he won't know how vulgar it is. You want my help; this is how I offer to help. Take it or leave it.'

'But I… You *promise* you'll be discreet.'

'For what it's worth, yes. But you're the victim of a crime, James. The least that crime is is vulgar.'

'You must promise me that anything you learn will be kept entirely private.'

'I won't break the law for you, if that's what you mean. But I'll keep it all to myself until doing so means crossing that line.'

James stared into his brandy for many seconds, at last said that he'd send the names tomorrow. Moments later, he put the brandy down and asked that Atkins be sent for a cab. While they waited, he said, 'I have told you something I have never told another human being, Denton. You hold my reputation in your hand.' Two minutes later, he was gone.

To Denton's surprise, Janet came down the stairs a few seconds after James's cab had clip-clopped away. She said, 'A rather remarkable thing.'

'I thought I heard you.'

She held out her hand. He took it, started up the stairs with her. She said, 'I found I couldn't sleep after all. I looked out the front window. There was a woman opposite—watching your house.'

'Professional?' The street had its share of prostitutes, mostly at the other end; the public house next door didn't like them hanging about.

'Middle-class *hausfrau*, I think. I watched her for a long time. Dowdy, completely dowdy. What was remarkable, when Atkins came out, she walked off, hiding her face. But she didn't go far, and more or less drifted back and stood there again until your guest got into the cab. And then she went off in a great hurry in the same direction!'

'Henry James—my guest, I mean.'

'Well, then, she was following Henry James.'

'An admirer.'

'No, she—'

She was sitting on the bed. He sat next to her. 'Can't we talk about this tomorrow?'

She struggled out of her robe. 'You don't mean "talk about it tomorrow"; you mean you don't care.' She lay down. 'You might as well undress if you're going to take that line.'

Next morning, Denton thought idly about James's story, decided that there was little he could do immediately. Or at all, perhaps. The woman Janet had seen seemed inconsequential, not connected to James's letters and box and Balzac. More important to him just then was his own worry about a new book. He spent the morning staring at the wall of his bedroom, also his workroom.

That afternoon, a note came from Henry James. 'I find I *must* have the little dog. He works on me powerfully. I shall call him Nicco, as he is a Neapolitan *cane pastoroso* and reminder of my dear Nick. I am going down to Rye in two days—will you and he come with me? You can survey the scene of the crime.'

Denton, having nothing better to do, supposed he might as well. The thought didn't delight him as perhaps it should have.

CHAPTER 2

Denton sprawled in Janet Striker's sitting room. His long body, almost horizontal, took up a good bit of the space. There was a faint uncouthness about him that success and London couldn't erase, visible at such times as now: we are what we begin as, after all, and he had begun as a child of rural poverty.

'Henry James wants the little dog. He wants me to go to Rye with the dog and him.'

She was playing her old square piano; without pausing, she said, 'He "wants" you? Is he like that?'

Denton knew what she meant, but he said, 'Like what?'

'Denton, really. Is he "so"?'

'What difference does it make?'

She whirled to face him. 'I've upset you!' She was grinning. 'I'm just surprised that you'd ask.'

Her grin faded. She had been a victim of gossip herself—former prostitute, former inmate. Her breath hissed out in exasperation at herself. 'I'm so sorry. It was stupid of me. Partly it was seeing that woman spying on him.'

'I don't know what James is or what he does with his Johnson. He's a fine, fine writer. And a pretty good man, I think.'

'A better writer than you?'

Denton made a sound, a kind of single laugh with the ends cut off. 'Like the lion and the mouse.' He pulled himself up into a somewhat more graceful position and said, 'Anyway, James wants the little dog, and Atkins is upset. It appears he was hoping nobody would take him and we'd keep him.'

'But he has Rupert!'

'And that's who the little dog was supposed to be for, in Atkins's secret plan. Rupert's getting on and he's none the better for being poisoned last year. Atkins thought they'd be pals and then he'd have the son when Pa crosses over Jordan.'

'I don't think dogs do that. Will you sing?'

She bought old music in Charing Cross Road, and she'd been playing some of it one day and he'd begun to sing, something he'd sung in clapboard churches in the American West. He had surprised her, first with his singing—'You have a voice!'—and then with his past—'You went to church?' He had said, 'I'd go anywhere there were women that didn't smell of sweat and dirty clothes.'

So now she said, 'Will you sing?' but he shook his head, held out his hands instead.

She said, 'I have to go out soon. Work.'

He slipped down on his spine again. 'Wish I could say the same.'

'Nothing's come to you?'

'I let down the bucket and bring up dust.' For the first time since he had started writing, he was unable to produce even the beginning of an idea. 'I think I've lost the knack. From a knack to the knacker's. Maybe I should just do hack-work.'

'Oh, don't feel sorry for yourself, Denton! You never feel sorry for yourself; don't start now.'

'I was hoping for sympathy.'

She came and sat next to him on the sofa; he started to push himself upright but she pressed him down, lay half on top of his right shoulder and arm. 'It will work out,' she murmured.

He grunted, then said, 'Is this compassion for the fallen?'

'I thought you liked women who smelled good.' She kissed him and leaned back. 'I have three dogs and Atkins will have only one now, so why don't I give him The Boy?' Rupert had sired five dogs on Janet's Sophie. Two had been given away; Denton had got the dog James was taking; and she still had The Girl and The Boy, two pups left nameless in hopes they'd be got rid of.

'I thought you were getting to like them.'

'I do, and so does Sophie, but if I gave you The Boy he'd be close by in your house, so everybody could see everybody in the gardens. That way Atkins would have somebody to replace Rupert when he dies, Rupert would have a chum, and I wouldn't have to care for three dogs.'

'And you could give The Girl a name.'

'But Rupert and The Boy have to be neutered, because I'm not going to have any more pups dropped on me.' She stabbed a finger into his chest. 'And *you* are going to see to it!' She leaned back again, her hands behind her head, her face in shadow and the long, knife-cut scar down the left side of her face barely visible. There was enough light to see that she was smiling at him. He hoped that the smile showed affection and not mere tolerance, a point that was always iffy. She said, 'What did James really want? He didn't come to you for a dog.'

'You really couldn't hear? He's had a robbery. Something personal.'

'I suppose "personal" means blackmail. And he thinks you can help him because he doesn't trust the police? Are you going to?'

Denton leaned back in the same posture, hands behind his head. 'I haven't got anything else to do, apparently.'

'What you mean is, if you do it, you won't have to think about writing.'

He took his hands down, kissed her. 'You know too much.'

'Don't start anything; I'm going out.' She kissed him, but without encouraging his starting anything. 'Don't forget that Walter's coming.'

'How could I forget? The end of privacy.' Walter Snokes was an eighteen-year-old whom Janet was trying, so far unsuccessfully, to adopt. He was 'backward', a strange mixture of obtuseness and an extreme, selective intelligence. It didn't help that he disliked Denton. Now, Denton said so.

'He doesn't dislike you; he distrusts you. He distrusts everybody.'

'Except you.'

'I'm tolerated, I think. It's only the rest of the summer, Denton.'

'I can't sleep here if he's here.'

'Of course you can; what you mean is you *won't*. That American prudery of yours.'

'How would you explain a man in your bedroom to Walter?'

'I wouldn't. Walter has to take me—and you—as we come. Anyway, he knows perfectly well about people sleeping together. He isn't an idiot.'

'I didn't say he was. He's just—I don't know what he is. He's unnerving. He's got some furniture missing upstairs.'

She kissed his cheek. 'Three days. Paddington, half-eleven.' She jabbed a finger into his chest again. 'And you're going with me."

He heard the iron in her voice. He looked into her face and laughed. 'You're such a tough old bird,' he said.

Once a week, towards evening, he met a detective named Munro in the Old Red Lion for a pint. Thrown together by a murder several years before, they had become friends of a sort. Usually it was Munro who was there first, glad of a reason to be out of New Scotland Yard; today it was Denton who sat over a glass and watched each man who came in, his irritation growing with the crowd and no Munro. Munro was in fact twenty minutes late; when his big body loomed through the door, Denton felt his annoyance collapse, and he made an exaggerated show of getting out his watch. Munro limped towards him, shaking his head at the pantomime. 'Coppers have a right to be late,' he said when he got close. 'We're the slaves of the rate-payers.'

He fell into a hard chair. Denton was big, but lean; Munro was as tall but a good deal wider. His head was huge, and the face sloped outward from forehead to jaw, giving him the look of some animal with a ferocious bite and big teeth—a hippo, maybe 'I've been at it since seven this morning—some stupid bugger killed his wife with a hammer and then beat himself about the head to make it look like somebody'd tried the same on him. You in the dumps?'

'I'm not singing and dancing.'

'Writing books.' Munro shook his head. He took his hat off, pulled a handkerchief from it and mopped his face. 'Too bloody hot. Walked too fast because I knew I was late.' He pushed the handkerchief back into the hat band and put the hat back on his head. 'I'm to be congratulated, so you're to buy me a pint of the best. I'm now Acting Chief Inspector Munro.'

'Are you really! That's worth a pint. Two pints, even.' Denton got him his pint and put it down in front of him and said, 'What does "acting" mean?'

'It means it's a test, and if I don't do a whip-round on N Division in six months, I'll be for the pension list. If I do it right, I'll be permanent and I'll take over CID in one of the divisions for good.' He grinned. 'Or bad.'

Denton congratulated him, repeated himself, felt his own failure. 'N Division's Islington, isn't I? George Guillam's still there?'

Munro was letting huge swallows throb down his throat, glass high but his eyes on Denton. He took the glass away and gasped with pleasure, said, 'Georgie it is. Going to be my good right hand.'

'Lots of luck with that.' Denton had had his troubles with Inspector Guillam.

'Georgie's learned a lot of late. Some of it due to you.' Munro picked up the glass and took a single swallow. 'You'd be surprised to hear him go on about you.'

'Surprised? I'd be astonished. You know an inspector named Wragge?'

'"Course I do.' Munro contemplated his mostly empty glass, seemed to reach a decision. 'And he knows you.'

'What's that supposed to mean?'

'Seems to think you're mucking about in one of his cases, as a matter of fact.'

'I'm not...! What the hell's he talking about?'

'You poking that big nose in where it doesn't belong again?'

'Munro, who've you been talking to?'

'Wragge himself. The man bent my ear about a case he's on for some literary bigwig; bad enough he got it when the locals should have taken care of it, now he says you've put your oar in and who are you when you're to home?'

'Well? Who am I?'

Munro drank off the rest of his pint and sighed with satisfaction. 'Acting Chief Inspector Munro told him you were all right most of the time, not as great an arse as you seem, he ought to talk to you himself. So he'll be here in a few minutes.' He extracted a watch from a pocket and looked down over his big chest at it. 'Twelve minutes, if he's prompt.' He cocked an eyebrow at Denton. 'You can scarper if you like.'

'Christ, you've got a nerve, Munro.'

'Chief inspectors can do as they please. *Are* you horning in on a case of Wragge's?'

Denton told him about Henry James. Not about the box and not about the letters, only about who James was and what sort. 'He's a great writer, but he's no good at rough and tumble. He's a gent, Munro. I think he's tougher than he lets on, but he's been robbed and he feels hurt and... *You* know how people feel when they've been invaded, Munro.'

'Bit sensitive, is he? Too good for the world? Wragge spent most of his time in Whitechapel before he got kicked up to the Yard. Wouldn't take to the la-di-da type one bit.'

'Good Christ, he isn't a "la-di-da type", Munro! James asked me to stand by because he doesn't know how you cops behave and he doesn't know what his part is. Told me he didn't even know he could ask to have New Scotland Yard in until his legal genius told him. So he asked, and he got Wragge.'

'Who he despised on sight? Wragge didn't wipe his feet? Didn't curtsey?'

'In fact, he said Wragge seemed to be doing a fine job, and he didn't say a word about finding fault with him, so what's Wragge got the spike about?'

Munro gave a quick, insincere grin. 'You, I suppose.' He pushed his glass across. 'You can ask him after you get me another congratulatory pint. That's him coming this way.'

Denton was standing by then. He saw a short man headed towards them, using his shoulders to make his way through the crowded room. He had a blue chin and cheeks, a belligerent scowl, hands balled into fists; his suit was too heavy for the weather and he was sweating. Denton lifted Munro's empty glass as the man came up and said, 'One for you when I fetch Munro's?'

It wasn't what Wragge had expected, if he had expected anything. He looked at Munro, turned red, stammered something about standing a round in his turn. Denton went off, glad of the crowd at the bar to give him the time to calm himself. It annoyed him that Munro had dragged somebody else into their weekly jaw session, which was usually Denton's chance to hear the gossip from the Yard. How could Munro bring in this hostile outsider to what had become their one chance in the week to relax together for a bit? The more so when Denton had done nothing in Wragge's case except listen to James's account of his burglary. And, perhaps, agree to collude in a small omission of evidence. But Denton knew Munro pretty well. Normally, Munro wouldn't give tuppence for another copper's complaints about Denton. So what was going on?

He set the two glasses down and sat.

'You not drinking?' Munro said.

'Not as much as you soaks from the Met.' He thought he'd try the jocular on Wragge. Wragge, however, looked disapproving. And harried. He pulled out a big turnip and studied it. As levity hadn't worked, Denton said, 'So, Inspector Wragge. You wanted to talk to me, I understand. I'm Denton, by the way. Munro's forgotten his manners, if he ever had any.' He put his hand partway across the table.

Wragge tucked his watch back in his waistcoat. He ignored the hand. 'This isn't a social call I'm making. I know who you are right enough. Munro got me here because he thinks the two of you'll persuade me to be a nice chap about you and the H. James case. Well, I'm not a nice chap. I'm a policeman trying to do his job, and it doesn't help to have folk like you nipping at my boots. Whatever Munro told you, the reason I'm here is to tell you to cut along. Go write a book. The same goes for Mr Henry James, who's going to get a piece of my tongue re: interfering with the police if he doesn't stop meddling. There!'

Munro seemed so unmoved it was hard to believe he had heard. 'Drink up, Wragge. We're all friends here.'

Denton tried to smile. 'Inspector Wragge, all I've done was listen while Mr James told me about the burglary. I'm not interfering.'

'You're going down to his place to look it over, ain't you? That's what he told me. You denying it?'

'He told you that?'

'This morning. Bellowing down the telephone like a banshee. Kept saying how it didn't mean anything and he hoped he wasn't stepping on toes and it was only seeking advice from a friend. You've heard of protesting too much? Well, I have. What's he going on so much about, I ask you, if it isn't bringing you in to show the stupid coppers how to do it?'

'You've got the wrong end of the stick, Wragge.'

Wragge slapped a hand on the table. 'I can see I'm wasting my time here.' He tried to stand.

Munro put a hand on his arm and forced him to stay where he was. 'Just sit a minute, can't you!'

Denton pushed his mostly empty glass an inch away. 'James doesn't know anything about the police or how they operate. He asked for my advice. That's *all*.'

'About what?' Wragge had a harsh voice, as if he'd been shouting all day. He looked the kind of small man who shouted a lot to make himself bigger.

'Making sure he does the right thing, I suppose.'

'What right thing would that be?'

Denton ignored the tone, tried invention. 'He told me you lot had taken fingerprints in his house and his housekeeper had cleaned the whole place afterwards, and I guess I winced or made a face, and I suppose he saw that he shouldn't have let her do that. Men like Henry James don't like to do things wrong.'

'He could have asked me.'

'But he didn't.'

Wragge's eyes narrowed. He glanced at Munro, sipped his bitter, scowled at Denton. 'So you're going to be his personal adviser in police manners. By appointment, is that it?'

Denton was tired of it. He said, 'Wragge, if this really gravels you, I can send James a note and tell him I won't help him. Except that I have to deliver a dog to him.' He turned to Munro. 'One of Rupert's pups. We've tried like hell to get rid of them.' He turned back to Wragge. 'You want me to do that?'

'And have it come back on me by way of the Commissioner's office and my super? No thank you. I know how it works when you people have friends in high places.' He took his watch out again and glanced at it.

Munro groaned and told Wragge to get off it. 'Denton's a friend of the Yard, Wragge; he isn't going to put a spoke in your bloody wheel.'

'I know his reputation.' Wragge pushed his glass aside as if it might get in the way of the hostility he was about to aim at Denton, and he said, 'I don't want you poking your pego into my case! I can't say it plainer. You understand that sort of plain speaking? I'll make it plainer: shove your oar into somebody else's business and leave mine be!' He gave Denton a full red-faced glare, then stood. 'Thanks for the pint, I *don't* think.' He clapped his hat on his head and whirled away.

'Rude little sonofabitch,' Denton said when he was gone.

'My doing. I thought he wanted to talk.'

'Well, he talked.' Denton chuckled.

'You don't sound much like a man who's just had the meat carved off his bones.'

Denton made a gesture, shoving it all aside. 'What he didn't say is a lot more interesting than what he did. That wasn't about some Yank author sticking his nose into police business. What's put the wind up him?'

Munro's lips came forward; his nose wrinkled. 'He's a bit waxed, is all. Overworked, maybe.'

'It was an act. And he was in a hurry to get it done and get someplace else.'

Munro shook his head. He stared at his glass, thought better of a third and pushed it away. He grunted. 'Odd, when you think about it, that he came to me, too. Only knew the man to speak to until he did.'

'Maybe because it's Henry James?'

'No offence, Denton, but nobody at the Yard gets his drawers up his crack over a *writer*—eh?'

'What, then?'

Munro shook his head. 'Usually, it's politics, but I don't see any politics.' He tried to drink from his empty glass. 'You might best drop out of it, you know. Just to be on the safe side.'

'I told James I'd do it.'

Munro set the glass down with a knock that served as a full stop and reached for his hat. 'Give my regards to Mrs Striker.'

Denton stood. 'We never got to the latest gossip.'

'Yeah, we did. *This* is the latest gossip.'

The next morning, he woke to hear bumps and crashes from the basement. It was barely seven. He pulled on an extremely ratty old dressing gown and hurried to the head of Atkins's stairs. 'What the hell's going on down there?'

'Cleaning.'

'Sergeant, the sun isn't up yet!'

'Couldn't sleep. Seize the day.'

Denton went down. Atkins, already dressed, had on a canvas apron over a shirt and waistcoat and was in the middle of rolling up a carpet. Denton said, 'Your nose is out of joint because of that dog.'

'Surprised you'd think it of me.'

'Well, get over your surprise; I do think it of you. Atkins, you're going to get *another* dog.'

'Me! What've I got to do with it, I'd like to know. Dog's nothing to me. It's Rupert I feel pain for.' He finished rolling the carpet and made much of trying to lift it. Denton crossed the room and grabbed one end. 'Where is this thing going?'

'Out back, where else do you think people beat carpets?'

'You start whacking a carpet now, you'll have the neighbours coming over the wall with clubs.'

They got the carpet outside and draped it over a line of chairs that Atkins had already set up. Rupert and the little dog who was going to Henry James were already out there, Rupert slow, the little dog quick and eager. Atkins looked at them. 'Doesn't know what's about to happen to him, does he. Doesn't know he's going to the lap of luxury. Leaving the life of below-stairs.'

'Oh, Atkins, for God's sake!'

'Rupert and I will have to make do with each other.'

'And the new dog.'

'Perfect stranger.'

'Atkins, Rupert is his father!'

'We don't know that for a certainty.'

Denton groaned. 'Yes, we know it for a certainty. I saw Rupert and Sophie at it. That was the only time. Rupert is the father!'

'Very different from each other, those pups. Chalk and cheese. Highly dubious.' Atkins picked up a rug-beater from the wet grass. 'It's a wise child that knows his own father, they say.' He swung the beater back like a cricket bat and said, 'I suppose you'll be wanting breakfast.'

'If it isn't too much to ask.'

'Oh, no.'

THUMP! Dust sprang from the carpet and rose towards the clear summer sky. One of the chairs fell over. Both dogs flinched, and Rupert lay down.

Denton said, 'You need to hang the carpet from someplace high.'

'Haven't got anyplace high.'

THUMP! More dust, and another chair went over.

Atkins dropped the rug-beater. 'This isn't working.' He stared at the rug. 'Only an idea. What you want for breakfast?'

'Would an egg be too much of an imposition on your house-cleaning?'

'I'm in the midst of blacking the stove. I'm also washing all the crockery. Cleaning out the ice cave, shocking in there. I can give you an egg boiled on the spirit stove. Toast if I use the gas ring. Got some quince jelly someplace, as I remember.'

'We have blackberry jam! You just bought it!'

'Cupboard's blocked. Furniture.'

Denton's peculiar relationship with Atkins was based on a high salary and a desire for a democratic master-man relationship. The result was that Atkins was allowed a lot of leeway, and Denton was able to have an in-house confidant and sometime pal. Now and then—as now—Denton got irritated. He fought his irritation, wrestled with it, breathed deeply, and said with the slowness of a man holding back terrible things, 'In fifteen minutes, I'm going to appear in the sitting room. So are you. With two boiled eggs, one for each of us; toast for two; and the goddam blackberry jam, even if you have to take an axe to whatever's blocking the cupboard! And we're going to have this crap about the dog out!'

Atkins nodded gloomily, muttered to himself.

'What?'

'I said, it isn't just the dog.'

'What, then?'

Atkins shook his head. 'Maybe later.'

Denton snorted, turned and fell over Rupert, who, almost excited by the noise, was awake. He raised his head a few inches and opened an eye as Denton went by, then fell back with a groan.

Fifteen minutes later, Denton and Atkins were seated across a small folding table in the sitting room—general sense of gloom, green drapery and upholstery, curtains closed against the morning light—with not only the blackberry jam but also a jar of wild *fraise de bois* preserves unearthed from somewhere, and a pot of honey. And toast in, if not quite great lashings, a sufficient quantity for two.

'Sorry about all that, General,' Atkins said. 'Making a point with the chores, I seem to have done.'

'My grandmother used to do it. Pots and pans became major outlets for anger. A mop and a pail of water could be more eloquent than a scream.'

'Daft time to clean. Mrs Char comes in on Monday, anyway. Oh, well, I'll put everything back. Egg all right?'

'Egg's perfect, as usual. Well, I'm sorry about the little dog, Sergeant.'

'Dog's only a provocation. Not a provocation—a *causus bellus* or whatever it is. An ostensibility. Is that a word?'

'I doubt it. Dictionary on my desk.'

'Anyway, the dog isn't it. Rupert and I will, as they say, learn to love the new one. At least he looks like Rupert. The missus wants the males clipped, doesn't she?'

'Pass the blackberry. Did she say something?'

'To Rupert's face! "Those things are coming off or Sophie and I're moving away." Her very words. Hurt his feelings. Mine too. Butter?'

The toast was already dripping with butter. Denton pointed his chin at a small covered dish. 'What's in that?'

'Cinnamon and sugar. First-rate on buttered toast. Said to be a favourite of a late princess royal. Which one, history don't relate.'

Denton tried the cinnamon and sugar on his toast, found it good, rather what a child might like. 'Is it another of your schemes?' Atkins was always looking for ways to make enough money to get out of servitude—'the soul of a servant, the mind of a bleeding capitalist', as he'd said once.

Atkins cleared his throat. 'Would the name "Atkins Cinemantics" appeal to you?'

'You're going back into the film business?' Several years before, Atkins had made a film called, rather grandly, *The Boer War*, which had put the entire war into four minutes of moving pictures, mostly of his pals (Atkins had many pals) in borrowed uniforms and Oom Paul beards, running about Hampstead Heath. Then the almighty American holder of the patent on the camera had found that Atkins was using an unlicensed machine and had gone to court. The camera was seized, the film supposedly destroyed, and a small amount paid to Atkins when he in turn went to court over his lost intellectual property.

'Another pal of mine who emigrated to Canada saw my *Boer War* at a local cinema there recently, some God-awful place called Toronto. Well, that didn't seem right to me, so I dug about and discovered my motion picture—mine!—was being shown all over the US, Canada and South America. You remember that lawyer you had to do with down in Finsbury?'

'The one who broke wind all the time?'

'Memorable, that. Yes, that one. Well, I went to him—you said he was cheap but sharp—this was while you were in Naples this last time—and he wrote some letters, and I wound up with a smallish amount of money. He wrote some more letters, and yesterday the shyster told me that they're offering a spanking-new camera and a licence to supply the American company with actualities of British events. Now, what do you think of all that?'

'There's money in it? And you could take enough pictures this time to make it worthwhile?'

'Question of putting the Atkins nose to the grindstone, isn't it?'

'You get Sundays and Wednesday afternoons off. Not a lot of time.'

'And the news don't happen only on Sunday and Wednesday p.m. And it happens in places I can't get to. Been thinking about all that. They're launching a new dreadnought up on the Clyde, for instance, supposed to wipe the German's eye, a natural for a moving picture, but can I get up there and back in time to meet my contractual obligations to you? I cannot.'

Denton had slumped back in his chair. He studied Atkins, who was studying him. Denton picked up another piece of cinnamon toast. 'But you have an idea, I'll bet.'

'I'm working on it. You're the one keeps talking about all men created equal, Major. You want me to advance myself, don't you?' He stacked Denton's plate on his own, brushed crumbs into a palm with a wadded napkin, and said, 'It isn't as if I was born to answer doors, is it.'

A few minutes later, the table emptied of everything but crumbs, they went their ways, Atkins to the lower regions, Denton upstairs to his desk, where he stared for an hour at some blank paper and then rose to look out the window. Below in the garden, the Henry James dog and the Boy dog were sniffing each other fore and aft, the door between the gardens was open, and Rupert and Sophie were tail-wagging. Janet and Atkins, like somewhat nervous parents, were looking on.

There should be a novel in that, Denton thought. *There should be a novel in everything. Why can't I see it?*

An hour later, he was packing a pebbled leather Gladstone bag to go to Henry James's, regretting now that he was going, when he heard Atkins, one floor below, shouting for him. Atkins, he knew, would be standing by the telephone earpiece and covering the speaking tube with his other hand and shouting over his shoulder. Denton tumbled down the stairs and reached for the earpiece.

'You deaf?' Atkins said. 'I been bellowing like Basham's bull.'

'Cork it, Sergeant.' He leaned into the flower-like speaking device. 'Denton here!'

'It's Munro.'

'Yes, what?' Denton hated the telephone, couldn't get used to its tinny sound and the need to shout. He also hit his upper arm on the speaking thing about one day in three, passing by too fast on his way to the stairs.

'Have you talked to Wragge?'

Denton had to remember who Wragge was, recalled yesterday's scene in the Old Red Lion. 'Only in the pub. That was enough'

'You didn't see him last night?'

'Why the hell would I see him?'

Munro let a pause form, then said, 'He said he was going to have it out with you.'

'Have what out?'

'At least we think it's you. He was going to have it out with somebody, and you seemed likely.'

'Munro, you're not making sense. Look, I have to catch a train in an hour, and I've got to water and box up a dog first. I haven't seen Wragge and I haven't talked to him. Why don't you ask Wragge?'

He heard Munro's sigh—remarkable achievement for the telephone. 'We're looking for him.' He cleared his throat. 'He didn't come home last night. The super's looking for him, in fact.'

'Why?'

'Because we can't find him! His wife came to the Yard this morning—all the way from Wandsworth, no telephone—this morning early. He was supposed to meet with the super, sparrow-fart. I just thought you might have, you know...'

'When he slammed out of that pub, he slammed out of my life. Who says he was going to have it out with me?'

'None of your business. All right, we were wrong. Have a good time with the great author.' And Munro rang off.

Atkins was still standing nearby. 'Miss anything?' Denton said.

'Didn't think you'd mind. Usually, you order me about if you want privacy.'

'You didn't get any messages or visits or calls from somebody named Wragge, did you?'

'You think I wouldn't tell you if I had, Captain? Fair dying to tell you that somebody named Wragge called by. Wouldn't miss the opportunity. Who's Wragge?'

'A policeman.'

'Oh, bloody hell, can't the police keep track of their own? We won't be safe in our beds next.'

'Wragge's the copper in charge of the investigation of James's burglary.'

'Ah, and now he's been stolen. What times we live in! You better hop it if you're going to meet Henry James on time.'

'Ah!' Denton ran back up the stairs and threw a shirt in the bag and closed it. When he ran down again, Atkins and Rupert were waiting with the little dog. Atkins held it out. 'Go ahead—break a father's heart.'

Denton took the dog. 'Think how happy he'll make Henry James.'

Atkins nodded. There was actually a tear in his eye.

Henry James was standing on the railway platform in the middle of what seemed to be the luggage of the entire train. It was, however, all his; behind him, two porters were loading one of his steamer trunks on a luggage wagon. James himself was carrying a large wicker hamper-like thing that had windows in the ends. Denton, coming along the platform, saw the boxes and hampers and trunks seconds before James saw him; when their eyes met, James waved somewhat wildly and held up the wicker object.

'For Nicco!' he called. 'For the journey!'

Denton had Nicco in a wooden crate that had held cabbage, picked up that morning in Covent Garden. The crate seemed fine to him, certainly large enough, if not so easily carried. James's wicker, he saw when he got closer, could have held several Niccos.

'As I thought, as I thought, you hadn't a proper container for the little fellow. Doesn't he look anxious, poor chap. Staring out between the bars of his prison. Well, let us transfer you to your travelling home—careful, careful—we don't want him scurrying down the platform—how he's shivering; it's the noise, I'm sure—there, there, in he goes—in—and all's well and the gate is barred and the dear little chap can settle in.' James was squatting, with some difficulty, and peering into the wicker carrier with his Roman nose almost touching the dog's. He looked up at Denton. 'What an intelligent face he has!' He put a hand on an upended trunk and pulled himself upright. 'I am a foolish, fond old man, Denton, in a *crise* of anxiety about a dog! I thought you might appear with him in your arms, and he would escape, and in this crowd...!'

Denton had put the now empty crate on a luggage wagon. 'We'll make a gift of that to the railway. The dog will be fine. You always travel this heavy?'

James was watching another trunk go on the wagon. 'The result of months in America. A very changeable climate. And gifts people *insisted* upon making. Did you know I was in the deepest South?' He hectored the porters for several minutes, then led Denton to a first-class carriage. James carried the dog and was panting when he threw himself back on the seat. 'I took the entire compartment,' he gasped. 'That way, Nicco can be at large.' He put his face against the wicker window again. 'But not until the train is under way, little one. No, no...' He mopped his forehead with a startlingly blue handkerchief. 'I allow myself to become *far* too anxious over trivia.'

Denton sat opposite him. Henry James, he found, interested him. He had just recognised that James was vain; the handkerchief, which was coordinated with a very wide cravat, told him that. Why a plump man of sixty or so should be vain, Denton couldn't understand. He was still years short of that himself, and... Was he vain? Surely not. Or...?

'Why are you laughing?' James said. 'Have I done something so risible?'

'Not you. Me.' Denton grinned. 'Human folly—always funniest when you find it in yourself.'

'I resolved long ago never to so find it.' That look of impending laughter that writers call a twinkle showed in James's face. 'I am sure we are both far too serious to share in anything so mundane, so, so lamentable, so outré as human folly!' And he laughed a great belly laugh, throwing his head back and showing his false teeth.

Doors were slamming along the train. Late arrivals were scurrying, a woman in tight skirts trying to run and unable to.

A male voice called out, the pitch rising almost to falsetto, to tell them that the train was leaving. And it began to move, at first so slowly that it seemed to be the platform that was gliding away behind them; then the train was going as fast as those who had missed it but were still trotting. Denton looked out into a face that seemed part of the train as it kept pace; he could have opened the door and let the man in, and then it was too late and the man was falling back and then was gone. Black smoke drifted by. The tracks began to knock at the wheels as if they, too, wanted to get in.

'Under way at last,' James said, smiling. He opened the wicker carrier. The dog put his head up, looked around, seemed to flinch away from the moving panorama of the windows, now only gas lights spinning by between pools of blackness in a tunnel. James took the dog out and put him on his lap, muttered something about continence.

'Atkins had him out just before I left.'

'We shall hope for the best. And you must try *very* hard to be a good lad, Nicco.'

James seemed content to give his attention to the dog, surprising Denton, who thought of the great man as a talker, one who lived in his words. Left to himself, Denton leaned back and stared as they came into daylight—the ugliness of the railway cuttings, then the more comfortable look of back gardens and allotments.

As so often when alone, he thought about Janet Striker. They seemed on quite good terms just then, he thought. She was never romantic, but often—he might have tried 'affectionate', but he knew the word was wrong—responsive. Never sentimental. Never 'loving'. He had almost lost her the year before; she had actually left him but come back within hours, not out of any longing for him but out some sense of—fairness? obligation? respect?

Whatever it was that kept Janet by him, it wasn't love. Without knowing it, he sighed

'"What a sigh is there",' James said.

Denton looked up.

'You made a sound. Even Nicco thought so. But that is your business, to be sure. I tend towards chattiness, Denton, as you've no doubt noticed; you, I think, are a man of silences. Shall we while away the journey with my ways or with yours?'

Denton chuckled. He began to make talk, more to keep from sombre thoughts than for having anything to say. Inevitably, they came to the burglary and James's loss. Denton mentioned meeting Wragge, said only that the inspector seemed put out that he was involved. 'Anger of that sort is so often really about something else. Maybe his wife burned the toast.' He didn't mention the meeting with Munro, turned instead to books and writing, critics they'd both suffered from, the vagaries of publishers. Inevitably, James said, 'I read your last.'

'Too bad.'

'Not at all; it has some very fine, some magnificent things in it.'

'It's a disaster in terms of sales.'

'"Caviar to the general." Not that I mean to say it was without fault, but whatever faults it has cower in the shadow of what you attempted to do.'

'They've demolished me in the States. Absolutely pulled me down and smashed me to bits. One paper in Ohio said if I came there they'd buy the tar if somebody else would provide the feathers and the pole.'

'I say this only in the snug confines of our compartment, and it will never go beyond these swaying walls, but most people are rabble and have the rabble's mental equipment.'

'You know that Mrs Humphrey Ward has more books than you and I together on the Army and Navy Stores' list?'

'One is tempted to conclude that sales are inversely proportional to value. We are coming into Rye.'

'Coming through the Rye' was so close to what James had said that Denton was confused. It was only a moment; then he was on his feet; the train was slowing, jerking Nicco almost to the floor so that James caught him up, held him until they were gliding along a platform in another cloud of coal smoke, when he deposited him in the carrier and pushed the pegs through the loops that held it closed.

'I telegraphed ahead,' James said, 'but I made it quite clear that there was to be no committee to welcome me. People *will* make a fuss if given the opportunity.'

In fact, two men were walking along with the train; one, recognising James, nudged the other; they waved, knocked on the window and trotted ahead.

'For you?' Denton said.

'For the luggage.'

With the two had come a horse-cart and a sturdy, bored-looking horse a bit larger than a pony. James insisted that he must oversee the unloading of *all* his luggage—indeed, a hatbox and a small trunk would have been left in the baggage car if he hadn't—and then he had to instruct the two men on the loading of the cart. Denton managed to get him away at that point, thought he saw a look of gratitude from one of the men. He had meanwhile had the care of Nicco, whom he now took from the basket and handed over to James, who produced a spanking-new leather leash and a kind of harness, into which the two of them wrestled the dog in no more than six or seven minutes.

'He doesn't like it,' Denton said.

'Nor would I, nor you. But he will grow accustomed to it, as we all must.' James's eyebrows went up and down. 'Although our harnesses are metaphorical. But none the less irritating for that. Good lad, Nicco!'

Nicco had deposited a pile among the stationmaster's flowers.

'I must learn again to carry a trowel,' James said. 'One forgets these things. It is curious how they become invested with the emotions we have ingrained in ourselves for the little animals themselves. I couldn't bear the sight of the trowel I used with my poor Nickie after he'd gone.' He stared down at the alert little dog. 'So, Nicco, I shall carry a trowel for you, and suffer as much for you, I suppose. Unless you outlive me.' He looked up at

Denton. 'Always a concern after a certain age—what will happen to the beasts if we go first? Shall we climb the hill?'

And so they did, although it was less a climb than a progress. The word of James's return had gone 'round. It was an event. Rye was a small place; James was its principal 'personality', its main emissary from the great world. If he amused them, these people who greeted and actually curtseyed (two of them, anyway) and tipped their hats, he also greatly impressed them. If perhaps he was guilty of behaving like a squire, perhaps they were as guilty of behaving like tenants. Or relatives of tenants, anyway.

As they climbed towards the top of the town, James gave him a short history of the place—medieval glory as an important port, then disaster and the silting of an estuary, loss of status. Denton, half listening, thought that Rye looked a good place for a certain literary type, thought it would drive him crazy in about six days. It was pretty, quaint, historical, 'nice', safe-seeming, a very odd place for a crime. Nicco, indifferent to the humans, sniffed at stones, urinated on gates and first approached and then fled from two strange dogs, tangling his leash around James's legs. James seemed charmed.

'And this,' Henry James said at the top of the village, 'is Lamb House.'

The approach was along a narrow street, at a bend that gave a little widening of the road—a rather narrow front, behind which was actually a large brick house that was also pretty, quaint, historical, et cetera. James had already told him that one of the Georges had slept there. Not George Washington, Denton thought.

They were met on the doorstep by the housekeeper and two new maids. The housekeeper was disapproving and angry, a grim woman in her sixties who refused to smile even at James but who stood back, giving off waves of unhappiness. The maids, newly hired, were embarrassed and awkward and flushed, women still not yet twenty and only just off the local farms. One was pretty and, Denton guessed, as dumb as a stump, the other rather more intelligent-looking, also solid and a little beefy. Denton wondered if they knew that their employer was famous, or why. Their names seemed to be Mavis and Emmeline, but he didn't get which was which.

He was shown a pleasant bedroom (not the one where a king had slept) that looked down into a big walled garden framed by two cottages near the far end. The garden was impeccable, a little over-perfect, full of flowers that Denton couldn't name but that he was sure James could. Perhaps Nicco would take care of the perfection. At the far end were several round stones mounding up from the sod. Dogs' graves?

'Well!' James said when they met downstairs. 'Let me give you the grand tour.' He looked apologetic. 'I am what is called "house proud", I'm afraid. I love Lamb House. It is everything I ever wanted in my home.' He frowned. 'It hurts me that it was invaded.'

A crash came from somewhere at the back. James flinched and murmured something about Mrs Esmond.

'The housekeeper?' Denton was thinking of Atkins and his own grandmother, domestic items used as language.

'She, poor woman, is more upset over the burglary than I. Guilty that she was away, I fear, and blaming herself for abandoning her post. She is also wroth with the police for what they did, although I must say, everything is sparkling now.'

Sparkling, indeed. Denton had given up already on the idea of finding any vestige of the burglars or the burglary. As he was shown around the house, he kept seeing freshly washed windows, waxed floors, woodwork like shiny satin, pictures and books and bibelots without a speck of dust. There were no hints that anything was missing; if pictures had been stolen, they had been replaced. He was shown the window through which the burglars apparently had come; there had been broken glass, he was told. There was nothing now but a new, houndstooth-clean pane in a French door. He was shown where the Florentine box had lain; all he saw was a space on a shelf, the shelf itself polished and dusted and wiped. The ghosts of the box's corners were just visible where years of weight had pressed.

'You didn't mind leaving the box here while you were in America?' he said.

'I told you, my enthusiasm for the contents was long since damped down, and it was only a pretty box *bien agé*. Who would want it?'

That was Denton's question.

He was shown a large sitting room, perhaps more properly a drawing room. A small grand piano was covered with a Paisley shawl, on which sat a lot of framed photographs, several of them recognisably having been taken in the garden. James named some of the people as if he were ticking off the greats and near-greats of literary England—Wells, Hardy, Hueffer, Mrs Wharton, the two dead Americans Crane and Frederick, the Bensons. 'I have no photograph of you, Denton.'

'Nor will you, I daresay.'

'I should really have my own camera, then I'd "shoot" you.' James smiled. 'Unfortunate expression.'

Denton looked at some of the photographs. Most of them were of men, the exceptions Mrs Wharton, a large-nosed woman he thought was Violet Hunt, and a couple of others. One part of the piano lid held newer, rather more professional-looking photographs, half a dozen young men and one woman in individual frames. 'My protégés,' James said. The pouchy lines around his eyes became those of an indulgent smile. 'Desmond MacCarthy, *most* promising.' He mentioned a couple of others, the names meaning nothing to Denton. He touched another frame. 'Raphael Neville.' He smiled at Denton, who recognised the name as that of the author of a new, somewhat queasy-sounding novel. 'I help all my literary friends to improve their writing.' This was followed with a pregnant silence, to which Denton didn't want to play midwife. He didn't want James's help, that was certain. Eventually, James put the photograph back and said, 'Neville is,

I fear, misbehaving with a much *older* woman of whose literary experience, I suppose, he hopes to benefit—although I could assure him that she's not capable of it.'

That sounded familiar to Denton. 'Violet Hunt?'

James pulled in a sharp breath. 'You know? I didn't like to utter her name. One ought never pronounce a woman's name in a questionable context. That is not meant as a criticism of you, Denton. Violet does behave abominably. I cannot have her here while this goes on, of course, although she's a dear friend.' He glanced at the photo of the woman with the big nose.

They went to another room. Denton started asking questions about the burglary again. 'And what's become of the two maids—the ones who worked here then?'

'Sent away, of course. I shall ask Mrs Esmond what's become of them, if I, mmm, have the, mmm, the effrontery, the, mmm, *daring* to approach her. She is in a mood, rather a towering one, I fear. Quite ancient Greek at times, Mrs Esmond. Clytemnestra, and so on.'

'I'll also want that list of the people who knew the house—house guests and the like.'

'The police have all that.'

'But they won't share it with me.' He waited. James nodded but made it clear he was displeased. Denton pushed on. 'Do you remember if people knew that nobody would be in the house but the two maids?'

'Oh, why... I wrote a great many letters to tell my friends that I was coming back. A great many. I suppose I may have mentioned that Mrs Esmond was going to see her mother. It was a small vexation, as it meant I couldn't come direct here from the crossing, so I may have mentioned it—may have.'

'I'd like a list of the people you wrote to before you left the US, then.'

'I could hardly be expected to remember such a thing. Is all this really necessary?'

'I'm afraid so. And so is telling Mrs Esmond to answer some questions. Where shall I wait for her?'

James pushed out his lips, frowned, shook his head and sighed. After making it clear that he was displeased, he showed Denton to a small sitting room and went off, presumably to get the housekeeper. Denton was looking at one of several etchings of Rye when she surprised him by coming in quite quickly, even briskly. She shut the door, then stood against it. 'You wanted to talk to me, sir.'

'I want to ask you a few questions, yes.'

'I told the police everything I know. Which isn't much.' She had a husky, mannish voice, but, even though her resentment showed in it, she didn't put up much resistance. She came and sat in a chair, not upright but somewhat sprawled, as if her strings had been cut. He thought she was physically tired, also drained by a sense of having let James down. She was no ogre, rather a tired old woman who was sick of herself.

'I'll make this quick, then. My name is Denton, and Mr James has asked me to help him with the burglary and trying to recover the things that he lost.'

'That's the job of the police, I'd have thought.'

'It is, but dealing with the police is new to Mr James. It isn't new to me.' He meant that to be a warning, but it sounded fatuous in his own ears. 'You were away when the burglary took place, Mrs Esmond?'

'I was, to my shame. I never should have left the house with them two stupid girls. It was only for a few days; I had sickness in the family. Still—I shouldn't have. I know it was my doing.'

'It's no good blaming yourself for a crime you had nothing to do with.'

'I should have been here!'

'You had Mr James's permission to leave, as I understand it.' He looked at her, she at him. She hugged herself, shrugged, looked away. He said, 'What was the house like when you came back?'

'Mess everywhere. The police had tracked in mud from the garden on their boots, and they'd done what they call "dusting" places for something about people's hands. I'll give them "dusting"—they don't know the meaning of the word. It was a pigsty. I left it looking entirely proper and I came back to... Oh, it was terrible.'

'You didn't report the burglary, then.'

'How would I have done? I wasn't here. It was Gammon, the gardener, that found the broken window. You ask him, he'll tell you. He called the constable, and then Mr James returned and he brought in Scotland Yard. One pack of them after another, acting like tramps on a tear. Not the least consideration for the people who have to make things clean and want them clean! Filth, they were, just filth, though I'm ashamed to say it of the police, that I trusted until I walked in the door and saw it.'

'The maids were gone by then?'

'Them two! Running off in some Jew's motor-car and coming back to find the constables here and half the house stolen. They didn't so much as wait to make a cup of tea. Packed their trash and left us. Baggages!'

'A Jew?'

'He was a Jew-boy, is what I heard in the village. He was seen. And them two with him, laughing and holding their hats on in the wind he made driving too fast. Then he took them some-place the far side of Romney Marsh and broke his motor-car down and they had to spend the night, they say, him on the ground under the car and those two hussies in it. Perishing of the cold, I hope they were. They weren't seen back here until tea-time next day, according to Gammon, but you can ask *him*.' She clutched herself and stared miserably at an etching of Rye Harbour. 'And all my fault!' She put her head down and began to weep.

'There, there—Mrs Esmond, it's all right... It isn't your fault. Mrs Esmond. Please, one more question.'

She looked up. Anger and guilt and now weeping made her ugly—nose and cheeks red, eyes pink, watery. Denton said, 'You helped Mr James make a list of things that were missing, didn't you?'

She nodded. She was mopping her eyes with a pocket hand-kerchief, apparently a man's. 'For the police. And the insurance.'

'And at that time, so far as you know, those things had all gone missing in the burglary.'

'Well, when else would they have gone?'

'Small things could have been taken by somebody else—a constable, maybe. The gardener.'

'Gammon is as honest as the day is long! He's a decent, hard-working man without blemish or stain to his entire life. I won't hear a word against Gammon!'

He wondered if Mrs Esmond had an eye on Gammon. If so, could they have been in on the burglary together somehow? Hardly very likely. Class among servants was as powerful as it was among their employers.

She had got to her feet. 'I'm sorry if I spoke sharply, sir. I'm that upset I don't know what I'm at. I'm sorry.'

'You've nothing to be sorry for. One thing before you go, though—Mrs Esmond, did any of Mr James's visitors, in your presence, ever show unusual interest in anything that was then taken in the burglary? Asking questions or spending a long time looking at something or...' He shrugged. 'Acting oddly.'

'How acting oddly? And why would they do it with me about? I don't have time to be in this part of the house when there's visitors, Mr... I'm cooking or following after the maids or seeing to the shopping. A thousand things a man wouldn't think of. What sort of thing are you thinking of?'

'Oh—a picture, or...something like the red box Mr James had in his study.'

'Oh, that box!' She seemed disgusted.

'Why do you say that?'

'I had more trouble from that box with them two layabouts than anything else in this house. They *would* not dust under it. Always a line of dust around the edges, if you understand me. Too bone lazy to pick it up, which they said was not wanting to drop it, to which I told them things could be picked up without being dropped if you have any sense and know what you're about, but the lazy ticks would only snigger and say we'll do better next time, and did they? They did not!'

'But only the two maids who've gone.'

'Aye, only them, and then it wasn't attention, not what you'd call attention, it was *not* paying attention. It was all thinking about Jews in motor-cars and what colour ribbons the princess was wearing in her hat.'

'I'm sure you did the best you could with them, Mrs Esmond. What they did wrong isn't your fault.'

She was plunged back into self-blame by that. When she left seconds later, she was weeping again.

He expected her that evening to have taken out her unhappiness on the supper, but in fact it was remarkably good. Pride of craft, he thought. It reminded him of his own inability to write, made him wince.

'Terrible thing, blaming yourself,' Denton said as they ate. James was working his way through a bottle of claret, growing even more talkative. Denton could drink by the quart if he chose, but he did not so choose. He sipped at the same glassful throughout the meal, studied his host.

'My housekeeper, you mean. Yes, quite dreadful. It comes easily to a certain type, I believe—Calvinist, perhaps. A certain kind of American, too.'

'Me, for example.'

'Do you? Are you? You seem, if I may say so, so ruggedly self-assured. May I ask for what you blame yourself?'

Denton smiled but said nothing, chewed.

James put down his knife and fork. He refilled his own glass, looked at Denton's half-full one, raised the bottle; Denton put a finger over his glass. James's eyebrows went up. He said, 'You were in the war.' Between two Americans, it was not necessary to say what war; there was only one, the civil war that had torn the country apart.

Denton nodded.

'I was not.'

Denton nodded again.

'You knew, of course. This is something for which I blame myself, indeed. Cowardice, in a word. I didn't—I couldn't... The possibility that I might kill a human being...' He picked up his fork, stared at it, spoke without looking up, attacked his wine glass. 'Did you?'

'Kill anybody? Probably. I did later, if not then. You've heard the story, I'm sure. Everybody's heard the story.' It had happened thirty years before, but the killings still pursued him. Once, there had been dime novels about them. He had even spent a year with Cody's Wild West as a 'crack pistolero' because of them.

'Yes, mmm, some small place in the West, several, mmm, villains...'

'Four. With a shotgun.' The 'crack pistolero' had been Cody's invention.

James was moving a green pea around his plate. 'Might I ask—please don't be offended—do you blame yourself?'

'I was paid ten dollars a month to be the lawman in a little town. For ten dollars, I killed four men. There's a lot to blame yourself for in that.'

'Is it... Isn't it...possible to kill and to, mm, feel, ah, nothing?'

'If you're a monster, I suppose.'

James drank, poured more, went again through the pantomime of offering wine to Denton. 'I live in a way, of course, that quite precludes anything so crude as killing. And burglary, I'd have thought. But one can imagine murder, and I should, mmm, posit, that is to say, mmm, suppose, *think it possible*, that killing could be done without later resonance. Is that not possible? A kind of numbness, rather?'

'As I said, if you're a monster.'

Neither said anything. One of the maids cleared the plates and brought in a pudding. As James poured the last of the claret into his own glass, he said, 'So guilt at killing—regret, self-blame, anguish—are you think only the normal human lot.'

'Essentially human.'

'I had thought there might be...men who could do such things without qualm *because* they were men. I mean, that this was an inward sign of a certain kind of manliness.'

Denton ate some of the pudding, which had a syrupy red tartness curled through its pale custard. He said, 'After a war, many men go insane. The West was full of them. I was one, I suppose. You see too much; you do too much. Then you can't believe what you did and you have...demons. Some men kill themselves. Some men kill other people. They turn into what people called "gunmen", killers. Guns for hire. They were monsters.'

There was bitter coffee, and brandy. James, despite having drunk most of the bottle of wine, seemed as sober as he had that morning; it was by then almost dark, the night soft with the promise of rain. Denton went to look for a book to take to bed; when he came back, he had to search for James and found him beyond the French doors that opened on the garden. Denton stepped out into the near-dark. Henry James was standing a little to his left; a blur at the end of the garden was, he thought, the little dog. There was a faint sound he couldn't place, and then he realised that James was pissing on the grass.

'One of the small pleasures of life,' James said, 'watering one's own garden. A variant of Voltaire.' He chuckled. 'Do feel free to join me.'

It seemed foolish to say he'd already stopped by a WC; in fact, it seemed foolish to say anything. James bent slightly and worked at his flies. The two of them stood and watched the sky, where thin clouds were beginning to slide across the stars. 'I am home again,' James said. 'I can't tell you how happy that makes me.'

Denton had been asleep, or in that jumbled state that is half-sleep, bastard sleep—images coming and going, phantom bits of thought. He came to abruptly, aware he was in a strange place, then knew where he was. He recognised the soft sound of rain outside. Still, an old habit of sensing danger made him slit his eyes and give no sign he was awake.

He had left his bedroom door closed but unlocked. Now the door was open. Faint light from the window showed a pale blur, man-sized, movement on one side of it.

'Are you awake?' The voice was thin, tentative, as if trying not to wake him to ask if he was awake. Denton realised that it was James in the doorway, wearing some sort of nightshirt; the movement was the little dog, held in his arms.

'I'm awake.'

'I have a...confession to make.' James's voice actually trembled. Denton wondered how much more he'd drunk after Denton had gone to bed; the trembling suggested tears or their nearness. He waited: what was there to say? He heard James inhale, then blurt out, 'I've never told this to anyone! But I must...to you...our talk of killing.' James shifted the dog's weight; it did something, moved, perhaps licked his hand.

James moved into the room a step. He seemed to be panting. 'When I first came to Lamb House, I was...desirous of having peace. Whatever the days contained, I treasured the peace of the night. Not to sleep; I slept rather little then, but I would lie in the dark and...luxuriate in it. One night...' He sucked in his breath. 'One night, terrible sounds came from the garden. A cat. A female, I think, howling without cease. Destroying the night for me. I did everything I could—I covered my head; I pulled the pillow about my ears; I closed my windows. But it went on and on. And I... My equanimity was fragile at that time. I...pulled on a robe and threw myself down the stairs, and as I passed towards the garden doors I—without thinking, without meaning anything—I caught up a walking-stick. I tore open the doors with great force and impelled myself into the garden. There was the creature. She looked at me. I meant to drive her away; I thought my very presence would send her away, but...she only looked at me and gave the loudest, the most terrible of the howls she had given all night. I was enraged, I was, I was...crazed. I raised the stick and...I hit her. I hit her!' His voice broke, and now he was weeping. 'I struck her again and again. I thought I could never harm anything. I thought that in a war I shouldn't have been able to lift a weapon. And…I killed her. I *killed her!*' His breath shuddered. 'I am so sorry. *I am so sorry.*'

'It's all right, James. You were human, is all.'

'But. I—*I*…I cannot bear it!' He went away down the corridor behind him, weeping.

In the morning, Denton was up before daybreak, tiptoeing down the stairs, shoes in hand, then setting the shoes down at the closed door that led into the rear of the house and opening it, fearful that Mrs Esmond or Emmeline or Mavis would be up ahead of him. The dark passage beyond was empty, however. He made his way to a door that led outside, felt over its barely visible surface and found two stout bolts, both closed. His groping fingers also found a barked log propped under the doorknob. He shone his flashlight on it. It was oak, more than three inches thick, its upper end worn as smooth as a piece of furniture where years of grasping had polished it.

So the thieves couldn't have come through this door even if they'd had a key. He was looking for the way in if it had really been an inside job and the broken windowpane had been a feint.

He retreated and made his way to the garden room where James dictated his books to a secretary working directly on a typewriter. The method sounded daft to Denton, who demanded privacy when he worked, but maybe he should try it, he thought; James's results were certainly better. He expected a door to the outside from this room, but the only other door led into the walled garden. So not this way, either. Unless they came through the garden.

It was getting light enough to see outdoors. He went into the garden, finding it wet with dew and seductive with the smell of roses, hoisted himself up on the brick wall in several places and hung there, looking over into the back gardens of the adjacent cottages and the lane behind Lamb House. He found a narrow door in a corner near the French doors that he knew led back into the house, but it was locked and solid; he pictured more bolts and another log.

James had said that the police believed the burglars had come over the garden wall. If they had, they had left no sign that he could find.

He let himself out the front door and walked around to the lane and looked at that side of the garden wall. Lamb House was a complex structure, its outer perimeter uneven, with nooks and crannies it would have been easy to hide in. He saw where they might have put up a ladder and been mostly hidden—at night, invisible—from the few windows nearby. And there was the lane, convenient for a cart or barrow to carry the loot away.

To where? Not the train. Not storage in the town, surely; everybody in Rye must know what went on in every outhouse and shed. Some sort of cart? How far? And how much stuff? Too much for a couple of men to carry? Three? Four?

Denton walked along the lane as the sky brightened and, in the space framed by a house and an ancient oak, the sky turned golden, pregnant with light. He walked to that end, then turned and went back to the other, looking at the cottages that flanked James's garden, a couple of other houses, a small field. Nothing seemed to suggest that it had been used to store stolen goods.

When he turned back, he saw a figure heading towards him, barely visible in the brilliance of the now risen sun. Denton meant to take a path that would lead him again to the front of Lamb House, but he saw the figure turn in along the first cottage and he hurried to follow. There was a narrow passage, the cottage on the right, and beyond a kind of tunnel, its roof a leafy one, and another door into Lamb House.

'I'm a guest of Mr James's.' Denton was breathing hard from running. 'Can I get in this way?'

The man was old, gaunt, hard-worked. 'Don't know as I should, sir.'

'Are you Gammon?' He'd rather baulked at thinking somebody could be named Gammon, but then there were Bacons and Hams, too.

'I am.' He had an odd dignity, some of it simply the slowness of his speech, as if he had measured the world's pace and decided not to match it.

'My name's Denton. Mr James has asked me to help him with the burglary.'

Gammon looked him up and down and said, 'I heard about you.'

'From Mrs Esmond?'

'Maybe.' He held the door open; perhaps Mrs Esmond's name was Denton's bona fides.

There was a tiled passage, a room with boots and a tattered mackintosh and gardening tools. Denton said, 'I wondered where these things were kept.'

'Can't have them in the garden, spoil the sense of it.'

'Awkward for you, I'd think.'

'Could be.' Gammon got a pair of secaturs and gloves and led the way to a narrow door that to Denton's surprise opened into the garden and proved to be the unexplained door he'd seen in the corner. To get out, Gammon had had to undo two bolts and remove another log from under the knob. Denton said, 'Are all the doors bolted and secured this way?'

Gammon, chary with words, nodded.

'The one we came in, too?'

Gammon nodded again, thought it over, said slowly, 'The girl undoes it first thing she gets up. They know I come early.'

Denton followed him into the garden. The grass was still wet. When Gammon began to move among the roses that clung to the walls, their scent redoubled. He clipped dead flowers, the odd twig.

'You found the evidence of the burglary?' Denton said.

'I found yon broken window.' Gammon nodded towards the French doors.

'Glass on the step outside?' He knew better than that, but he wanted to know what the man would say.

Gammon shook his head and snipped off a spotted leaf. 'Inside.'

'Did you go in?'

'No key. That door we come in will get us into the garden but not into the house. Inside door is locked.'

'But...' Denton was seeing it as he supposed it happened. 'If the first maid up opens the door we came in by and the inside door, and the maids were away that night, the doors should have been locked.'

'Didn't say they wasn't. Fact, they was both locked fast, so I was locked out. I thought, them lazy scuts's done it again. The third time since Mr James went away. Them two was the worst we ever had here, each one worse than the other. Good riddance they're gone.'

'How did you get into the garden, then?'

'It happened before, didn't it? So I knew what to do. Got the dustbin from Simons's cottage and got up on it and come over t' wall, which you'd think spry of a man my age, wouldn't you?' He put his nose into a full-blown rose and inhaled, then for the first time smiled. 'A beauty, this one. At its perfection this very moment. Be going by afternoon. Two days, I'll be cutting its head off. Beauty don't last.'

That was a platitude Denton could hardly argue with, so he went back to the wall. 'Up you went and over, and nobody saw you or cared?'

'No, sir.'

'Do you think that's how the thieves got in?'

'Not my business how the thieves got in. Fact, they got in. Nought to do about it now.'

'Then you called the constable.'

'I called nought. I walked down to the police post and told the lad there about yon broken glass, and by and by they sent somebody up. That was that.'

'Why do you think the thieves didn't try to go in through the door from Mr James's writing room, the garden room? It doesn't have bolts.'

'No need, was there? That door has a lock would keep out an elephant. Patent lock. Takes two turns round of the key and is picklock-proof, was what the smith told me when he put it in. Mr James is very strict about keeping his house safe.'

Did this suggest, Denton wondered, that the burglars knew about that lock? Or had they tried it and found it too much for them? A good lock man ought to be able to get into anything, in his view, but maybe in the middle of the night, in a strange town, not wanting to make noise, wanting to get in and out fast, maybe breaking a pane of glass had been the easy and safe way. But they'd known about the other doors, surely, as they hadn't even tried them. Had they?

He examined the lockplate of the door to the garden room, then went out and looked at the outside of the other two rear doors. So far as he could see, there were no evident scratches or nicks. So perhaps they had known something about Henry James's doors.

He went back and talked some more to Gammon, who was now on his hands and knees to pull all but invisible weeds out of the crumbly soil. Nothing more came: to Gammon, the crime had happened, he had seen the broken glass, the constable had come, he had done his work and gone home. No, he hadn't seen the two bone-lazy maids again. No, he hadn't been there when Mrs Esmond returned. Yes, the police had questioned him. No, he'd seen no sign that anybody had been up on the wall, and he knew of no ladder that was easy to get at and close by; on the other hand, if he could come over the wall on a dustbin, why couldn't they have?

Female figures had been passing back and forth behind the French doors. Smelling breakfast among the waves of roses, Denton rapped on the glass and was let in by, he thought, Mavis.

'Breakfast now, sir?'

'Tea, anyway, if I could.'

'Oh yes, Miz Esmond's been up ever so long.'

The breakfast was served by the less pretty of the two maids. The food was too abundant, too rich; Denton did his best to satisfy Mrs Esmond, although he wasn't hungry. James appeared a few minutes after he had sat down, freshly shaved, talcum-powdered, dressed in rather over-tailored country clothes, as if he were going to play a village squire in the West End. He showed no sign of last night's drinking, and he gave no hint of remembering the evening's end.

James produced two sheets of paper with names from his guest book—everybody, he said, who had visited him in the months before he'd gone to America. The recent tenants and whatever guests of theirs Mrs Esmond remembered were listed separately. Denton began to study the pages.

James clapped his hands together. 'The rain is over, a fine, soft rain, as the saying is, capital for the garden and coming by night; what could be better? I shall have only a boiled egg, Mavis—is it Mavis?—Emmeline, then, and tell just that to Mrs Esmond, she will know how I like it. No, my child, don't ask me about toast and so on; *she will know*. Off you go.' He beamed at Denton. 'You slept?'

'Very well. You seem to have a lot of literary guests.' He saw the names of H. G. Wells, one of the Bensons, Violet Hunt and then Edmund Gosse, and he remembered Harris and the dinner for George Meredith.

'I wish you were staying, Denton. We could have a walk in Romney Marsh. On the roads, I mean. I used to "take a spin" on my bicycle there. Miles and miles! I was quite a sight, I am sure, much laughed at, but the bicycle is an *inspired* mode of transportation. Will you have more muffins? Mrs Esmond's muffins are rather famous. You must try at least one. I can't afford to hurt her feelings. Difficult at best, between you and me. Preserves? Cooper's? You seem very lucky in your servants.'

'Only the one.' Denton's mouth was full of muffin. Butter ran down his chin. James's guest list, he saw, included a member of Parliament; should he be impressed? Probably not, he guessed.

'Yes, yes, the one. Seemed quite a sound chap. A nice sense of tone, I thought.'

Denton thought he'd have to tell that one to Atkins.

James said, 'Ah, my egg. Thank you, Mavis, and now you might get the door, as the bell is being rung. Good, yes, well done.' He cracked the top of the egg with a spoon. 'Girls come from the farms; Mrs Esmond teaches them and they become quite competent, but in the beginning they know nothing.'

'Who're Mr and Mrs Gaddis?'

'Who, indeed? The name means nothing to me. Ah, wait—members of a party that stopped at tea-time and had motor-car difficulties and had to be put up overnight. Rather awkward.'

Denton folded the list and put it into an inside pocket. 'I suppose the police have questioned them all by now.' He patted the pocket. 'God knows I won't.'

Mavis, if indeed her name was Mavis (Denton thought that the other one was Mavis; this was Emmeline), came in with a yellow envelope on a silver salver—Mrs Esmond must have intercepted her between the front door and the breakfast room, salver in hand.

James snatched the telegram from the dish, tore the top off the envelope in little strokes, as if he were peeling a fruit, and read the folded yellow paper inside. He flushed; his eyes rose to Denton's, and he pushed the telegram into a side pocket of his jacket. 'Publishers, publishers,' he murmured.

James was a good liar. Most men who have been out in the world for a while are. But Denton knew he was lying; the initial look had been alarm and perhaps guilt. Because of the telegram.

'I have to go,' Denton said.

'To be sure, to be sure! I shall just finish my little egg and be with you...'

Denton said there was no need; James said yes, yes, he walked every morning and he would walk Denton to the station. When Denton came downstairs with his Gladstone, having sent Emmeline (he thought) away when she had offered to carry it for him, James was waiting for him at the front door. He had changed his clothes, now looked like a city gent.

'Going to town, James?'

'No, no, only I must seem of a certain gravitas in Rye. They expect a successful author to look like a banker, you know.'

In that case, Denton wondered why he'd appeared first in the country clothes.

'Bringing Nicco?'

'Ah, poor little chap, not this time. He's in the kitchen, being made fat by the maids. Shall we go?'

It displeased Denton that he thought that James was lying to him again.

The walk down through the town was again a progress. A damped-down excitement seemed to have a grip on James; his greetings were just a touch too effusive, his smiles a quarter-lip too broad. He talked; he babbled. More history of the town—French attackers and the old town wall and the tower built for defence. When the train appeared, he bundled Denton into a first-class compartment and stood only part of a minute saying over again some of the things he had already said, and then he all but jumped down and said, laughing, 'I don't wish to be carried off to London!'

After James had left the platform and, presumably, the station, Denton moved to the other window of the compartment to give himself a better view of the rest of the train. Again, voices called; compartment doors slammed; the whistle tooted. And then, just before the train began its slide away from Rye, James scurried across the platform and opened a door and struggled aboard.

Denton wondered if it was the first time in his life that Henry James had travelled second class.

At Victoria, Denton hurried out of his compartment and got into a stream of people to make himself as inconspicuous as a tall man could be. At the cab stand, he jumped into a hansom and said, before the driver could ask, 'We're waiting for somebody else. Put the cab someplace where I can watch people come out.'

'Oh, right, then.'

'He's going to take another cab and you're going to follow it.'

'You having me on, guv?'

'Truth.'

'Well, I've heard of it but I never done it before.' The cab jiggled as the driver seemed to settle back, then jiggled again as he swung forward and opened the hatch. 'You a detective or an ill-treated husband?'

'Both.'

The cab shifted back again and the hatch slammed. Almost fifteen minutes later, Henry James came out. As Denton had expected, he hadn't taken the underground and had waited until the train was empty—waited until Denton was sure to be gone, was what the delay really meant—and now Denton hoped he was going directly to the source of the telegram and not to the Reform, where he kept a room.

'That one,' he said. 'The plump fellow in the wide hat.'

'Don't look the type. Don't look the type at all.'

Denton had to think about that, decided that the man meant that James didn't look the sort to steal another man's wife. He wanted to say that looks weren't everything, or something equally sage, but it was too late by the time he thought of it.

They headed east on Victoria Street and into the Strand, a dubious decision because of the traffic, but Denton's driver said that it wasn't his fault, was it; on they went, maddeningly, into Fleet Street.

'Ought to lose his licence, that chap,' the driver said. 'Running up the fare something awful.' They turned into Queen Victoria Street. Denton wondered if perhaps it was James who had chosen the route, relishing the ride because of what seemed like a triumphant mood. Maybe he enjoyed the London of the old jingle that ended 'London is a man's town, with power in the air.' Or maybe he was early for whatever appointment the telegram had made and was killing time.

The cab ahead drew up at an unmistakable complex of buildings: the Royal Exchange. Denton jumped down, his eyes on James, who was getting down more slowly and with more dignity from his own hansom. 'Wait here,' Denton told his driver.

'Here now, don't you run off on me.'

'I've left my grip, haven't I?'

Denton followed James up the broad steps and inside. James seemed to know exactly where he was going, crossed the vast court and headed for a staircase at the east end. A uniformed porter said to Denton, 'Help you, sir?'

'What's up those stairs?'

'That's Lloyd's, sir. Mercantile insurance and so on.' He said something else, but Denton ignored him, instead ran up the stairs, went through a doorway that looked large and important in time to see Henry James's portly figure vanish through a door at the far end of a big room filled with desks but mostly empty of people. Denton started to follow but was intercepted by a quite formally dressed man with a chairman's manner and an actor's voice.

'May I be of service, sir?'

'I, uh, wanted to see the famous Lloyd's.'

'Yes, many gentlemen do, but there's little to see, I'm afraid, sir.'

'What's through that door?'

'The reading room for our Members only, I'm afraid, and beyond that the Captain's Room, our restaurant for Members and their guests. Are you perhaps a guest of a Member, sir?'

'Uh, no. No, I'm a tourist. American.'

'I thought as much from your voice, sir. If I could answer any questions...'

'I just saw somebody go through that door.'

'Yes, sir.' Meaning, you may say that, but I'm not adding to it.

'Does Lloyds do insurance for household burglaries?'

'Here at Lloyd's, sir, we are proud that we *pioneered* house-burglary insurance.'

'I see. Good. Good. Thank you very much...' Denton bowed himself backward as if leaving a potentate. He supposed that James was meeting somebody who could penetrate the inner reaches on a Sunday, and there didn't seem to be any way to follow him.

He climbed back into his cab. 'That's it, then. Take me to Lamb's Conduit Street.'

'Caught him, did you, guv?'

'I let him go. Drive on.'

On the ride to his house, Denton brooded as he had brooded on the train. Henry James had lied to him. That was the essence of it. There was a measure of deviousness in James's face, his eyes, at best; that look of shrewdness, of avian intelligence, also suggested a tolerance for deceit. But how did all that square with the blubbering confession of the killing of the cat?

James was a man who held himself back from intimacy; he was known for it. He had pierced that defensive wall, it was true, to ask Denton to help him, but since then their relations had been merely courteous, merely conventional—until the question at supper about war and killing, and then the story of the cat.

The cat, the cat—why had he told Denton about the cat?

A confession, he had said. And the astonished tone in which he had said 'I killed her!' As if Henry James couldn't possibly have killed something. Was that it, that he had disappointed some deep moral self-confidence?

And then to lie to Denton. First a difficult truth, then the easy lie. Was the lie the revenge for the telling of the truth? That would be very human of him. There had been a certain glee to James after the telegram had come and while he was walking Denton to the station—the pleasure of tricking the man he had confessed to? A kind of mortar to stick together the new bricks he was laying up around his private self?

At any rate, Henry James had lied to him. In word and in deed. And had seemed pleased with himself while doing it, utterly unlike the man who had suffered such anguish over killing a cat. And what had set off his pleasure, apparently, was a telegram that had something to with insurance; enough, in fact, to bring him back to London from his beloved Rye. And his new dog.

Inside his own house, giving his hat and coat to Atkins, Denton said, 'Why does a man lie about something that's connected to insurance?' The question was mostly rhetorical, partly to get Atkins's corroboration of what he had worked out.

'That's an easy one. Because he's on the fiddle.'

'What fiddle?'

'Collect the insurance and pretend something's happened to something he owned, which he says was burnt or nicked or otherwise lost to his use and quiet enjoyment.'

'But what if it's an insurance company that he goes to visit after he's lied?'

'They're on to him.' Atkins used a foot to push away the new dog, which, more enterprising than Rupert, was interested in Denton's crotch.

'He seemed too pleased for that. Beside himself with delight, in fact. Have you got a name for this animal yet?'

'I'm thinking of Sammy. Or possibly Henry. Like Mr James. This fiddler you're asking about *is* Mr Henry James, I take it. The one that wanted your help in recovering a certain object. Well, putting two and two together and getting three, I'd say he's heard good news about his losses. Maybe got his object back.'

'Why lie to me about it?'

'Doesn't want to hurt your feelings.'

'That's weak.'

'You don't pay me to be a bleeding genius, Major. This comes off the top of my head, *extempore*.' He looked with disgust at the young dog, who had collapsed on his side, exactly like his father.

'James says you have a nice sense of tone.'

'What's that mean, I toady nicely? Thank you, sir, very good, sir, very good of you, I'm sure. You know he gave me sixpence when he left here? I've had worse.'

Denton started up the stairs, stopped. 'But why would the good news that made him so happy come from the insurance people and not the coppers?'

Atkins was heading for his own regions but came back. From his position on the stairs, Denton could see that Atkins's hair was getting thin on top. Had they been together that long? Atkins said, 'The easy answer is that it's the insurance found the swag, not the coppers. Maybe that's the fiddle. What my suspicious mind makes of that is that money is changing hands.'

'Insurance companies are in the business to make money, not pay it out.'

'Yes, they are, but if a contract says they got to pay shilling for shilling to the party of the second part if he loses his goods, then they'd scratch like Billy-O to be able to get the goods back for him at, let's say, sixpence in the shilling, what about that?'

Denton put a foot up on the next stair tread and stopped. 'They've made their own deal with the thieves, you mean.'

'Would be my humble opinion.'

'Which wouldn't please the police overmuch.'

'Might even rub them up the wrong direction.'

'If they even knew about it.'

'They'd have to, wouldn't they?'

'I'm wondering.' Denton went up a step. 'Speaking of coppers, has Mr Munro called?'

'Not a peep out of him. If you're going out again, change that suit. Looks like you slept in it. Bleeding railways.'

Denton tried to call Munro to find if there was anything new about Wragge, but Munro was 'out' from Scotland Yard. During the afternoon he called twice more, once to ask for Wragge himself—'out'—and then once to be told that Munro had moved to N Division and might be at the Angel station, but it was thought he was touring the sub-divisions.

Denton gave it up. He had thought that if Wragge had appeared, he might talk to him about James and the insurance business and the telegram, but, overcome now by inertia, he saw that he probably wouldn't have done anything about anything, even if Wragge had turned up in his sitting room. The lassitude he had been feeling at the dinner where James had grabbed him settled into numbness—the familiar sense that nothing was worth doing.

He astonished Atkins by going to bed at eight. Janet was working—the apprentice solicitor's life. He slept for an hour, dreamed bad dreams about cats and his dead wife and failure, then woke and lay there, still numb. Angry with himself, he threw on some clothes and went through the dark garden to Janet's. She was just home, tired but to his relief glad enough to see him. She ate the cold supper that had been left for her; he nibbled; they made love. Lying close with her in her bed, he said, 'Henry James isn't being forthright with me.'

'Is this the proper time to tell me that?'

'I can't get it out of my head.' He waited for some sharp reply. When none came, he said, 'He dodged around the name of whoever wrote him the letters. The letters in the box. I told you about the—'

'The box, yes, the box; I'm not an idiot.'

Denton was thinking out loud. 'James likes to keep his hands on the reins. And nobody else's. He thinks he can keep me in the dark about part of it and then I'll just look into the burglary for him. Not look at the whole story. Are you asleep?'

'How could I be?'

'It's no good me running around like a chicken with its head cut off, talking to people the cops have already talked to. What I need to find out is who knew about those letters. Is that impossible? Easy enough to find when James was first in Paris—that'll be in something he wrote about himself, probably—and then? The family name? How do I get that?'

She sounded drowsy, but she said, 'You'll do better starting with Balzac. Find whom he wrote *his* letters to.'

'I don't read French. Or know how the French do things.'

'Oh, you can get somebody to do that if you pay a bit.'

He made the mistake of saying, 'You read French.'

She rolled towards him, propped herself on one arm. 'Denton, I make time for you as my lover, but I'm damned if I'll make time for your enthusiasms! Find your own damned French speaker!' She threw herself down and rolled back the way she had been, pulling the bedcovers half off him. He was irritated— *enthusiasms* seemed harsh—and then he wanted not to have angered her and he tried to think of what to say, but before he could get anything out she rolled back partway and said, 'I'll do this much: I'll stop at University College and put up a notice for you. "Fluent French required." You'll have to pay. Can you pay?'

'Some.'

'Some is all it will take; students always need money. Now go back to your own house and let me sleep.' She rolled away and pulled the rest of the bedclothes off him.

CHAPTER

He was back in his own house and still awake a little after two, a nearby church bell just struck, when the telephone rang. He was surprised because of the hour but glad of it, something to do. He kicked the bedcovers back and shrugged into a ratty old robe as he went down the stairs, and he was standing at the telephone with the earpiece at his ear before he ever heard Atkins stumble out of bed below him.

'Ready! Denton here.'

The voice was distant and metallic. 'It's Munro.'

'Munro! You know the time?'

A garble of sound, then '...be damned. I want you and that motor-car of yours.'

'No you don't.' He stopped himself, tried to think. 'Why?'

Another garble, and '...business. They called me out of bed and I had Hell's own time getting to the Yard. Last tram of the night, half-dressed. I want you and your motor-car and I won't take no for an answer. And tell that man of yours to be up and awake; I want to talk to him.'

'Munro, it's after two!'

'We can be there by three in your motor.'

'In God's name, where?'

'I told you!'

'You didn't!'

'Stoke Newington! Are you deaf? Now you get that car! I'll be there as fast as a carriage can bring me!'

He rang off. Denton thought of going back to bed and letting Atkins deal with Munro. The policeman didn't have the right to do such a thing. It was worse than an imposition. He wouldn't do it.

'News from town?'

'I'm supposed to get the car. Inspector Munro.'

'What I thought.'

'And he wants to talk to you, he says. He'll be here shortly.'

'What about? What have I done?'

'Stay awake and you'll find out.' Denton started up the stairs. 'I'm going back to bed.'

'Here! You leaving me to take the brunt of it?'

Denton looked down at him. His inertia swung the other way: it was easier to get the car than to put up with Atkins's justified outrage. He swore. Of course he'd get his car and drive to Stoke Newington. Could it be worse than lying awake in the dark or lying asleep and dreaming of failure? Or giving Atkins a reason to complain for days?

He pulled on the oldest suit that Atkins would let him keep and a pair of soft boots. He put on an old cloth cap and went out. It was still warm enough to go without an overcoat, despite the hour.

He kept the car, a tiny three-seater Barré, in a shed several streets away. Once out, he found himself enjoying the darkness and the near-silence of the city. The air smelled of flowers and green leaves and dust, summer heat and manure. His long legs devoured the distance; he was sorry when he reached the shed. *I should walk more at this hour. Often awake anyway. Force myself out of bed and be the only one about.* Maybe it would be a cure for the inertia.

He hadn't had the car out in a week, hoped it wouldn't give him trouble. It was more than two years old, starting to act up. He pushed it out into the open yard and closed the shed doors, then set the spark and did his own cranking and was surprised by having it catch on the first crank.

Wake everybody within half a mile.

The car was noisy—one cylinder, which sounded like a trip-hammer, and a chain-drive mechanism that had started making a noise like cracking nutshells. He passed a policeman, who looked at him with a frown that said he was thinking of making an arrest. Denton waved and went on, turned into Guilford Street and then Lamb's Conduit and found Munro just waving a police carriage away from the kerb.

Munro watched him pull in where the carriage had been. Denton reduced the throttle and withdrew the spark and the car died. In the silence that followed, he almost whispered, 'What's this about, Munro?' He went very close to the policeman.

'Tell you later. Where's Atkins?'

'Where would he be at this ungodly hour? He's in the house.'

Munro moved to the door. Denton reached for the bell, but the door opened and Atkins and both dogs appeared. As if it were his own house, Munro warned Denton off with a hand and said, 'You stay out here. I won't be a minute.'

Denton leaned against his gate. It was ridiculous to be kept outside your own house at the dead low of the morning. He breathed the night air again, thought idly that he would never find London's air sweeter. It would be fine air to be breathing if you were twenty and coming home from some dance in Mayfair and had a girl who was crazy about you. That was what such air was for, the young and their follies. He breathed it again and laughed. He should thank Munro for bringing him out of his dumps and into this.

The door opened and Munro came down in a rush. 'Let's go.'

'What's up?'

'Tell you as we go. Come on, come on...'

'You crank.'

'Oh, cripes, I all but broke my wrist the last time!'

Denton turned a half-circle in the empty street, swung right into Guilford, and then three streets on crossed Gray's Inn Road and went into Calthorpe Street.

'Where are you going?' Munro shouted over the noise.

'You said Stoke Newington.'

'This isn't how you go to Stoke Newington! You want Pentonville Road.'

'No I don't.'

When he crossed King's Cross Road, Munro howled, 'You should have taken Farringdon to Clerkenwell!'

'If I'd wanted to show you the beauties of Hoxton by night, you mean, I could have. Shut up, Munro.'

'Turn right up here at City Road! Now I'm telling you!'

'Who's driving this hack, you or me?'

'You want to get to Kingsland Road. That's the way to get to Stoke Newington—Kingsland Road!'

'Tell me what's going on.'

'Are you going to Kingsland Road or aren't you?'

'I'm going by the quickest way I know. What's going on?'

Munro withdrew into his suit jacket, chin on chest. Denton, delighted to be able to fly at twenty miles an hour through the empty streets, the car lamps leading by their thin wash of yellow light, began to sing. When he drove right through the intersection where Pentonville turned into City Road, Munro banged a fist on the dash. Denton grinned, tried to pull the throttle out still farther, and bent the beams of light into Essex Road.

'Now tell me what's going on, or I'll turn down into De Beauvoir Town and push you out at a crossing.'

'You're interfering with police business.'

'I'm saving twenty minutes of driving is what I'm doing. Munro, what the hell is going on and what's the rush?'

Munro sank still lower, although his knees were already jammed against the dash. He growled, 'Somebody found a body in my new parish. Welcome to N Division.'

'Misadventure? Wrongful death?'

'Guillam thinks something like that.'

'What's Guillam to do with it?'

'I told you, didn't I? He's been in N for two years, knows his way about. I've made him sub-divisional inspector up there.

Station sergeant took the complaint, called Guillam because it looked like...looked bad.' He wriggled himself partway back up. 'Guillam called me. Where the hell are we now?'

'Getting on for St Paul's Road. What aren't you telling me?'

'Tons of things. For now, anyway.'

'Is it about Wragge?'

Denton could feel Munro stop to think. 'Why should it be about Wragge?'

'Because day before yesterday you called me because he'd gone missing.'

'I don't see the connection. Your mind works strangely.'

'It's about Wragge somehow, isn't it? Is the body Wragge?'

'Would I know, never having seen it? Would I tell you if I did know?'

Denton pulled right into St Paul's Road and turned again almost at once into King Henry's Walk. Munro bellowed, 'What the hell are you doing?' He tried to rise from the prison of the seat to look around but was wedged. He might have been about to say something, but he turned his head, looked back and shouted, 'Slow down! Turn around! Can't you see we're here?'

'Where? The high street's up ahead.' But Denton was slowing and preparing to turn.

'Boleyn Road! That was Boleyn Road and you went right past it.'

Denton turned while spluttering that Munro had said Kingsland Road, and Stoke Newington High Street was a continuation of Kingsland Road; who had said anything about a Boleyn Street?

Munro wiggled himself upward. 'Go left at the next crossing. Then immediately right. You see? Right. The police station is the one with the blue lamps in front.' Said in a tone of profound sarcasm.

When the car was stopped, Munro climbed out as if he were getting over a stile and looked at his watch and said, 'Not too shabby. Now I know why I asked you to come.' He went into the police station. But, Denton thought, the car wasn't the reason

Munro had brought him. Wragge was the reason: a dead body, some very short questions to Atkins ('Where was Mr Denton last night?'), Denton's supposed dust-up with Wragge.

When Munro came out thirty seconds later, he had the station sergeant right behind him. 'You in front,' Munro said to the sergeant; to Denton he said, 'He's going to direct you.' Munro headed for the rear of the car. Denton started to say that the rear seat was too small, but Munro was already backing into it—it faced rearward—and then both he and the station sergeant got in at the same time. The Barré was nominally a three-seater, but it was best if two of them were children. The springs groaned and gave up, settling down on their supports. Denton could imagine all four tyres going at once. 'Drive on!' Munro shouted.

Denton pulled on the throttle. The engine banged, and the car moved jerkily forward. 'We're a bit of a load.' He gave it more throttle and turned out into the road. If he hit a bump, it would be the end of a tyre for sure. At the first crossing, the sergeant pointed right and Denton turned as slowly as if he were pulling into a street paved with eggs. Three slow streets on, he was pointed left.

'Where are we going?'

'Cemetery, sir.'

From the back, Munro groaned, 'Can't you put some speed into this thing?'

'No.'

After the exhilaration of the drive up Essex Road, these fifteen minutes were agony. Munro said once that he could have walked it as fast; the sergeant said it was a lovely night. Denton treated the car as if it were made of glass. At last, however, he saw a sign that said 'Abney Park Cemetery', and the sergeant pointed into the maw of a pair of open wrought-iron gates, behind them utter blackness.

'They're somewheres th'other side of the church.'

Denton drove on. He never saw the church, but the sergeant, who had already had to get out once to lead him along what seemed to be a gravel path, pointed ahead at a glow of light. 'That's them.'

The motor-car's lamps barely brought the first headstones out of the darkness. The stones dropped behind and new shapes appeared, arches, angels, tiny temples. When the sergeant said, 'Stop!', he stopped.

'Down there, sir.' This said to Munro. He hopped down. 'If you won't be needing me, Inspector, I'll walk back.'

'Denton can drive you.'

'Good night for a walk, sir. Just as fast.'

Denton didn't tell him that with only two of them, he'd go faster. Instead, he got out too and followed Munro towards the light. It was intensely dark; they both stumbled, Munro almost falling headlong over a stone. Denton caught him, pulled him up, and Munro said, 'You still here? I told you to wait at the motor-car.'

'You didn't, actually.'

Munro strode on. Denton followed, stumbled again, found himself going down a gentle slope where the light from several coal-oil lanterns, faint as it was, seemed bright by contrast. Ahead were several dark figures, four lanterns on the ground, deep shadows.

'About time,' a hard male voice said. Denton recognised it as Guillam's, an inspector he'd sometimes got grief from.

'Bloody slow motor-cars,' he heard Munro say. So much for gratitude. Munro, ahead of him, joined one of the dark figures and the two stepped a few feet away from the rectangle of lights. Denton came closer; a uniformed constable said, 'Are you with Mr Munro, sir?'

'I am.' That seemed to be taken as authoritative. Denton started to take a step closer to the lanterns, and a man on the other side of the rectangle said, 'Don't walk there! If you please, sir—trying to preserve the scene.'

'Of course.' Denton had already seen the crumpled pile of clothes at the centre of the lanterns. A man's shoes, soles towards him and the toes pointing into the dirt, were most recognisable, then a dark trouser leg that might have been blue. He could make little of the head. One hand was a pale smudge that disappeared into what he supposed was ivy or creeper.

'The bad penny,' a voice said at his left side.

'Hello, Guillam.'

'You have a way of turning up.'

'I was asked.'

Guillam grunted. He was as tall as Denton, heavier; his pock-marked face was ominous, otherworldly with the light shining on it from below. He said, 'What do you know about this?'

'Munro's been mum.' He looked at the form on the ground and lowered his voice. 'Is it Wragge?'

'Don't know yet.' Guillam, who had been looking at the dead man, too, turned his head towards Denton. 'Who said it might be?'

'Putting two and two together.'

'You're always a great one for that.' Guillam was wearing a light overcoat, although he hardly needed one that balmy night. He plunged his hands deep into the pockets. 'We've been waiting for the surgeon since midnight. Bloody slacker. Some local quack.'

They were speaking very low, but the constable said from a few feet away, 'He's on his way, sir.'

'He's been on his way since yesterday.'

'Burns spoke to his wife, sir. He was out on a call, coming here next.'

'What was he doing, consulting in Paris?'

'Delivering a baby, I think, sir.'

Munro came out of the darkness to join Denton on his other side. 'Recognise anything?' he said.

'I'm not much on shoe soles.'

Munro called over another man in plain clothes, the one who had spoken to Denton and turned out to be a detective sergeant. Prodded by Munro, he said, 'There's nothing in his pockets. First constable on the scene went through them. Probably shouldn't have, but it's done.'

Munro sighed. 'Coppers up here are living in the nineteenth century.'

'Constable found him?' Denton said.

'Courting couple, as the expression is. Apparently they were having a grope and she had to relieve herself, came over this way and found this gooseberry. The lad at least had the gumption to tell the station sergeant. Walked the girl home first—she was having herself a fine case of the jim-jams—then he walked to the station. That was an hour lost. Then the sergeant called Inspector Guillam...' He directed his voice at Munro. 'Your orders, sir.'

'Right they were.'

'He got here after midnight, that was another hour lost.'

'And then they called me, and that was two more hours lost! I know. Where the devil's the surgeon?'

'He's just coming, they say.'

They stood around. Another constable came with a metal pail of tea and some tin cups that scalded the lips but were welcome. Another twenty minutes later, an old man preceded by a bobbing lantern came slowly towards them. He seemed infirm and supported himself on headstones when he could. Close to, he looked ancient and unwell. He said, 'It was a girl. Nine hours of labour, extremely vexing. What have we here?' He was putting on a pair of gold-rimmed glasses that reflected the lanterns' light and made his eyes invisible.

'Corpse,' Guillam said.

'It could have waited till morning.' The old man smiled, a rather terrible sight. 'He's not going anywhere.'

'He'd be going to the morgue now if you'd stirred your stumps,' Munro growled.

'Stirred my stumps! I've a mind to turn right 'round and leave you to find yourself another surgeon. If you can!' He laughed again and looked around them.

Munro's face suggested that he was going to be looking to put a new surgeon under contract at daybreak. 'Get on with it,' he muttered.

'Indeed, indeed. Birth to death, all in a night's work. Where's my satchel? Somebody took my... Oh, thank you. Right.' He stepped past a lantern, almost knocking it over, and put his foot down next to the body, and the detective sergeant howled. The doctor looked towards the noise, blinked, squinted, muttered something and walked all the way around the body as if to make sure to obscure any traces that the first constable might have left.

Munro groaned, 'Good Lord.'

Guillam whispered, 'I took my shoes off and had a look first thing with my flashlight. No marks except the constable's boots.'

'You can't be sure until daylight.'

'Daylight won't do us any good now.'

Munro shook his head and swore again. He looked at Denton and said, 'What are you still doing here?'

'You brought me.'

To his surprise, Munro laughed. 'So I did.'

The surgeon was discouragingly quick. He had a constable roll the body over, studied what was left of the face with the help of two lanterns, went through the pockets, put fingers on the carotid artery and raised a lid on the one eye that was still an eye and said, 'Dead. Cause probably violent blows to the head, but I won't stand by that until the autopsy.' He stood. 'You can remove him now.'

Guillam stared at him. 'We've waited three hours for you, you bloody fool! You haven't given us two minutes!'

'He's dead! That's my job, to say if he's alive or dead! Don't you call me names, you hulking Irish brute!' He supported himself on a constable's shoulder and pointed into the darkness—the wrong way, actually. 'Lead me out of here!' He turned back to Guillam. 'I'll lodge a complaint on you. What's the name? I want this lout's name!'

'It's Guillam, George. Detective Inspector Guillam. Sub-Divisional Inspector First Class.'

'Well, your superiors will hear about it!'

Munro raised his hands. 'I'm his superior, and you're an idiot! Get him away from here!' He shook his head. 'It's all right, George; he's done in this division.' He motioned to the constables. 'Hold those lanterns up. At the head, the head, lads. Guillam, Denton, get your flashlight on him, will you? Let's see what we have.'

Guillam and Denton went close. Denton leaned in, curving his body to keep from casting a shadow on the destroyed face. The nose had been moved to one side; one eye was missing. The left side of the face was red pulp. The blood had dried and had matted into the hair all the way to the top of the head.

Guillam said, 'I couldn't find any blood under him. He didn't bleed here.'

'Killed someplace else?'

Guillam lifted one of the dead man's arms. 'Been dead a while. Rigor's subsided. Yesterday? Night before?'

Munro said, 'All right, Denton. What do you think?'

He wants to see how I'm taking it. Good God, he thinks I might have killed him. That's why I'm here. At the same time, he was as sure that Munro was trying to eliminate him as a suspect, the suspicion not real. But why entertain it at all? He said, 'Is it Wragge?'

'I want to hear what you think.'

Denton took a bit of the suit jacket between thumb and two fingers. 'Wragge was wearing a heavy suit like this when we saw him. I remember thinking it was too warm for it.' He looked up at Guillam. 'You know him?'

Guillam shook his head.

Munro, who had been kneeling by the body, pushed himself up and groaned as his knees clicked. 'I think it's Wragge, but I'm not sure. Now listen to me, the lot of you.' He looked around—four men besides Denton and Guillam and Munro himself. 'If you heard us say anything, keep your gobs shut. No identification has been made. Victim is male, and that's all, full stop. I don't want to hear a ghost of a breath of rumour coming out of this station tomorrow. Understood? All right, get the mortuary jockeys in here and let's clear him away. Upshaw, secure the scene and leave a constable and two lanterns here. Guillam, I want the area searched at first light; get yourself a kip at the station and might as well plan you'll be here until the autopsy report's in. Denton, you come with me.' He picked up a lantern.

He led Denton into the shadow of a mausoleum that seemed to have a murky resemblance to the Parthenon.

'That goes for you, too. Keep mum.'

'I'm not a journalist, Munro.'

Munro perched his buttocks on a headstone and took off his hat. 'It's Wragge, I'm pretty sure.'

'That's why you brought me.'

''Course it is.' Munro fanned himself with his hat.

'You think somehow I'm involved.'

'I don't think so for a minute, but somebody at the Yard heard Wragge say you were a right shit and he was going to have it out with you. I want to spike that notion right off the reel. Where were you last night? Not this night we're in, but the one before.'

'Rye, staying with Henry James.'

'You got witnesses to that?'

'James, obviously. His housekeeper, two maids.'

'I'll have somebody down there check, just to nail it down. Some of the hard nuts at the Yard would be glad to see you brought up on a charge. Not loved by all.'

'But adored by some. Thanks for thinking of me.'

'Yeah, well… We're pals, after a fashion.' Munro put his hat on. 'Look here, I'm going to have to go by the book on this. Once we get a time of death, then it'll be where were you and who saw you and…you know the drill. Ditto your Mr Henry James; not that I think an author's going to murder a cop, but he's connected to Wragge through the burglary. A formality in his case, too.'

Denton thought about James and the hurried, deceitful trip to London. He said, 'Do you know something you're not telling me?'

'I'd be a hell of a cop if I told you everything I know. But it's early days yet; I don't even know what's worth knowing yet.' He hoisted himself up, one hand on Denton's shoulder. 'You up to driving me back to the Yard?'

'You're not going home?'

'And turn right around and get on a tram to the Yard? I'll maybe have a lie-down in the duty office.'

Denton found himself alone with Guillam while Munro talked to the constable who had first seen the body. 'How've you been?' he said. Guillam nodded. Both the question and the nod were a kind of code. Each of them knew something damning about the other—Denton about Guillam's sporadic need for sex with another man, Guillam about Janet's assistance in an illegal abortion. The two secrets had cancelled each other out when they were first learned, but time had made them mostly irrelevant. Guillam's nods meant that things were the same as always—furtive sex, the risk of discovery. He said, 'How's the lady?' Meaning, don't forget I know about her.

'She's fine. Walter Snokes is coming to stay with her this week.' Guillam had been there when Walter had entered their lives, had shown an odd sympathy for him.

'I'd like to see the lad. If that's all right.' Meaning, if you don't think I mean to bugger him.

'Of course it's all right! Do you think I...' Denton bit down on the idiocy of any supposed danger Guillam might be to Walter. 'I'll tell Janet.'

Guillam nodded again. 'Better if she's there. Always better if somebody else is there, eh?' He walked away.

Denton drove Munro to the Yard through the lightening city. The first drays and omnibuses were already rumbling along Kingsland Road. By the time they reached Bishopsgate, the earlier grey was showing colour. At Denton's instigation, they detoured to Covent Garden and had breakfast at a place both knew in King Street that existed to make life bearable at dawn if you'd been up all night, misbehaving. It was mostly full but rather quiet, the haunt of those for whom it was still last night and those for whom it was already tomorrow—men and women from the market, other policemen, even a few prostitutes, one or two real beauties. They were fuelling themselves with sausages and eggs and tea from an urn before they pushed on to work or bed.

'It wasn't kind of you to keep Atkins up,' Denton said across his fried tomatoes and bacon.

'Had to nail it down. Where you were.'

They ate and said little. Munro seemed to know half the people there, nodded and smiled and now and then shook a hand. Denton finished with toasted bread soaked in the puddle of grease on his plate, horrible but wonderful. 'This whole Wragge business is a bit off.'

'Including your part in it. You never tell me everything you know, Denton. But it comes out, finally.' Munro pushed his own plate away and stretched. 'Time to face the day—those of us who must.' He yawned. 'On with the dance.'

Denton was putting the little motor-car away as the sun rose, walked home through streets whose roofs and treetops were just being touched by the first sunlight. He was at his own door before six; he used a key but was met in the downstairs hall by Atkins and the two dogs nonetheless, Atkins in a faded velour robe and slippers.

'Out on the tiles?' he said as he took Denton's hat.

'Looking at a body. The far reaches of Islington.'

'Had any food yet?'

'Grease at Covent Garden, guaranteed to return in three hours or your money back. I could use some coffee, though. Do we have coffee?'

'What do you take me for? Of course we have coffee.'

'Italian. In the little turn-over pot. With hot milk. And sugar.'

'I'm delighted you're not particular about what I give you.' Atkins looked down at the dogs. '"Coffee?" he asks me, and then he adds six things you didn't mean when you said "coffee". Well, come on then, boys, we've work to do.' He looked back from his doorway. 'Toast?'

'I have bad memories of toast at the moment.'

'With cinnamon and sugar?'

'That might drive out the taste of petroleum. Let's give it a try.' He went up to his sitting room and threw himself into his armchair. He was tired, the night almost sleepless, but he felt a kind of exhilaration. The inertia was gone. In its place was a sort of vibrating anticipation, like the slight quiver of a setter on the point. And something was tickling the underside of his brain that might have been the beginning of an idea for a novel. Nothing much, only a feeling like the beginning of a sneeze. But reassuring. He got rid of his boots and went up for slippers and came down again.

'All right, then!' Atkins, with dogs, was coming down the long room. 'Dago coffee *with* hot milk *and* sugar *and* it was made in the turn-over pot you brought back from Naples.' He put down a tray with a teapot and two metal pitchers—one coffee, one milk—and unfolded a little table.

'Try some?'

'Wouldn't let it past my lips. Tea for me, Britain's best, the Army and Navy Mixture, two and eight pence the pound. Cinnamon toast. Butter, but there's butter already on the toast and you professed an aversion to grease. Mind if I sit?' He pulled up a side chair. 'Coffee acceptable?'

'Couldn't be better if you were Italian.'

'Ha-ha. Perish the thought.' Atkins poured himself tea. 'I've had an idea.'

'You already mentioned it.'

'But no details. Not ready to talk then.'

'Now you are.'

'I think.'

'Will it wait until tonight? Mrs Striker wants the evening with Walter Snokes.'

'Not in the mood now? Bit jiggered up, I shouldn't be surprised.'

'I'm thinking of going back to bed for a couple of hours.'

'Spend the day.'

'No, I want to be out by nine. I need to catch Mr James before he leaves his club.'

'They're on the telephone, I daresay.'

Denton shook his head. 'I want to surprise him. Not a social call.'

Atkins looked up from pouring himself more tea. 'Do I smell a rat?' He put the teapot down. 'First it's an insurance fiddle, then it's a body in the middle of the night, now it's jumping out of the wainscoting and saying boo to Henry James. You at it again, Colonel?'

Denton yawned and stretched, then pushed himself out of the green armchair and wiggled past the little table. 'Call me at a quarter past eight.' He started up the room and Atkins called out, 'Don't forget the missus and the lad at Paddington, half-eleven!'

Denton was headed for the stairs. 'I know, I know...' He bumped his shoulder on the telephone and swore.

Denton came up Pall Mall Lane and into Pall Mall itself. He was mostly immune to the West End, certainly to this bastion of the stuffiest kind of privilege, although he'd had a friend who had tried to get him into a club once. It was entirely irrational on his part: he was in his own way a snob—about ability, about having a personal code, about everybody's putting his pants on the same way—but he didn't like the sort of privilege that thought it was Nature's dictate. He didn't like the ideas of 'the right people' and 'the better sort'; he didn't like people who talked about 'the little people'. Still, there he was, going through the doors of the Reform Club as if he belonged.

'Mr Henry James, please.'

'I believe Mr James is at breakfast, sir.'

'Good. I'll join him.'

'Oh, if you would just wait while we announce you, sir. Who shall I say...?'

Denton thought about some way of getting out of it but couldn't. 'Mr Denton.'

'Mr Denton.' He wrote something, touched a bell, gave the slip of paper to the aged flunkey who shuffled by, murmured, 'Mr James.' Then, to Denton, 'If you'll just be seated, sir.'

Well, there were times when privilege was to be preferred. If he'd been his late friend Hector Hench-Rose, Bart., he'd probably have been ushered into the breakfast room solely on the strength of his name. And title. Why hadn't he given himself a title?

Sir Alfred Denton. Lord Francis Denton. Earl Denton? That led to thoughts of money, from money to a new book. He'd have hours between talking to James and meeting Janet at Paddington. Was it a good time to see his editor, ask for an advance on a book he hadn't yet invented? Beard the lion? To do so would be another admission of defeat, another—

'Mr Denton? If you'll follow me, please.'

The aged flunkey went off at a pace that threatened to delay arrival in the breakfast room until lunch. Denton almost bumped into him, thought of going around him, realised he was in the clutches of British tradition. Old Beezer had probably been delaying people at the Reform since Prince Albert was alive. Probably part of the Reform myth.

'Mr Henry James is sitting in the corner, sir. Oh, thank you, sir.' He pocketed Denton's coin without a glance. James, who was chewing, half rose, his napkin held over his groin as if something awkward had happened. He was smiling, however.

'Denton, how nice. However did you find me here? You are prescient, I'm sure. Tea? Coffee? I haven't quite finished breaking my fast...'

They both sat. Denton said, 'I knew where you were because I followed you to the Royal Exchange yesterday. I don't like being lied to, James.'

James looked startled, then wary—worse than wary, threatened. His eyes narrowed; his nostrils flared; the face became suddenly closed and dangerous. 'What a thing to say.'

'You pretended to go home but got on the same train with me. Because of the telegram you got. You went to one of the insurers, one of the Lloyd's syndicates.' A cup and saucer appeared in front of Denton. Another elderly personage whispered that he could have tea or coffee. 'Neither. Nothing.' When the servant had gone away, Denton said, 'You asked me to help you. Now you lie to me. What's going on?'

'Your tone is offensive.'

'I mean it to be.'

James put down his napkin. He started to push himself away from the table. 'In that case, we have nothing to say to each other.'

'Say it to me, or say it to the police.'

James's hard eyes flashed at him; his mouth became as Roman as his nose. 'I am already in communication with the police. I expect to hear from Inspector Wragge at any moment.' He stood.

'Wragge may be dead. Sit down.'

James remained standing, perhaps to show that people didn't tell Henry James to sit. Then, because perhaps they did, he sat. 'I don't understand.'

Denton leaned forward and lowered his voice. 'I've been up most of the night because a murdered man was found up in Islington. It may be Wragge. He's been missing since you and I went to Rye.'

'Missing! But he can't be. I was expecting to...Wragge? It makes no sense. Why do you think it's Wragge?'

'Two senior policemen believe it's him, although what they're saying right now is they don't know. If it's Wragge, they'll want to talk to both of us.'

James absent-mindedly picked up his teacup, then looked into it as if he had never seen such a thing before. 'Why?'

'Me because I had a run-in with him day before yesterday, and you because you were working with him on your burglary. Once they have some idea of the time of death, they'll want to know where we both were. You won't be able to hide things from them, James. It won't be like getting into a second-class compartment and thinking you're invisible.'

'You are quite insulting,' James murmured. 'I am, I am, *disappointed* in you.' He put the cup down, raised his eyes to Denton.

Denton accepted the direct look, held it. He said, 'What was it the telegram told you, and why did you need to hide it from me?'

'I can't tell you.'

'Then tell the police, because I'll tell them what happened.'

'Wragge *is* the police!'

'Were you supposed to meet Wragge at the insurer's yesterday, is that it? You said you were 'expecting' something. Look, James, Wragge's wife reported him missing the morning you and I went down to Rye. It's odd for a policeman's wife to do that; they know what kind of lives their husbands lead; they get accustomed to absences. But this one worried her. And her reporting it worried Scotland Yard enough that an inspector called me. And Wragge was still missing at midnight last night when two lovers found the body of a man who'd been bludgeoned so badly that two of us who'd seen Wragge couldn't tell if it was him or not. Now: are you going to tell me what was going on yesterday morning, or shall I quit the whole business?'

'I assume that neither of us would care to continue in a social relationship after what has been said.'

'Oh, for God's sake, James! Stop acting like the juvenile in a genteel melodrama! *You lied to me.* I'm asking you to make that right and tell me the truth, and then what you call our "social relationship" can maybe continue.'

'I do not choose so to go on.'

Denton looked at him. Then he threw himself back. He chuckled. 'Well, so be it. I still think you're the best writer of our generation. No hard feelings.' He stood.

'For the sake of the little dog...' James's voice seemed strangled. 'That you gave me, at a time when I needed him... Do sit down.'

Denton sat. 'I thought you were mad at me.'

'I am not *mad,* I am angry!'

'I'm twitting you, James. All right, are you going to tell me anything?'

James looked around the breakfast room, which was slowly emptying itself of men remarkably like himself—well beyond fifty, well beyond slender, well beyond any public show of self-doubt. 'Wragge was negotiating the return of my stolen possessions. It was as simple as that. Nothing nefarious, nothing underhanded. I was cautioned most severely to say nothing until the arrangement was brought to a satisfying conclusion.'

'Where does an insurance firm come in?'

'This will sound perhaps outré to you—I believe you have a, mmm, Puritanical respect for the law—but I am assured that it is entirely legal and unassailable. My insurer is to pay a certain amount for the return of my things.'

The fiddle. 'But the police weren't to know.'

'How many times must I say it? Wragge *is* the police.'

It occurred to Denton to wonder how many times Wragge had been involved in such an 'arrangement' before. And what he had got out of it. He said, 'And the burglars were to get off scot-free?'

'The transfer of money is to be done privately, of course, with no intercourse that involves me at all. Indeed, I believe that Wragge—Wragge can't have been murdered; the idea is absurd—Wragge will perform that part himself. Then my insurer will be told where the stolen articles are, and we are to go to them and I shall identify them. It is all quite straightforward, Denton, and hardly the sort of business arrangement that in any way prevents the police from continuing their pursuit of the guilty persons.'

Denton had to remind himself that James didn't know any cops. The man's naïveté was remarkable to him. This angry, impressive Roman was in fact a child when let loose in the world that Denton knew. 'So you received the telegram yesterday morning, and it told you—what? That the deal was made and you should come to London? And to tell nobody. And do Wragge and your insurer know that you had come to me about the Florentine box?'

'Of course not! I told you why. A great mistake on my part, as I see now.'

Denton poured some no longer hot tea into the unused cup. 'Here's the situation, James. If the dead man is Wragge—no, let me finish; it's very possible that Wragge's been murdered—then the police will look into everything he's been doing. They'll be attracted by the case of your burglary and the "arrangement"

Wragge was making between the thieves and your insurance man, because what they'll see is a policeman involved in a possibly irregular act—with criminals. And then he turns up dead. And immediately a policeman's mind focuses on those criminals.' He tapped the table. 'When there's a murder, you look first at the victim's family. I'd look at Wragge's wife, certainly. But I'd look at your burglary, too. A criminal gang? Money to change hands?' Denton thought of Henry James's being sweated by two tough cops at Scotland Yard. A moment's thought and he guessed that James would come out of it pretty well: naïve he might be, but he, too, was a tough old bird.

'I hardly think they can be so ignorant as to suspect me,' James said.

'There are a lot of shades of grey between innocent and suspect. You'll be of interest the moment they know of the "arrangement".'

'They need not know.'

'They do. I'll tell them if you don't. You'd be a fool to try to hide it from them, even if I weren't such a Puritan.'

'You will cause me enormous embarrassment.'

'There are worse things than enormous embarrassment.' He tapped the table again. 'As soon as he's sure that that body is Wragge, a very good copper named Munro is going to telegraph Sussex Constabulary to ask them to send a detective to Rye to question you. Sussex Constabulary will be unhappy when they find you're in London, and they'll make sure that Munro hears about it. *My* advice is to head them off: call Scotland Yard and ask for Wragge, and when you can't get him, leave the message that you're in London at the Reform Club. That way, you've done the right thing, and if Munro checks Wragge's desk, as I think he will, he'll find out you're here.'

'And he will send detectives to *question* me? Here?'

'He'll maybe even come himself. Or send a detective named Guillam, who's very sharp.'

'I feel like a hunted animal!'

'Well, don't. Tell the truth and you're out of it.'

'But the arrangement! My things—the box is probably among the stolen things!'

'If Wragge is dead, so is the arrangement. The police will want to talk to your insurer, too. The murder of a policeman really gets the police's dander up, James. There's going to be no avoiding it. You can have a solicitor with you, if you like, although that can be a sign of a feeling of guilt. You don't feel guilty, do you?'

'I feel betrayed.' The noble Roman face was stern.

'I feel lied to. I daresay we'll both get over it.'

He retraced his walk along Pall Mall and Pall Mall Lane. The morning was warm, the sun a little weakened by haze, the air no longer the sweet air of the night but the odorous air of a great city by day—horse, dust, river, a ghost of something in bloom. He turned east and found his way to the Strand, strolled, tried to argue himself out of going to his publisher's. Nearer the Temple, the lawyers were out, many with furled umbrellas despite the day (no rain for at least twenty-four hours, was Denton's view), several in chauffeured motor-cars with polished brass and great folded tonneaux like arms embracing the rear seats. Add the smell of burned petrol and oil to the city's other daytime smells.

He was thinking off and on about Henry James's problem, then his own of finding a new book subject. Got nowhere with either.

Before the bottom of Chancery Lane he turned left, then right into a tight worm-coil of buildings that had lasted since Izaak Walton had lived there. His publisher was in one of them, up a flight of worn stairs to off-kilter floors and stone fireplaces and books, books everywhere, The firm had been in business a long time, and they had one old employee whose only function seemed to be to make sure that nothing was ever thrown away.

'Lang. Good morning.'

Diapason Lang (named by an organist father) was even leaner than Denton but with an unlined face, rosy as a boy's, shrewd as a money-changer's. Denton thought him in his sixties, knew he could have been off by twenty years either way. Lang was his editor.

'Ah, the very man!' Lang rubbed his long fingers together. He was a little fussy, could have been believable in some ways as an old woman, but he was also tough, if personally austere. 'How good of you to visit us.'

'I need some inspiration. I also thought that a modest advance might inspire me.'

'Oh, my dear!' Lang tittered. 'Well might you say.' He waited until Denton had sat down on the other side of his Queen Anne desk (the real thing, although one corner was held up by a pile of books), keeping a smile fixed on his face and the face fixed on Denton. 'I shan't try to disguise the truth.'

'Nor should you. British sales of my last are a disaster.'

'Sales are a disaster, indeed.' He sighed.

'*British* sales, I said. You sold the Russian rights.'

'Oh, well—Russia!'

'And America.'

'My dear man, America was *worse* than a disaster. The word "decadent" was used. In a place called Salt Lake City, they hanged you in effigy.'

'And I was banned in Boston. It's selling better as a result.'

'But not well.' Lang would have insisted on that if in fact the sales figures had been a world record. He didn't like Denton's last book—*Worship Street*, about a possibly insane man's pursuit of God or a god or gods through several religions; he hadn't liked it when it had been proposed, and he now wanted the pleasure of having been right.

'All in all, *Worship Street* will make you a profit.'

'In how long, Denton? In our lifetimes?'

Denton put his hat under the chair. Asked, he said he would take tea; Lang sent a plump young man after it. Denton said, 'I want to write another book.'

Lang smiled. 'And we want you to write another book! But not a book like the last, whose title causes the bookkeeper to make squirming motions on his stool. We need you to write a book that will *sell*, Denton.'

'You're such an idealist, Lang. I don't have saleable books dropping out of my pockets just now. In fact...'

'You don't have an idea for a new one at all?'

'I thought you might make the usual advance for an unspecified novel. To egg me on.'

Lang opened his eyes quite wide and leaned his head back, one hand over his heart as if something might be going on there. He took a deep breath and blinked. 'One of the vexations of publishing is that we must constantly play off Melpomene against Mammon. We should, of course, prefer to have utterly clean hands—lucre is filthy—but we cannot and stay in business.' He tipped his head forward and joined his hands on the desk. 'I have an idea.'

Those were words Denton dreaded to hear. They were bad enough when they came from some stranger at a dinner; they were worse when they came from Lang. Lang had got the bee in his bonnet that Denton wrote horror books and belonged in a category with Le Fanu and Stoker. There was no shaking it. If Denton had written *Tom Jones*, Lang would have said it was the funniest horror novel ever written. 'You always have ideas for me, Lang.'

'Meaning, you never act on them. This time I want you to. This is an excellent, I may say a *magnificent* idea.' He leaned still farther forward. '*The monster.*'

Denton sighed the way adolescents sigh when they're trying to make a point about parents.

Lang jumped up, took a glance at the coloured print on his wall—always an inspiration to him, at least with Denton: a hideous man-beast lurking over a mostly naked young woman. He turned back to Denton. 'Perhaps I should say *the creature*. Dr Frankenstein's creature!'

'It's been done.'

'Exactly! And I want you to do it again! In our world of today—the creature stalks the city—his yellow eyes—women tremble...!' He looked back at the print. 'Let me tell you my idea.' Lang perched his narrow buttocks on the desk, hitched up a beautiful pantleg of light flannel. 'The creature is frozen into the Arctic ice. Round and round the pole for almost a century! Then comes a ship—an attempt to open a Northwest Passage— the creature is found! A great block of ice is brought up on the deck with his remains, as they think, frozen into it. They are unable to force their way farther north, so they head south. The ice begins to melt. And melt. The horrified crew are appalled as the creature *moves*. Can you see it so far?'

'All too clearly.'

'The ship arrives at a port, and...'

'Everybody on board is dead,' Denton finished for him.

'Exactly! How quick you are. And then the creature makes its way to London—I don't know how, but you'll work that out—and so on, and so instead of a lot of Transylvanians in fur waistcoats we have a huge metropolis and its civilised inhabitants terrorised! Gore. Screams in the night. Women...' He swung about as if he were in a swivel chair and gestured at the print. 'The idea of a monstrous male and unprotected, mmm, vulnerable females, mmm...'

'Sex and abuse of women, you mean.'

'Well, not quite in so many words, although the times *are* changing, Denton. Some quite startling, rather *racy* works coming off the presses. Ouida. Elinor Glyn! I have it on good authority that her new book, not yet in press, is quite shocking. Well, you know what I mean. We've had this conversation before. What Stoker managed to do in *Dracula*...'

Denton groaned.

'You must listen to me! He made biting women's throats thrilling! To women! They couldn't put it down!'

'I'm not going to rewrite *Dracula*, Lang.'

'Of course you're not! You're going to write *The Return of the Creature*, and then a whole series of luscious, disturbing books that pit the creature against other great mythic bugbears—*The Creature Meets Dracula*...'

'Oh God...'

'I know, I know, that name's taken. We'll make up our own. Or take it from that old play, *The Vampire*. I think he was English, which is even better. Then those other things that are so horrible—the ones that turn into wolves...'

'Werewolves.' Denton sounded exhausted.

'*The Creature Meets the Werewolf*! That could be in Scotland, I think. Lots of atmosphere. Then, then—well, that's three books; one hardly need plan beyond that at this point. What do you think? Five hundred pounds a book. In advance.'

Denton stared at him. He pushed out his mouth so that his long moustache moved. He got his hat from under the chair and stood. 'We'll pretend that this conversation never took place.' He put the hat on. 'That's what I think.'

He'd never got his tea.

Paddington was for some reason a station he didn't like. It made no sense to like or dislike railway stations; they were places to be got through, after all. But Paddington weighed on him, and he didn't need to feel its weight to want again to go somewhere and lie down, sink into the old inertia.

'You don't want to be here, do you?' Janet said this as she took his arm. She had been on the platform ahead of him.

'It has nothing to do with the boy.'

'Of course it has to do with "the boy". And Walter's eighteen now.'

'I don't like Paddington.' *And I don't like being lied to and just now I don't like Mr Henry James and I don't like Diapason Lang's daft ideas.*

'Does anybody? For God's sake, Denton, cheer up a little. It's going to be hard enough for him just coming here—all this damned noise.' She squeezed his arm. 'He doesn't like to be touched, remember.'

'I remember.' He had last seen Walter Snokes in a ruined pub where the boy had tried to hide after he had run off from a terrible place where he had been a 'guest', actually an inmate. All the boys there had been 'backward', difficult, some idiotic, but nobody, Denton had thought, deserved to be kennelled up in such a place. 'Has the new school done anything for him?'

'They seem to think so. We shall see. Not right away, but perhaps when he's settled in.'

Denton nodded as if he agreed that Walter should settle in. The truth was that he knew he resented Walter, even was jealous of him. He resented anybody who took part of what he thought was Janet's small store of affection. *I'm a selfish, small-minded bastard. No wonder people lie to me.* He said, 'Guillam would like to see him.'

'Oh, good. Walter liked him.' It had been Guillam and Janet who had walked Walter out of the ruined pub where he had hidden, Guillam who had told the boy that his mother was dead.

Heads were turning to the open end of the vast shed; men who had been standing close to the edge of the platform now pulled back. Wreathed in coal smoke and steam, an engine muscled its way into the great space and came towards them, inexorable, unstoppable as fate. They walked slowly down the platform. Compartment doors opened and a few daring types jumped down while the train was moving. Janet stopped and stopped Denton. A great hustle and bustle began, men helping women down, porters grabbing cases and boxes, a few people running as if to catch other trains.

'There he is!'

Two cars down, a solid youth was cowering in the doorway of a compartment. One hand was pressed to the ear that was turned towards the platform. Behind him and above him, a young man with a cheerful face grinned at them and then waved. He said something to Walter, who again cowered back. Janet took a few steps forward. The cheerful young man put out a hand as if he were a policeman, and she stopped; he didn't look at her but went on talking into Walter's uncovered ear. Then he looked at Janet and pointed at her, and Walter looked, too.

He took a step down. Another engine a couple of platforms away let out a jet of steam with a sound like a small explosion; Walter started back up but was stopped by the young man, who pointed again and urged him down. Walter put one foot on the platform, then the other. The young man nodded at Janet and invited her closer with a hand.

Denton, watching them, realised how tense they both were. It astonished him that Janet, always so self-contained and so often unfeeling, could be unnerved by simply meeting a boy she didn't know very well. And Walter seemed as tentative and as wary. He had expressed little emotion that Denton had ever seen, his feelings mostly negative and temporary: his hatred of noise, his loathing of being touched, his contempt for what he saw as other people's stupidity.

They approached each other. The young man waved Denton in, too, but he stayed where he was. Janet and the boy were close to each other now. She blocked Denton's view of Walter. She was saying something. She was nodding, apparently at the young man in the compartment, who grinned and waved and called something to Walter, but Walter didn't turn and the young man vanished. Janet waved Denton closer.

'And Walter, this is Mr Denton, whom you met last year.'

Walter's answer was terse, given mechanically: 'How-do-you-do-Mr-Denton-sir.'

Well at least he didn't say 'I don't like you', which would have been his greeting last year. 'Hello, Walter.' There was a pause. 'Did you like the train journey?'

'No.' Again said mechanically, as if he had been asked about somebody else.

'Well...' Denton looked at Janet. 'Shall we?'

'Yes. Where would you like to go, Walter? Is there something you'd like to do?'

'Yes please, I would like to visit the men's convenience.'

'Of course. Mr Denton will take you.'

'I can take myself, thank you, but it was gracious of you to think of me.' This was said as if he were reading it off a card. They walked up the platform, and Denton pointed out the men's toilets. As they waited for him, he said, 'Is that what they've taught him, memorised things to say?'

'They "replace some responses with more acceptable ones". It's part of their method.'

'He sounds like a machine.'

'Denton, don't start! He just got here!'

They waited in silence until Walter came out. He said, 'Thank you very much for waiting for me,' in his soulless voice.

They walked to the cab rank. Janet said, 'And now what? Where shall we go?'

'Somewhere quiet, please, miss.' Walter's eyes were twitching over the street, the cabs, the crowd. Janet looked at Denton: she had told him that the school had written her to avoid too much stimulation at first. It wasn't only noise, it appeared; movement, bright colours, things novel and fast-moving also distressed him. Her expression told Denton that he was supposed to think of something. He was tempted to say it wasn't his party; the boy was hers to entertain, but he loved her too much. He said, 'I have to see a man who has a shop full of art, Walter. Pictures and things. Would you like to go there?'

'Is it quiet?'

'Very quiet.'

'Yes, please.'

Janet tried to chat as they went along, but nothing could be started: the boy was a pile of wet wood that resisted her flame. She pointed out famous sights, places people were supposed to want to see; he didn't care. He looked ahead over the horse's back, after a few minutes put his third fingers into his ears. It was remarkably rude, and the school was trying to teach him not to be rude, but Janet only looked at him and then at Denton. She seemed helpless. It wasn't like her, to allow herself to be helpless. But Walter Snokes made Denton feel helpless, too.

Along Piccadilly, the rush and crash of traffic made the boy shut his eyes. When they got down, Denton didn't dare touch him but pointed into the mouth of Burlington Arcade, and the boy dashed into it with his hands over his ears. Janet came almost as fast behind. Denton paid off the cab and strode in and found them partway along, Janet simply standing there, the boy panting, leaning against the pillar between two shops.

'I forget how noisy London is,' she said.

'Shall we go in?' He was pointing down the arcade to a shop with a sign, gold on black, that said it held art and objects of virtue. He wanted to talk to the owner about James's stolen box, although he wondered now why he should bother, except that it was a quiet place to take the boy.

Janet got Walter moving and they went the few steps to the shop. Walter looked around the enclosed arcade with too-wide eyes. Yet when Denton opened the shop door, the boy ducked under his arm and wriggled in, apparently glad of a still smaller place.

Geddys was waiting at the back. He was a small man made smaller by a deformed back and a twisted neck; he had to look at people Denton's height upward and sideways. His bearded, rather good-looking face allowed itself an ironic smile when he saw Denton. 'Come for more paintings to cover the cracks in your walls, Mr Denton?'

'You've done very well off me, Geddys; don't mock.' Geddys knew Janet, who had been in with Denton before. She introduced 'my young friend, Walter Snokes.' Geddys came forward as if he were actually interested, rare for him.

Walter said in his mechanical voice, 'I-don't-shake-hands-excuse-me-sir.'

So the school had taught him some manners of a sort.

Geddys actually smiled. 'That's all right, my boy. Foolish custom, anyway. Do you like pictures?'

Walter seemed set back by the question. 'I—I don't know. Sir.'

'I have lots of pictures.' Geddys waved a hand at the walls. 'Enjoy them.' The shop was a catch-all, two glass-topped counters and many small tables, every surface covered with things, trifles, ornaments of all periods, all countries. The walls were almost hidden by pictures large and small, the highest not quite touching the ceiling, mostly photographically precise renderings of daily life in ancient Rome and scenes of bibulous monks with lots of alizarin crimson in the faces.

Denton said to the art dealer, 'You have a moment to talk?'

'If you're not buying, I suppose I have to.' Geddys turned towards the back of the shop but swung around, his bent back like a gantry that was carrying his head, and said to Janet, 'Don't touch anything, please,' meaning, Denton thought, that Walter wasn't to touch anything.

Walter seemed to think so, too, because he said, not in his mechanical voice but in a warmer one, 'You do not touch things that do not belong to you. That's a rule.'

Geddys smiled. 'And a very good one.' He led Denton to the back, stood with his arms folded and said, 'Well, what is it this time? Somebody murdered?'

'Something missing.'

'You think I deal in items that go missing, Denton? What a slanderous thought.'

'I thought you maybe got notices, catalogues, whatever they'd be called, that would list things if they came on the legitimate market.'

'I might.' Geddys was watching Walter, who was across the shop with Janet, staring up at a picture. 'What's wrong with the boy?'

'A kind of ugly story.'

'It would suit me, then; I'm rather an ugly man. A bit touched, is he? Backward, as they say?'

'He was a child prodigy. Music. There was an accident and now he's as you see him.'

Geddys's eyebrows lifted. 'Is he the lad whose drawings you showed me last year? Intricate little figures twining around musical staves? Oh, is he! I see, I see. These missing things have to do with him?'

'No.'

'Who, then?'

'I can't say.'

Geddys nodded as if that confirmed what he'd always thought about Denton. Denton told him about the Balzac novella and the letters; he left out the letters James most wanted, which wouldn't, he was pretty sure, come on any market, legitimate or otherwise. Geddys tilted his head to look up at him. 'Five love letters and an unknown novella by Balzac, and you're asking if I'd hear of them?' He laughed. 'I wouldn't be much of a dealer if I didn't.' He exhaled and shook his shoulders. 'You always want something from me, Denton. What is it this time? What am I supposed to divert my attention to now?'

Before Denton could answer, Walter gave a kind of howl. He and Janet had moved along the wall; now they were looking at quite a small painting that was half hidden from Denton by a piece of garden statuary. Walter's howl turned into laughter, or at least his kind of laughter, which was loud and uncouth and seemed mocking to people who didn't know him.

Walter backed a little away from the painting and pointed at it, trying to show something out to Janet. 'A bird in the hand! Miss, a bird in the hand! See—see?'

'Walter, I don't—oh, the little bird... Yes, but—'

Geddys had moved quickly, perhaps at first because he thought something was going to get broken, but that had lasted only a step or two, and then he was saying, 'Yes, yes, very good, my boy. He's very acute, Mrs Striker. Not one person in a hundred would see that!' He was behind Walter. 'Well, my boy, what else do you see? What's the painting about?'

Walter was still pointing. 'A bird in the hand is worth two in the trees. And she's got the bird!' He gave his terrible laugh again.

'I don't see it,' Janet said. 'I see the bird, but...Walter, what are you going on about?'

Denton had come close. The painting, he saw now, was what he called 'early', meaning that it was older than any of the stuff Geddys usually sold. In the foreground, a young woman was sitting at a table on which were a gold coin, a tiny fish on an earthenware dish with a blue line around the rim, and two letters. Her open hand was palm up on the tabletop, in it a small bird. Through the window at her left, a somewhat fanciful tree held two other birds, although they had to be searched for. Behind the young woman hung at an angle a spherical mirror that apparently reflected the room, because Denton could certainly make out the window and the girl's back, distorted, in it.

'Very nice,' he said.

'Very nice?' Geddys snarled. 'That's possibly a Vermeer!' Janet made a sound, and Geddys changed his tone and muttered, 'Well, school of Vermeer. Attributed to.'

Janet moved in front of Walter and studied the painting. Unsatisfied, she turned and looked at Denton and then at Geddys and then at Walter. She said, 'What is it you see that I don't?'

Walter sniggered. 'The man. She has the bird.' He laughed.

'Walter, explain it to me. Please.'

Walter pointed again. 'I won't touch it, as I'm not allowed to. But you see the bird. She has the bird. Now look at the mirror. Look over at the side where it curves the most. You see the man?' He sounded impatient. 'He's wearing a dark red—I don't know the word, some kind of coat—and a dark red hat and he has a bag in his hand. You see?'

'Y-e-e-e-s...'

'He's the bird.' He laughed, a single sound like a cough. 'He has a big nose and one droopy eye, but *she's got him.*'

'Oh.' Janet chuckled. 'He's the bird in hand who's better than two...' Now she pointed. 'The two letters? Is that it?'

Geddys grinned at Denton as if he'd put something over on him and said to Janet, 'It's a betrothal painting. Probably commissioned by her father, or maybe by the groom. Groom would either have been blind or very tolerant, once he saw it.' He chuckled. 'The bag is probably supposed to be money. He's rich, so he's a good catch, wall eye or no. The letters mean she has other suitors, but they haven't come to the point and this one has. She's making up her mind, but we know what she'll decide.'

'And the little fish?'

'A sign of fruitfulness. She's probably fifteen or so.' He began to point out other details of the painting, other subtle symbols. He said, 'An art critic would talk mostly about the light.' He didn't mean it as a compliment.

'Damn the light! Walter, do you like it?'

'Yes, I like it, thank you for asking, miss.'

'No, I mean, do you *want* it?'

Walter seemed uncertain what 'want' meant. Finally he said, 'It would be very nice to be able to look at it every day.'

'Then we shall have it, and it will hang in your room in my house.' She smiled at the boy, and, for the first time, he smiled back. They stood there, smiling at each other. Denton's heart turned over.

'It's a somewhat expensive item,' Geddys murmured.

Janet was no fool. She had money, but she knew how to hold on to it because she had for so long had none at all. '"Attributed to the school of" can't be too expensive, Mr Geddys.'

'Well, yes, but consider the quality and the age. I have letters of provenance and a very sound appraisal.'

'I'm sure we can come to an agreement.'

Geddys sighed. He had dealt with her before.

As he wrapped the painting, he said to Denton, 'So what is it you want from me about these Balzac papers?'

'Notification if they come on the market.'

'Stolen?'

'I'm not sure.'

'Most thieves wouldn't know Balzac from Bishop Berkeley. Such things usually get sold any-old-how for a farthing on the pound and I'd never hear of them. A knowledgeable thief, on the other hand, a specialist, might have a buyer before he ever did the theft—a dealer or a collector. Not, of course, that there are any such dishonest folk in England. Not within ten yards of where we stand, at any rate.' He began to wrap brown twine around his package. 'If you're lucky enough to have had a thief who knows the papers are worth something but doesn't have a buyer, then they might show up at auction, probably on the Continent or in the US. Lots of crooks in your country, aren't there, Denton?'

'They're in politics, not antiques.'

'Ah, like England.' Geddys snipped the twine and handed the package up to Denton. 'She got a bargain. She always does.' He put a hand on Denton's arm. 'Bring the boy back any time you like. He has a remarkable eye. Most people don't *see* what they see, you know?' He nudged Denton to go ahead of him. 'If I hear anything about the Balzac materials, I'll let you know. Don't hold your breath. And for God's sake, buy something from me once a century.'

Denton thought he'd done pretty well by Geddys—three paintings of the sea to replace two of cows he'd found he couldn't stand—but he supposed that Geddys wouldn't have been satisfied if Denton had walked in and bought the shop.

He held out the package. Janet took it and gave it to Walter. 'That's our painting, and you're its guardian. Shall we go?'

When they were in a cab, Walter said, 'That man was in pain.'

'Who? Geddys? Why do you think so?'

'They teach us at the school. You must be specially nice to those in pain because you are in pain yourself. That's what Richard said.'

They left Piccadilly and got into leafier, quieter streets. Janet asked if Richard was the young man who had brought him on the train.

'Of course he is.' His tone would have been just right if he'd finished with *you idiot*. The school hadn't, it appeared, taught Walter everything about manners yet.

CHAPTER

'Inspector Munro *again*. For you.'

Denton tried to wake. His inertia had returned; all he wanted to do was sleep. He had pulled a book down, sat in his armchair, and here he was, an hour—no, two hours—later.

'What's he want?'

'You.'

Denton struggled up. His eye caught the book he had seemed to want to read. One of Henry James's. *The Golden Bowl.* Trickery and deceit; he'd already read it once.

'Denton here.' He leaned against the wall by the telephone, head tipped against the door jamb, eyes closed.

'It's Munro.'

'I heard.'

'It's Wragge. The body. Keep it to yourself.'

Denton pulled himself away from the wall. 'Positive identification?'

'No question. He had an old injury he got on duty, a couple of his mates in H Division recognised it. Took them to the mortuary specially. Seems he liked to show it off when he'd had a few. Plus the wife said it's him.'

'Did you have to tell her?'

'No, Guillam. Hard thing to do.'

'How'd she take it?'

'Like he'd told her big hats were coming back, according to Guillam. Stoic. They'd been married donkey's years. But still.'

'Kids?'

'Grown and gone. Yes, we're looking at her, Denton, but I don't think she's it.'

'Man friend someplace?'

He heard a sound that the telephone made seem like a seal's bark, probably a laugh. 'You'd have to see her.'

'I don't want to.'

'We're going to have to interview you, get it on the record. Pro forma. Also your Mr James.'

'He's here in London. The Reform.'

'I know that. He left a message for Wragge. Any chance of finding you in tonight?'

'As a matter of fact, yes. But I'd thought early to bed might make me healthy and wise.'

'What's that about?' Munro was Canadian, now British, probably didn't know Poor Richard. 'Anyway, Guillam and I have had about three hours' sleep between us since yesterday. It's to your advantage to talk to us quick.'

'Yeah, yeah, come along. Guillam too, eh? Any time before eleven. After that, no.'

After he had put the earpiece back, he bent his head down towards Atkins's domain. 'Inspector Munro and Inspector Guillam are coming later. They might want a word with you.'

Atkins's voice rumbled from below, unintelligible. Later, he came up and said he was going to the Lamb for a chop, and could he bring back anything for Denton? 'We could talk while we eat.'

'Supposed to be bad manners. Get me steak and kidney, something like that. Potatoes, whatever they're laying on and pretending is a vegetable. I'll drink my own ale. You too?'

'Um. Might have a half while I wait.' He started away, leaned back. 'I've decided to call the new pup Bill. He seems to be fitting in.'

They sat in the old kitchen to eat, possible in summer with the evening light coming in the high windows. With only the gas in winter, the place was greeny-grey and unpleasant after late afternoon. Atkins had set out the food on the work table; they sat on high stools. Denton had brought down six bottles of Bass from his stock.

'How's the chop?'

'The chop is a shepherd's pie tonight. You want to talk or don't you?'

Denton waved his fork. 'Talk.' Gravy dribbled out of his over-full mouth and he pushed it back up with a thumb. Atkins offered a plate of bread, then peered into the shepherd's pie and said, 'It's like this, General—I got to have more time or give up the film idea. Like every other business I ever tried.'

'Bitterness doesn't become you.' Denton looked up. 'In fact, I never heard it from you before.'

'Well, I'm that tired of starting things and chucking them, I could spit! Here's the gist of it—I don't have the time and I don't have the legs to do the moving pictures the way they need to be done. What I need is more hours in the day and another man.'

'Time and money.'

'In a nutshell.' Denton tore off a piece of the bread and pushed it into the pie until it was viscous with gravy. He shoved that into his mouth, chewed, swallowed, and said, 'We can do something about the time. The money, I don't know.'

'I ain't asking you for money. What I would ask for is the motor-car.'

'What, outright?'

'No, kind of shared, so to speak.'

'Then I'd be without it.'

'We could work that part out. So many hours a month. Pay my share of the petrol and upkeep. Anyway, that's a detail. The poser is my time.'

'You could quit.'

'Couldn't afford it. Anyway...'Struth, I don't want to. Maybe it's habit. Once a servant, always et cetera.'

'And I don't want you to. How do you suppose the walnut ketchup would be on the veg?'

'Depends on the veg, don't it? Can't do any harm, if it's the same veg as I got. I'm using anchovy sauce, myself.'

Denton tried the anchovy sauce, shrugged. 'Give me the figures. Lay it out. Then we'll talk about it.'

'There's more.'

'Oh-oh.'

'My time. This is how I see it: I go on shared time. Like the car. There'd have to be somebody hired for when I'm not here. Now, it wouldn't have to be somebody of my quality. That lad you had some years ago that was sent in by the day, he was all but useless but could answer the door well enough. One like him. Of course, I'd contribute to the cost. By rights, I should hire him myself and pay for the entire kitamaboodle, but I can't afford it yet. Puts you in the position of supporting my enterprise financially, the which I intend to repay with shares in Atkins Cinemantics. Could make you a millionaire. In time.'

Denton laughed. 'You're a prize, you are. A pearl of great price. And getting pricier.'

'Well, what do you think?'

Denton thought about his dwindling money but admitted to himself that what was dwindling money to him would have been riches to most of London. 'You can scout about for a kid who's cheap to get the door. I'll give you two days off a week extra until we see if your motion pictures are going to catch on.'

Atkins jabbed a finger. 'You're a prince among men. And now a major stockholder in Atkins Cinemantics.'

A custard had appeared—not from the Lamb, Denton thought, but cooked up from powder on the gas ring. Atkins said, 'It's a risk. Like betting on yourself.' He set the bowl down and spooned some out for each of them. 'And then there's Rupert.' He put a smaller bowl and a spoon in front of Denton.

'What's Rupert got to do with it?'

'Medical expenses. Something that boy of the missus's said. I was out in the garden with the dogs and he looked through the gate. You know what he said? He said, "That dog's in pain." He meant Rupert.'

'Don't call her "the missus", and it's what he said about Geddys the art dealer, too. Something they teach him to say at that school.'

'Might be something in it, though. He's sensitive.'

'In some ways. In others, he's a block of wood.' Denton ate a spoon of custard. 'What flavour's this supposed to be?'

'Lyons's almond. I don't take those claims too seriously.' He tried it, made the face that means 'Oh well.' He said, 'About the boy. Marches to a different drummer but ain't necessarily wrong. I think I'll have in that chap from the horse barns that saw to Rupert when he was poisoned that time. Can't do any harm. But it costs.'

'While he's here, you might see about getting the dogs clipped. She won't let you get out of it, Sergeant.'

'I know, I know. But it just makes me...' Atkins took more custard. 'What you're saying is, you're not saying no to my idea.'

'Yes, I'm not saying no. But I want the figures. And you know I'm not particularly flush just now myself.'

'All I dared hope for. You're a prince, General.' He offered Denton more custard; Denton refused and got up to go to his own part of the house.

Atkins was piling dirty dishes. Denton said, 'I never help you with the washing-up.'

'Nor would I allow you. There's boundaries we don't cross, Colonel. Something the army teaches you. Go on, march.'

Denton went. He wondered again about their arrangement. It seemed to him that Atkins did everything and all he did was supply the money, and what Atkins was trying to do with the film business was get out of all that and himself become somebody who paid somebody else to do the hard work. Was that fair? Humane? Christian, if he might unfairly claim the word?

Munro and Guillam looked like hell, Guillam the worse of the two. He hadn't shaved in two days, the bristles black against his pocked skin. His eyes were red, the lids pouched, dark underneath, his suit rumpled. Both men moved oddly, as if their balance was a fraction off.

'Tea? Coffee? Spirits?'

'Been guzzling tea all day, the both of us, insides probably tanned like old boots. And spirits and duty don't mix.' Munro cocked an eyebrow at Denton. 'We are on duty here, remember.'

'Let's get it over with.'

Guillam grunted. He got a cheap notebook from an inner pocket and leaned his elbows on his knees to read it, now and then holding it up towards one of the electric lamps for more light. Whatever was in the notebook inspired his questions: where was Denton three nights before from seven to midnight; who was with him; how do you spell the name Emmeline, one M or two; what were you doing in Rye?

'Visiting Henry James, I told you.'

'Close friend?'

'I'd given him a dog. Mrs Striker's dog had puppies by Atkins's dog. It's a long story.'

Guillam was writing in the notebook. 'You took the dog to Rye.'

'We both did. James and I.'

Guillam looked up at him. 'He couldn't take the dog down there by himself?'

'Well, it was a social thing, too. You know.' When neither Guillam nor Munro gave any sign of understanding, he said, 'We're both Americans. Both authors.' Although he despised the word 'author'.

Guillam shifted his weight to lean an elbow on the arm of his chair. 'Have a chat about writing? Make jokes about other writers? You two close?'

'Not at all.' He thought he sounded defensive, was reminded of Janet's question: was James 'so'? That wouldn't do. He said, 'We'd run into each other a couple of nights before at a dinner for another author. James was just back from the States. We got talking.'

'And then he dropped by later.' This was from Munro, who'd been sitting there quietly.

'Atkins tell you that? You got a lot out of him in a short time.' Now he sounded testy. Small-minded. 'What is it you want to know? Spit it out.'

Guillam said, 'What's the story behind James asking you to put your oar into his burglary?'

Denton remembered what he'd promised James—that he'd keep quiet about the Balzac papers until keeping quiet meant breaking the law. He didn't think he'd quite reached that point. 'James isn't used to dealing with the police. Much less burglars.'

'He wanted your expert opinion,' Munro said.

'I guess he thought I knew more than he did about such things.'

'And so you talked about that at Rye?' Guillam said.

'Among other things.'

'The gardener—' He looked at his notebook. 'Gammon. He says you looked at the garden wall and the locks and asked a lot of questions.'

'I suppose I did. You haven't been to Rye already, have you?'

Before Guillam could snarl something at him, Munro said, 'Sussex Constabulary. Don't ask questions, Denton.'

Denton sighed. Guillam looked in his notebook, then closed it and put his hand in his lap. 'Did you and James talk about Inspector Wragge?'

'Not that I remember.'

'Did you tell James that you'd already had a call from Munro asking about Wragge?'

'Had I?' Was that the same day? Yes, before he'd met James at Victoria. 'No, I don't think so. Have you talked to James about it?'

The two policemen simply looked at him. They wanted his story and James's story to be given separately, no cross-pollination.

Guillam asked a few more apparently perfunctory questions, the only one that seemed serious being had he seen or talked to Wragge after meeting him and Munro at the Old Red Lion?

'No.'

Guillam wrote something in his notebook, put it away, nodded at Munro and then put his head back and pressed thumb and fingers against his eyes. Munro said, 'All right, that's that. If I can find a typewriter in N Division who can actually use the machine without a bushel of mistakes, I'll have a constable come by tomorrow with a statement for you to sign.' He sighed. 'Cripes, I'm going to have trouble getting out of this chair.'

'Am I allowed to ask questions now?'

'Probably won't get answers. Do we have to stay awake?'

'What did Wragge die of?'

Without removing his fingers or opening his eyes, Guillam said, 'Blunt force. At least five blows with something hard and round. Maybe a piece of pipe.'

'But not where he was found.'

Munro gave him a faint shrug. 'He was moved there—probably.'

'Any idea when?'

Guillam raised his fingers and opened his left eye. 'Why?'

'You know why. It doesn't make a lot of sense that he wasn't found earlier, does it? That cemetery's still used. People coming and going.'

Munro growled, 'Medico thinks he lay somewhere else on his side for a while. Has to do with the way the blood settles.'

'So he was already dead a day and was taken to the cemetery the night he was found?'

'We don't know that. And this isn't for public consumption.'

'I'm not the town crier. Mrs Wragge was "stoic", you said, when Guillam told her that her husband was dead. She capable of moving a dead man?'

The two policemen looked at each other. Munro then looked at Denton but said nothing. At last, Guillam pushed himself up in the chair and said, 'We ought to get going.'

'Mrs Wragge isn't a subject I'm allowed to ask about?'

Munro cleared his throat. 'There's no boyfriend, if that's what you're thinking. And she's a small woman.'

'Wragge was a small man.'

'How would she get him to a place like that cemetery? In a cab? With the driver's help? I grant you that a woman in a rage could kill a man with a piece of pipe—woman scorned, and so on—but she couldn't have done the rest of it. Not alone.'

'Two women?'

'Oh, for God's sake, Denton!'

'Another woman might have been willing to help if they were close. And if she knew the wife was justified. Wragge having it on with another woman, maybe? Or beating the wife?' Both policemen were silent. 'Her coming to the Yard to say her husband was missing after only a few hours was kind of strange, after all.' He waited, feeling himself getting annoyed. 'Munro!'

'Yes, it was, and keep it to yourself.' Guillam looked at him, frowned. Munro said, by way of apology to Guillam, 'Denton's been a good friend to us in the past, Georgie.'

Guillam's tired eyes locked on Denton's. He seemed to be weighing something—Denton's knowledge of Guillam's own secret life, never betrayed? For the first time, Denton wondered if Munro knew about Guillam. Munro was a fairly stiff moralist, a church-going man, but he and Guillam went back. Guillam said, 'Wragge's private life's police business. I understand you asking, but we can't talk about it. If we knew.'

He stood. Munro began to unfold his huge body from his chair. Munro said, 'We're seeing Mr Henry James in the morning. At the Yard. Mr James didn't want to "bring the police into the Reform Club". Sacred premises.'

A minute later, they were gone.

Denton went up to his desk and sat staring at a piece of paper on which he'd written *The Monster*. It was a title, no doubt about that—provided by Lang, in fact, but not for the sort of work that Lang had had in mind. Denton was sure that he'd meant something when he'd scribbled it in the middle of a night. Something he and James had talked about—killing and its aftermath. James's story about the cat had been involved, too. *A monster. What is a monster?* What was monstrous and also real, even mundane, that he had thought it worth a title? What the hell had he meant by that title?

Denton was in Janet's house at an indecent hour next morning. She was still wearing one of her flowing, gaudy gowns, this one some sort of wrap or robe in leaf-green and very dark red and lavender. Austere in her business clothes, she was a bright-coloured bird at home. Now, she stared at him, yawned, smiled, asked what he could be thinking of. 'Walter's still asleep. Will be until noon, I suppose.'

'That woman you saw outside my house when James was there.'

'Do you need breakfast? I'll share one piece of toast with you; after that, I have to call Mrs Cohan for help. A woman. Yes, I remember.'

'Tell me what she looked like.'

'I told you, not like a whore.'

'Tall or short?'

'Short. Dumpy.'

'Old? Young?'

'Middle-aged, I should think. Much added to the hips along the way.'

'Pretty? Ugly?'

'Hard to say in the dark. I did get the sense when she passed under a light that she had noticeable eyes. Boiled eggs, you know.'

'Protruding?'

'Isn't there an illness that causes that? Some people have them naturally, too. Why does all this matter? More Henry James?'

'I'm wondering if it was Wragge's wife.' He had told her all about Wragge, the run-in at the Old Red Lion, the body at the cemetery. 'Munro and Guillam came to see me last night. I told you that Guillam wants to see Walter, didn't I? I thought I had. Anyway, they "interviewed" me. It's definitely Wragge, and he was killed with something like a lead pipe. A woman could do that.'

'What's that got to do with her following Henry James?'

'I don't know. But Munro said something about a woman scorned, and he was joking, but jokes come from somewhere. When I asked if Wragge had something on the side, they both shut up.'

'I shouldn't think Henry James was somebody one had "on the side". I'm joking.'

'Suppose her husband had told her he'd be out with James working on the case and she thinks he's lying. Maybe knows he's whoring around.'

'And if she follows Henry James, she'll either catch her husband in a lie or satisfy herself he's where he says? God, I wouldn't be married for all the tea in China.'

'And then when he comes home, she kills him.'

'Bit far-fetched.' She cocked an eyebrow at a half-eaten piece of toast. 'I tried to push my husband down a flight of stairs once, which is why he put me into the institution, but I had provocation. I suppose we all believe we have provocation. Well, good for her if she did it.'

'But she can't get the body out of her house alone. Would another woman help her?'

'I would. But in a proper middle-class area full of proper middle-class virtues...'

He searched his memory for something that Munro had told him. 'Wandsworth.'

'An accomplice would be hard to find. Easier in the places I used to live. The barely working poor are clearer in their loyalties. She hasn't got a lover? Not too likely? A woman friend who'd risk hanging? Not very persuasive, Denton.' She gathered her colours about her. 'The law requires me.'

'If I find Mrs Wragge, would you take the time to have a look at her? To see if it's the same woman?'

She looked put out. 'You're in danger of making me think you believe that what you do is more important than what I do. The day I'm certain of that is the day you'll see the back of me.' She finished the dregs of her tea and clattered the cup down. 'Look, I have my work and I have Walter. That's enough just now.'

He said he hadn't meant that, he'd asked not demanded, of course he knew the importance of her work. And of Walter. But of course, she was right: he wasn't working; she was. What was it that he was doing, then? *My enthusiasms.*

She said, 'I'll give you my luncheon hour. If you can get me down to Wandsworth and back in an hour, I'll look at her.' She was ready to go, but she held herself back for a few seconds and then kissed his cheek. 'We never get this quite right, do we?'

He walked down to the Museum and into the Reading Room, where he knew they kept the London directories. They were difficult things to use, not all alphabetical and not all either up to date or accurate. Wragge didn't have a telephone, he knew: Munro had told him that. Nor could he ask anybody he knew in the police what Wragge's address was.

Wandsworth was lumped into a Kelly's with Putney and Barnes, but the towns were entered separately. He had to go through it page by page, running his finger down the columns for the name Wragge. His inertia returned, became drowsiness, warmth, the conviction that it wasn't worth it. If he'd been at home, he'd have slept. As it was, he got up and walked about, had a look at some Saxon gold, sat down again and found Wragge— or somebody named Wragge, at any rate—almost immediately. It might not be the only Wragge in Wandsworth, however, so he had to go down the columns of twenty more pages before he was done.

There seemed to be only the one Wragge in Wandsworth.

And what was he doing in Wandsworth? he wondered. A policeman should want to live near his work, although Munro lived in Peckham and Guillam somewhere almost to Kingston—

he remembered that Guillam had been posted to East Ham as a punishment at one point. But perhaps Wandsworth wasn't so bad if you were at New Scotland Yard. Hop across the river and you were at Victoria. A long hop, nonetheless.

At home, there was a note from Atkins.

Insp. Guillam phoned & wants you to call him NOW. Also a female from University College named Heckham about something French was all Greek to me. Coming by fiveish.

There was a number that Denton took to be in Islington. He called, but Guillam was 'out.' People were always out when you wanted them—another fault of the telephone. Denton left his name and number, then thought he ought to go the second mile and got from Central the number of the Stoke Newington station. This struck gold: Munro had set up his murder investigation there, and Guillam was in charge. The first number, he supposed, was Guillam's home station at the Angel.

'Where the hell have you been?' The night hadn't improved Guillam any; maybe he still hadn't slept.

'I don't sit at home and wait for you to call.'

'I talked with your Henry James this morning. You weren't forthcoming with us.'

The insurance scheme. James has told them and I'm on the hook. Did he tell them about the box, too? 'What now?'

'I'm not going into it on the bloody telephone. Get your arse up here or I'll have you carrying it in your hands.'

'Seems a little rough. What have I done?'

'It's what you haven't done, and you know it. Get up here. For your own good.'

Atkins had taken the car. Denton looked in the guide and found that he could get a tram from Holborn up to Dalton, which was good enough; he hoped it would dump him in Kingsland Road. Off he went, finding the tram oddly exhilarating, the regular sway back and forth unnerving at first but then somewhat pleasant. He remembered the tram tracks from the motor-car ride with Munro, that fear, mostly mythical, of getting the narrow tyres caught. By consulting with the conductor, he got himself let down at what was supposed to be the closest place to Stoke Newington police station, and the conductor's arm pointed the way from there.

'Inspector Guillam? Inspector Guillam. Ah, he's the officer in from the Angel, right. I'll just send for him, sir.' The duty sergeant scribbled something and sent a constable off with it. Some minutes later, Guillam himself walked through, first pointing at Denton and then waving him in. Denton opened the gate in a wooden barrier and went through, stung by Guillam's manner. When he saw the man up close, however, he understood: Guillam was exhausted. Denton said, 'You need to sleep.'

'Spare me the advice.' They were in a small room with poorly distempered walls, pencilled scribbles just above a wainscoting the colour of spoiled meat. 'Sit.'

There were a table and two chairs, two more against the walls, none comfortable.

Guillam put his forehead in a hand and opened his notebook on the scarred table. 'Mr James says that Wragge had negotiated an "arrangement" with an insurer and he told you all about it.'

'Not very willingly, he didn't.'

Guillam slammed his free palm on the table. 'Why the hell didn't you tell us last night?'

'Because I'd told him I'd leave it to him to tell you, and if he didn't, then I would.'

'That's withholding information. I could—'

'Have me up on a charge, I know, I know. Guillam, I didn't know about his damned arrangement until yesterday morning, and then all I knew was that there was one. No details. Nothing. And I wouldn't have known that much if I hadn't followed James to some sort of meeting with his insurer.'

Guillam raised his head. 'James made it seem like you knew the whole thing.'

'Not true.'

'You weren't in on it?'

'Of course not. Why would I be?'

'You're conniving with him, aren't you? Forget I said that; the word was ill-chosen. Working with him, all right?'

'I was trying to help him. I don't think I am any more; the last I heard, he'd got the hump about me. But it looks as if Wragge was setting up some sort of deal with the insurer. You make it that way too?'

Guillam leaned back and massaged his forehead. He took his hand away and said, 'You make yourself a hard man to like, Denton. It was your obligation to tell me and Munro everything.'

'Would it have made any difference if you'd heard it last night instead of this morning?'

'That isn't the point, as you well know. Look.' Guillam pushed the notebook aside and put an elbow on the table, his head in the hand. 'Whatever deal was in the works, it's likely blown by now. Munro's talking to the insurer. What it could be now is that Wragge was killed because of the deal—got crosswise of the burglars or too smart for his own good. Time, Denton, *time*. If we'd known earlier, we could have moved earlier. You should have told us yesterday morning.'

'You didn't know for certain that dead body was Wragge yesterday morning. And I knew almost nothing!'

'Is there anything else you do know? I'm worn down to a frazzle, Denton. When I get to this point, I'm unforgiving. I don't make allowances. We've had our ups and downs, you and me, and if you hold anything else back, this will be a down. Way far down.'

What had he said to James? That he'd keep silent until silence conflicted with the law. That time had come, he thought, although perhaps not for every crumb of every detail. He said, 'Two things. One, when James came to my house a couple of nights ago, a woman was seen across my street. She might have been waiting for him. I don't know who she was and she may simply have been one of the tarts that wander through there. Second thing, James brought me in because he lost something personal in the burglary and he doesn't want it made public. For the rest, you'll have to ask him.'

Guillam waved a hand. 'The woman doesn't sound much, but I'll follow it. Good. What's the personal thing?'

Denton shook his head.

'I mean it, Denton. Goddammit…!'

'Ask H. James. You have all you need from me. And all you're going to get.' Denton waited for Guillam to start filling out a charge sheet.

Instead, he locked eyes with Denton and tapped a fingernail on the table, turned away abruptly and picked up his notebook. 'I'll give you twenty-four hours to think it over. There's no point in dubbing you up; that swank lawyer of yours would have you out in an hour.' He stood. 'You've actually been good to work with sometimes, Denton, and you've been…understanding, but goddammit, you can be a pain in the arse.'

'Mrs Striker says you're welcome to visit the boy any time.'

Guillam seemed to go numb, recovered. 'I'd forgotten. All this mucking about with Wragge. Yes, when it's over.' He went to the door, paused as if he were going to say something, then shook his head and went out.

Denton went home to find another note from Atkins: *Been and gone again. Car is yours for rest of today.* He mused that that was generous of Atkins. But it made it possible for him to take Janet to Wandsworth to have a look at Mrs Wragge. He got the Barré and racketed over to Goodge Street, trying not to listen to the off sounds from under the car, somewhere between a scrape and a thump.

Janet was working in the office of a determinedly female solicitor who had made it clear she didn't want Denton about the premises. Nothing personal; it was a question of distracting Janet. And perhaps Miss Mercer's distaste for men in general. He scuttled across the tiny waiting room—two weary-looking women, four unhappy children—put his head in at the door and signalled to Janet. She raised her eyebrows, blew out her cheeks and exhaled as if he was the last straw. Still, in four minutes she was in the motor-car with him.

'One hour,' she said.

He was already under way. 'Less.'

'I shouldn't be taking any time at all. We're drowning.'

He made his way to Tottenham Court Road and managed to get up to fifteen miles an hour for a hundred yards, then caught up to the parade of goods wagons and 'buses and carriages that were flowing like melting tar down into the centre of London. He saw at once what a mistake he had made: he'd have been wiser to take them on the underground. Was it still possible?

Janet said, 'Perhaps we should have taken the underground. Now it's too late.' She watched the people on the pavement, moving at about the same rate they were. 'It's no good, taking all the time to get there and turning right round to come back.'

Oxford Street would have been impossible. Charing Cross Road was no better, but short; he sweated through Trafalgar Square and into Whitehall. Once, he heard Janet say, 'It's ridiculous.' The motor-car was making irregular clanging noises now, as if he'd picked up a bell in the undercarriage.

'This will work,' he said, coming off Westminster Bridge into Lambeth Palace Road.

'Everyone wants his lunch this hour. You're fighting British appetite, Denton.'

Then it was suddenly not so bad—perhaps nobody down here ate lunch—and he had the Albert Embankment on his right, and then he was in Wandsworth Road. 'You see?'

'I see that it's almost time to turn about and go back!'

He found Goshawk Street only a street away from the High and pulled over to the kerb half a dozen houses along from number 12, the house recognisable as Wragge's by the black crêpe on the door. Janet was holding on to her hat with her right hand. 'Now take me back,' she said.

'Good Christ, Janet...!'

'Don't start cursing, Denton; it's unbecoming. You did magnificently, but the fact is my time's a bit more than half gone.'

'Only have a look at the woman, Janet. Please!'

'Ah, you never say please. Nor should you have to. Let's get on with it, then.' She was out of the tiny car, which quivered from her getting down. 'You might have parked right in front of the house,' she said as he piloted her along the pavement.

'I didn't want her to hear us before we were at the door. Don't ask me why.'

'Because you want to surprise the poor woman, of course.' She was walking very fast, her skirts kicking out as her long legs scissored. He thought of her legs. Pleasant thought.

At the house, she held out a card for him. 'Send our cards in. Let's don't just barge.'

The card had her name and *Articled Solicitor's Clerk*, then *for* in small letters and then in much bigger letters *Theodora Mercer, Solicitor.* She said, 'Teddy gave them to me to tide me over until I've passed the examination.'

Denton added a card of his own and pulled the bell. Janet looked at her watch. The door opened. A rather bent woman in her sixties stared at them.

'To see Mrs Wragge,' He held out the cards.

'Not seeing nobody.'

'It's a matter of some importance.'

'I was told to say she ain't in to people.'

Janet swayed, perhaps took a short step with one foot, at any rate got between Denton and the maid without seeming to have done so and said, 'The police were here yesterday. We are following up.' Denton flinched internally but showed nothing.

The old woman took the two cards. Could she read? Probably. At least she seemed to be mouthing the word 'solicitor'. 'Come in, please, miss.' She ignored Denton. He followed the two women.

They were left standing in a cramped, dark entry while the maid laboured up a flight of dog-leg, rag-carpeted stairs, one hand on the black oak banister, the other holding up her skirts, her back bent. A minute passed. Janet looked at her watch. Denton looked at his watch. Janet looked at him and shook her head, unsmiling. After another minute, Denton heard the whisper of skirts upstairs, then a heavy foot on a tread.

She was, as Janet had said, dumpy—badly dressed in a black gown that was years out of fashion and creased where it had been laid away, as if she didn't experience many deaths. There was an odour of camphor. She was homely, the obvious feature the pop eyes that Janet had told him about. She had chipmunk cheeks like the aged Victoria, a chin so weak it seemed simply part of her throat. But her principal feature now was her fatigue: four steps above them, she stopped and leaned both her hands on the banister as if she were too exhausted to come the rest of the way.

'Mrs Wragge?' Denton said.

She nodded. He glanced at Janet, who nodded: *It's the same woman.*

'Are you the police?' the woman said in a voice like two bricks scraping together.

'No.'

'Mary said you were a solicitor. There's no business for you here. Please go away. This is a house of grief.'

This seemed too dramatic, but he found himself tempted to think that such an unattractive woman couldn't possibly be feeling grief for a man like Wragge, and then he saw how stupid that idea was. Of course she could: how was her grief any less than, let us say, the late Queen's over Albert? He said, 'I'm sorry to intrude, Mrs Wragge, but I have to talk to you.'

'Please go away.' She looked as if she might collapse, but she pushed herself erect and turned to go back up the stairs.

'Mrs Wragge, you stood outside my house in Lamb's Conduit Street for an hour two nights ago. You were seen.'

She didn't look at him but kept her eyes on a square, oak-framed window at the turn of the stairs. 'That wasn't me.'

'You were seen. There's no question of it.'

She stood still for several seconds, said, 'Please go away,' and started up again.

Denton went to the stairs and stood below the sloping banister. 'Mrs Wragge! Why were you following Henry James to my house? Mrs Wragge...!'

She went out of sight.

Janet put a hand on his arm. 'You can't go up there. I'm already late.'

He started to object, looked at her, exhaled noisily, turned to the door. She went ahead of him to the street and took his arm as soon as he joined her. 'She's most certainly the woman, Denton; she's unmistakable. Drive me to the nearest station and I'll find my own way from there.' She looked back at the house. 'You must talk to her.'

'You'll be late.'

'Of course I shall. No use going on about it.'

He protested that he'd drive her, but she seemed to have got over whatever she'd felt about being late. In fact, she seemed more interested in Mrs Wragge than in herself. 'There's something very wrong, Denton. Her hands were trembling; that's why she held the banister.'

'Maybe she has palsy.'

'She was frightened out of her wits.'

He thought of Walter's saying that Geddys and Rupert were in pain. He didn't put much stock in intuition. 'Is Putney Bridge all right?'

'Good God, no, it's miles from here.'

'But you can get to Euston Road on that line.'

'Oh Denton, you can be exasperating! Didn't they open a station at Clapham? Take me there.'

'I can drive you back to the—'

'Take me to Clapham at once!' To his surprise, she began to laugh. 'Words I never expected to hear myself say.'

He let her out at the Clapham Road station. 'Don't shut down the engine; I'm quite able to get out.' She did so, stood on the kerb, then bent close and said, 'Come over this evening for supper. Spend the night.' She smiled. 'It's impossible for me to stay angry with you just now. Is that you, or is it me?'

Spending the night meant spending it while Walter was in the house. She had done it deliberately, he knew; she confronted things, got them out of the way. He, often brusque enough with other people's feelings, got tentative when it came to his own. He would have temporised.

Driving back, he realised how much he resented Walter Snokes. He admitted that he was jealous of him, of Janet's interest in him. Jealous of a mentally not-all-there eighteen-year-old! Then he felt ashamed.

He left the Barré on a cross street and walked down to Goshawk and along to number 12.

'Not here,' the elderly maid said. She didn't sound sorry.

'Where has she gone?'

'I don't know, I'm sure.'

'The High Street? Doing the shopping?'

'I done the shopping this morning, didn't I?' She straightened, her feathers ruffled.

'But did she—Was she walking?'

'She went to get herself a carriage.'

'A carriage? Where would she find a carriage?'

'On the High Street, wouldn't she? Where the carriages are.'

'Where?' He was fumbling in his pocket for a coin, having his usual uncertainty whether by feel he would find one that was big enough. Or small enough.

She glanced at his hand. 'By the butcher's.' She took the coin and closed the door, as if to make it clear that that was all she'd get out of him.

He headed for the High Street.

The butcher's was announced by a once-golden calf's head. Two bored horses and two hansoms were standing at the kerb in front of it. Denton thrust his hand into his pocket again and felt for coins.

'Somebody just took a lady in black somewhere,' he growled at the first driver who pushed himself out of a bit of shade under a plane tree. 'Where did the lady go?'

'Who wants to know?'

Denton held up a shilling for answer. The driver, who looked a little like Atkins but had committed the mistake of a moustache, shook himself into his clothes as if they didn't feel right and took the coin. 'Got in Jack Mumford's hack not ten minutes ago. Not back yet.'

'Where was he taking her?'

'I *think* he was going to Clapham Road station, as he said he'd wait there for a fare coming back.'

Denton thought with some grimness that he'd just been at Clapham Road station and had undoubtedly passed her going the other way. He said, 'Another shilling if you get me there while Jack's still there.'

'Plus the fare.'

Denton pulled himself into the hansom. As they trotted off, he remembered the Barré. All in all, the cab would be faster.

Clapham Road station was almost the end of the City and South London Electric line. Denton got to see some of the sights of Clapham on the way but ignored them to keep urging the driver faster. The promise of more cash got the horse into a trot, which seemed to inspire it, as its head went up and it began to flash its tail. Denton had great sympathy for horses, having ridden a great many and seen many more abused, but this one was young and brisk and seemed to like Clapham.

'There's Jack!' The driver rapped on the roof with his whip and then pointed it. The horse slowed, turning towards a line of carriages and hansoms along the dark brick wall of the station. 'Eh, Jack!' Twenty heads turned. Then one of them grinned; a hand waved. Denton's driver manoeuvred his hansom until it was next to the other. Denton looked up at Jack—plump, thirty, red-haired, cheerful—and said, 'Did you bring a woman in mourning here from Wandsworth?'

'Indeed I did. Mrs Wragge. Just lost her husband.'

'Where did she go?'

'Into the station, where else is there to go?'

Denton jumped down, all but threw money at the driver and began to run. He dodged people going into the station, coming around them from behind and startling several; unkind remarks were made. He cursed as he waited to pay his tuppence, cursed again the crowd that filled the space in front of the elevator. He saw no dumpy figure in black. He threw himself down the stairs, threw himself forward again and reached the platform in time to see a train ready to leave; a guard waved an arm, shouted, 'Train leaving!' and the doors made a tentative start at closing, then opened as somebody along the train went in, then started to close again. Denton flung himself inside and sprawled on the floor. The train started.

Several women had drawn their skirts away from him. He got up, smiled foolishly, tipped his hat. Nobody was pleased. He brushed the grit off his hands, then his knees. Atkins would scold him.

And Mrs Wragge? Not to be seen.

A guard prevented his walking between carriages. He fell back into a window seat and stared out until the train stopped at Kennington Oval, then stared out at the people who got off. No Mrs Wragge. So, too, at Kennington New Street and Elephant and Castle. He pictured what was up above; was it a likely stop for the sad, defeated Mrs Wragge? Who knew.

At Borough, a great many people got on; fewer seemed to get off. He wondered what that meant. He knew Bermondsey, the Borough area. It didn't seem Mrs Wragge's kind of place. But that was foolish; what did he know about the woman?

They went on. They rumbled under the river, London Bridge far above them. Unsettling, going under a river.

Monument was the end. Denton was standing at the doors when they opened; he jumped out and retreated to the platform wall so he could look up and down the train. His head went back and forth like something on a clock. She would be one of the last off, he thought; she was slow with weight and age and sadness. Then he saw her. She was in the midst of a clot of people, apparently carried along by them until she could drop behind, a hand on her heart, her eyes searching for something. Help? Relief? Not for Denton, anyway, for they passed over him without a flicker. Nonetheless, he tried to make himself shorter, tipped his head down so his hat would hide his face.

She didn't care. He might as well have worn a red nose and a fright wig. She wanted only to get out. He followed her up a flight of stairs, then along a seemingly endless tunnel, at last past another ticket window—threepence this time—and so to the Metropolitan Line. They waited almost together on the crowded platform. She all but backed into him when the train came shrieking in, then stumbled forward and wouldn't have got on the train at all if he hadn't put his arm forward between her and a brute who meant to brush her aside. The brute looked at him, ready to rage, and decided it wasn't the time or place.

She got off at Aldgate. She was slow, her gait that of a woman with a bad hip, but she didn't hesitate. She didn't have to read the signs to find her way out; she didn't need to look about to see which way to walk. They went along Aldgate High Street, he thirty feet behind her, hating the slow pace; then left into Goulston Street and so up to Bell Lane and onward. It seemed a long way for her to be walking; why hadn't she got a cab or a 'bus at Aldgate station? At the far end of Bell Lane she turned again, and then he knew where she was going: into that curious maze of small streets east of Bell Lane that were locked into themselves like parts of a Greek key design. He knew better ways to get there, but, he decided, this was the way that *she* knew.

There was still no hesitating. She plodded into Shepherd Street and turned into Freeman, and then to his surprise, because he was accustomed now to her walking, she laboured up the three steps of a newly painted house and rang the bell. Some of the street was decayed, but this house and several others shone as if they'd been polished: sparkling black on the railings, gleaming brass on the knobs and plates, white that hurt the eyes on corners and soffits and window frames. And flowers! Astonishing— boxes full of reds and yellows at the windows, the only one that Denton recognised the trailing ivy.

And on the varnished wood of the door, a huge black crêpe bow.

He watched the door close on her and walked along past the house, walked to the end of the street, crossed and came back. The curtains at the windows of what, he thought, would be the front parlour were drawn. Upstairs, too, the curtains seemed to be closed. A house of mourning. As he watched, a man and woman stopped at the house, went up, handed in cards and went away. Rather prosperous-looking but very conservative, even stuffy; both in black, taste restrained to the point of asceticism.

And, he thought, possibly Jewish. No skullcaps or tassels, not that kind. Assimilated, and self-conscious about it. And it was a Jewish neighbourhood.

Denton crossed the street and went up the front steps as he had seen them do, a calling card ready in his hand. He wrote, 'To pay his respects' on it and then pulled the bell. The maid was Irish, youngish, briskish; she took the card and stood back and herded him towards the closed door of the parlour with hardly a word. She opened the door.

Five people were seated in ways and places that suggested that two were couples and one a singleton, and they didn't know each other. None of them was Mrs Wragge. On a sideboard were plates of food and a decanter of a very dark, heavy-looking wine. Three rectangles on the flocked walls had been draped in black to cover the paintings inside them. At the far end of the room to Denton's left was a table also draped in black, on it several photographs in heavy silver frames, two burning candles in thick silver candlesticks.

Denton bowed. The men bowed their heads. The women moved on their chairs. Everybody was in black. Black lace handkerchiefs were being used to dab at invisible tears. The closed curtains gave the interior the look of a recently opened tomb in some dry, dusty country. *As rendered by our artist.*

Denton walked on thick Oriental carpets to the long table. He studied the framed photographs. He was not quite surprised to find that they were of the late Inspector Wragge.

But if it was Wragge who was being mourned, why, so far as Denton could tell, were none of the mourners policemen?

Denton put dabs of food on a small but very good porcelain plate and ate small bites while he waited, not sure what he was waiting for. Mrs Wragge was in the house, he knew. If she left, he thought he would hear her, although that wasn't certain. He would have to force matters soon, he decided, but he'd missed lunch and the food, although rich, was good. He finished it, dabbed his mouth with a black-edged napkin from the sideboard, and stood. He bowed at the others again. They looked resigned.

Denton went out into the hall that divided the house down its middle. The furnishings, even in the near-dusk of mourning, were as bright and aggressive as the house's exterior. If the taste was not good, it was certainly showy—lots of polished wood with shiny brass all over it; paintings of people in brilliant scarlet coats jumping horses over gates and walls; Paisley shawls as peacock-coloured as some of Janet's at-home clothes. What it all announced was that good money had been spent here.

'Sir?' It was the Irish maid, who had materialised from the back of the house.

'I'd like to see Mrs Wragge, please.'

'I don't know a Missus Wragge, then. Is it somebody in the parlour, maybe?'

'She's not in the parlour. Is your mistress at home?'

'Mistress is upstairs, sir. This is a grieving house.'

'Indeed. Still, if you go up, I believe you'll find Mrs Wragge with her or nearby somewhere. If not...' He took out another card and wrote on it, 'In the matter of Inspector Wragge. Urgent.' Give this to your mistress, please. At once.' He produced yet another coin, handed it over.

'I was given orders not to disturb Mistress.'

Another coin? 'I have to insist, I'm sorry. She will understand.' The maid went up the polished, vividly carpeted stairs.

He thought that he would make sense of it all when he saw the mistress of this house. He had figured out at first, he thought, that she would be a close relative of Wragge's, maybe a sister, and that would explain both the photographs and Mrs Wragge's visit, even her knowing the way so well. But he was not so sure. Wragge wasn't a Jew, though he could, perhaps, have a sister who had married a Jew. But would that justify all this showy mourning?

He waited. And waited. The single man came out of the parlour and, after bowing to Denton, looked around for a bell-pull, found it, pulled with a funereal discretion. He was all in black. His hat, Denton thought, would have black crêpe around the crown. His hair was black. He was quite handsome, no older than thirty-five, habitually grave.

Denton said, 'I think the maid is upstairs with her mistress.'

'Ah.'

With that, the maid came from the back of the house, saw the man, vanished, and returned with a hat and a light black overcoat that was still too heavy for the day. The hat did have black crêpe around the brim. The man bowed again and went away.

'I told Mistress.' The maid eyed him without expression. 'I done what you asked.'

'What is your mistress's relation to the man whose photographs are on the table in the parlour?'

'He's her husband, isn't he?' Then she went away towards the back.

Denton waited. And waited.

And then he heard a footfall, much muffled. *Nice carpets upstairs, too.* Another sounded some seconds later at the top of the stairs. *On tiptoe.* Denton moved closer to the stair and looked up at the left-hand half of a woman's face as it tried to peek around a corner. It was not Mrs Wragge.

'Please come down, ma'am. And bring Mrs Wragge, if you would.'

He thought she'd run, but she gave it up and came down slowly, one hand on the dark wood of the banister, the hand seeming the paler by contrast. She was tall for a woman, big, olive-skinned, a rather flat face diminished by a huge mass of wiry hair and marked on the left side with a bruise she'd tried to hide with powder. Her dark purple mourning didn't suit her, nor the jet bib she wore at her throat. She might have been forty, possibly younger.

'I don't know you,' she said. Her voice was husky, as if she had shouted too much for a long time.

'My name is Denton.'

'I got your card.' She led him across the hall to a closed door, trailing eau de cologne and a more powerful menstrual smell. Behind the door was a small sitting room, perhaps once an office when this house had belonged to a merchant who did his business here. She sat in a stiff chair, didn't offer him one. 'Who are you?' She had the accent of the East End; even Denton could recognise it.

'I came about Mrs Wragge.'

'I don't know a Mrs Wragge.'

'She's in your house.'

'What do you know about my house? What are you doing here? This is a house of mourning!'

'Yes, for Mrs Wragge's husband. I saw the photographs. Is he a relative of yours?'

She didn't look at him. 'Yes, he is.'

He thought she was lying, but he wasn't sure. He said, 'This is difficult for both of us. Am I correct that Inspector Wragge was your husband, ma'am?'

'My name is Ruth Gold. I am called Mrs Gold.'

'But the man who is being mourned here is a policeman named Wragge. Mrs Wragge is his wife.'

'You are making no sense. Are you a crazy person? There is no Mrs Wragge!' But she didn't look at him. 'I am Mrs Gold. This is my house. I don't want you in it, you're a vulgar, a nasty, an un-un-uneducated person! Get out of my house or I will have you put out!'

He wondered by whom she meant to have him put out, wondered if she would threaten him with the police. *Not likely.* He said, 'I'm very sorry to have upset you, particularly at such a time.' He bowed. He went out of the room and closed the door.

The maid brought him his hat when he rang, said nothing, stayed locked within herself as she opened the door.

He had reached Commercial Street before he had decided what to do. Traffic was heavy, dust raised by it as if it were on a country road. It struck him how long the summer heat had lasted without rain, how the taste of heat and dust was there on his lips like something he had eaten. He was looking north for a 'bus when a four-wheeler appeared, and he shouted. It would be uncomfortable, expensive, but it was there.

'The nearest telephone room!' he shouted to the driver.

The man turned about. 'Telephone room.'

'I want to make a telephone call. The Company have rooms all over London!'

'O-o-o-h.' He wasn't old but gave that impression, perhaps deliberately, seemed to have got his persona from a *Punch* cartoon—yellowed moustache, dented bowler, watery eyes, cockney accent (all working-class accents were cockney to Denton). 'A *telephone* room.'

Denton sighed. 'A telegraph office will do. Cannon Street's always open.'

'No-o-o...' The man massaged his small chin with a thumb and a forefinger, a part of the persona got from pre-Delsartean acting. 'There's a telephone room in Oxford Court. You saying Cannon Street made it come right into my head. Right into my head. Cannon Street it is.'

Denton didn't figure it out until they got there that he wasn't going to send a telegraph after all, because there really was a telephone room—a very large one—in the offices of the National Telephone Company in something nominally Oxford Court but effectively Cannon Street. He was sure they'd passed half a dozen others on the way, but at that point he was resigned to taking what he could get.

'Funny how the mind works,' the philosophical driver said as he took his money.

'Comical, in fact.'

Denton paid sixpence for the first three minutes of a call and agreed that he would pay more if he ran over. The room was full of small tables with high sides like horses' blinders, a deliberately uncomfortable chair, and a telephone. He asked to be connected with the Stoke Newington police station, then asked for Guillam. Not surprisingly, Guillam was unavailable.

'Chief Inspector Munro, then.'

'Haven't got a Munro in my list, sorry.'

'In the murder room. The Wragge case.'

'Oh. Right. I can try that. Hold on. Let's see...' Thirty seconds later, Munro came on.

'It's Denton.'

'Got the case solved? Can we all go home?'

'You won't like it. I certainly don't.'

He told him about the two Mrs Wragges.

Munro's face was lined with something like disgust, as well as middle age and fatigue. 'You were right. I thought it was daft, but you were right. We had constables waiting for Mrs Wragge when she got home. The Gold woman has scarpered.' He belched slightly. 'Won't get far.'

It was evening, Denton's sitting room. Denton had had supper with Janet and Walter, was now back in his own house to talk to Munro. The supper had been hard work, Walter sullen, Janet's attention all on him, and Denton trying to be jovial. 'Has Mrs Wragge said anything?'

'She's about ready to, but she hasn't yet. We had a Wandsworth detective put some questions to her. Got her to the point where he was going to have to charge her if she said yes and stopped and told her to get herself some legal help. Smart man. He's bringing her up to N Div in a carriage.'

'She admitted they killed him?'

'Not yet, didn't come right out with it, but she will when we ask her outright. According to the Wandsworth copper, the woman's got no will left, no spine.'

Denton thought of the woman on the stairs. No will, yes, that would have been his notion, too. 'So she didn't go off to Mrs Gold to confront her. She went for help.'

'Or collusion, however you want to put it. They're both in it.'

'You don't know that yet.'

'I do. Why else has the Gold woman scarpered? *She* has a will. She doesn't want to hang.' He belched again, fist over mouth, his supper not sitting well. 'We'll catch her.'

'I think you're getting ahead of yourself.'

'Me! You're the one that telephoned me to say you'd solved it! You should have seen Guillam's face when I told him. He looks like hell, anyway. Like I'd hit him with a cross-beam. But Georgie's at heart a good sort. You know what he said? He said, "Denton was right and I was wrong."'

'Generous of him.'

'Mmm.' Munro had a bottle and glass next to him, untouched. Now he looked at it, studied it, poured himself a few ounces. 'What was your impression of the Gold woman?'

'Pretty tough cut of meat, but pretty well jiggered, too. And she had a big bruise on her face.'

'Hmm.' Munro smiled. 'Nice house for a policeman's wife?'

'Especially a policeman's second wife. Where was Wragge getting the money?'

'That has some people at the Yard clenching their arseholes very tight. Because I'll tell you something you *don't* know.' He leaned forward, the glass of ale like a shaft of amber light in his hand. 'Guess who your Mrs Gold is.'

'I don't like guessing, you know that.'

'You'd never get it.' His smile was friendly, but just slightly malicious. 'She's the daughter of Ginger Goldensohn.'

'That helps a lot. Now if I knew who Ginger Goldensohn is, I'd know something.'

Munro inhaled noisily, then drank off the glass and poured himself more. 'Fifteen years ago, Ginger Goldensohn was the biggest crook in the East End. I wouldn't say he ran *everything* between the Minories and Limehouse Cut, but I wouldn't insist he didn't, either. It was Guillam who got it. I said "Ruth Gold" and he said, "Judas, Ginger Goldensohn". Like that. Knew she was his daughter, knew she was married—there's two kids, by the way, still sprats—said there was no way Wragge could have got Ginger's ugly daughter without being in Ginger's pocket.' He started to drink, put the glass to the side to say, 'She was famous for being ugly, apparently. Fact, maybe Wragge got something from Ginger for marrying her.'

'Marrying after a fashion, you mean.'

'It puts a whole new colour on your friend James's burglary. Also on the 'arrangement' with the insurance people. If Wragge was Ginger's man—well, no 'if' about it; his bleeding son-in-law, even bigamously—then we've got a dodgy copper standing between a bunch of thieves and the people ready to pay down money to get their swag back. It stinks. It stinks worse than a po at five in the morning. And Ginger would have been looking on and smiling.'

'Jewish?'

'Ginger? Unnh. Officially, I suppose, but a damned bad one. I got on the telephone to the head of CID in H Div. He filled my ear about Goldensohn, but as if he was talking about ancient history. He says there was a dust-up between Goldensohn and the head rabbi years ago and Goldensohn lost. There's old Jewish gangs in the East End—that's how he got his start—but there's all sorts there now, anarchists and Black Hand and Camorra and Fenians. Ginger's in a manner of speaking a pensioner, which doesn't mean he's any better than any other crook with blood under his fingernails, only that he's old and out of it.'

'What did your H Division man say about Wragge?'

'I didn't ask. The lid's on. Orders from Whitehall. Bad enough a cop gets murdered, wait till we admit he was crooked.'

'You don't know that yet.'

'Don't I? Do I know that beds have bugs?'

The telephone rang. Denton heard Atkins pounding up the stairs. He started out of his chair, fell back. 'More ale?'

Munro started to say something, looked down the room at Atkins, who was holding up the earpiece like a trophy. 'For Chief Inspector Munro.'

'That'll be Guillam. He's the only one knows where I am.' As he passed Denton, he rested a big hand on Denton's shoulder and said, 'Yes to that bottle,' and went on.

Denton watched him take the earpiece and lean into the telephone horn. Atkins looked around him to meet Denton's eyes. Both men raised their eyebrows. Next to the telephone, the dumbwaiter doors were open, meaning Atkins had been listening from downstairs. Atkins shrugged. Denton shook his head. Atkins went back down.

Munro was being monosyllabic. Huh, mmm, when, good. When Denton passed behind him to get the ale, he heard Guillam's voice as a scratching from the other side of Munro's head, unintelligible and apparently inhuman.

The wonders of the twentieth century.

Munro rang off and came back up the room, his limp more pronounced than usual. He fell backwards into his chair and acknowledged the fresh bottle with a nod. 'Mrs Wragge's being charged.'

'That was quick.'

'Guillam had somebody there to represent her even before she arrived—grabbed him out of the night magistrate's court. The shyster took her aside, came back and said she wasn't ready to make a statement and he'd advised her to say nothing.'

'She'd have broken down without some sort of legal advice.'

'Aye.' Munro studied his bottle, blew out air with puffed cheeks. 'Not always a job I like, mine. But it has to be done.' He stared at nothing. 'Funny—you said a woman could have done it.'

'But Mrs Wragge was the one scorned.'

'No, both of them. Wragge had somebody new. This is according to Mrs Wragge this afternoon. She admitted to the Wandsworth tec that she was outside your house a couple of nights ago. She was following your Henry James because Wragge had told her he'd be out all night with him.'

'And Ruth Gold? Following Wragge himself?'

'That's for her to know and us to learn.' He looked at a big pocket-watch. 'We checked her neighbours and the boat trains; sounds as if she and the two kids and a maid were on their way to Calais. Special Branch have two coppers over there; they've been sent a wire. Have her by morning if that's where she went.'

'Not with her father?'

'H Div say Ginger's on the go someplace. He's got a big house—no bollocks, he's tried to make himself legit—but he travels, some Zionist thing. Maybe he wants to be a Jew again in the little time that's left.' He raised the glass. 'Here's to the death of ancient villains.'

'You make him sound like Old Parr.'

'He's getting on. This Ruth was a late child. Didn't fall too far from the tree, did she?' He looked at his watch, sighed. 'Guillam's got to get some sleep or he's going to be no good to anybody, least of all me.' He stood, leaving half his bottle of ale. 'How's Mrs Striker?' By which he meant, from the context, that he knew he was keeping Denton from her bed.

'She's well. She has Walter Snokes with her.'

'Right. That a problem?'

Denton hesitated. 'He and I don't get on.'

Munro stamped a foot and flexed his knee. 'Bloody thing goes to sleep. Same old injury. You mustn't expect to get on with a kid that age. He's how old? Eighteen? Not a hope.' He banged his foot on the floor twice more and stood there, one hand on the back of Denton's chair. 'I'll tell you about kids. Don't expect too much from them in the way of considering anything but themselves. It's the nature of the beast. They grow out of it. I've had three.'

Denton decided that Munro was a good friend and he could be frank. 'I found myself today being jealous of him. Because of Janet.'

'That's wrong. Kids'll play you off against each other, but she's better than that. She won't let him do it. You just be yourself and be honest. If he doesn't like you, that's his worry.' He stamped his foot again. 'Guillam thinks well of him. Says there's a lot there. But Guillam doesn't have a lady in the mix, so I think that's the difference and you're being foolish.' He patted Denton's shoulder. 'Think of kids as dogs. You get more out of them with a biscuit in your hand than a stick. I have to go.'

Denton shouted. Atkins appeared with a huge hat. Munro took it, scowled at it as if he'd been handed a summons. He eyed

Atkins somewhat sideways. 'Not a word of this business to your chums, get me?'

'What business is that, sir?'

Munro chuckled and put the hat on. 'I'll have your hide if there's a peep. Let me out.'

When Atkins came back up he said, 'So you were right about the women.'

'Right for the wrong reason. Not much to pat myself on the back in that.'

He was cleaning up his and Munro's bottles. Atkins took them from him and started downstairs. 'New recruit coming on duty tomorrow.'

Denton raised his eyebrows in question.

'Lad we talked about. To get the door when I'm away. The new dispensation, remember?'

'That was quick! I don't get to vet him?'

'That's what he's coming for. On probation. Doesn't know anything about anything—sixteen and spent his entire life in Bermondsey. Crossing the river's like going to China. Nice enough lad, mind.'

'How'd you get him?'

'He's the nephew of the current Mrs Char. I figured that'd give us a bit of added weight in keeping him up to snuff. Mother's a posy-seller, father's an odd-job specialist. Seven shillings a week. They ought to be paying us, as he'll be fair useless for weeks if not months, *and* getting trained by me, which is like going to the Sandhurst of servant academies. Name of Alfred. Don't scare him to death.'

'Me? What have I done?'

'Mrs Char has filled the family with tales of her employer, a Western gunman who regularly shoots up the landscape and kills miscreants. If you reach for your pocket, the poor kid will probably faint.' He moved his jaw sideways and cocked an eyebrow. 'You made it up with Henry James yet?'

'Not that I've heard.'

'Too bad.' Atkins went down. 'Let me know when you do. Things are moving.'

Meaning that Atkins had had another idea. Denton shook his head. He wasn't up to dealing with both James's indignation and Atkins's ideas. All he wanted was to crawl into bed with Janet and hold on to her and make sure she wasn't angry about the dismal scene at supper.

He was stewing about that—*What should I have done differently? Is Munro right about simply being myself? Why the hell am I jealous of a kid I ought to feel sorry for? Well, I do feel sorry for him, but goddammit*—when the doorbell rang. He shouted, 'It'll be Munro again; what did he forget?' He looked around his sitting room, seeing nothing that didn't belong there. Nothing of Munro's.

There was conversation at the front door, to Denton merely mumbles. Atkins appeared. He whispered, 'An old gent to see you. Won't give his name. Bespoke clothes, top quality, talks like a docker. A bit off, I'd say.'

Denton frowned. Atkins made a face, suggesting an iffy smell. Denton took a Remington derringer from a box on his mantelpiece—habit, nothing but habit—and dropped it into a pocket, then said to show the man up. Atkins raised his eyebrows and shook his head as if his employer had lost his buttons.

The man was short, poor in his wind, paunchy, elegantly dressed. His lavender cravat might have been a shade too bright, his diamond ring a fraction of a carat too big, but he suggested wealth and position. His posture did not: he bent. He was mostly bald, the sides of his head silver, the backs of his hands spotted and hairy. Red spots along the sides of his nose and on his forehead. No moustache. Little eyeglasses on a ribbon. A voice like gravel coming out of a crusher. He said, 'You don't know me.'

'I'm afraid not.'

'I know you. By name, Denton. I don't send up cards.'

Denton shrugged, waited.

'My name is Samuel Goldensohn. They call me Ginger.' He had to look up at Denton, but his eyes, pouched and lined as they were, were hard and humourless. 'I knew you was busy with the copper, so I waited.'

'How did you know he was a copper?'

'How do I know a turd is shit?' He made it sound almost like 'toid'. 'I seen him come in, I seen him go out. I want to talk to yous.'

'In that case, let's sit down.'

Goldensohn took Munro's place opposite Denton's armchair. When he moved, a slight tinge of urine reached Denton's nose; he had a flash of eating a kidney—when was that?

The room was deeply shadowed, the curtains drawn and only two electric lamps burning. Goldensohn made no attempt at courtesy, did not even look around to see what sort of place he was in. When he was settled—the chair too big for him, his breathing heavy—he said, 'You know why I come.'

'I don't, in fact.'

'You was to my daughter's place this p.m. You got her all riled. How you think I feel about that?'

'I don't give a goddam how you feel about that.' This wasn't somebody nice he was talking to, and it definitely wasn't some-body he liked. 'If your daughter's on the warpath, it's her own doing, not mine.'

'You come into a grieving house where you wasn't invited.'

'Tell me another.'

'You know who I am?'

'You're the pa of a woman who married another woman's husband and, I think, bludgeoned him to death. That's supposed to make me squeamish about going to her house? Don't make me laugh.'

Goldensohn stared at him. If he felt insulted, he didn't show it. Maybe he had no feelings.

Denton said, 'What do you want?'

'What you said about Ruth killing him, where did you hear that? From that copper?'

'None of your business, Mr Goldensohn.' He put his hands on his knees, ready to get up. 'That it?'

'You got *proof* she did that?'

Then Denton saw that the old man really didn't know what his daughter had done. He wasn't appalled by the possibility; he wasn't frightened; but he didn't *know*. And that squared with Denton's suspicion that the two women had taken Wragge's body to the cemetery themselves: Ginger Goldensohn's daughter hadn't asked her pa to do it for her. Why? 'Ask her.'

'You're being a big pain in the arse to me, Mr Denton.'

'I'd say the same for you if asked.'

Goldensohn stared at him some more, then turned to look down into the empty coal grate. Slowly, his voice even more like gravel, he said, as if he were talking to the grate, 'You know I might have fellas like you killed?'

'Come to the point.' Denton allowed himself to sound fed up.

Goldensohn sat on. Denton was tempted to offer him port or beer, an absurd idea; politeness would be wasted on him, even ironic politeness. So he waited the old man out. At last Goldensohn said, 'Here's the deal.' And then said nothing.

'Well? The deal?'

Goldensohn finally took his eyes off the grate and offered them to Denton. 'If my daughter done something, I'll trade wit' yous. Maybe your friend's goods. Maybe I heard something where they are.'

Friend. He could mean only Henry James. A tiny alarm rang in Denton's head. 'You won't trade with me, because I'm not a policeman, and if you think you can trade murder for some housewares, you're barking loony.'

The hard little eyes, two stones found on a beach and dropped into white dough, stayed fixed on his. 'See, what I see wit' you is a go-between. You know this James, you know the copper. I see you're a sensible man and you know what's what. When I'm ready, I make an offer, I bring it to you, you go to other people.'

'I'm nobody's go-between.'

'Ruth is a crazy girl. She marries this copper, she knows he's got a wife awready but she was fucking him, so what should she do? She wasn't the prettiest girl on the Ratcliffe Highway, here's her big chance. I tell her, a copper in the family is good, I give you a house, whatever you want, but don't tell me later you made a mistake. What I'm saying here, Mr Denton, is that I don't go too far for Ruth Gold, but I go some of the way. I got things to offer that the coppers want. Maybe I know about some other things than this James's goods, too. Things that coppers might like to know. If Ruth Gold don't hang and goes to chokey five, seven years, I could accept that. No longer than that, though.'

Denton let their eyes hold. Finally, without breaking the look, he said, 'I'm not a judge and I'm not a jury.'

'But you got a pal in the police. It all starts with the police. Then the prosecutor.' He pushed a hand out between them and waggled the spread fingers. 'Maybe this, maybe that. Maybe a deal, maybe money. Maybe I got friends you think I don't in the City. Maybe in the Houses of Parliament. You got no right to say what happens to Ruth Gold, because you're ignorant of what I got.' He gathered his legs under him and put his hands on the arms of his chair. 'Nobody ever made a deal the first meeting. You and me meet again. You tell your copper that Goldensohn got things in his pockets he maybe wants to trade.'

'Not on your life.'

'Oh yeah, you'll tell him. Because now I'm evidence. The famous Ginger Goldensohn come to your house and talked about his daughter. That's evidence. People like you, Mr Denton, don't withhold evidence from the coppers.' He pushed himself up. 'Tell that flunkey to bring me my stuff.'

Atkins would have heard through the dumbwaiter shaft, but he waited for Denton's ring for appearance's sake. All the time Goldensohn was waiting, all the time he was slowly assembling his gloves and silk hat and cane, he said nothing. Nor did he say good night.

'Nasty piece of work,' Atkins said when he'd returned from the door. '"Flunkey," indeed.'

'He thinks he's a nasty piece of work, anyway.'

'Don't rub him too hard, General. That kind's got no sense of humour.'

'Neither have I, just now.' He consulted his watch and saw that it was nearly midnight. Janet would have given him up and gone to bed, and she'd be furious with him if he woke her.

But Atkins said, 'The missus come over while I was watering the boys and said she was waiting up for you.'

That sounded fairly positive. Denton smiled. Atkins nodded.

'And he rode away in a closed brougham with a driver got up like an undertaker.'

'He actually said he might kill you?'

'Nothing that definite.' He was lying on his side, his knees fitted into hers, both of them wearing sleeping clothes. They had arrived at an agreement of a sexless night without saying the words—small signs, offers given and refused, the practised signals of long-time lovers. She wasn't angry about the supper, as it had turned out; she was not even resigned. She wanted to cuddle.

'Does he know who you are?'

'He knew my name.'

She pressed her buttocks into him. 'I used to hear about him in Bethnal Green.' When she was poor, she meant, and working for the Society for the Improvement of Wayward Women. After she'd been a wayward woman herself.

'Guillam said he was into everything.'

'I suppose he was.'

'He ran girls? Women?'

'Not directly, not that I ever heard. He took a bit every week, was how he worked. The girls said he ruled who could work what streets, who got which corners. But mostly he took his bit for not doing anything. "Give me tuppence a week and nothing will happen to you."'

'What we call protection in the US. And did he protect them?'

'I never heard a girl complain about him. The money wasn't much. That's how he worked, they said—he took a little bit from everybody and nobody kicked over the traces.'

'He must have had something to threaten with.'

She shifted again, then put very cold feet on Denton's. He complained; she laughed, pushed them up his calves. 'You have to be good for something, Denton. My feet are cold.' He put a hand over one of her breasts and she sighed but said he wasn't to get ideas; it was so late. Then she said, 'Goldensohn had a gang. Or gangs. But I think most of the violence was already old when I lived in Bethnal Green, so he was going on his reputation. Which isn't to say he was harmless. He was vicious, but he was very far away. Like God.'

'You never ran into him?'

'Not himself, as the Irish say. Two of his toughs came to the office once and looked about and asked what we did there. I told them the truth—that we tried to get girls out of the life. They strutted about for a bit and said we weren't to upset the apple cart, and they went away. Goldensohn was a realist, maybe—we never succeeded enough to cut into his supply of tuppences, so what was the point? In fact, after that, we got a contribution from him once a year. It's how a monarch behaves—bleed the peasants all year long, but give them a bun on Michaelmas.'

'King Goldensohn.'

'And his daughter the princess. Why do you think she called herself Gold?'

'Maybe the old man's idea. Or Wragge's. One in the eye of his fellow coppers. "I'm Mr Gold, if you only knew." Raking in the gold.'

'You think he was twisted?'

'Like a corkscrew, but don't tell Munro I said so.'

She put a hand over the hand that was on her breast. 'I'm almost asleep.'

'Good for you.' He pushed the thin blanket off so it lay more or less between them. She was very warm. A little later, he felt the regular rise and fall of her breathing. He was surprised when she murmured, 'You were very good with Walter. Thank you.'

'I wasn't. I was a complete dub.'

'That was why you were good. You were just yourself.' She stirred, pulled away from him, lay on her back, and found his hand and put it back on her breast. 'I think what Walter looks for in people is authenticity. He can't *like* people, but he more or less believes in them if they're real to him. Authentic. I think it's what he sees in Guillam.'

'He was with Guillam only a couple of hours last year. But Guillam was good to him.'

'No, he saw something in him. Maybe it isn't authenticity. Maybe it's...I don't know...'

'Pain?' Denton said. She had nothing to say to that.

To keep her awake, he told her about a young woman from University College who had appeared that afternoon and was going to look at Balzac's early life for him. 'I told her I was an author, much as I think the word's too good for me, and said I was working on a book about interesting romantic events in the early lives of famous authors. Which isn't such a bad idea, actually. Might be something in it. Anyway, she's writing a monograph on Balzac and said she thought she knew where to look. Named Heckham, wears little round glasses, freckled, kind of spirited. So I have you to thank for her.'

But she was asleep.

He lay there and thought about what he had said earlier. Did Walter Snokes really look for, and so recognise, pain? He'd said it about Geddys, and he'd warmed to Geddys; he'd said it about Rupert, and he seemed to have some sort of attachment to the dog.

And that's what he doesn't find in me, because I don't feel that sort of pain.

I think.

The Monster?

Janet insisted that he stay for breakfast, but he insisted that he have his usual morning exercise, so he went back to his own house for an hour. It was too early to call Munro about Goldensohn. He went up to the attic and worked with his dumbbells and his rattletrap rowing machine, and then he stood with his old cap-and-ball Navy Colt and held it out at the end of his arm, sighting without wavering for five minutes, and then he fired twenty rounds with his parlour pistols. They sounded like birthday crackers. His neighbours never seemed to hear them.

'I'm going back to Mrs Striker's for breakfast,' he said to Atkins.

'Less work for me.'

'I thought I'd try to fix the motor today. It's making noises.'

'Just at the time I want to use it more. The story of my life.'

Denton went off, rather awkward in a new summer suit that he thought too colourful, as if it were Boat Race Day. Atkins had insisted it was proper, however. In fact, *de rig-ew-err*.

He went into Janet's garden, found Cohan, husband to Janet's cook and seamstress, shadow-boxing. Cohan had been a prize-fighter, now ran a boxing school in east London. Seeing Denton, he feinted at him; Denton parried, and then they were boxing. Cohan had only one eye and a game leg, but his hands were so fast that Denton could hardly keep up. When he was sweating and panting in his new suit, Denton said, 'Ever know somebody named Goldensohn?'

'That sonofabitch they call "Ginger"?' Cohan had an accent—pure Stepney. He'd fought as the Stepney Jew-boy, throwing that name into his Gentile opponents' teeth. '*That* Goldensohn?'

'What about him?'

'He's a crook, a criminal. Worse! A Jew who stole from Jews. Why d'you ask? He's dead, I hope.' He feinted twice at Denton, dropped his hands. '"Pay up, I'll take care of you", that's what he said to everybody who made a penny in the East End.'

'Did they get anything in return?'

'Sure, they got not to have their hands and feet broke. A *shaitan*.'

'Was he ever in things like burglary? Fencing stolen goods?'

'He was in everything!' Cohan was wiping off his sweat with a rag. He tossed it to Denton. 'Keep that elbow in more. I could of basted your guts twice just now.'

Denton went in to Janet's.

'Good morning, Walter.'

'Good-morning-sir-I'm-well-thank-you.' And the boy did look well. Living in Janet's house seemed to have given him colour. And he was cleaner.

'I wish I had seen Rupert doing it to Sophie.' Walter was looking at a place where nothing was. 'Janet told me about it. It's how they made the puppies.'

'There wasn't much to it. Rupert looked like an old rug that had been dropped on Sophie's back.'

'Still, I wish I had seen it. I've seen humans do it but not dogs. I like dogs.'

Janet came in, severe in her working clothes—grey from top to bottom. She smiled at Walter but didn't touch him, kissed Denton's cheek, said, 'You'll find you mustn't talk in public about dogs doing it, Walter.'

'Why?'

'I've told you—people don't talk about their bodies. It upsets them.'

'These are dogs.'

'Dogs, too.'

'But I see ladies walking their dogs and waiting while they do caca on the pavement.'

'But they don't talk about it. And you'll find that if you look at them, they'll look away.'

'I can still see what they're doing.'

'But they can't see you seeing them. A lot of being grown up is knowing what not to see.'

They were eating soft eggs and toast made a little earlier by Mrs Cohan downstairs and brought up and left on a sideboard. It was one of the disappointments of breakfast at Janet's—the food was always good but cold. Cool, anyway. Denton said, 'I'm going to try to fix something on my motor-car later, Walter. Would you like to help?'

'Will it be noisy?'

'I'm trying to get rid of a noise. I won't have to start the engine, I think. Want to come?'

'Yes, please.'

They finished; Walter went off. Denton said to Janet, 'Wragge's wife is going to need a lawyer. You might tell Teddy.' He meant Theodora Mercer, Janet's solicitor-boss *cum*-mentor. 'The woman's been ill-used, and now the law is going to steam-roller her if she doesn't get help.' He kissed her cheek and went through the gardens to his house. He got himself more tea and took it up to his sitting room and thought it was time to call Munro.

Munro wasn't at Stoke Newington, however. Guillam was, and sounding less as if he'd been shouting for hours into a sandstorm.

'Get some sleep?' Denton said.

'Made me a new man. What do you want?'

'Two things. One, you were going to visit Walter Snokes.'

'I haven't had the time.'

'He needs to see people.'

Guillam was silent. Denton pictured that pocked, brooding face. Guillam said, 'I can't just drop in on them.'

'You can, but you think you need an invitation.'

'Mrs Striker should be there.' The other side of what Janet had been trying to teach Walter: part of propriety is not seeing, part of it is being seen.

Denton thought of ringing off and trying Munro at New Scotland Yard, but remembered that Wragge's murder was Guillam's case. He said, 'There's a second thing. You ready?'

'Why wouldn't I be?'

'Munro came to see me last night. After he left, I had a visitor. Ginger Goldensohn.'

Guillam laughed, not pleasantly. 'He's not short in the brass department, is he!'

'He wants what he calls "a deal".'

'I'll "deal" him. What the hell's he farting about with you for?'

'I'm to be the go-between.'

'Like hell.'

'Not my idea.'

'What's he think he's got to trade? It's about his daughter, I suppose.'

'He seemed confused.'

'Ginger Goldensohn is about as confused as a ferret in a henhouse.'

'He's old.'

Guillam grunted. 'Mrs Gold is on her way back. They caught her in Calais.'

'Sounds like a song.'

'Her and her two daughters. Special Branch tecs went out on the Customs launch, found her first crack out of the box. I've sent a detective and three constables to bring them from Dover. Sometime tonight or early tomorrow.'

'She did it?'

'I got warrants last night; there's two crews searching the women's houses. It's a right cock-up—two women that should have hated each other but they don't. Wragge's housemaid says Mrs Gold is a pal of Mrs Wragge, been dropping in regularly for donkey's years and came there late on the night Wragge was murdered. Word in the Met is Wragge's always had something on the side, but nobody seems to have tumbled to the second family. My guess is that he had a new one and maybe she looked to the women like becoming wife number three. Too much for them.'

'That's all hearsay and guesswork, is it?'

'I'll know by tonight.'

'You're thinking of Mrs Gold? She won't talk, especially with the kind of lawyer the old man can afford. She certainly wouldn't talk to me.'

'You're not a cop, one, and two, you didn't find a blood spot in her clothes press where Wragge lay for a day and a night.'

'Your people have found that?'

'They've had all night, haven't they? Thanks to you. I mean that, Denton. We've had our differences, but this time you pulled a diamond out of the shit. Forget what I said about you and James and his box.'

'What about a murder weapon?'

'We do, but we don't. At Wragge's house—his real house, where he lived with his real wife—they found a policeman's billy hanging on a nail beside the bed. Medico says it could have been a billy that made the wounds on Wragge. Tecs in H Div say it was his billy from his uniform days; he'd had it drilled and filled with lead. Home protection. Used to show it to his mates. Problem for me is, it appears to be clean. We'll see when the experts put their magnifiers on it. Killed with his own billy? Serve him right, if he was bent.'

'But that would make Mrs Wragge the killer.'

'There should have been one exactly like it hanging next to the bed he shared with Mrs Gold. There's a nail there. But we didn't find one. So what I think, the Gold woman killed him, then she went to see Mrs Wragge, used some excuse to go upstairs, switched billies and it's a dolly.'

'Put the killing on her friend? And why didn't she hang Mrs Wragge's billy on the hook in her own bedroom?'

'I don't know yet. But I will. Anyway, I'm grateful to you for what you did. Which doesn't mean there's going to be any deal with Ginger, and it doesn't mean you're going to be any mucking go-between. You hear me?'

'Couldn't agree more. It isn't as if it's something I signed on to do, you know.'

'You don't have to sign on; these things come to you like you've been dipped in honey.' Guillam mumbled to somebody at the other end of the line, then came back on. 'What did the old man think he was going to trade for? His daughter's neck, right?'

'He thought he could get the prosecutor down to five to seven years.'

Guillam laughed. 'That's rich. They'll be going for the noose. Maybe let the Wragge woman off a bit, but maybe not. But Gold is for the drop. What's Goldensohn got to trade?'

'James's stuff.'

'What, from that tuppeny-ha'penny burglary? He *is* old.'

'He implied there were other things.'

'Like what? Didn't say, did he! Doesn't know, in fact. What's he going to give us, another Jubilee Plot? Fuck him. Every copper in the

East End has been trying to bring him down their whole careers; you think there won't be cheering? You think they'd let anybody trade away a treat like seeing his daughter hang? It's out of the question.'

'What if she didn't do it?'

'She did do it. Don't rub me the wrong way. I've got work to do.'

He rang off. Denton tried Munro at the Yard. No luck.

He collected Walter from Janet's house and walked him the several streets to the old carriage shed where he kept the Barré. He and Walter pushed it out. Denton pointed to the crank and the spark lever and said that those were what you used to start it.

'I know that.'

'How?'

'I read a book.' *You idiot.*

Denton got the canvas tool bag from the tiny boot under the rear seat and wriggled under the car. Moments later, Walter wriggled under and lay on his back next to him but wriggled out after thirty seconds; Denton thought the boy was bored or puzzled, but his boots marched around the car and he wriggled under from the other side and lay so that his head was next to Denton's, his right ear almost touching Denton's right ear, but upside-down to Denton's. 'I couldn't see,' he said.

Denton took off a nut and a sprocket and began to wrestle loose a branch that had wedged up there. When he needed the big wrench again, Walter handed it to him without being asked. Dirt sifted down from the undercarriage on both of them, and Denton, blinded, tried to get it out of his eyes. Walter took Denton's pocket handkerchief and wiped Denton's eyes, then his own. When Denton's arms tired from being held up so long and he dropped them to his chest, Walter took the tools and finished the job.

Standing in the watery sunshine, Denton said, 'How did you know how to do that?'

'I told you, I read a book.' Said again in the voice that implied that Denton's brain had been removed.

'Want to take a ride?'

'I don't like noise.' *You idiot.* Then, neutrally, 'Thank-you-for-asking-sir.'

They pushed the motor-car back into the carriage shed. Denton said, 'I'm going to buy you some hearing protectors.'

Denton walked home, Walter for reasons of his own going round the long way to Janet's; Denton put his key in his front door and was starting to open it when the door was pulled hard from the inside and he careened through the doorway. He caught himself, found himself a few inches from a frightened young man in baggy clothes. The boy yelped, then said he was sorry, then asked who he was. He had an accent so thick Denton had trouble understanding.

Atkins appeared in the doorway to his quarters. 'This is Alfred. Alfred, your new employer. He's pinned up behind, General. Trying to make some of my old rig-out fit. There isn't much to him to fit to, I don't mind saying.'

Denton said, 'Maybe I ought to—'

Atkins leapt in with a loud 'His mother will sew them up to perfection, Colonel!' Meaning, *Don't waste money on clothes for him, he may not last.* He motioned for Alfred to disappear; as he passed by, Atkins muttered something to him about how to open a door. When the boy was gone, he said to Denton, 'Rupert has his doubts about him.'

'Rupert's a snob.'

Atkins held out a yellow envelope, obviously a telegram, and a single piece of mail. 'You've got grease on that jacket.'

Denton tore open the telegram and read it:

URGENT STOP COME YARD NOW STOP MUNRO

'You'd think he had to pay for it, he's so curt,' Denton muttered, crumpling the paper in his fist. The other envelope held heavy notepaper headed 'Lamb House'.

My dear Denton, I have returned here to lick my wounds, and from this refuge I send my apologies for any harsh words I may have spoken. I realise now the position I put you in vis-à-vis the police. Please write to say you have forgiven me. Most sincerely yours, Henry James.

Denton laughed. 'And this one isn't curt at all. I have to go out again.' He started up the stairs.

'You and Henry James have made it up, then?'

'It appears so.'

'Gives me an idea.'

'I've got to go.'

'You change those clothes! I won't have it said you were seen looking like a mechanic!'

CHAPTER 8

Inside the Gothic splendours of New Scotland Yard, the corridors were uncarpeted and his footsteps rang like hooves. A porter who was supposed to be guiding him kept making little half-skips to catch up. 'I know the way,' Denton said.

'Matter of orders, sir,' the porter panted.

Munro was in the CID detectives' room, his desk a small centre of quiet in what seemed to be a madhouse. A boy was running, actually running, with his arms full of papers; two men in saggy suits were shouting at each other; a telephone was ringing at the far end, where three phones hung on the wall. Somebody bellowed, 'Who the H has stolen my pens?' There was a general smell of dirty floors, spilled ink, bodies, as if it were a schoolroom.

'You took your time,' Munro growled when Denton was still several strides from his desk.

'I was fixing the motor-car. What's so urgent?'

'Politics.' Munro showed his teeth, a non-smile. 'Surprise, surprise.'

'I don't get it.' Denton fell into a scarred wooden chair. 'What's it got to do with me?'

'Ginger Goldensohn.' Munro was at the same time trying to write something, bending his head over the paper and holding out his left hand, fingers splayed, as if he were stopping traffic—meaning for Denton to shut up. After some seconds of scribbling, he wrote something that took his hand almost off the paper—probably a signature—and threw the pen down. 'You're Ginger's go-between. The Great Ones want some going between.'

'I'm not anybody's go-between! What the hell is going on?'

Munro got up, motioned to Denton. 'We've a meeting. Already late, in fact. I told them you'd be late. Won't do any good.'

'Munro...!' He followed Munro's broad back out of the CID room and down the corridor. Munro's limp almost disappeared as he sped down a flight of stairs, crossed a landing, went down another flight. 'Whitehall,' he said as they turned towards the north end of the building. 'Home Sec's office. Not his *personal* office.'

Denton could in fact walk faster than Munro, was striding next to him, half turned back so as to look into his face. 'Why?'

'Word has come down from Caesar Augustus that they don't want to hang a woman just now. Election coming—Liberals may win. Especially they don't want to hang a woman with two kids. Home Sec wants to know what Ginger's offering, thinks he can kill two birds with one stone. This is all strictest confidence, of course.'

'Of course. Jesus God, politics!'

Munro, a pious man, flinched. He led them through a secondary doorway and into a small lobby that was far better kept than the upper floors of New Scotland Yard. A top-hatted porter more or less bowed; Munro muttered a name, and the man pointed upward and said they were expected. Munro charged up the stairs. 'Before I fell, I could take bloody stairs three at a time.' He was panting. 'Look at me now—feel as if I'm pulling a bloody cart!'

On the second floor, they were waved at by a very thin Arthur Balfour type who was leaning out from a doorway, obviously waiting for them. They were still far enough away for Munro to whisper, 'Garnett—Home Sec's private sec's hatchet man.' When they were closer, he said aloud, 'Here we are then, Mr Garnett.'

'You're late.' Garnett was all of thirty, Munro fifty; Garnet spoke as if Munro had come to clean the windows.

'I said we would be.'

'You're keeping *everyone* waiting!' He pointed through a door, rushed in behind them, let the door slam—not much of a slam; the door was ponderous, oak, nicely balanced—and actually pushed Denton forward. Denton almost said *You ever push me again, you'll get a push back,* but thought better of it for Munro's sake. He was irritated, more than irritated: he knew he was being used. First Henry James, then Goldensohn, now the damned Conservatives!

'Right on through, all the way...' Garnett pushed past them and opened another door.

Three men were sitting in what looked like a small drawing-room that somebody had dropped a desk into. Good carpet on the floor, good pictures on the walls (at least Denton thought so; they were certainly better than what he got from Geddys), a great many books in sets. Garnett went behind the desk and sat. The four of them looked at Denton.

'Mr Denton,' Munro said. As nobody spoke, he made the introductions. 'Mr Garnett you've met; Superintendent Morriss of CID; Brigadier General Hales, our Assistant Commissioner of Police; and...' Morriss was compact, ruddy; Hales was young for a brigadier, terrific-looking in Nietzsche moustache and sideburns. The fourth man, rather faded-looking, forties, high-voiced, said, 'Ransome, Office of Public Prosecution.'

Munro gave Denton a look that meant *Don't queer me with my bosses.*

Denton looked around for a chair, found two set out a little separate from the others and sat, his hat on his knee; Munro followed but put his hat on the floor under his chair. Munro apologised for being late; the others murmured, looked at their watches.

Garnett cleared his throat. He was, Denton saw, one of those polished young Englishmen who had come up through public schools and the Varsity and the Debating Society and the Union and who could say that black was white with a straight and authoritative face. He would have been trained from knee pants to know whom he could bully and which rumps he should plant kisses on. Denton supposed that he never lied because he didn't know what lying was; he knew only saying what was needed, and saying it always as established fact. 'We are here at the behest of the minister,' Garnett said. 'I wish to emphasise the seriousness of the matter and the absolute need for secrecy in our discussions. Mr Denton particularly needs to be cognisant of the requirement that he say nothing outside these walls of the matters that will be discussed. Mr Denton?'

'Depends on what the matters are, I suppose.'

'That's not good enough,' the Assistant Commissioner said. He had made his reputation in India, may have thought that Denton was from one of the lesser tribes.

'I think what he means,' Munro said quickly, 'is that he can't say what he can or can't do until he knows what's going on. Which is only fair, sir.'

Garnett looked authoritative. 'This comes from the very highest level. The *very* highest. You *will not* break this confidence.'

'Then maybe I should leave. Before anything's said.'

The CID super looked at Munro and then gave Denton what seemed to be a sympathetic glance. 'Mr Denton's essential to the matter, gentlemen. He's been a good friend to the Metropolitan Police in the past; he understands what's what. No offense, Mr Garnett, but you're not dealing with an unruly schoolboy. Get on with it.'

Garnett dilated his nostrils. The CID super, after all, had *not* been to the Varsity. 'I *must* have his assurance that he will be discreet.'

'Fine. I'll be discreet. But I'll say to you the same thing I said to somebody else recently—I'll keep it to myself until it crosses the line of what's lawful. Then all bets are off.'

The Assistant Commissioner said that he hardly thought anybody there was thinking of committing an unlawful act. It was Denton's feeling that that was exactly what they had in mind, but what he said was 'We understand each other, then.'

Garnett shook his head and looked pained. Nonetheless, he put his hands on his desk and said, 'In the matter of the woman who calls herself Mrs Gold, then. I have been instructed to tell you that my minister, and others at the highest level, do not believe it is in the best interests of the Crown for her to face the ultimate penalty if some other just and adequate punishment can be found.'

'Why?' Denton said.

'That is not yours to question.'

'It's mine to question or nothing is. I'm not particularly fond of hanging, but it's your law and your custom. Or is British law made of India rubber?'

The Assistant Commissioner cleared his throat and said, 'The new government want to present a somewhat kinder face to the little people, I think.' Meaning that the government, in office for donkey's years, didn't want the cheap papers calling for Liberal reform. And the Home Secretary probably wanted to starve the newspapers of any embarrassing facts about Inspector Wragge.

The representative of the Public Prosecutor said, 'It's like this, Mr Denton. The Gold woman's best plea is probably self-defence. That's a powerful argument just now—suffragettes and women's rightists everywhere, men presented as brutes. And the fact that her "husband" was a policeman, and a policeman with a legal wife somewhere else, could be made to look as if she was very much an injured party.'

'And the fact that her father's the biggest crook in the East End doesn't matter?'

'Superintendent Morriss's men are looking into that. But you can see how it would be put in court—married to get away from her father and his crimes, set herself up as a law-abiding woman. Lured into marriage by a man who didn't tell her he was a bigamist. All her neighbours speak well of her. A very good mother, they say.' It was as if he were rehearsing the defence strategy for court.

'And we can't give them an excuse for throwing Wragge in our faces.' The Assistant Commissioner meant by 'them' not the neighbours but the papers. 'Scum.'

Denton said, 'You've moved very fast. You know a lot.'

The Assistant Commissioner stared at him as if he were a subaltern. 'Seize the day!'

Morriss, the CID head, leaned forward. Denton knew him by reputation, had met him once or twice—fair, forthright, not above pushing his own career, a holy terror when stupid mistakes were made. He said, 'The fact is, Mrs Gold's to be handled what I'd call "humanely". Those are our orders. Munro says you had a contact from that villain Goldensohn. He doesn't know that we mean to treat her humanely; therefore, it may be that we can negotiate what's already been decided and get something worth-while in return. What did he say to you?'

Denton gave a précis of Ginger Goldensohn's visit.

'What did he ask for?'

'No hanging, maybe five to seven years.'

The prosecutor's breath whistled as he inhaled. 'Perhaps— perhaps... We'd have to hope the coroner's jury didn't come up with a verdict of deliberate murder.' He glanced at Garnett. 'Would you make a note that someone should see to that?' Garnett began to scribble.

Denton smiled. 'Have you seen the body?'

'Yes, yes, I know it looks like murder. Still... Death by misadventure? Well, we shall see.'

The Assistant Commissioner said, 'Get on with it! What did this Jew offer? What's his devil's bargain?'

'He was vague. Maybe information about where the stuff from the James burglary is. Maybe something more, but that was maybe just a try-on.'

Garnett, who perhaps felt that he was not sufficiently the centre of their attention, said, 'We must move this matter along, gentlemen. We all have things to do. I think we need do no more now than inform Mr Denton what it is he is to do, and we can adjourn.'

Denton turned dead eyes on him. 'Who says that Mr Denton is going to do anything?'

Morriss jumped in. 'Right, quite right, there's no pressure on you and there's no presumption that you'll do what we ask. What we're *hoping* is you'll see it as the right thing. The just thing.' He looked honestly at Denton; his eyebrows rose a fraction of an inch: *I think Garnett's as great an arsehole as you do, so let's you and me press on.*

Denton said, 'Tell me.'

Garnett broke in very loudly, talked right over him. 'And you might benefit, Mr Denton, by helping your friend Mr Henry James recover his possessions.'

Morriss waited him out, didn't look at him, spoke to Denton. 'We'd like you to get in touch with Goldensohn. Ask him what he wants. Arrange a meeting—you, Munro, him.'

'Why me? What have I got to do with it?'

'He picked you. He won't meet with a couple of coppers. He'll meet with one, who will speak for all of us. Munro's the copper.'

Understanding, Denton said, 'There have to be two people because you want a witness.'

'And you're our bona fides. Believe me, he'll want you at any meeting we have. Don't ask me why he picked you, Denton, but he did.'

Because I've killed people and he knows it. Because I'm more like him than like you four. He said, 'I don't know how to get in touch with him.'

Munro shifted in his hard chair. 'We'll take care of that. H Div've got an ear to the ground. Goldensohn's got a house along Commercial Road, he's maybe there by now. Anyway, we know people who know him.' He eyed Denton. 'Meet at your house again, that all right?'

Denton scowled. 'I should charge rent.'

Morriss laughed too heartily. 'Now, now! Well, well, are we agreed then, Denton? You and Munro will have a slap at it?'

Before Denton could answer, the prosecutor said shrilly, 'But you can't make any promises! You can't!'

'Of course they can't, and they won't.' Morriss sounded weary. 'Gentlemen, let's assume there's a grain of common sense in a detective chief inspector and a famous author, shall we? But while we're on the subject, Ransome, you need to be prepared to say exactly what you will promise when we come to it. Munro and Denton will do the preliminaries; then there'll be a meeting that includes you and me, at the very least, and you're going to have to promise him something. Goldensohn's no fool.'

'Five to seven years for murder won't make it past my superiors.'

'Then don't make it murder. Justifiable homicide? Manslaughter while mentally impaired? You lot will come up with something.'

Garnett stood. 'This is not to the point, gentlemen. We have accomplished what I asked you to do; the rest can be done in subsequent meetings among yourselves. We are adjourned.'

'Except for discussing Mrs Wragge,' Denton said. He might as well have broken wind. He looked around the pained faces. 'Is she going to get the full shot while Ruth Gold waltzes away?'

Garnett banged something on his desk. 'That is a different issue and cannot be discussed here. The meeting is over.' Everybody but Denton seemed to agree.

Walking back to New Scotland Yard, Munro laughed and said, 'Our betters.' He laughed again. 'How do you want to play this?'

'What, meeting with Ginger? What are my choices?'

'You don't have any. Well, the time, maybe. But I think, as our Assistant Commissioner said, we have to seize the day. Ginger won't wait long to see if we take his bait; then he'll go looking for something else. Come on in.' They had reached the entrance to the Yard.

'I thought I'd get lunch.'

'Good. You can take me. I want to check for messages first.' Back they went to the schoolroom smell and the noise. Munro looked at scribbled-on bits of paper and then took Denton's arm and started them out again. 'Goldensohn's already got his daughter a high-priced solicitor. She'll be advised to say nothing—Guillam'll have her in nick but she won't say boo. Where are we going?'

'How's an ABC?'

'Are you that stony? I'll take you to Kettner's.' He signalled for a cab.

Record of interview with Mrs Arthur Wragge, widow. Present: Inspector Guillam, Metropolitan Police, Mrs Wragge, Miss Theodora Mercer, solicitor.

Inspector Guillam (hereinafter IG): You've been told your rights, Mrs Wragge, and you know why you're here, I think. I warn you again that you're a suspect in the illegal disposal of the body of your husband, Inspector Arthur Wragge.

Miss Mercer (hereinafter MM): She understands all that. (Mrs Wragge nods her head.)

IG: What can you tell me about the day of your husband's death?

Mrs Wragge (hereinafter MW): Nothing. I don't know when he died.

IG: August twelfth, late in the evening.

MW: I was at home.

IG: Had you seen your husband that day?

MW: In the morning, of course. But not since.

IG: Was he often absent from your home?

MW: Two or three days at a time. He'd say police business, but (stops)

MM: You needn't answer if you don't want.

IG: She does want. What I'm asking is not incriminating. Mrs Wragge?

MW: He had other women.

IG: Who, specifically?

MW: You know.

IG: I want to make sure you know, Mrs Wragge. Who?

MW: I don't know the latest. He had a new one. I could always tell. But I don't know her name. Not like (stops) Not like Ruth.

IG: For the record, please tell me who Ruth is.
MW: Ruth Gold. His other wife.

Denton stopped reading. '"His other wife." It looks so cold-blooded on the page.' He was at home. It was evening. Munro had just arrived to prepare for the meeting there with Ginger Goldensohn. He had brought the testimony with him.

'It's the typing. Looks mechanical.' He grinned. 'An idea I got from that man of yours—finding somebody who can take down verbatim on the typewriter.' Atkins had had one toe in that business a while back.

Denton said, 'Henry James writes that way, did you know that? Dictates to a typewriter.'

'Well, it's a great saving of time. And eyesight. Though it does look cold, I admit.'

Denton went back to reading.

IG: How long had you known about her?
MW: Donkey's. Six or seven years, anyway.
IG: How did you find out?
MW: She came to see me. She'd found out about Wragge and me. I think maybe from her father. He was an evil man; he'd say things to hurt her. Anyway, she came to see me and we got talking.
IG: And you became friends?
MM: Please don't put words in her mouth, Inspector.
IG: I'm not.
MM: You're leading her.
IG: This isn't a trial.
MM: You're leading her right down the garden path to the matter of collusion in disposal of a body. I won't have it.
IG: Mrs Wragge, you said Ruth Gold came to see you six or seven years ago. What happened then?
MW: She found out Wragge had somebody else, other than her and me, I mean, not to be married to, but

you know. She was weeping and she was that angry.
It was a funny situation, when you think about it.
Like something in a farce. But not to us.

IG: Did you see her again after that meeting?

MW: She took to coming once or twice a week. It was like
we had nobody else to talk to about being Wragge's
wives, and him having other women. Sometimes I
went to her house. I suppose we were like sisters.

IG: In what way were you like sisters?

(MM whispers to MW.)

MW: I'm warned not to go ahead with that.

IG: Being a sister is somehow incriminating?

MM: You know where it leads, Inspector. I won't allow
her to pursue it.

Denton looked up. '"Like sisters."'

Munro grunted. 'She's bang correct about it's a farce. Women.'

'They were lonely. They found a friend in each other. Don't
look so sceptical. Women can't be friends?'

'Sisters?'

'A manner of speaking.'

He went back to the transcript.

IG: Mrs Wragge, on the day your husband died, how
recently had you seen Ruth Gold?'

MW: Two or three days before, I suppose. Not the
Sunday, certainly. Nor the Saturday, because she
took her kiddies to their church, which was the
Jewish one, you know, the synagogue. She's Jewish,
you know. She thought Wragge was Jewish when
she married him. Two kiddies by him, lovely little
girls, and she finds their father's a *goy*. (Recorder
has to ask for repetition of word; MW repeats it.)

IG: Goy?

MW: It's what they call us. Folk who aren't Jewish.

IG: So maybe it was Friday you had seen her.

MW: No, Thursday. Wragge told me he'd be away for
the weekend on a case. I remember thinking he must
be going out of town with some new woman, he was
probably going to leave Friday p.m. There was a time
I thought he'd get over it. That it was just a phase, you
know—the women. Ruth was more forthright than I
am—she'd spit in a tiger's eye, she would. She'd told
him to quit it. He hit her once. More than once.

Denton said, "'He hit her once. More than once.'"
'You never know if that's true or if it's something they say to
make their case. Though hitting women is something a copper
runs into all the time when you go into their homes.' In a wispier,
sadder voice, Munro added, 'In coppers' own houses, some of it.'
Denton grunted.

IG: Did he ever strike you, Mrs Wragge?
MW (looks at MM; whispering): Not hard. More like
a slap. Now and then. He said he was a policeman
and knew the law and the law said he could. He
said it's in the Bible.
IG: Did you and Ruth Gold talk about him hitting
both of you?
MW: It was something we knew about each other. We
had all that in common.
IG: All right, Mrs Wragge, the night your husband
was killed. Did you see Ruth Gold that evening?
(MW looks at MM.)
MM: I advise my client not to answer.
IG: Did you see Inspector Wragge that evening?
MW: He came home for his tea then went out.
IG: Did you see him after that?
MW: No.
IG: Did you see Ruth Gold that night?
MW (stopped by MM, whispering): I've been advised
not to speak.

IG: I want to go to the next morning, Mrs Wragge. You went all the way to New Scotland Yard to report that your husband was missing.

MM (after a pause): Was that a question?

IG: Why did you go all the way to New Scotland Yard to report him missing?

MW: We're not on the telephone.

IG: Why did you report him missing after only a few— after only, it can't have been more than fourteen hours?

MW: I was fed up. I wanted the Yard to know what he was.

IG: Explain that to me, if you please.

MW: I thought that if they went looking for him, asked him why I thought he was missing, they'd get it out of him. About the women.

IG: Had you ever reported him missing before?

MW: No.

IG: Why that particular morning?

MW: I was fed up.

IG: And you hadn't talked to Ruth Gold for four days?

MM: She won't answer that.

IG: Let's take a short rest.

Denton put the papers down. 'You don't want Goldensohn to see those.'

'I surely don't.' Munro tapped the papers together, folded them lengthwise and put them into an inner pocket of his suit jacket. 'Finished with them?'

'No. Had enough for a while, though.' Munro handed the papers back and Denton put them in his own pocket. He took a cigarette from a box on the table beside his armchair, offered it to Munro. 'Guillam's being pretty hard on her.'

'She's guilty of a crime.'

'You don't know that yet.' He lit a crown vesta, held the cigarette in the flame. 'Is Mrs Wragge included in Goldensohn's hoped-for "deal"?'

'I don't know why she would be. He didn't say so, did he?'

Denton blew out smoke. 'If Mrs Gold slides on murder and Mrs Wragge gets time for conspiracy, I'll scream holy hell. That's when it'll have gone beyond the law, Munro, and I won't have it.'

'What the devil do you care?'

'Mrs Wragge's a beaten-down woman. She's been burned by life—burned by marrying a shit like Wragge, burned by being the soft one in her connection with Mrs Gold. She looks like an old woman, walks like an old woman. She's given up! And so she helps get rid of the body of the man Ruth Gold has murdered, and then Gold skates and Mrs Wragge gets ten years hard? No!'

'Gold won't skate, and Mrs Wragge won't get ten. Anyway, maybe it was Mrs Wragge killed him and Gold that helped.'

'A conspirator could even hang, Munro.'

'No, no.'

Denton stood over him. 'Guillam's going for a conspiracy that started right after one of the women killed him. You can see it in the interview! He's obviously making a conspiracy out of the fact that Mrs Wragge reported Wragge missing—two women covering their tracks. All right, it's what I thought originally too, that Mrs Wragge had killed him and she went to the Yard to cover herself. But she didn't kill him. She couldn't—she's too beaten, too soft. You know that. But all Guillam has to do is keep pushing and pushing and get her to admit she saw Ruth Gold the night Wragge died. Then it's a conspiracy, and she's an accomplice in murder.'

'Desperate people do desperate things.'

Denton mashed the cigarette into a porcelain ashtray with a portrait of the King on it. 'I feel dirty.'

'Welcome to police work.'

'Oh, put a cork in it.'

Denton took down a book and stared at it without reading until Ginger Goldensohn showed up. When they heard the horse's hooves and the whine of the carriage brake, Munro moved quickly to the window and used one finger to open the drapes an inch. He looked down, waited.

'He's got somebody with him. Maybe some kind of body-guard. Looks tough enough.' He dropped the curtain. 'Here he comes.'

'You're the spokesman?' Denton said.

'I'll do the talking, if that's what you mean.' Munro pointed a finger. 'None of this about Mrs Wragge, all right? Don't muddy the waters.'

'We wouldn't want justice interfering with police business.'

Munro shook his head. 'You wear me out, you really do.'

Atkins announced Goldensohn and the old man shambled in, wearing what looked like the same black frock-coated suit. His bald head looked brown and shiny in the electric light. 'Well, well,' he said and clapped his hands together. He looked at Munro. 'You the copper?' When Munro said nothing, he all but shouted, 'You got a name?'

'Chief Inspector Munro, Metropolitan Police.'

Goldensohn looked at Denton. 'I know who you are, don't I.' He went to the same chair he had sat in before and fell back into it; Denton thought his legs weren't strong enough to let him down easily. Goldensohn said, 'A chief inspector! Should I be honoured?'

'You wanted to talk to the police. Talk.'

The old man shrugged. Denton indicated his own armchair opposite Goldensohn, meaning Munro should sit in it. Munro started to refuse, thought better of it, lowered his bulk majestically as if showing off the strength of his hams. Denton backed to a side chair against the far wall. Munro said, 'Talk. About your daughter.'

'Not about my daughter! About what you can do for me.'

'The question is, what can you do for the Metropolitan Police? Mr Denton was under the impression you wanted to offer us some information.'

'Nothing comes for free. I learnt that early. So did you, eh?' He grinned, showing china-white false teeth. 'I don't *offer* information to you; I trade it with you.'

'I can't promise you anything. You seemed to think last night that we'd let your daughter off scot-free; well, that can't happen. Depending on the charge and the coroner's verdict and the public—'

Goldensohn was waving his hand, palm towards Munro. 'Don't tell me what I know! I know how it works; I could have been a barrister, I know so much!' He leaned forward. 'I tell you what I also know: the Met can fix it so my daughter does short time on a ticket—*if they want*. You know why Justice is blind? So she can't see what the coppers are doing.'

He laughed, showed his teeth to Denton, turned them back on Munro, who waited him out and then said, 'Talk. You're wasting my time.'

Goldensohn looked angry, a kind of sneer pulling his upper lip back. 'I am, am I?' He settled back in the chair. He looked like a child in the big wingback. 'Hoity-toity.' He looked at Denton again, grinned, looked back at Munro. 'So, Mr Chief Inspector, you wouldn't be here if what I asked for isn't possible. Would yous? So we take it as acceptable that the Met can help my daughter if they choose to. And I accept that the Met will choose to when I give them what makes it worth the while, eh? Yes. So, here's what I offer you: I happen to know, by a circumstance that is my business, where the swag from the burglarising down in Rye got itself to. That's what I offer you—case solved, house-holder gets his goods back. We have a bargain?'

'No. But I'll take your statement on what you know about the burglary.' Munro looked at him. His face might have been cut out of a block of wood. Goldensohn held his eyes, then looked at Denton and said, 'He says no. Some bargainer.' He looked back at Munro. 'Don't ever go into the old clothes business, Chief Inspector.' He chuckled, apparently pleased with himself.

Munro stood and spoke to Denton. 'Have your man get my things. We're through here.'

'You said you wanted to talk!' the old man shrieked. 'So talk to me!'

'You're the one who needs to talk! If you think His Majesty's Government are going to let your daughter slide on murder in exchange for a housebreaking, you ought to be committed.' He turned his back on Goldensohn, waited by the door. Denton in fact hadn't rung for Atkins; he hated calling a human being with a bell; he'd let Munro play out his drama. Goldensohn flailed at the chair arms as if he meant to get up but then abandoned the effort. 'Sit down, sit down! I got things at stake here! Yous think I was finished? Don't yous know nothing about bargains?'

Munro turned around but didn't go back to his chair. 'Offer me something the Met wants.'

'You want the loot from the burglary.'

'More.'

'There isn't any more!' He turned his head towards the wall like a spoiled child. 'What d'yous want? Want my blood? Want my skin?'

'You might offer us the people who did the Rye burglary, to start.'

'I can't do that.'

'That's too bad. For your daughter.'

'What I hear, that burglarising was special, not something I would hear about, not something I would... Nothing I had connections to, yous know what I mean.'

Meaning, Denton thought, *I didn't get one percent off the top.* Hard to believe.

Munro strolled to the armchair, sat, got a cigarette from Denton's box. 'Time was, Goldensohn, they used to say that nobody farted in the East End without you smelling it. Now you can't get a whiff of a run-of-the-mill household job.'

'Run-of-the-mill! You think run-of-the-mill?' Goldensohn shook his finger at Munro. 'This wasn't the run of some mill! What I hear, it was outsiders. See, I give you that for free—it's what I know, outsiders.'

Munro lit the cigarette. 'What kind?' When Goldensohn didn't answer, he said, 'Russians? Italians? Irish?'

'I'm telling you, I don't know.'

'Then you'd better find out.'

The top of the old man's head seemed shinier. *Sweat.* He put out a hand. 'Give me one of those.' Munro held out the box, followed it with the box of vestas, waited. Goldensohn blew out smoke, coughed, said, 'You're right, it ain't like the old days. Don't get old. Eighteen seventy-five, nobody on the docks pulled his meat until I said so. Now...' He puffed on the cigarette again. 'You lose your stand, you don't care so much any more. It's like you give up without meaning to give up. These boys who went down to Rye, what I hear, they're a cruel lot. That's all I know.'

'You're not going to get your daughter off for some household goods. We want names; we want addresses. We probably want you to set them up. You understand? Get them together for us, make it an easy nick. You offer that, we'll see what we can do—*after* the arrest and the recovery of the goods.'

'I can't do that!' Goldensohn smashed his cigarette into the King's face at the bottom of the ashtray. 'These people are dangerous!'

'Dangerous housebreakers? Tell me another, Ginger.'

'They, they...' Goldensohn was breathing hard. 'You don't understand me. I'm out of the business, I don't have the, the... people, the protection. Look at me! I'm old!'

''You could use a violin, Ginger, and I still wouldn't shed a tear. I'll take your statement now.'

'I don't make no statement!'

'You're a witness. It's here or at the Yard, take your pick.' Munro poised a pencil over his notebook.

Goldensohn squirmed but finally gave a statement that was terse and vacuous: he 'had heard' about the Rye burglary; 'people' had told him where the loot was stashed; no, of course he hadn't seen his daughter for weeks; no, he never saw his son-in-law Wragge, that lying sonofabitch. Munro said he'd have it typed and ready for Goldensohn's signature tomorrow.

Munro pushed himself up from his chair. 'Let me know when you find out who did the burglary and where we can get them. It'll be much better for your daughter if it's by tomorrow midday, when we have to lay charges. After that, we can offer less and less.' He turned to Denton. 'I'll take my hat now.'

Denton called down the stairs to Atkins. Goldensohn made angry noises, then heartbroken noises; then he fell silent. When Munro was ready to leave, he turned back to Goldensohn and said, 'Before you sign your name to this statement, you'd better think about what the penalty for lying to the police is.'

When the front door had closed on Munro, Goldensohn said, 'That shit.'

'You'd better do as he says.'

'You think I got all this in my hat, like a music-hall magician? He don't know what he's asking. He don't know what he's dealing with!' He struggled out of the chair. 'You—flunkey! Get my goods! I never should of come here. I've gone soft, soft in the head, too! Fuck the lot of you! *Fuck* you!'

He felt his way down the stairs, his legs unsteady, both hands on the rail. Denton watched him down, watched as he went out the door. It was raining; Atkins held an umbrella over him and saw him out to his carriage. Back inside, Atkins slammed the door, shook the umbrella as if it were his worst enemy, and brushed rain from his hair and his shoulders. He looked up at Denton. 'Well?'

'Difficult customer.'

'Gone soft! He's about soft as a cobra. And no tip.' He went off, muttering.

Denton called him back. 'You said you had some idea about Henry James.'

'Oh, yes. Well. Only a thought.'

'Now's the time.'

'Well you see, General, I was thinking, what goes on in my world that I can make a motion picture of? And I thought, why, here I have two famous men practically at my fingertips. As it were.' He glanced at Denton.

'I'm listening.'

'Well, think how pleased the public would be to see a picture of two famous men meeting. Make it a bit of an event—"Famous Author Returns from America"—that's Mr James. "The Two Authors Together"—that's the two of you. Talking, reading books. Give the great unwashed a peek into the literary life.'

'You want to make a motion picture of me and Henry James?'

'An *actuality*, Colonel—the real thing, everyday life of the great, artists as they are, et cetera.'

'Trade on my connection with James, you mean.'

'A bit hard, that. Grasp an opportunity would be my view. Anyway, it might sell some books for you and him.'

Denton grunted, chuckled. 'You have no shame, Sergeant. I think Henry James would run from the idea as if it had horns and the clap.'

'But you aren't saying no!'

Denton sighed. 'I'm not the one you have to worry about. We'll see.'

Atkins went off. Denton went up to bed. When he undressed, he found in his jacket the papers Munro had given him. Munro wouldn't be happy that he'd forgotten them. Denton got into bed with his reading glasses and the papers and took up where he had left off. It was dispiriting stuff: a fragile, hopeless woman was being chivvied by a man with no pity for her.

But the interview had stopped before Guillam had got what he wanted.

> IG: Mrs Wragge, you should know that your maid has told us that Mrs Gold came to your house the night after your husband died. She says that Mrs Gold stayed about an hour and then you went out with her. Is that true?
>
> MW: I don't... It wasn't quite...
>
> MM: That's enough. Inspector, you're leading a suspect into self-intimidation, and I won't have it. This interview is over.
>
> IG: I'll only ask her again.
>
> MM: Not tonight you won't.

Thank God for Teddy Mercer, Denton thought. He threw the papers aside. He felt worn out, dirtied. He went to his desk, pulled over notepaper and wrote to Henry James. He had been first amused, then touched by James's apology. Now, he wrote conventional things but didn't dare mention Atkins's daft idea: there was nothing to forgive; they had both been strained by circumstances; he hoped to have good news about James's stolen possessions soon. Perhaps they could meet for lunch when James was in town.

Perhaps we could be friends, he meant. He doubted it.

'Ginger's delivered the goods.'

It was only a little after nine the next morning. Denton had been up since five, playing with his dumbbells and his pistols, then sitting in his bedroom-study and staring at the piece of paper on which he had written *The Monster* several days before. He had been boiling an egg on his spirit stove and drinking Italian coffee and hot milk and thinking about an idea for a novel when the telephone rang. Atkins was out doing the shopping.

'You mean he's come up to scratch?'

'Gone the second mile. Or so he says. Offering the gang's next job.'

'That was mighty quick, Munro.'

'Aye, aye, it's a mite suspicious.' He didn't hear Munro sigh over the telephone, but Denton thought that was what he would be doing. 'But the dark view is he knew all along and was only waiting for the moment. He may have been behind the whole thing, and behind their next job, for all of that. I wouldn't put it past him.'

'But he'd be cutting his own throat if he gives you the next robbery.'

'Ginger Goldensohn never worked where his hand could be seen. If he was behind something, he was way behind. Somebody else does the fall.'

'I was thinking of the money.'

'Ginger's got all the money he'll ever need. Losing whatever he'd get from the James job would be the easiest thing he could do.'

'Well—hold on, I've got to put down the earpiece...' Denton rushed into the alcove, turned the spirit stove off, got the egg out of the water with a spoon. 'I'm back. Are you there?'

'I am, and I'm to tell you His Majesty wants you at the south entrance of New Scotland Yard at half-ten. Don't be late this time.'

'What the hell for?'

'We like you. That's an order from above, Denton. Just do it, all right? Please don't make trouble for me, man.'

Denton ate his egg and stared down into the empty shell, hoping for another taste of congealed white. If it were winter, he could have made toast in the grate. He disliked it from the spirit stove, which gave the toast a taste; his only hope was the gas ring. Janet had given him a peculiar metal contraption called a toaster that was supposed to work on the gas, a truncated pyramid of tin with vanes cut into it up and down the sides. The bread went on the four sides; the vanes conducted the hot gas to the bread; toast resulted. Sometimes.

He went downstairs and got butter from the ice cave, paused to scratch both dogs, got upstairs to find the toast smoking. He turned the toast over, burned the other side for a bit, sat down to burned toast and blackberry jam. Not so bad as it could have been.

He stared some more at the piece of paper on his desk. When he heard Atkins come back, he went downstairs and said, as Atkins unloaded cans and bottles from the Army & Navy, 'What do you think of *The Monster* as a title?'

'Need to see what was inside, wouldn't I?'

'Just the title, the title, Sergeant.'

'Can't judge a book by its title. Like saying of a woman, do you fancy somebody named Mary Jones?'

'You're useless. I'm going out at ten.'

'Would you like me to apply my uselessness to laying out clothes?'

Denton laughed. 'I deserved that. I can get my own clothes together.'

'Where you going?'

'New Scotland Yard. Bunch of bigwigs.'

'I'll lay out your clothes.' He started away, came back. 'Me and Walter took Rupert to see the chap at the horse barns yesterday.'

Denton had to think who that was. A rough-and-ready animal expert—hardly a veterinarian, but he'd saved Rupert from a poisoning once. 'Well?'

'Spleen's swollen. Says he's got to see the vet. Money, money, money.'

'You hard up already?'

Atkins shook his head. 'I was just crabbing. It isn't the money; it's Rupert. But the boy was right—he's in pain.'

'The sort of thing you'd rather he'd be wrong about.' Denton patted Atkins's shoulder. 'Maybe it'll work out.'

At ten twenty-five, Denton crossed to the south doorway of New Scotland Yard, where a constable was waiting. The constable saluted, asked if he was Mr Denton, then led him up to the second floor to an unfamiliar corridor that grew a carpet, then larger and more elegant doorways widely spaced apart. Denton was shown into a cluster of offices with north-facing windows, finally into a large room that looked like something in a men's club. To his relief, Munro was already there; so were Ransome, the man from Public Prosecution, and the CID super, Morriss.

'We should give you a room here, Mr Denton,' Morriss said. He sounded jovial, like a man to whom something good was going to happen. This time, they shook hands, as did Ransome, who kept hold of Denton's elbow and said very low, 'I understand your worry about Mrs Wragge. We'll run her prosecution in tandem with the Gold woman's—sauce for the goose, and so on. If we make a concession, it will be reflected in the treatment of Mrs Wragge.'

Denton wondered if Guillam knew about that.

Hales, the Assistant Commissioner, bustled in, then held the door for a very fat man who was introduced as Sir Somebody from the Home Office. Garnett had apparently been thrown overboard. The fat man said with the absolute authority of somebody whose eyes had seen the glory of real power, 'The PM is cognisant. He'll go along, but if he gets a question down the line, heads will roll. We all understand that, do we? Which of you is Denton? Ah. Mr Denton, a word to the wise: you're a guest of the Crown in Britain. Don't imperil your status. Now where's this Jew criminal we have to deal with?'

An elderly but militarily erect man came in, whispered in Hales's ear and went out.

Hales said, 'Goldensohn is downstairs. They're bringing him up.' At that point, Denton realised that the office was the Assistant Commissioner's.

They waited. Everyone had his eyes on the door. After several minutes, it opened; the elderly man appeared, flattened against the door as if blown there by a high wind. Many seconds later, Goldensohn appeared. He looked years older to Denton, perhaps ill. He came a few feet into the room and stood with his head hanging forward, only his eyes moving. No smile, no false cheer.

'You're killing me, you lot,' he said.

Hales jerked to a sitting brace. 'You mind your manners in this room, sir! We know who you are.'

'I'm telling you the simple truth. You'll be the death of me. But you'll get what you want.' His eyes jerked over them. Rested momentarily on Denton; was there appeal there? The eyes moved on. 'Who's the lawyer here?'

Ransome stirred. 'I represent the Public Prosecutor.'

'We have a deal?'

'You've told us nothing as yet.'

'For my daughter, three to five on a ticket. No time inside. For that I give you where they're keeping the goods from the Rye house burglary, and I give you the ones who did it. If you're quick, you catch them doing another job. In the act.'

Denton saw Munro and his superior trade a glance, both frowning. Hales said, 'If you try to trick us, your daughter will hang.'

'You think I don't know that? You think I want *mercy*?' He laughed. '"Soft! The Jew shall have all justice."' He laughed again, somewhat recovered now, sneered. 'Get on with it.'

And they did. Two minutes later, there was a nodding of heads. No handshakes. What Goldensohn had had to say was pretty simple: the loot from James's house was in an outhouse in Deptford. The gang were at that moment tunnelling into a diamond merchant's in Paul's Road from a house in the street behind, where one of them rented rooms.

'*Now?*' Morriss had said.

'They was supposed to start last night. They have to go through the walls of both houses.' At that point, Morriss and Munro had got up and left. Goldensohn, his bargain made, was not far behind. Denton followed, his going apparently regretted by nobody.

'You got that motor-car of yours?'

Munro had grabbed him halfway down the corridor. 'I walked.'

'Why, today of all days? Look, we've caught our hand in the wringer over what Ginger told us.' They were heading, Denton thought, for the CID room. 'By rights—if he's telling the truth— an attempted burglary in Paul's Road is H Div's collar and they've got to be given it. But all but a couple of their tecs are out on some hooroar near the big synagogue. Plus it's in a way my case because of Wragge. Super's on the telephone to the H super to sort it out.'

He led the way through the noisy room to his desk. Several other detectives looked at him as if they knew something was up.

Munro sat, leaned his forearms on his desk. 'It's a right tangle. I don't want a tiff with H just now. We don't know how many of these supposed burglars there are, but we're sure they have axes and picks and shovels, so there's weapons to hand. Something like this, you want two weeks to plan; we've not even a day. I've alerted my tecs up in N; the moment I give the word, they'll head for Paul's Road. Plus the super insists on two men from the armed squad, which I don't have to wait on H for, although I think it's maybe laying it on too thick, having fire-arms. I don't know. Doesn't hurt, I suppose.'

'Goldensohn said they were cruel people.'

'And you believed him?' Munro ran his hand over his thick but greying hair. 'We'll have to post men both in Paul's Road and in the street behind—what is it? Clemence—where they're actually working. I've got my people ready to go into the diamonds place and clear the building. Once that's done, we can go in from Clemence Street. I've got somebody looking out a detailed map. Oh, crikey.'

'I'd have more than two armed men.'

'That's because you're American. Shoot your way in, right? The London police have a reputation for not using weapons, and we're proud of it.' He stretched. 'Assistant Commissioner wanted no weapons at all. Super got him to allow sidearms. Safer, probably.'

'I'd like to be there.'

'Not a hope.'

'I've been in it this far, Munro. I brought you Goldensohn. I brought you his daughter and Mrs Gold, for that matter.'

Munro eyed him. 'You'll stay out of the way? Do as you're told?'

'Of course.'

Munro grunted. 'Of course. Don't you want to be in Deptford when we open up Ali Baba's cave?'

'What? James's stolen goods? You're not doing that now, are you?'

Munro shook his head. 'Don't want any chance of tipping them off. They might have a lookout down there, a—Here comes my map. That's my lad!' A constable, who had put a roll of maps on the desk, blushed. Munro said, 'Show me, show me!' and the boy unrolled them. Denton came around the desk—so long as nobody stopped him, he'd press on—and looked over the seated Munro's shoulder. The map's scale was big enough to show individual plots. The constable's fingers tapped two back-to-back properties. The one in Clemence Street actually held several buildings, arranged around some kind of court or yard, perhaps once a well. The building through which the burglars were trying to get into the house on Paul's Road ran almost its entire width. A tenement, Denton thought.

'We can close off the entrance to the courtyard,' Munro said. 'That's good. We don't want the public hanging about.'

The constable's not entirely clean finger rested on a broken line on one side of the court. 'This looks like some kind of walk, little alley, something like that, sir. There's an opening, see? Then I think there's maybe a walkway, like a tunnel—see?—that goes through this building here.' He tapped the one to the east of the square.

'Have to get somebody there. Plain clothes. They'll have lookouts, or they're even stupider than most criminals.' Munro pushed the maps together. 'All right, good job. On your way out, tell Parsons I want to see him. The tall one over there by the window. Yes, him.' Munro opened the map again and looked at it, went quickly through the others. 'This one's best. Ah, Parsnip!' A thin, yellowish man had joined them. 'Busy?'

'Always.'

'What I mean is, have you got an hour? I need a plain-clothes job done in H Division.'

'Ask them.'

'I can't find them. You want me to get the super to order you to do this?'

'I can't go on H's pitch without they give permission.'

'I don't have time for the bloody rules!' Munro stood and grabbed the much smaller man's arm. 'You come with me.' He started off, looked back at Denton. 'You're on your own.'

'I'll get the motor-car.' But Munro paid no attention.

Denton jumped into a hansom and went home as fast as the traffic would allow. There, he changed into a rougher, more comfortable suit of tweeds and a light mackintosh—it was raining again—and hesitated with his hand on the box that held the derringer. What use would a derringer be if something went wrong in what was about to happen—a gun that was no good at more than a pace or two? He dropped the mac on his chair and ran upstairs and got his Smith and Wesson from a locked drawer. Six shots, decent accuracy, a bullet big enough to do damage. He checked that it was loaded, slipped it into a side pocket of the already baggy tweed jacket, poured cartridges into the other. Retrieving the mac, he hollered to Atkins that he was taking the car and ran down the stairs. If Atkins heard him, there was no sign. His hand was on the front doorknob when he heard the telephone ring. He hesitated. Atkins should get it. But it rang again. And again. Denton swore and ran back upstairs.

'Denton here!'

He heard Munro's voice. 'Not in any hurry, were you?'

'I was getting the motor!'

'Good. Just why I called. Drive up to Stoke Newington as fast as you can go, chop-chop, and pick up two of my tecs. Take them down to the corner of Turner Road and—I've got it here somewhere, dammit—and Edward Street. I think it says Edward. Anyway, opposite the Burdett railway station. Somebody'll meet them there. *You stay out of the way.* Nobody's to go closer than that to the scene. Then you come back here and get me.'

'Munro, that'll take time!'

'I've got plenty to do. You just do as I ask and don't complain.' He rang off.

Denton shouted again for Atkins, again got no answer, and ran down the stairs. Minutes later, panting, he was opening the shed and pushing the car out. He went through the rigmarole of starting the car alone—advance the spark, run to the front, crank, wait for the engine to catch, keep from getting the wrist broken when the crank rebounded, run to the driver's seat before the car either stalled or ran him over.

Errand boy, that's all I am. But he didn't mean it. It was activity; it was movement. He was weary of inertia. Get on with things!

The two detectives were waiting outside the station, already prepped by Guillam for Denton and his toy car. Guillam stood in the station doorway and waved but didn't smile. Denton pointed at the two seats, got the usual laughter at the rear-facing one, and was off as soon as the two men were aboard. The bigger one had taken the rear, of course. It wasn't as bad as the night he had driven to the cemetery, but he felt the car complain. *I need a better car. Damned ridiculous, having to go slow because you've got two passengers.*

'Big hurry,' he said.

'Hurry up and wait,' the man sitting next to him said. The two coppers weren't going to talk about what was happening, Denton decided. Maybe they didn't know. He drove along, thinking for no good reason about the war. His war. He didn't know how he'd got on the subject, then saw—confusion, things patched together too late, men going forward without knowing why. The fog of war. The fog of police work, too.

A freckled young man in plain clothes picked them out as soon as he got near the railway station. It was the car, of course. He could imagine Munro's saying it: *A comical little thing that looks like it's made for a pantomime and sounds like a shitepoke in spring.*

'I'm Allingson. Detective Constable. You gents from N Division?'

The gents said they were, in a tone that let the young man know they weren't detective *constables* and had been sergeants since he'd been pissing his nappies. Denton turned the car around and waved and headed back on the long haul to New Scotland Yard—Commercial Road East, because he had to get over the canal, then Commercial Road and fiendish traffic, Aldgate and Fenchurch Street and then a rat's nest of twists and wiggles to the Embankment, crowded with carriages in the rain. He had his mac on and his hat pulled low, but he was wetter with every furlong.

Munro was standing in the lee of the south entrance. *Thank God he's alone.* Munro's weight was enough. When he got in, the Barré tilted far over and didn't right itself. *Bang down on the springs.*

'I'm the last,' Munro said. They were going east on the Embankment. 'Sent off a wagon full fifteen minutes ago. H Div's in a dither. Screaming over the telephone to keep the bloody hell away, then asking for help. Their super slammed down the telephone on my super, then called the Commissioner's office and asked for more men from the divisions! Well, there aren't more men from the divisions. There are men from N Division, because I'd already got them moving, and there's the two tecs you brought down and the chaps from the armed squad and half a dozen or so uniforms I picked up at the Yard. We'll have to make it work. Have to be enough.'

'Who's in charge?'

Munro bounced, held his hat, snorted. 'A chair-filler from H named Mellors. I've run into him off and on. Plodder, but thinks he's the hare in the race. And prickly as a cactus about being given his due!' Munro hunched against the rain. 'We'll be all right. It'll all come together.'

A song ran through Denton's head. 'Just Before the Battle, Mother'. He thought of what it was like, just before the battle. No mother; he'd never had a mother. Just before the terror, Mother. Just before I crap my pants, Mother. I'm not thinking, dear, of you; I'm thinking of what a bayonet looks like coming at my guts. 'You get nervy, this sort of thing?' he asked.

'I'm out of it. Nothing to be nervy about.' Munro looked at him. 'I'm an onlooker, just like you. It's Mellors's show.' He settled deeper into his seat. 'And Hales's. Hales has decided to take part.'

'They're damned fools.'

'I know.'

Mellors had commandeered a storage room in an ABC. Everybody was crowded in there: Denton counted eleven uniformed constables, the two plain-clothes detectives from Stoke Newington, two more who were probably from H, two obvious armed-squad men, uniformed, with duty belts and service holsters that held .455 Webley top-breaks. He whispered to Munro, 'That's all the weaponry?'

'Four-five-five's a first-rate revolver.'

Denton didn't disagree, although he thought the revolver too big for what came out of the muzzle; but his question had meant, no shotguns? No rifles? Munro, apparently by then understanding what he had asked, muttered, 'Hales won't allow anything else. Public perception of the Met.'

The room was packed with men smelling of wet wool and nervous sweat. Mellors got up on a wooden crate and told them that they all knew what they were to do, and the Met and the people of London were counting on them. He got down. Hales got up and harangued them about duty and showing what they were made of. Several of the young constables looked wide-eyed. *Just before the battle, Mother, the General says I'm not to piss my pants.*

They moved out. Denton and Munro stood aside to let them pass. Two of the uniforms picked up a standard-issue battering ram that had been leaned against the corridor wall.

'We're last,' Munro said. 'On sufferance. Anybody asks you who you are, just point at me and keep going.'

'What about the crooks' lookouts?'

'Already taken out. Two kids and an out-of-work lumper who was standing outside the door where they're trying to tunnel through into the diamond shop. Said it was the first day's work he's had in two weeks and he's got kids.'

They moved along Burdett Street. The uniforms were marching two abreast in cadence. Denton said, 'Shouldn't the Brigadier be going first?'

The detectives peeled off at Paul's Road and headed for the diamond shop, already empty and, Munro told him, the diamonds moved out by the owner.

They turned into Clemence Street, marched along a short street and crossed, and, halfway down another, stopped when Mellors ran to the front and held up a hand.

'This is it, boys! You know what to do. Armed squad with me, please. Fellows with the ram right behind me—right—

where's Baker and Pedloe—right, off you go, lads, don't let anybody out of that passageway... Everybody ready?'

That was clearly rhetorical, for he turned around without waiting for an answer and set off between two tall houses. Denton pictured the map, knew where he was: ahead of them, the courtyard; the house where the gang was working straight ahead across it; on the right at the far side the narrow passage that turned at right angles and came out on Clemence Street.

'We're not to go into the courtyard,' Munro said. 'Observers to the rear.'

'Where's the Brigadier?'

Munro jerked a thumb to the right and up. 'Royal enclosure.' A window, Denton assumed he meant.

Munro stopped where the passage between the houses opened into the courtyard proper. He leaned his left shoulder against the sooty brick wall. Denton, not wanting to be noticed, did the same, his view partly blocked by Munro's hat. What he saw rather stunned him with its obviousness and therefore its audacity. Straight ahead of him, Mellors had take up a position facing the doorway of the house. One of the armed squad was placed on each side of him, ten feet away; both men were checking their weapons. No attempt at secrecy was being made; on the contrary, it was a show of force. Mellors—or Hales—had decided that they would frighten the criminals out.

Seven other constables were in the courtyard, four of them now holding the ram by its handles the way they might have carried a stretcher. Five more were ranged along the houses to the right, beyond which Denton could see the narrow passage. Two more constables would be in there.

Mellors looked around, nodded. He glanced up and to Denton's right—checking with Hales. He turned back to face the house. He walked forward, knocked with his fist on the door and shouted, 'Police! Please open your door!' He waited, then pounded again, this time as loud as the crack of doom. 'Police!' And put his hand on the doorknob and pulled.

The door opened, and Mellors came stumbling back as if he had been pushed, blood spraying into the air as he arched his back and fell from the last step. At the same time, a fusillade of gunshots exploded into the enclosed space. Denton thought *Gatling gun* because there were so many shots and so fast. The front windows of the house erupted; glass flew out, fragments of wooden mullion. Not a Gatling gun, he realised, but several guns firing from inside faster than he thought they could be fired.

Both armed constables went down, their hands still reaching for their weapons. One of the ram-carriers fell to his knees; the weight of the ram, suddenly unsupported at his corner, pulled the others off balance, and they twisted, tried to recover. Two fell or threw themselves down; the fourth man, still holding the ram, let it pull him halfway down and looked around, his eyes wild, and then jerked and fell and lay bleeding. The front door opened all the way and two men burst out, spraying the courtyard with fire. Denton had his own pistol out.

He heard Munro grunt, then saw him swing back against the brick wall and begin to slide downwards.

Two more men rushed out, ran forward. One of them shot the bleeding ram-carrier at close range. The other ran straight at Denton, firing, shooting high; Denton heard the round buzz above his head. Then again, even higher. Denton shot him.

The man staggered back and sat down. Seeing him, the one who had been shooting the ram-carriers started forward, saw Denton's pistol, fired and ran towards Denton's right—the passageway.

A fifth man had come out of the house. He stood on the top step, looking around the court. He seemed calm, unhurried. He came down the steps, bent over Mellors and put the muzzle of his pistol almost against his temple.

Denton shot him.

All the shooting was from his right now. Denton stayed in the cover of the brick wall, looked right, saw two of the shooters there. One was reloading; the other was firing at fallen policemen. Denton watched the shots climb a wall, bits of dust and stone bursting out as the shots hit first along the cobbles and began to climb the wall to the left. Had the police cleared all the houses? Were there people in there? He heard glass break.

He dashed into the courtyard, firing to his right without looking, feeling the mackintosh billow around his legs. *The Deadwood Dodge, they called it. The would-be gunmen wore big dusters because they believed the billowing cloth confused their adversaries.*

The first man he had shot was still on his knees and was trying to raise his pistol to shoot. Denton shot him again, kicked him in the head when he didn't fall, and threw himself down so that his body would give him some kind of cover. He put an aimed shot, his last, to the right and saw the only shooter left there stagger. He picked up the weapon of the man behind whom he lay and tried two shots to his right, felt surprising recoil, the rise of the muzzle from it, knew the second shot would go too high but saw the staggering man go down.

Denton stood. He was deafened. Then, the sounds: screams.

He looked up and to his right. Hales was standing behind a window staring down at him. He looked like a stuffed fish, eyes popping and mouth open.

Munro lay on the pavement by the blackened wall.

Denton looked around him. The smoke-darkened brick walls had bright red spots like drops of blood where bullets had knocked the surface grime away. Dozens of them.

He threw the gun down and stumbled to Munro. The front of Munro's blue suit was black with blood. Denton ripped it open and tore the waistcoat buttons loose. Blood was welling on the right side, then subsiding, a hideous sucking noise that Denton hadn't heard in forty years coming from it.

'Get a doctor! Call the hospitals! Somebody get a doctor!' He was screaming. He put his hand over the welling blood. Munro was drowning. He pushed down until the sucking noise stopped, then turned and looked into the courtyard. Two uniformed constables were standing, one bending to vomit.

Other men were trying to rise, some wounded, one getting up and falling down, getting up and falling down.

'I need a doctor!'

His bellows got the attention of a young constable who had lost his helmet. He stumbled towards Denton. He was one of the ones who had been wide-eyed during Hales's speech.

'Constable!'

The boy stared at him.

'Constable! Doctors! Get doctors!'

The boy came towards him, ran his shoulder into the corner of the house, looked about. Denton grabbed his wrist and pulled him down. 'This is Chief Inspector Munro. Put your hand where mine is. Flat. *Flat.* Keep the wound closed to the air. You see? See? Nod your head!' Denton was screaming.

The boy nodded. 'You said doctors.'

'I'll do it, I'll do it...' Denton took three unbalanced steps into the courtyard, reeling as if he were drunk. The scene had changed: one policeman was helping another to walk; two others were kneeling beside a fallen one. To Denton's left, a sergeant was standing by the battering-ram crew, trying to help a man up and bellowing for assistance.

'Sergeant!'

'Sir.'

'Where's the police wagon?'

'In the... It was behind us.' The sergeant supported the injured man with an arm and a shoulder, at the same time shouting at another constable, 'Get on a bloody telephone and get us some help!'

'Yessir...yessir...'

Denton took several slow steps to his right. He felt as if he were exhausted, parched, hardly able to stand. He looked at the men on the ground, knew at once that one was dead, three serious. The two by the fallen man were trying to give some sort of first aid. 'Good. That's good,' he muttered.

He turned. Hales was standing there. He said, 'What can I do?

Denton put out a hand and supported himself on the pocked wall. 'Call University Hospital on Whitechapel Road. Tell them—tell them to send ambulances. Wounded men coming in.' He was panting. 'Tell them to send ambulances!'

'Yes, yes—good...'

'And ask for Dr Bernat! In the Jewish Infirmary!'

'Why?'

Denton wanted to hit him, but felt too weak. 'He was a military surgeon in a war.' Bernat was Denton's doctor; he had been with the German army in the Franco-Prussian War. He had seen plenty of bullet wounds.

Hales shambled off. Denton made his way out to the street. The police wagon was standing there, its doors open. The young constable and another one were loading Munro inside. Denton pointed at the boy. 'Go with him. Keep your hand on that wound!' He ran to the front and shouted at the driver, 'Go to University Hospital on Whitechapel Road, you hear me?'

'I was thinking St Bart's.'

'University Hospital!'

He found the two detectives he'd brought down from Stoke Newington behind him. They'd come round from the diamond shop. The bigger one said, 'We heard the shooting. Thought it was fireworks or motor-cars.' He looked at two bleeding men being carried towards the wagon. 'Christ, what happened?'

'They had Mauser automatic pistols. It was butchery.'

One of them said, 'We've got to set up a perimeter somehow.' He jerked his head towards a small crowd staring at them from the opposite kerb. The other one said, 'We've got to find if there's anybody hurt in these houses, too; those bastards were shooting everywhere.'

Before they could go off, Denton held the smaller one by the arm and said, 'Two of them got away, I think. That little passage down there.' He pointed east on Clemence Street. 'There were two unarmed constables in there.'

Then the two H Division detectives joined them. They had been into the courtyard. One had been sick and smelled of it; the other one was white. He said, 'I've already been in that passage. Both the uniforms are down. One's dead, I think.'

The detectives began to confer. One of the H Division detectives said, 'Did our armed squad shoot the villains?'

Denton was leaning back against a house wall. He had lost his hat somewhere. He still couldn't get his breath. 'They were the first to go down after Mellors. They never cleared their holsters.'

The detective nodded grimly. 'I saw one's gun at his side. Who, then?'

Denton shook his head and went back into the courtyard. There was a kind of order now. The sergeant had taken charge. He remembered that about battle: first the noise and the death and the horror, and then the human attempt to make things right. The criminals lay where they had fallen, nobody near them; the dead policemen had been left, too, probably because somebody— the sergeant again, he thought—had realised that it was a crime scene. He was now shouting directions about closing the little passage to the east. Denton drifted back out, one shoulder rubbing the side of the passage. There was nothing for him to do in there.

A kind of triage was being done by a middle-aged constable with one arm in a rough sling. He was hurrying along those who came with the badly injured, holding back those who could walk. 'Next car, lads, next one is yours; we got to take care of our own as best we can! You've hearts; you're policemen; you know the drill—'

He was interrupted by the clamour of an ambulance's bell. 'Here they come!' he shouted.

Hales appeared from somewhere. 'I found a telephone.' He seemed to be more in charge of himself. 'Ambulances coming. More constables from the Yard and the local stations. I've put out an alarm about the one that got away.'

'Two.'

Hales frowned. He looked at the bloody but ambulatory men leaning against the wall. He shook his head.

Denton said, 'I'm going to the hospital.'

Hales patted him on the shoulder. 'Good man. Good man.' Shook his head again.

Denton saw the rear doors of the wagon closed and climbed up beside the driver. 'University Hospital, as fast as you can.'

The driver looked him over, made a decision. 'Right.' And used his whip.

Sitting down, Denton found he was shaking.

'Lie down, please.'

'Sister, I'm not a patient. I'm quite—'

'Lie down, *please*. You're covered with blood.'

'But I'm not hurt! It's other people's blood.'

She put a hand on his chest and another behind his back and tilted him as if he were a log. He found his legs willing to go to horizontal. They felt weak. His head ached and his hands were still shaking. *If you don't feel something afterwards, you're a monster.*

'There. You just lie there until somebody comes to look at you. We're overwhelmed just now.'

He lay there and thought of it and tried to get it out of his head and thought of it. *Thank God there were no horses.* In the war, the wounded horses had always been the worst. His dead wife had had a horse she loved. She had killed herself and left him with two children and her horse, which he couldn't afford to feed, and he'd had to—

'Sir? Just lie there now.' He was very young to be a doctor. Irish. Maybe he wasn't a doctor. He had more blood on him than Denton did. He parted Denton's suit jacket and then his waistcoat and looked at his shirt. 'This will be your old suit now. They can get the blood out, but it's never the same. Do you hurt anyplace? Look in my eyes. Yes. Look at my finger. Yes. Can you stand up? Easy, easy—a little weak on the pins, is it? You might as well slip out of that coat and waistcoat while you're up. Good. Now sit over here, if you please, and let me listen to you.' He put a stethoscope against Denton's chest and then his back. 'You're very fit. A policeman ought to be fit.'

'I'm not a policeman.'

'Oh, and I thought you were. You can go home, if you like. Just be careful, you're still a bit shocked.'

'I came to see about Chief Inspector Munro.'

'I don't know about that. I've just come out of surgery, where I've been sewing up the poor lads that were shot. Would you be up to giving one of them some blood, do you think? We're taking people in off the street, we're that hard up for blood.'

'Is it for Munro?'

'I wouldn't know, we've so many. They brought everybody here, police and criminals, willy-nilly. We've sent the ambulatories on to St Bart's; we haven't the room nor the surgeons. How about that blood?'

'Not if it's for one of those bastards who did the shooting!'

'Ah, I can't say who it's for, can I? We have an oath, you know, goes back to the Greeks; we heal, we don't check their morals first.'

Denton started to say *I do*, saw it was pointless, shrugged. 'How do you take my blood?'

'We find what blood you are, first. We have to match it. I'm sure you're a match for somebody, we need so much.'

Twenty minutes later, he was lying in a ward with a tube running out of his right arm and through a small gap in curtains that surrounded another bed. He wasn't to know who was in there, he supposed. The ward was long, a row of beds down each wall, smelling of carbolic and floor wax and blood. The cases from the shooting were all at his end of the room, they'd told him. He could see six beds on the other side; if there were six over here, that would be everybody who'd been left alive. Although if some of the beds were people giving blood, there wouldn't be so many of the victims. Or was this where they had the shooters, too?

A figure appeared at the end of the bed. Denton raised his head. A nursing sister put her head around the curtains and said, 'Don't you move that arm!' She disappeared again. Hales was standing at Denton's feet. He said, 'I've just finished giving.'

Giving. Ah, blood. 'Good.'

'I want to say how terribly sorry I am, Mr Denton. It was my fault, you know.'

'How is Munro?'

'They won't tell me.' Hales came a couple of steps along the bed on the side where the tube ran out. 'I don't know how to…' He gulped, as if he couldn't speak.

Denton couldn't say that it hadn't been Hales's fault, which was what he supposed Hales wanted. Hales had ordered that the armed squad have only sidearms. He must have approved the plan that had everybody standing up in that courtyard like targets. He'd been at the gathering just before they went in. Denton said, 'It's honourable of you.'

Hales recovered himself. He lowered his voice. 'Why did you take a pistol?'

'I often do.'

'You knew something?'

'No. Guns breed guns. And it was put together too fast.'

'They were waiting for us.'

'Maybe.'

'With those automatic pistols! Those were the new Mausers. They sounded like machine guns. It was butchery!'

Denton nodded at that. He didn't want to think about it. He'd thought about it enough. He said, 'Find out about Munro, if you can.'

Hales went away. A sister came and took the tube out of Denton's arm and told him to lie there and drink all the water she was putting next to him. Then he could leave.

'I'm not going to leave. I want to know about my friend.'

'Drink all that water'.

It was a pitcher that held several glasses. He was dizzy when he rolled up to drink it. When most of it was gone, Bernat came to see him.

'Too soon to know about your friend,' he said. 'He hangs on.' Bernat was Hungarian, a Jew who had been drafted into the German army as a doctor. He was kind, sceptical, pragmatic. 'And you?'

'When will you know about Munro?'

Bernat gave him what Denton thought of as a European shrug. He was wearing an apron of the sort butchers wore, bloodier than any butcher's. Where his shirt cuffs showed below his suit jacket, they were crimson; the lower part of the dark blue jacket's sleeves were black and wet. Bernat sat on the edge of the narrow bed and said, 'He was shot in the right lung. The bullets they used, they were made to open up inside the body—scored, and a hole drilled. The chief inspector has lost much of the lung. And there is damage to the muscles of the back. Plus, much loss of blood.' He sighed. 'I see so much blood. Like the war again.' He looked at Denton, his eyes soft, sad. 'You send them to me because I knew war wounds, yes? Well, that was right.' He looked exhausted. 'You go home. You cannot see him; you cannot do nothing for him. Go home. Tell my wife I stay the night here.'

'Do you want more blood from me?'

Bernat walked away shaking his head, making a gesture behind with one hand as if shooing him away.

Denton finished his water in time to fend off a brief and embarrassed visit from the Commissioner of Police, who warned him that the vultures of the press had gathered in their flocks. He let himself be led to an exit from the kitchens. He made his way home on the underground and remembered too late that he'd left the motor-car somewhere. He didn't go to Janet's house but took a bottle to his bedroom and behind a closed door drank himself to oblivion.

CHAPTER 10

He woke at five, ravaged by drinking and the terrible dreams it allowed, most of them of his wife's suicide, in which this time a cat had figured somehow. Usually it was a horse. The cat had been crying and had been his, he remembered that much. Then he had lost the cat and was trying to find it. These were always dreams of failure. Killing was failure. He had killed how many yesterday—three? Four?

He had said to Henry James that if you felt nothing after killing, you were a monster. He was not a monster; he knew he was not, had proof in the nightmares, saw it in his willingness to numb himself with whisky. And the hangover, made worse by having given blood. A penance? Retribution: for their blood, take mine?

He fell asleep again, woke, hated the light, pulled the pillow over his head, slept. Once, he heard Atkins come to the door and then go away.

I am not a monster.

And something more had happened in his drunkenness: there was the new book. *Two men, one murderous, one civilised. Denton and James. But then, to take them through lifetimes and show that in the end it is the civilised man who does something monstrous. What? Murder the other? More likely destroy him somehow. But that wouldn't be James. James had only been the instance; throw James out. And throw himself out, too. He had been only an instance. Go again to the American West, those raw towns where killing still happened. A gunman and—perhaps a clergyman. A lawman and a clergyman. Law and piety. Violence and...hypocrisy? And then bring them forward in time, the town becoming a small city, electricity, trolleys, the first motor-car, and the gunman now a quaintness, a bit of residue, the other a 'big man'—landowner? Developer? Yes, that sort of monstrosity.*

He stumbled out of his bed at ten and drew a bath and stood looking down into the rising water, his hands on the oak surround of the tub, his head bursting. He had used to joke in his drinking days of the perfection of drunkenness, the sin that brings its own punishment next morning. He careened to the water closet and tried to vomit but could not, then spent half an hour in the hot water.

He came out like something crawling out of the sea; he took headache powders; he shaved and saw himself in the mirror, bloodshot and lined. *A monster.*

He was back lying naked on his bed when Atkins knocked. 'Telephone for you.'

'Not now.'

'Inspector Guillam. He says it's important.'

Denton cursed, wrapped himself in a long robe, tottered downstairs barefoot.

'Yes?'

'Ginger Goldensohn's dead.'

'What about Munro?'

'How would I know? Did you hear what I said?'

'Yes, well.'

'You're not surprised. Constable found him on his own front doorstep at five this morning. Tongue cut out. Bled to death.'

'They knew.'

'Yes, but who? That's Italian, isn't it—the mouth?'

'For informers, I suppose so. Not just Italians. Why did you call me?'

'Because you're the only one that was in those meetings who'll talk to me! The rest won't give me so much as a cross look. I'm acting as divisional inspector up here with Munro out; H and Central are running into themselves because of this cock-up and all the men they've lost. Plus now Central have told me to fold your Henry James's burglary into the Wragge case. It ought to be Central CID's, but they're totally jiggered up by yesterday. I want to talk to you.'

'No, I don't think so.'

'I have a warrant to search the place where your Henry James's goods are supposed to be. You get your arse in your little motor-car and come up here and we'll go together. You can see the loot.'

'Not in the car. I'm still drunk.'

'Oh, it's that way.'

'I gave them some of my blood. Then took it back as whisky.'

'Then there's Wragge's wives. The Public Prosecutor sent me a message yesterday that he was changing the charges, knocking them down to a kiss on the cheek. Then after the massacre in Clemence Street he said that was off, they're to be prosecuted to the full extent. What the hell happened in that meeting?'

'It'll change again with Goldensohn murdered.'

'Change the charges again? Hell, no! Anyway, I'll be there in thirty minutes in a police carriage. We'll talk as we go down to Deptford.'

Denton sighed. He knew that he had to see the loot from James's burglary—the Florentine box might be there, although it seemed trivial after yesterday. He said into the telephone, 'Find out how Munro is,' but Guillam was gone. He thought, *I forgot to tell Mrs Bernat about her husband last night.* One more thing to feel bad about. He tried to call the hospital and talk to Bernat, but he wasn't there and they wouldn't tell him anything.

The morning newspaper had yesterday's disaster on the front page:

POLICE MASSACRE IN WHITECHAPEL
Four Dead, Seven Injured
Brig. Hales: 'Entirely My Fault', Resigns

After a long opening paragraph, there was a leader, 'Chief Inspector Munro "Grave",' and farther down, 'Well-Known Author "Heroic".' An artist's rendering of Denton's head was added.

Denton went into the downstairs WC and managed to vomit this time.

'Tea?' Atkins said when he came out.

'Tea, I suppose, yes.'

'Taking it hard.'

Denton looked at him.

'Sorry.'

He drank tea with sugar, later ate dry toast. He refused a raw egg in Worcestershire sauce.

'You coming back for lunch? I ask because the missus is worried about you.'

'Tell her not to worry. I'll see her this evening.'

'That female from University College came by again. You wasn't here.'

'Oh, God.' He had to think who that was. *Balzac. French.* 'One thing at a time.'

'She said she'd come back. Relentless, that sort. Wants her tuppence, I suppose.'

Denton waited in his armchair with a pounding head. Atkins called to him when the police carriage pulled up. Denton, outwardly neat in a greeny-brown tweed suit, stood. He reached for the box where the derringer was. His hand was shaking. He looked at it, made the hand into a fist. *Not today. Today I daren't go near a gun.*

He got in beside Guillam, who said, 'I hate these bloody carriages. They smell like a stopped crapper and I can't see worth tuppence. You look better than you feel, I suspect.'

Denton grunted, said he'd tried to call Bernat but couldn't get him. He told Guillam what his pounding head remembered of the meetings with the Great Ones and Goldensohn. Guillam shook his head as if he couldn't believe it. He said that if he had his way, Ruth Gold would hang, and Mrs Wragge next to her. 'The loaded billy-club at Wragge's didn't work out as the murder weapon. Clean as a whistle but for the maid's and Wragge's fingerprints all over it. Nobody else's. We can't find the one from Gold's. If there was one.'

Denton tried to fall asleep. The cab swayed steadily side to side; their shoulders touched. Guillam said, 'Munro's really bad. All they'd tell me was there's no change. He's dying, I think.'

'He'd better not.'

Guillam told him again what a shambles H Division were. 'They have all the work of investigating yesterday's disaster, now there's Goldensohn murdered, and they lost two tecs yesterday. Chickens with their heads cut off.'

'Pull it into the Wragge case.'

'No fear. I've enough for two as it is. At least we don't have to put up with that stupid bugger who put yesterday together.'

'Mellors. That's harsh. He's dead.'

They swayed along. Guillam kept hitching himself forward to look out the small window. 'How did Munro get shot?'

'He was a bystander. Mellors put Munro and me at the back. Supposedly, we were out of it. In fact, we were right in the way when the mugs tried to get out.'

Guillam swayed forward and back and said, 'I wish you'd killed more of the bastards. How the hell did it go so bad so fast?'

Denton knew but didn't say. He subsided into feeling like hell until they got to Deptford, a sad street of warehouses behind the cattle market, where two constables who'd been keeping watch pointed them towards a line of tumbledown carriage sheds. Denton spotted three men from the armed squad carrying rifles as well as sidearms. He looked around, saw another on a housetop. *Locking the barn door after the horse is gone.*

Guillam examined the shed's door, a large padlock. He said something to one of the constables, who went off and came back with a large young man who apparently had been kept out of range in case the gang came back for its loot. He was a locksmith. It took him twenty seconds to have the padlock off. Guillam and the constable pulled the doors open; the bottoms caught on the earth and grass, and the wooden doors, curved by the pulling on them, threatened to smash as they were opened by main force. An evil smell crawled out. The constable turned grey-green; Guillam frowned, then wrinkled up his nose. Denton, already sick, felt himself get woozy and then clear. He looked inside, saw a pile of household things, arguably James's, in a corner, but most of his attention was on a huge black puddle, now dried, on the cobbled floor.

'Christ,' Guillam said. He sent the constable off to notify H Division. 'It's Goldensohn's blood, as sure as eggs are.' He barked out some harsh orders about keeping people away, staying clear, not dirtying the scene. When he had tiptoed around the puddle and then walked up and down, he motioned at Denton. 'There's nothing to see on these cobbles but filth. Come on in, but stay tight along the walls.'

Denton tottered in. The blood smelled like spoiled meat. Flies were walking on it and in it where it was still viscous and shiny between the cobbles. They buzzed and swarmed. Denton wished he could be sick again. It was the smell of a battlefield a day after the shooting stopped.

'Doesn't look like much this way,' Guillam said of the stuff in the corner. The pile was mostly indistinguishable but had put out some tendrils that proved to be, as Denton's eyes adjusted, silver candelabra. He made out the carved back of a mahogany chair, several large crates. Guillam went the other way down the shed. 'Oh ho, ho, ho.' A large grey shape sat at the far end. Guillam put a hand on it and pulled at a heavy canvas, which slipped off as he backed away, revealing a bright yellow touring car. 'Bit bigger than yours,' he said to Denton. 'Constable, get those things in the corner out of here and laid out so I can see them outside. Wear gloves! And don't walk through the fucking blood. Who else is here besides you? Get somebody in to make an inventory.' He looked at Denton. 'You all right? Of course you are. I suppose we'll find more blood in the car. Probably how they moved him around.'

Denton grunted when Guillam cautioned him to touch nothing. Fingerprints had been new two years before; now they were the first thing the more forward detectives thought about.

Not, so far as Denton could see, that they were doing much good in court yet. He walked along the inside of the doors to the motor-car, a Panhard et Levassor. He leaned his buttocks against the bonnet and massaged his forehead. 'You think this is the stolen car that was used at James's?'

Guillam was standing by the blood, looking at items that were being taken from the pile and laid out on the canvas in the light. 'Stolen car? Oh cripes, there's something in Wragge's notes.'

'The car they used to lure the maids away.'

'What if it is?'

Denton pushed his pelvis away from the car and shambled along a wall to Guillam. Guillam said, 'We'll check for fingerprints. Maybe the thief'll turn out to be one of the dagos you killed yesterday.'

Denton thought about the men who had erupted from the house firing their Mauser pistols. 'Not dagos. Anyway, there may be no connection.'

Guillam had wrapped a hand in his handkerchief and was examining a gold statuette of a dog. 'With this and Goldensohn? What a hope.'

'Why would a gang who were trying to raid a diamond shop and who carried Mauser pistols do a burglary in Rye? It's chalk and cheese. What do you do for hangovers?'

'Prevent them the night before.' Guillam made a puking sound. 'Although you've seen me drunk enough.' He had come drunk to Denton's house once and tried to start a fight. Atkins had hit him with something heavy. 'I don't do it so much any more.' He held up the golden dog. 'Nice, this. Your Mr James mad for dogs? There's another one in silver.'

Outside, a constable was kneeling on the canvas and unpacking one of the crates. Denton said, 'Have you come across a wooden box, painted red and gold?'

Guillam turned on him. 'What's that about?'

'There was a box James particularly wanted back. Sentimental value.' Too late, he knew he shouldn't have spoken.

'Is it on the list?'

'No idea.'

'Is this the "personal thing" you told me about?'

Denton shrugged and went off looking for water, anything he could take more headache powders with. In the end, he took two with cold tea from a constable's flask. The taste was terrible, too reminiscent of the blood—more punishment.

Guillam squinted against the pale sunshine, said, 'No point me standing about wasting time. I'm going back to Stoke Newington. You?'

'You can drop me. Did that box turn up?'

'Not yet. They're still at it.' Guillam looked up at the armed man on the roof. 'I suppose the pistol-packers better stay until they're done. Never know after yesterday.'

'What about the car?'

'The car, the car, Christ. Somebody has the owner's name, I suppose. In Wragge's notes, maybe, but they're a shambles. One more straw for Inspector Guillam's back. Come on.'

When they were in the carriage, Guillam said, 'Now what's going on with this box you mentioned?'

'I told you, it simply has sentimental value to James.' Warning signals went off again; Guillam was a very acute copper.

'Is this why James came to see you, way back? That's more than sentiment.'

Denton didn't respond. *Way back.* How long had it been? Only a week. He looked out of his window. It was true, he couldn't see anything, as Guillam had said; the window was placed wrong. After several minutes, he asked if he could tell James that his things had been found. Guillam said no. 'I'll tell you when. Or I'll tell him myself. After we've been over them.' Then they were both silent, and then Guillam began saying back to Denton what he'd said earlier about Goldensohn and the meetings in Whitehall and the Yard. 'So you think he was afraid of being found out.'

'I think he knew he'd be found out.'

'Which do you suppose killed him, the diamond gang or the burglars?'

'Only two of the diamond lot got away. Do you escape by the skin of your teeth at midday and murder somebody that night?'

'You do if you're waxy enough.' Guillam said something to the driver because they were nearing Denton's street. 'I'm going to murder somebody myself if Donnie Munro dies.'

Denton got down and waved the carriage away. Atkins went off to the Lamb for lunches. When Denton was halfway through a plate that was mostly pickles, the telephone rang. It was Guillam again.

'Thought you'd like to know. Two men with fast-firing arms tried to assassinate Brigadier Hales half an hour ago. Peppered his car with bullets but missed him, wounded the chauffeur. Poor bastard resigned but they still went after him. This is bad, Denton—you'd better be careful. Your face is in the papers.'

'Burglars on the warpath?'

'It isn't a joke. They've got those pistols; they mean to use them.'

'Well, all right. I'll keep a lookout.'

'CID might squeeze out a couple of plain clothes to guard you.'

'You're short enough as it is. Maybe I'll hire somebody. Would they go after Munro and the others in hospital, do you think?'

'Central're putting uniforms in the wards. Fat lot they'll do without firearms!'

'Who's in charge—this going to be yours, too?'

'The CID super, Morriss, has taken Clemence Street himself. But he's short two detectives, plus Munro. I'm supposed to meet with him every day until we get a handle on all of it—that was before Hales got ambushed, anyway.' He added, as if it were an afterthought, 'I've sent a telegram off to Henry James about his stuff.'

Denton warned Atkins about the attack on Hales and went to Janet's house and told Mrs Cohan to tell her husband, who was off at his boxing school, then went back and put his head together with Atkins's. 'What do you think?'

'You worried, Colonel?'

'I've seen those pistols in action. They're terrible to shoot because you can't control the recoil, but you have to take them seriously. You want to go away somewhere for a while?'

'What, on my lonesome? And leave the dogs and the motion-picture business? If something's going to happen, I'd rather be here to put it on film for posterity.'

'I was thinking I might get Fred Oldaston for a bit.' Oldaston was a former prizefighter who had been the muscle at Ruth Castle's whorehouse when Janet had worked there. 'He could maybe patrol around the house at night. You two get along?'

'Nice enough chap, the little I know of him. We might put him in the box room down on my level, if he's to be here nights.'

'See if you can find him, tell him what's wanted. The sooner the better. And you'd better send Alfred home until it's over; he's not up to it.'

Two hours later, a constable on his beat was shot twice in Camden Town.

In the afternoon, Miss Heckham, the young woman from University College, came again. She was eager, a bit like the dog that they had given to Henry James, also rather bouncy. Also rather pretty, although he hadn't told Janet that. She had a tinge of accent that Denton thought was well-off, even upper class.

It didn't help his understanding that she started her report in the middle, saying, 'It was ridiculously easy, as a matter of fact. Maybe I shouldn't say that.' The Clemence Street shootings and Goldensohn's murder had driven the rest of it from his mind; he had trouble understanding what she was talking about. She said, 'It went like this: one of Balzac's biographers said that in his youth Balzac fell madly in love with the daughter of "the Vicomte de G", an impoverished nobleman who lived in an ancient *hôtel* in the rue Jacob. Her name was Marie-Célimène. Well, it was child's play to pull down the new equivalent of the *Almanach de Gotha* and winkle out a family name starting with G in the 1830s and a daughter named Marie-Célimène! It's Guyenne, de Guyenne, the title, I mean; the family name was Sarmonteux. So there you are! She held up her palms. *'Tout fini!'*

Denton, who had caught up by then, wondered if she had found anything worth knowing, but he paid her anyway and asked her if she knew how to use modern Parisian directories. Would they have them in the British Library? Could she go and look to see what had become of the family? Today? For more money, of course. The hangover had reached the numb stage, also a rather stupid stage, but he felt mostly tired of talking to her.

When she was leaving, Denton said, 'I wonder how we'd find out what happened to the young woman—Marie-What's-Her-Name.'

'Oh, that's easy. I should have copied it down while I was in the book. She married, I remember that; there was a line and a name—not Balzac, ha-ha!—but I remember noticing because her husband had an English name. Shall I find it again? And the family. Today? Right. I'll be back!' And off she went, pleased with herself and the money she was about to make.

Denton went up to the attic and forced himself to exercise. He knew he wouldn't really feel better until the alcohol left his body, probably another day yet, but exercise gave the illusion of sweating out the poison. And it was punishment, which was, after all, the point.

Miss Heckham was back two hours later. 'Hardaker,' she said. 'The man she married, Joshua Hardaker. As for the Sarmonteux family, the de Guyenne viscounts, that is, there's nobody of either name in the rue Jacob any more. There is, however, a highfalutin' perfume manufacturer called Guyenne et Sarmonteux Frères in Lille. Looks as if they came into some money somewhere along the line. Or broke down and went to work. I brought their address.' She looked hopeful, probably of immediate payment.

Denton forked over. 'Who was Joshua Hardaker?'

'Not my province, I'm afraid.'

'But wouldn't there have been some sort of wedding notice?'

'The impoverished aristocracy? Might have avoided it to show how aristocratic they were. Rather Balzacian, that.'

'Did you look?'

'For a wedding notice? Good Lord, no. Wouldn't know where to start.'

'University College is pretty much closed now, isn't it? Why not have a go at it? At the same rate, I mean.'

The young woman sighed. Money was money, but she was apparently tired of the Guyenne-Sarmonteux. Still, money *was* money. She'd give it a try. Without enthusiasm now; the high spirits of the first discoveries were gone. *A burster, not a stayer.*

That evening, Fred Oldaston moved a suitcase into the box room and started patrolling around the house from dark to dawn. They went into a state of siege, Atkins with the derringer and Denton with his Smith and Wesson. When the doorbell rang about nine, Atkins kept one hand in a pocket holding the derringer, Rupert padding along to lend bulk. It was not, however, a killer with a Mauser automatic, but Dr Bernat. He had stopped in on his way to the hospital. Denton supposed he had gone home to change his clothes, could hardly have stayed long; he looked as if he hadn't slept.

Denton apologised for not having carried Bernat's message to his wife. The doctor waved a hand. 'I should not have asked.' He accepted a cigarette, puffed. 'Doctors are not supposed to make predictions. I will make a prediction. Your friend will live.'

'Munro?'

Bernat nodded. 'He is strong; he has will.' He smiled. 'Very Nietzschean. How well he will be, I will not predict. Maybe he will have the lung again, maybe not. But I think he lives.' He stubbed out the cigarette on the King's beard. 'We saved everybody but one that you brought to us. The one who died was one of the bad ones.'

He stood. 'You are a good shot.' He eyed Denton critically. 'You know they are putting police on the wards? Is there danger to you?'

Denton shrugged. 'They seem to be targeting the police.'

Denton sat on after Bernat left, his mind jumping like a drop on a griddle. First glad because of Munro. Then fretting about Hales and the policeman wounded in Camden Town. Then second and third thoughts about the new book.

The Monster. Two people. The reader made to think that the obvious one is the monster. A gunman or a murderer. The other one 'good'. Not a clergyman, too easy. A woman? Does it then seem anti-female? Maybe not if we see her made *into a monster. He rapes her. Have to show why he is as he is—the war. Feelings gone. Violence as normal. They marry. She grows and grows. Money-hungry? Story of the West, too, little town becoming city, his loss of place, function. She buys property? Destroys what was old—'development'. At the end, she dominates. And does something monstrous. Kills him? Too easy. Destroys. Destroys somebody else. Somebody he—can it be made love? Maybe friendship. Wilfully destroys his friend.*

The next morning, there was an invitation from Henry James—'on the very shortest of notice, but the weather is perfect'—to a garden party at Lamb House. That same day, the two remaining shooters from the Clemence Street massacre were besieged in a house in the Isle of Dogs. The Metropolitan Police put eleven armed policemen with high-powered rifles around it, and the Home Secretary called for the assistance of the army.

James's invitation distinctly included Janet. Denton was amused; he couldn't rememeber ever having mentioned Janet to the great author, but James was a connoisseur of gossip, so of course he'd know about her. Doubly amusing was that James said he 'couldn't have Violet Hunt' at Rye House because of an affair she was having with somebody, but he'd have a mistress and former prostitute—one who had her own money, anyway.

Given this inch, Denton took the mile of asking James in his note of acceptance if Atkins could do some motion-picture filming at the garden party. He repeated Atkins's notion that it might sell books. He added a line that he thought would get James's attention: 'We'd be seen by hundreds of thousands in America and Britain.' And a line that, he hoped, would gently pluck at James's sense of guilt: 'I should greatly appreciate this favour for Atkins and would consider it a return for anything I may have done for you.'

And a line about 'Mrs Striker's ward, who is staying with her and whom she won't care to leave behind.' Walter Snokes wasn't legally her ward, but that was a quibble. At any rate, he dared to ask if Walter, too, could come along.

Then he waited for James's refusal.

Before it could come, the two besieged anarchists walked out into a thin drizzle with smiles on their faces, their hands in the air. They seemed entirely pleased with themselves despite facing certain hanging. Their Mauser pistols were found inside the front door. They had run out of ammunition.

James's reply came. With obvious reluctance, he agreed that Atkins could 'use his machine' before the party started, but he begged that it be done 'entirely unobtrusively and with regard to one's sense of taste'. As for 'the young lad, the charming Mrs Striker's ward, he will be most welcome.' Denton had to conclude that the garden party was going to be a collection of odds and sods, and one more or less wouldn't matter.

CHAPTER 11

The front door of Lamb House opened and Denton stepped out, then turned back to say goodbye to his host. Henry James, squinting slightly into a watery sun, came out behind him and gave him a sudden, somewhat ghastly grin. Denton was a step below. He put out his hand. James put out his; there was a certain amount of fumbling, then a handshake so vigorous it looked as if James were hoping to bring up water. Then they stood there looking at each other as if they didn't know what to do next. Denton turned towards the street and said, 'For God's sake, Atkins!'

'Sorry, sorry, it was so good I just wanted to keep watching. Now, if we could do it one more—'

'No!' Denton's voice was a roar; James jerked back but looked relieved.

'You want this to be right, don't you, General?'

'We've come out that damned door four times, and we went *in* that damned door three times! Enough is enough!'

'Oh well, if you're going to take a tone...Mr James, my most sincere apologies for going on and on. I'm sure you understand the drive for perfection.'

James gave a weak, somewhat baffled smile. He said, 'Are we done, then?'

'Only a shot or two of the both of you together, if I may.'

'I really don't want it done *in* the house. There is such a thing as one's privacy.'

'Wouldn't think of it. Not enough light indoors, anyway. Come along, Ralph.' Ralph was Atkins's new dogsbody, an undersized forty-year-old from somewhere he described as 'south t'river'. The camera with its tripod was as tall as he, but he got it in his arms and carried it towards the front door. James fled. Atkins followed, tipping Denton a wink as he disappeared inside.

'I never think of Atkins as a martinet,' Denton said to Janet. She and Walter had been watching from across the road, where Atkins had found a little widening for the Barré.

'He was a sergeant, after all, wasn't he? Walter, what did you think of the motion-picture-making?'

Walter frowned. He was looking much better than when he'd arrived in London, less strained and less sullen. He said, not in the heavy voice that seemed to come from a machine but in one that was lighter and sweeter, 'Why did he do the goodbyes before he did the party? He says he has more to do in the garden, but Mr Denton's already left the house.'

'They'll fix that later, I think. According to Atkins, they can cut the pictures up now and paste them back together in whatever order they want.'

'But that isn't truthful!'

Denton was leaning on the motor-car with his arms folded. He laughed. 'I think it's coming at truth in a different way.'

Some of Walter's less pleasant voice sounded. 'But it's wrong!' He pointed at the side of the Barré, where a bright yellow sign with black letters had been attached to the doors: *Atkins Cinemantics—Actualities for Everybody!* 'He says *actualities*, but it isn't actual!'

'Well, I was actually sick of it. Come on, let's go inside before the rest of James's guests get here. James will have a stroke if Atkins is barging around with that machine while people are trying to drink tea.'

Janet took his arm as they crossed the road. 'You looked quite pompous,' she said. The tone was affectionate, pleasing him.

'It's hard to play yourself,' he said.

Walter brayed behind them, 'But you weren't playing! You *were* yourself. Weren't you?'

Denton wanted to explain it but couldn't. He wanted too to say that the whole thing had embarrassed him, but Walter didn't seem to have any sense of what embarrassment was. He paused in the open doorway and said, 'Would you mind having Mr Atkins take pictures of you, Walter?'

'No. Does he want to?'

'But would you mind if he put the pictures up on a screen and let other people look at them?'

'Pictures of me?'

'Yes.'

'I don't like people looking at me. But if they don't touch me, it's not so bad. If it was only a picture, they couldn't touch me, could they?' He laughed, not his uncouth laugh but almost a giggle. 'Maybe I could be a picture of myself, and then I'd be safe.'

Janet raised her eyebrows at Denton. They hadn't heard the concept of 'safe' before. First *pain*, now *safe*. Denton said, 'Well, I don't like having my picture taken. It makes me feel...as if I'm somebody else.'

Walter nodded. 'I'd like that.'

Inside, James's two new housemaids had been joined by two young men got up as waiters. Mrs Esmond was moving through the rooms, looking as if she meant to commit a murder. The four servants were laying out cutlery and glassware on a long table. Henry James came towards them and clapped his hands. 'We have been blessed, or at least favoured, perhaps I should say merely gratified, with a pleasant day of the sort that Rye can now and then provide—not entirely desert-like, the sun not a blinding light, but in all very pleasant. It is the influence of the sea, I think.' He paused by Janet. 'I'm so happy you were able to come.' He smiled at Walter. 'And you, my boy.' But the smile for Walter was uncertain, while that for Janet seemed genuine.

Janet looked mischievous but smiled. 'It's very good of you to have us.' Walter, who had been coached to say one positive thing when he was introduced—the notion of 'positive' perhaps not entirely clear to him—said to James, 'You performed yourself very well, sir.'

James hesitated, then hooted. He started to clap Walter on the shoulder but stopped his hand midway and turned it into a peculiar gesture, as if giving a blessing. He had been coached about Walter, too. 'Well said, my boy! "Performed myself." That's exactly what it felt like, wasn't it, Denton? Utterly unreal. My brother would have much to say about it.'

'Mr Atkins shouldn't call it "actualities",' Walter said stubbornly. Janet said, 'Walter!' in a voice he had learned to recognise, and Denton turned James aside and said that they'd best get the rest of it over, hadn't they?

James sighed. 'It's what I came to find you for. He wants us in the garden room.' His face took on the Roman look. 'It's my first experience of being "directed", as he calls it; stage-managed, *mise en scène* by a servant.' He took Denton's arm.

Atkins had set up in the garden with the camera facing the garden-room door. He came forward as they appeared in the doorway, a book in his hand. He held it out. 'You're talking about a book. I think, Mr James, if you would hold it? General, if you'd just look over his shoulder, like, pointing out something in the book?'

'What?'

James objected. 'Yes, why would I be looking in a book? This is one of *my* books. Not one of my best. What's Denton doing, pointing out a typographical error?'

'You're two famous authors discussing a book.'

'Well, surely we don't need the book in our fingers to do so!'

'It's what we call very-simmy-litude, sir. For the great mass of people. They've never seen a famous author. Famous authors have books—eh?'

Denton murmured to James, 'Best to humour him, or we'll be here all day.'

'I heard that, Colonel! Now, Mr James, you have the book— the Major's pointing a finger—good...' Atkins disappeared behind the camera. One hand appeared and began to crank. 'Good—good—somebody move, please—you, General, move that pointing finger—good—good—Mr James, say something to him, if you please—anything—good—smile, please—bigger smile—Colonel, could you manage a laugh? Big ho-ho-ho—no? Liven it up a little somehow...'

Atkins's head appeared. 'Oh, well, can't ask for miracles. I'll get a few seconds out of that, be a bobby-dazzler for about as long as you can say Nebuchadnezzar, after that goes quickly off. No matter. Now, gentlemen, if you'd just walk up and down in the garden, yes, walk, that's it, both legs, yes—good, Colonel, take his arm...' Atkins was walking beside them, got a step ahead and walked backwards. 'No, keep the book, wave it about, right, remind people you're authors—good—up and down—if either of you knows a joke, tell it when I say so, some laughter will go a long way towards making you seem human—good—keep it up, up and down...'

He backed to his camera, dodged behind it. The hand began to turn the crank.

Henry James said, 'I have never been so humiliated in my life.'

'Myself, I'd rather be shot at.'

'I am reminded that you *were* shot at recently. And behaved heroically.'

'Instinct.'

'And the wounded policemen? An inspector?'

'Munro. Still down but he'll make it.'

Distantly, Atkins could be heard saying, 'The joke now—tell the joke...'

'How long must we keep doing this?' James groaned.

'Think of it as a stroll in the garden.'

A somewhat muffled exclamation came from the camera. 'Out of bleeding film! Ralph—more film. In the box, yes, in the box—that box, there!' Atkins ran to them. 'Only a matter of seconds. Latest equipment, change film in a trice. Half a trice.'

'I really think,' James said, 'that my other guests are arriving.' Indeed, Denton had heard voices.

'Up and down, *please*. Can't emphasise too much the importance of this scene. Great authors—Henry James's own garden—we're permitted to look in on history—up and down, *please*—Ralph, you got that film in yet?'

Eventually, the crank turned again. James said, 'I saw my things. From the burglary. They recovered everything except—you know.'

'It wasn't there.'

'Hopeless now, I suppose.'

'We'll see.'

'And was it Inspector Wragge the whole time? He was what they vulgarly call "the brains" of the crime?'

'As I said, we'll see.'

'If he was the brains and he's dead, then perhaps...perhaps that's an end to it. Anyway, you've more than met my request for assistance, Denton. You needn't go on.'

Before Denton could speak, Atkins was standing in front of them, one hand up. 'You can stop now, gentlemen. Forgot I was here, didn't you? That's when it's best. Absolutely believable. Lovely. Couldn't have asked for better.' He shook James's hand, said the worst was over, he'd been extremely generous and under-standing, and, now that the other guests were arriving, might he just park the camera in a corner of the garden and shoot the few remaining inches on the new spool?

'Oh—oh...' James looked as if he wished he could launch thunderbolts. He glanced at Denton as if it were all his fault—as it was, of course. 'Do as you like!' He put on a smile and made for his new guests, who were just coming into the garden.

'Not half miffed, is he?'

'You went too far, Sergeant.'

'Tell you one thing I've learned in this business already—you don't get arrested for asking. And if they get shirty but say yes, you're still ahead.' Atkins was waving at Ralph, who had the camera and tripod in his arms and was walking around a big larch. 'To your left—your left, Ralph—yes, that left—in the *shade*!' He shook his head. 'I had a pal in the army, he was like that with women. Not like Ralph, like me asking James for more. My pal would see a woman took his fancy, he'd go up and say, "You're a peach, how about a jump?" Half the time he'd get it in the conk; the other half he eventually got what he wanted, which was about a hundred times more than the rest of us did. Moral: it never hurts to ask. Here comes the mob.'

Atkins trotted to the shade of the larch as Henry James led his first guests out. Denton saw about a dozen, more in the room behind, some of them the faces on James's piano, one or two writers he already knew: H. G. Wells, a neighbour of James's; Conrad, the same; Arthur Benson, only an acquaintance; Edmund Gosse, the establishment's pet man of letters; a fluttering party of Ladies This and That; a couple of middle-aged men Denton didn't recognise who seemed very sure of themselves; a couple of quite unsure young men, and one named MacCarthy who was sure to the point of the insufferable. Considering the shortness of notice and the nearness of the end of the Season—was it Cowes Week? Lord's?—James's net had brought up a pretty good catch.

Denton let himself be introduced to anybody and everybody. Behind them, Janet was watching from the French doors, Walter in the gloom behind her. Denton groaned at the thought of talking to all of them, but he supposed he had to. *Somebody* had wanted the Florentine box. The whole business seemed old now, faded behind the more recent, more spectacular events. Guillam had turned most of his attention to Wragge and his two wives, particularly the question of which of them had killed him and which only stood and waited. Denton found concern for Munro far more important than James's box; he had tried to visit Munro once in the hospital but had been refused. Old letters, old love, genteel fear of revelations—these seemed insubstantial now. But he would go through the motions.

He spoke first to the couple who had rented the house while James was in America, the Grahams. No, they'd never gone into James's study, of course; yes, it was always locked, except when Mrs Esmond let one of the maids in to dust; yes, of course it was locked when they moved out. Mrs Graham seemed unaccountably nervous, even flighty. She protested too much, he thought; she was probably lying, curiosity having been too strong to allow her to live in a house for six months without penetrating into every corner. Her husband muttered something about 'enjoying Lamb House while he got his legs back under him,' the reason for having his legs someplace else unclear.

He talked to Benson, at the moment so jovial he might have been drunk but apparently wasn't; he had the reputation of being sometimes 'difficult'. Benson congratulated Denton on his 'heroic aid to the Metropolitan Police'. He was delighted, absolutely *delighted* that James had got his things back; burglaries were shocking; all's well that ends well. Didn't know a thing about the study; hadn't been in Lamb House for a year until this moment. 'Although I wouldn't vouch for every face in this crowd,' he said in the tone of a stage detective doing an audience aside. 'Some rather rum artistic types.'

'Meaning?'

'Well, there had to be what's called an "inside man" for the burglary, didn't there? That is the expression, inside man?'

'Or woman. Why do you think so?'

Benson didn't like to be contradicted or, it seemed, questioned. His father was a bishop, or some such. 'It's perfectly obvious, I should think! I heard the broken window pane was a sham.'

'Where did you hear that?'

'Oh, you're being too tiresome.' He moved away.

'Denton!' a sharp voice said behind him. He turned, found the big moustache and little chin of Edmund Gosse.

'Oh, hello, Gosse.' He wasn't able to warm the engine enough to put any cordiality into the words. And Gosse, he was sure, was too grand to have had anything to do with a burglary, so there was no point in questioning him.

'A word with you.' Gosse was often called England's most eminent literary man, a laughable notion if you thought about who else was about; what was meant was that he got himself the best press. He was everywhere, doing everything, where there was 'literature'. He edited, he assembled anthologies, he did little biographies, he wrote endless numbers of essays, he gave graceful speeches after mediocre dinners. Now the holder of a sinecure in the Lords library, he was among the eight or ten men the newspapers treated as the nation's high priests of letters. Denton thought he was a leftover Victorian windbag.

Gosse peered at Denton through his ever-present pince-nez. He said in a schoolmasterish tone, 'I think you must be made to realise that you have been unfair to James by bringing that woman here.'

Denton had several instantaneous, not quite simultaneous thoughts: *What woman? Oh, Janet? I'm going to knock him into the shrubbery.* But he balled his fist behind his back and said, 'I don't think you want to pursue that line, Gosse.'

'There are *ladies* here!' Then, desperately, 'Lady Maud *Warrender* is here!'

'I think you'd best go talk to somebody else.'

'I insist that you take that woman away at once!' Gosse's pince-nez quivered. 'James is too polite to say it!'

Gosse and Denton were of an age. Denton was taller, leaner, fitter. His first impulse was to put his fist through Gosse's nose; then he wanted to let ten years of personal dislike pour out as invective; then he thought of Janet and the boy and James and controlled himself. He put his left arm around Gosse's shoulders; Gosse flinched away but Denton drew him back, tight against his own chest. 'Gosse,' he said. He made himself smile. 'Gosse.' As if to say, *You naughty fellow, how I do regret this sort of behaviour.* He tightened his grip still more and put his right hand on Gosse's right arm, effectively imprisoning him. Gosse struggled, but only for an instant—people might see. What men like Gosse feared most of all was that horror worse than any of Lang's werewolves or vampires—Making a Scene. Denton squeezed Gosse's upper arm with his left hand. His voice was genial. 'Gosse, you're a bum-sucker and you're a bully, but you don't have the weight to bully *me*. Let me give you a demonstration of bullying: if you ever again mention the lady I brought to this *swar-ay*, I'll put that nose of yours in a plaster so big it will never again fit into my business. Understand me? Hmm?' He let go. 'Now go suck a bum.'

Gosse lurched away, almost lost his balance, and caught himself while trying to smooth his hair and check his necktie and pull down his very tight jacket all at once. 'You vulgar ruffian!' He looked around. He pushed at the nosepiece of the pince-nez. He took a step and whirled back. 'Your last book was appallingly bad—gross, badly written, and an offence to Christianity!' He wheeled away, again turned back. 'All your books are bad—trite, coarse, *vulgar*! You are an offence to the English tongue!'

Denton smiled and bowed, then walked away, shook some more hands, murmured, tried to match faces to the names in James's guest book. Everyone pretended not to have seen what had happened.

He talked to a lot more people. James seemed to have invited, along with his literary friends, everybody of the middle class or above in Rye and the surrounding villages. They had all been shocked by the burglary, they insisted; now they were all delighted by the return of James's things. None of them had ever been in James's study, the words *inner sanctum* used several times. If Denton mentioned the Florentine box, they looked blank.

More and more people came into the garden. A surprising number of folding cameras appeared; a cluster of people would pose for a photograph, then wait while one member changed places with the photographer and a second picture was taken. A kind of game developed of taking Atkins's picture while he was filming the crowd. Denton heard one woman say that it was 'awfully smart of James to have a motion-picture person here'.

A group of new arrivals broke into twos and threes and made slowly for chairs that had been set out near beds of flowers. Denton, tired of asking questions and learning nothing, made his way to Janet, still sequestering herself indoors. 'You don't like James's guests?'

'James introduced Walter and me to them. I got "the look" from several of the women. And a couple of the men.' She had contempt for people who judged her by what they thought she had once been. 'Walter was very good. He said nice things to everybody. Congratulated one woman on her "fine bust", which took her a bit off-centre but was thought witty by a couple of the more bohemian men.'

'*You* have a fine bust,' Walter said.

'Yes, dear, but we're not supposed to say so. It's another of those—oh, let it wait until we're home. Ah, here come yet more.'

One of the maids had come into the room, then stepped aside. Behind her, an invalid's chair made its way in, piloted from behind by a good-looking young man (*one of James's young men*, he could hear Harris saying). In the wheelchair was a contorted woman in a green silk dress, expensive, Denton thought, but wasted on her. No, that was cruel; perhaps it helped her. She sat almost sideways in the chair, her left leg drawn partly up, the line of the bent leg clear in the drape of the skirt. Her head was lowered as if burrowing into the chair back, and when she turned it, as she did now, it had something of Geddys's contortion to it, as if her chin were attached to her right shoulder. She had to twist her whole upper body, the neck apparently frozen. Her right arm, the hand cupped into a claw, was carried across her torso, the shoulder low.

'I'm Raphael Neville,' the young man said. He looked cheerful and rather puppyish and oblivious, as if everybody pushed crippled women about in invalid chairs. 'And this is my sister Clara.' Two things registered on Denton: this was the young man who Frank Harris had said was having an affair with Violet Hunt, and he and his sister were on the list that James had supplied of guests who had stayed overnight at Rye House. What had Harris called him? 'One of James's laddies.'

Denton muttered his own name. Neville brightened still more, said that he admired Denton's work. Denton introduced Janet. There was no frisson of recognition from Neville, no disapproval, only an open, cheerful pleasure in meeting her. Clara Neville turned her tilted head and said in a strange, cracked voice, somewhere between a crow and a goose, 'I won't say I am glad to meet you, because I know you're not glad to meet me. Nobody should have to look at cripples at a party.'

'Oh, Clara...!' Neville muttered.

Walter stepped towards her. 'My name is Walter Snokes, and I'm a kind of cripple, too, only I'm a mental cripple. So I'm glad to meet you. I'm not glad to be here, either. Why are you crippled? Did you have an accident? I had an accident when I was seven and it destroyed part of my mind.'

Raphael Neville smiled but looked baffled. Clara Neville turned still more. If she smiled, it was a smile of malice. She said, 'I have a congenital disease. That means it runs in my family.'

'I know what "congenital" means, miss. I have no family. My father murdered my mother because she murdered two of his mistresses, and then he killed himself. Nothing runs in my family. Except murder.' He gave one of his uncouth laughs. Raphael muttered something, maybe 'No, no,' and Janet cleared her throat as a signal to the boy. He said, 'You're very pretty, miss. You have a very pretty face no matter that you're all crippled up.'

She looked up at him, gestured with two fingers to her brother and told him to put her near a window and go enjoy himself. 'Get me a book.'

'I'll get you a book,' Walter said. Janet looked at Denton: this was new. Walter and Clara Neville agreed that he would get her a book. She specified a book about great houses and told him where to find it. Walter actually ran out to fetch it.

'He likes you, Miss Neville,' Janet said.

'He doesn't know me.'

Raphael fussed over her, brushed some hair off her forehead. He said softly to Janet, 'Did the boy really lose his parents as he said, or...?'

'Exactly as he said. He has a sister who killed somebody, too, but she was a child at the time.'

Raphael looked harried. Clara said, 'My sort of people.'

Then Henry James came in and touched Raphael Neville. It was as if he couldn't believe what he was seeing, couldn't get enough of it once he did believe it. Walter came back with the book—the right book—and Clara took it without thanking him and began to turn its pages. Denton saw shiny paper, real photographs of great houses that had been pasted on otherwise white pages, a photo of a turreted and crenellated place that looked to him rather like New Scotland Yard, on which she seemed to linger. James spoke to Clara but was speaking really to Raphael, whom he touched again, now on the arm, then on the hand. The young man simply smiled, as if he expected it or were too polite to ask James not to do it. James held on to Raphael's hand and said to Denton and Janet, 'Raphael has a new book just out. His *first* book.'

'Thanks only to you, *cher maître.*'

'Oh, dear boy, you exaggerate. I had only a *very* small part in it!'

As did Violet Hunt, Denton thought.

Raphael seemed an unlikely 'new young man' for a voracious woman, if that was what she really was. Harris's word wasn't necessarily to be believed, but then James, too, had said that the young man was having a fling with her. Raphael kept smiling, more like somebody's well-mannered nephew just down from university than an older woman's fancy man. *Fresh as paint and nicer than cream pie.*

When Denton said this an hour later to Janet, she said he sounded jealous; Denton snorted. 'It irritates me to see somebody like James fawn all over somebody in public, if that's what you mean.'

'James is infatuated with him.' She was eating a small dish of ice cream the colour of primroses by then.

'Just what I mean.'

'Would it be any better if it was some simpering popsy?'

'Pretty much what it is.'

'No, Neville's a very attractive, very male young man. Take it from a woman.' She took his arm. 'Your nose is out of joint because you hated the filming. Well, cheer up. Atkins has packed up and gone, and so can we—*soon.*' Indeed, Denton had been aware of Atkins and the camera during the first half an hour of the party, filming a panorama of the garden and its colourful residents—women in bright summer dresses like flowers, pinks and pale greens and yellows, men in linens and white flannels, panamas, even one boater—all being caught in a medium that didn't register colour. Walter, after fetching Clara Neville's book, had migrated to a place behind Atkins and had seemed to be absorbed in the business of moving pictures. And then Denton, after again quizzing some of the guests, had realised that Atkins was gone and Walter was back hanging about Miss Neville.

'I want a word with Neville before we go,' he said.

'Well, don't tell him he's a popsy.'

Denton was looking around the large garden when a hand touched his elbow and H. G. Wells said, 'What was Auntie Gosse wetting its knickers about?'

'Hello, Wells. He thought my necktie was too colourful.' Denton's necktie was grey.

'He looked as if he was going to do the St Vitus's dance. You'll never get another good review in London if you offended him, you know. He has influence, our Gosse. In fact, he can be a bit of a shit if you cross him. You're asking a lot of questions of everybody, I hear.'

'Curiosity.'

'Mrs Graham thinks you're a copper. She seemed agitated. Benson says you were rude to him. If you think any of these people had something to do with James's housebreaking, you're off your nut. They aren't that clever and they aren't that practical. They weave not, neither do they spin. I'm trying to take over the Fabian Society, have you heard?'

'How's the campaign to use fiction to teach the middle class to be socialists?'

'It'll work, it really will! James doesn't get it—he still goes on about form and style and all that. Wants me to write perfect sentences, when what I want to do is change the world, the sentences be damned. He can be quite a pain in the arse about it. He ever tell you how to write your books?'

'I wouldn't let him.'

'Ehh, smart man. There's one of his protégés now, a piglet sucking at the Jamesian tit. "*Cher maître*." My arse.' Wells was looking across the garden with what seemed to be malice. James was talking to some personage while holding the arm of Raphael Neville, and two other young ones were glaring at the favourite. Denton looked at Wells again, saw real dislike, remembered that Wells had been having an affair with Violet Hunt himself. She did get about.

'You don't think James is generous to take on young writers?'

'He wants everybody to write like him.' Wells snorted, then eyed Denton. 'You ever think of making your books more political? I can tell you how it's done...'

Denton laughed and detached himself. He found Neville and the group that included James, who was still dithering around him like an adoring aunt. Denton managed to cut Neville out of the flock and, turning his back on the rest, said, 'You're very good about your sister, Mr Neville.'

'Oh...!' The young man blushed. 'She's the good one. She's put up with so much. She's very brave.'

'It must have been difficult for her, staying in this house. The stairs. When you were James's house guests, I mean.'

'It was, yes. She can get around a bit by herself with a cane, but not stairs. I tried carrying her up and down, but... When James invited us to stay, I insisted that she stay down in the town, where she could be on one floor.'

'That was before James went off to America?'

'Of course.'

'You weren't in the house while he was gone?'

'No, no—why would I be? I didn't know his tenants, although they seem very nice people.'

'But you know Lamb House pretty well, I suppose.'

'Oh, intimately! I'll never forget the sessions we had in the garden room. For a beginner, it was like—I don't know what it was like. Sitting at the feet of Homer or some such.'

'I'd have thought you'd work in the study.'

'Oh no. I think the study is James's last resort when he wants to brood. He has his moods, you know. No, the study was the inner sanctum.'

When, a few minutes later, they left (Walter, asked by Janet if he would go now, said, 'Oh yes please, miss'), James saw them to the front door. It felt false to Denton, the farewell too much like what Atkins had filmed. James held Denton's hand and whispered, 'I'm so sorry about Gosse. He so desperately thinks himself my defender—even when…I do apologise. I do.' He held Denton's hand tightly. 'You *and your friend* are always welcome here.'

As they walked down to the railway station, Walter said, 'Miss Neville wanted to read her book. I tried to engage her in conversation as you told me to, but she told me to go away. She is terribly unhappy.' He took another step or two and said, 'But she isn't in pain.'

Janet said, 'Some afflictions are like that.'

'You get what you wanted?' Denton said to Atkins as soon as he was home.

'Couldn't be better. Was back in London just in time to drop the film at the lab. Have a look at the raw stuff Monday p.m. Then one copy to America, the negative to the company offices here, and I watch the money roll in.'

'I never want to go through that again in my life. Not even for your ascent into capitalism.'

'You're not an actor, General. That's why you write books. Private personality, not a public one. Mr Henry James, too.'

'I thought he was going to throw you out.'

'He'd never do that, because of you. Sorry I had to trade on that. Not admirable. You want some supper?'

'I'll be at Mrs Striker's. Take the night off, if you like.'

'Well, I might, then.'

'You seem to have converted Walter to motion pictures, there at the end.'

'I thought he was going to get inside my jacket with me. Yes, kept trying to look through the focuser. As much as told me I was a liar for shooting the farewell before you'd left. Bit literal, he is.'

'It's the way he thinks. Or doesn't.'

With Janet, Denton went over the day, was able now to laugh at it all. 'Mostly comic somehow, James and his world. Not James himself, not in private. But with people…'

'Young Neville's very patient with his attentions.'

'That's what you said once about a whore with a client.'

She smiled crookedly. 'One wants to earn one's keep.' They gossiped about other people at James's party. They were sitting at a little table, eating cold chicken and homemade mayonnaise and a salad made of greens from the garden that Atkins and Cohan shared. She held up something on a fork. 'This is Italian, and I can't remember the name of it. Atkins keeps saying "that dago lettuce". He disapproves because it grows better than everything else. What did you think of Neville's sister?'

'I thought she was pathetic. Pitiful. Spiteful, nasty. Unlikeable.'

'Well, I'll tell you something about both of them—their accent's learned. They're up from somewhere. I used to hear that accent-that-isn't-an-accent a lot in the whorehouse. The customers, not the girls. *Nouveaux.*'

Denton shrugged. 'You English.' He chewed some chicken and sipped some white wine—Est! Est!! Est!!! from their most recent visit to Naples—and stared at the now darkened window. 'I didn't learn a thing from that bunch at James's. Not that I expected much.'

'You could give it up.'

'I could, couldn't I.' He threw down his napkin. 'Let's go to bed.'

'I'll just have a word with Walter.' By choice, Walter was eating alone in his room. She got up, laid her own napkin by her littered plate. 'You want it to be young Neville, I suppose, because you didn't like him.' She held out her hand.

Next day was Sunday: little doing. Janet was off to church. Walter, given the choice of church or nothing, elected nothing; church, God, piety didn't exist for him. Denton left him sitting in a window with a pile of books.

'You're off?' he said to Atkins.

'Day off, remember? Working holiday—going to the zoo to shoot a chimp. Got a pal looks a bit like a chimp, show him the pictures of the real chimp and then my pal imitates it. But then I switch the order, so in the film it'll look like the chimp is imitating my pal. Barrel of laughs.'

'Walter would be shocked.'

'Normal folk love it.'

Atkins went off for the car. Denton changed and made his way by underground to University Hospital. A policeman was standing guard in Munro's ward, but Denton's name was now on a list and he was allowed behind the screens that surrounded the bed. It was the first time he had seen Munro since the shooting; he was prepared to be shocked, but he was shocked beyond any preparation. Munro looked pale, his face gaunt, not so much that he had become suddenly old or broken-looking as that he was unrecognisable.

He woke from light sleep and eyed Denton and even tried to smile but at once closed his eyes again.

There was a chipped metal chair, once white. An equally chipped gilded stand held a pile of cards and letters and a picture of a woman Denton assumed to be Munro's wife. Vases and baskets of now tired flowers stood on the floor and on another metal table. Denton read one ribbon, 'CID Central'. He looked at a card: 'Your old mates in the Annexe'. That was where Denton had met Munro.

'Don't you wear him out!' The voice behind Denton was Guillam's. He turned, half rose; Guillam's big hand pushed him back down. In a lower voice, Guillam said, 'I want to talk to you. Don't sneak out.'

From the bed, Munro tried to whisper something.

'We're leaving in a tick. Your wife's on the way; she'll throw us out anyway.' Guillam leaned over Munro. 'You need a shave, Donnie. Want me to shave you?'

Munro's head moved back and forth. He whispered, 'Bea.' His wife, he meant.

Guillam said, 'You look better, but you're pale. They give you any more blood? They should. Beef tea and beet juice aren't going to make up for what you lost. Want me to speak to the doctors? You wear me out, Donnie, you really do. Exasperating. You need somebody to raise hell for you.'

Another large figure appeared—female, broad, smiling but ready to be tough. Denton got up. Munro's wife was polite but wanted them gone. 'And you, George Guillam, stop hectoring him!' She had a Scots accent. Then to Munro, 'And you stop humouring him! You just waste your strength on listening!' She made shooing gestures with her gloved hands and began to chatter at Munro about church as if they'd already gone.

Out in the tiled, echoing corridor, Guillam said, 'She's right, you know. We don't do them any good, just riling them up.' He tapped Denton's upper arm with a knuckle. 'The prosecutor is sweeping the whole Wragge business under the rug. And this is the murder of a policeman! I can't let it go like that.'

They passed through a side door of the hospital and into a now cloudy morning. Denton said, 'Rain soon.'

Guillam ignored him. 'Walk a bit with me. What I think is, if I tell Mrs Wragge we'll lower the charge if she'll blow, that female lawyer of hers will snap at it and we'll be able to convict the Gold woman. If not premeditated murder, then one of the crimes of violence with intent, plus concealing a crime.'

'Any murder weapon yet? Then it's all spit and moonshine. The prosecutor'll never have it.'

'The prosecutor will fucking well take what we give him!'

'Not if the PM's office still wants to let the women off easy.'

'Did you see the cards and flowers around Donnie's bed? Four other coppers dead and four more still in hospital, and the prosecutor won't come down on a woman who murdered a detective! There'll be a bloody police revolt if that happens!'

'The two aren't related, Guillam. You know they're not. In fact—no, let me finish—I could make the case that if one of the women killed a copper, he was a bent copper who was in on whatever got Munro and the others shot. Maybe the Met ought to be giving Ruth Gold a medal.'

'He was still a cop!'

'Bent or straight, you lot are sacred, are you?'

'Sometimes you make me sick.' Guillam pulled up in front of a coffee stall. 'Let's get something. I want tea. Two teas. From a bloody urn; imagine what the coffee's like.' He stepped away from the counter with two thick white mugs. 'Now look, Denton, you're not a cop, but you know us. There's a lot of rage out there in the force. Coppers want blood.'

'Throwing them somebody for Wragge's death isn't going to stop a police revolt, Guillam.'

Guillam was leaning back against the coffee stall. 'What I have to do is tie it all up and hand it to the prosecutor in such a way that they can't say anything but "Convict the bastards."' It was as if Denton hadn't spoken. Guillam scrabbled in an inside pocket and came out with a half-crushed cigarette box, white card stock with 'Lambert & Butler May Blossom' printed on it. He held it out without looking up, waited until Denton had taken one, then thumbed another out one-handed and took it out of the box with his lips. Denton held out a lighted match. When he had dropped the box into a side pocket, blown out smoke and sipped his tea, Guillam said, 'They recovered two more of those Mauser automatic pistols after the siege. I'll tell you something about those. The numbers are in the same sequence as the three they picked up in Clemence Street.' He puffed again. 'They're part of a box of twenty that was stolen in Germany two months ago. The two thugs that were captured aren't saying anything except that they're anarchists, but the wounded one is blabbing because they've told him he's dying. He isn't, unfortunately, but he thinks he is. He says...' Guillam forced smoke out the side of his mouth, dropped the cigarette on the pavement and ground it with his sole. 'Listen to this—he says that the Mausers were payment *in advance* for doing the James job. Does that wring your withers? Ever hear of a gang being paid in advance for nicking somebody's silver? This is between you and me and the piss-pot, by the way. H Div really put it to him, I s'pose. Stick a finger in a bullet wound, you get results.'

'Another anarchist?'

Guillam nodded. 'H says they all have accents. Dagos, Polacks. But smart. The two who came out of it whole say they don't want lawyers. They'll be their own lawyers. Big chance to make speeches before they hang, see? Good Christ.'

'Tell me more about the Mausers.'

Guillam took out the box of cigarettes again. 'They wanted them to kill somebody important.'

'But he admits they did the James burglary? And they left the goods where you and I saw them in Deptford? For Wragge to fence, or Ginger?'

Guillam reached around and put his empty mug on the counter by feel. Denton was still sipping his tea; it was harsh, tannic, fairly disgusting. Guillam ferreted out another cigarette. 'Wragge, I'm fairly certain. Goldensohn never wanted his hand seen. But he was in it somewhere or they wouldn't have known to kill him.' He lit his own match from a box and held it to the cigarette. 'The blabber says there were only the five of them. Five in the James burglary, five at Clemence Street. Plus Wragge and Goldensohn. Wragge wouldn't likely have provided the Mausers; I don't think he had the contacts. Possible, yes, but why? So he could rob your Henry James? The same goes for Ginger. If Ginger Goldensohn wanted to rob houses, there's at least three gangs in Whitechapel'd have been happy to oblige him. And they needn't have gone so far as Rye by a long chalk.'

It was the possibility with which Denton had started, back when Henry James had sat by his empty grate. 'James was targeted at the start?'

Guillam straightened and eyed him through thinning smoke. 'You were brought into this by James himself. For a "personal", "sentimental" reason. When we got to Deptford, you went looking for a box. Box wasn't there. The only thing that was missing. I ask myself, what's different about this house burglary that's worth bringing in five stolen automatic pistols?' He put the cigarette to his mouth and drew in, his eyes always on Denton's. 'Guess what I think.'

'I know what you think.'

'What's in the box?'

'Ask James.'

'I did. Or a Sussex Constabulary tec did. Answer, some letters of a French author. He didn't tell us, he says, because he didn't want to alert the thieves to their value. He's lying, or I'm a duck. What was in the box?'

Denton had been holding the stub of his own cigarette. Now he used it as a distraction by dropping it on the pavement and stepping on it. He threw the rest of the tea to the side and put the mug on the counter. He said, 'It's private. No, let me finish. Something personal. James could be blackmailed.'

Guillam was nodding. 'Worth enough for somebody to go through all this rigmarole?'

'James isn't rich. On the other hand...'

'Revenge? Just nastiness—torture the old man?'

'Maybe something like that.'

'Who?'

Denton shook his head.

'This straight? You're not pulling something out of your arse?' Guillam waited several seconds, then swung himself away from the stall and started up Whitechapel High Street. Denton caught up and they walked side by side, two tall men with long strides. They walked several streets before Guillam said, 'I've been over Wragge's notes on James's guests and his tenants and the servants. Wragge or his people interviewed everybody. Huge mob of people. Nothing struck a spark.'

'I was down there yesterday and met some of them. Had the same experience.'

'Somebody we don't know about, then? Christ, it means making a list of James's enemies. He'll have a crowd, won't he?'

'He's famous. He's written a lot about other people's books, that sort of stuff. Still...'

'No reason he'd have done it himself? Not something he's trying to get at you with? Or get some attention from?'

'Nah.' They strode along. Denton said, 'You've got to separate Clemence Street and Wragge from Henry James. No, don't start to splutter; what I mean is, when it started—the burglary, the plan for the burglary—if James and the box were always the target, then that was all there can have been. Let's say the anarchists did it because they wanted guns, all right, but they can't have *started* it. They can't have gone around London saying, "Look here, we want some Mauser automatic pistols, who'll give us some in exchange for robbing Henry James?" They wouldn't ever have heard of Henry James. So let's say somebody wanted to rob James—to get the box, all right, let's say that was the goal— and to him, the Mausers were just like money, they were a way to pay for it. So what happened with the Mausers afterwards had nothing to do with James or the box or his house. Nor did Wragge's murder. Unless you think that was something that happened between Wragge and the burglars over the goods or some such. They murdered Ginger because he betrayed them; could they have murdered Wragge for the same reason?'

'Wragge didn't betray them. And it's clear one of the women did it.'

'Clear to you, maybe.'

'If Wragge had betrayed them, I'd see it in his notes. And the fruits of it—arrests, reports, notes. If Wragge was going to betray some bad 'uns, he'd make sure he got credit for the arrests.'

They walked half of another street and Denton said, 'Blackmail can be lucrative.'

'You said James isn't rich.'

'He could pay out several hundred pounds a year, I guess.'

Guillam grunted. At the Aldgate underground, he stopped and said he was peeling off here. Denton said he was glad to see that Guillam got home sometimes.

Guillam looked away. 'I've taken a room up in Stoke Newington. To be close to things. I don't get home much these days.' He didn't look at Denton. Then he did. 'You give me a shout if you learn anything about this. Anything!' He put the tip of a finger against Denton's chest. 'I'll make a bargain with you: I won't pry into this box and what it contains if you'll keep me in the know on what you find. 'Cause I know you're looking and you'll go on looking.' He gave a non-smile that flashed over his face and faded. 'I've worked with you before.' He went into the underground.

Denton thought how lonely Guillam looked. How lonely he must be, in fact. Taking a room in Stoke Newington was a move away from his family—that was what he'd meant for Denton to understand. If he didn't go back to them when this was over, he'd be worse than lonely.

He hesitated at the door of the underground, not wanting to go down while Guillam was still down there, not sure why. Done with Guillam for now? Something about Guillam's new situation—fear of embarrassing him? He temporised, started north to walk home, then made a decision and turned around and went back along Whitechapel Road.

He wanted to find Goldensohn's house. The police would have long been finished with it now. What he wanted was Goldensohn's coachman, or the tough who had been with the old man in the carriage. If Goldensohn had been a spider near the centre of the James burglary's web, then somebody knew why, and perhaps what had happened to the Florentine box.

He had to ask at five places before he got directions to Goldensohn's house. Two of them wouldn't discuss Ginger Goldensohn and looked at him in disgust. Two of the others said they didn't know; maybe they didn't. The fifth, a greengrocer laying out pears in an outside bin, said, 'He's dead.'

'I know. I want a look at his house.'

'It's not much, take it from me. All the money he had, it isn't much. You're a newspaper fellow?'

'Close enough.'

He looked at the pears he was laying in orderly rows on the bare wood. He jerked his head to his left. 'Corner of Mile End Road and Cambridge Road. Next to the almshouses. Built himself a house where he could look right down on the people he drove to bankruptcy.'

'I was told it was in Commercial Road.'

'You was told wrong—that's my fault?'

Whitechapel Road was mostly middle class. Behind it, some of the blackest slums in London festered, but even there it was spotty, derelict squats and flophouses next to decent-looking houses where people made as much as a couple of pounds a week. The recent history was Jewish, but the area was changing, like all of London.

Goldensohn's house was ornate without being at all lovely, was in fact one of the uglier houses Denton had seen in a while. A lot of black wrought iron and a square turret were meant to make it seem medieval; so were rounded shingles and several arched windows. It was big enough, with enough varied rooflines, to give a kind of *trompe l'oeil* impression of a village, but the eye knew better and said it was all fakery. It was simply an unlovely house that had been designed on the cheap.

The curlicue-burdened iron gates were closed and locked with a chain and a padlock. A pasteboard sign on a wooden stand had apparently blown down from the front door and lay at the bottom of five stone steps, but Denton could read it by tilting his head: *Police Area Keep Out*. No bloodstains were to be seen. He hadn't expected any; Goldensohn had done his bleeding in Deptford.

Denton walked along the cast-iron fence, the spindles topped with points and flanking barbs to resemble, he supposed, spears. A gravel drive led back to a second, much higher pair of iron gates, through which he could see a porte cochère and, still farther on, part of something that was probably a carriage house in the same unlovely architecture. These gates, too, were chained and locked.

Denton shook the gates. They rattled but were very stable.

He shook them again. He called out, rattled, called, rattled, and finally kicked.

'Here, now!' A head appeared over a brick wall on his right. The face was rather round, suggesting fat farther down the body, but it had a big bristle of moustache and a lot of dark sideburn and hair. 'What's all this racket?'

Denton was trying to figure out if this was a householder or a servant. He said, 'I'm trying to see if anybody's here.'

'There's been a death in that house!'

'On the front steps, actually.'

'If you keep that up, I shall have to call the police.'

A householder, then. '*Is* there anybody back there?'

'Who are you? What do you want?'

'I'm investigating.'

'What? What are you supposed to be investigating?'

'Do you know how insurance works?' That was as close as he was going to come to lying.

'Do you know how an electric bell works? On the gatepost at your left. Which civilised people know about, *I'm* sure!'

There, indeed, at his eye level on the left-hand gatepost was a bell push. He hadn't expected to find one, and so he hadn't seen it. *Brilliant investigator.* 'Thank you, sir.' He pushed. If a bell rang, he didn't hear it. He pushed again. He shook the gates.

The head on the wall said, 'I'm going for the police.'

Denton put his finger on the bell and held it there. *What the hell, it isn't my electric battery.* After he'd kept the bell ringing for about forty-five seconds, a hoarse voice said from somewhere in the back, 'Wot the hell are you ringing like that for?' The voice got louder as it went on, and at the end of the question a short, angry and very drunken man reeled around the corner of the building. 'Wot is it? Wotcher doing driving me crazy with that bell?' By that time he was nose-to-nose with Denton through the bars of the gates. A combined smell of gin, beer and bad teeth wrapped itself around Denton's head. 'You cut it or I'll open these gates and rip yer guts out!'

'I'm looking for Ginger's coachman.'

'Well, go look someplace else and leave that bell be.'

'I thought a coachman who's about to be out of work would want to make a little money.'

'Wot for?' The man threw his head back as if he were near-sighted and Denton were a page of small type.

'Can't be much money with Ginger dead.'

The man tried to spit; much of it ran down his chin. 'You think Ginger gave me money by the ton, you got another think coming. Dead, he ain't much less of a miserly old shit than he was alive. What money?'

'Just some money. For some information.'

'You newspaper cunts can go fuck yerselves. You wouldn't pay me last week, I ain't giving you fuck this week.' He thought that was pretty good, laughed.

'I'm not from a newspaper.'

'Wot are you, a bloody bell-ringer?' That was a good one, too.

'What if I'm a copper?'

The man frowned. He was holding on to the bars of the gate, the caricature of a man in prison. 'If yer a copper, I'm a cunt.' He belched to show how true that was.

'Thought you might like a couple of shillings.'

'Shillings! You think I'm idiotic? Cripes! Shillings. I tole you lot last week I don't nark for less'n a quid!'

Denton thought that he could reach through the bars and give him enough grief that he'd talk for free, but the place was too public. 'Have to be a pretty good squeal for a quid.' Denton made a show of going through a pocket, then took out several coins. 'What d'you think?'

The coachman leaned forward against the bars. He reached through. Denton raised a coin just out of reach. 'Talk first.'

'And have you scamper off? My arse! Gimme—'

'Payment down for services to be rendered.' Denton held out a shilling. 'Take it. Go on, take it. The sooner you take it, the sooner we'll get to a quid.'

The man took the coin, put his head back again, then let his weight sway back so he was holding himself up by the gate. 'Yer trying to bugger me.'

'You drove Ginger's carriage, am I right? Did you or didn't you? Yes? All right, another shilling. Now—did you ever pick anybody up in the carriage and bring them here?'

'Women. Old fool kept trying.' He laughed. 'They had tales to tell when I took 'em back!'

'Ever pick up any men? No, I don't mean that; I mean men you brought here to talk with him. You know—private talk. About Ginger's business schemes.'

'Pretty much over. All that.'

'What? What's that?'

'Old bastard, out of the business, eh? Often and often he says, he says to me, "Don't get old, Farley." Like I could help it. "Don't get old. They don't mind you no more." Well, what'd he expect? Eh? Laugh at him these days, most of the tough boys.'

'He had a tough boy of his own, didn't he? Rode behind the carriage?' Denton was thinking of the man he'd seen waiting for Goldensohn the night of his first visit.

Farley—if that was in fact his name—staggered to his right and hit the brick of the house. He glared at it, then leaned on it for support. 'Don't talk about him.' He shook his head. 'Not fer all the tea 'n China. Mum's the word.'

'That fellow here now?'

'Mum's the word. See no evil.' He seemed to fall asleep standing up, then came to and said belligerently, 'Where's my quid?'

'You haven't told me anything yet, Farley. Where's my information?'

'Well, wotcha want t' know? Think I can guess yer bleeding mind?'

'Planning a job, Farley. Did you hear Ginger plan a job in the last couple of months?'

The coachman pushed himself off the wall, grabbed the gate with one hand. 'Think he was mental? You think a keen old cock like Ginger'd plan somefing where the likes of me could hear? You're the one is mental. Gimme my quid now, I'm done.'

Denton flourished the coins but held them high. 'He planned a job, Farley. A couple of months ago, it started. Come on, man—you must have seen something.'

Farley made a drunken pretence of thinking. One arm was extended through the bars as if he were begging for alms. He said, 'Tell you somefing.'

'Good.'

'I druv him twicet to Paddington station. Twicet. Now gimme my pound.'

'What's that worth? Paddington? So what?'

'Paddington railway station, dummy! Where do you go from Paddington? Reading, that's where. Always Reading. Wha's in Reading? The chokey. Who's in chokey? His old pal Miles. Miles o' the smiles.' He laughed. 'Now my story is all told, yer turn to hand over the gold.' He laughed and filled the air with stink.

'Reading prison? Miles? Miles who?'

'Quid. I'm done. Tole you the lot. No idea who, just Miles, knew that by him saying it accidentally. Pay up.'

Denton tried again, but it was no good. Farley really was done. He went off into insults and curse words and threats. Denton handed over some coins, although not a pound, and Farley lurched away without a word.

Denton sighed, turned, looked up to see the householder's face perched on the wall. The householder said, 'Insurance, indeed!'

'We're an industry that works in mysterious ways.' He headed for Mile End Road.

He was at Munro's bedside again. The sister had been surprised but had let him in, 'but only for a moment'. Munro was awake, muzzy from morphine. Denton bent low and said, 'A lag in Reading. Name of Miles. "Miles the Smiles".'

Munro blinked, rolled his head a little towards Denton. He whispered something that sounded to Denton like 'alpine'. Denton said he hadn't understood, but Munro wasn't having it. He was in pain, weak, tired. He whispered, 'Ask my super,' and turned his head away.

The sister came in, but Munro was asleep anyway.

CHAPTER

12

he Monster. Man and woman. She is black, a child at beginning.
Just after war. He rapes her, takes her with him—foraging, taking
what he can. Moves west. She pregnant, leaves her behind. Gunman—
railroads, cattle drives, small towns—sheriff? Marshal? She turns up
again with a child, prostitute. Or housemaid? Then long affair as she
slowly rises, he sinks. Marriage? Probably not. She becomes what he
made her. Avaricious. Ruthless. She destroys him—how? Both 'the
monster', changing roles, but the monster is slavery. No, race. White
assumption of power, superiority (ownership). Her assumption of fear,
hatred, revenge. End with lynching? Yes. But which one?

He re-read his scribbles as he dressed. He could see it now.
Time to talk to Lang again? Maybe smooth the way with a
proposal for the little book on the early follies of great men.
Sounds right. Then ease *The Monster* in.

We'll see.

Atkins greeted him at the bottom of the stairs with 'You
going out?'

'Business at Scotland Yard.'

'And on and on. You never stop. Be different if they'd pay
you, wouldn't it? But no, he works for free. Tea or coffee, jam or
cinnamon toast, porridge with milk or salt and butter?'

'Porridge! When the hell did you ever make porridge?'

'Alfred's back. Trying to fatten him up. Don't think it'll become a habit.'

Denton surprised him by saying porridge, salt and butter, the way his grandmother had eaten it. 'Tea, cinnamon toast. Alfred's already here?'

'On duty at seven.'

Denton walked down to Scotland Yard through a damp, clouded city, the air surprisingly fresh despite the street smells. He'd telephoned the Yard before he left, asked to visit the super of CID. He guessed—rightly, as it turned out—that time would be made for him because of his part in the Clemence Street disaster. In fact, Superintendent Morriss's sergeant was waiting for him when the porter left him at the door of a suite of offices. As he led Denton to the superintendent's room, he said, 'I'm speaking out of turn, sir, but I want to say I'm personally grateful for what you did. You saved a lot of policemen's lives.'

There was no way to answer that, so Denton muttered, 'Thank you,' and passed into the office as the sergeant held the door. Morriss made a little speech about Denton's service to the Met at Clemence Street. It was nicely done, apparently heartfelt.

'I happened to be there,' Denton said.

'An instance of divine help, some would say. What can I do for you, Mr Denton? If it's something I *can* do, I will. We're in your debt.'

'I saw Chief Inspector Munro yesterday. He suggested I see you.'

'How was he? Well enough to make a suggestion, anyway. That's good news. I saw him the day before; he wasn't in the condition I like to see my officers. That was a hellish thing they did to him and the others.' He shifted something on his blotter. 'Anyway, a suggestion?'

'Somebody gave me a name. Miles. "Miles the Smiles". Maybe in Reading prison.'

The superintendent sat back. A slight smile seemed to lift his lips. 'Galpin. Miles Galpin. What's this in aid of?'

'I was wondering if I could talk to him.'

Morriss worked his fingertips over his palms, rubbed the pads of his thumbs. 'Is this police business, Mr Denton? Much as we owe you, much as I trust you, I can't have you doing police business.'

Denton told him about Goldensohn's coachman.

'Didn't we interview him? We must have. Why didn't I hear this from my people?'

'Maybe he wasn't drunk. Maybe they didn't pay him.'

Morriss pressed a button; when the sergeant appeared in the doorway, he said, 'Get me the name of whoever caught the Goldensohn murder. Probably in H Division.' He began to twirl a pencil in his fingers. 'Look, I don't think I can let you talk to Galpin if you mean to ask him about Ginger Goldensohn. That's for a detective to do. If you're wondering why we haven't done it already, it's because we've had no reason. There was no connection. Not recently, anyway.' He dropped the pencil, looked at a wall clock, put his hands flat on the desk. 'Miles Galpin was a petty thief and confidence man—ran the runaway-boy trick with a kid. He somehow got into Goldensohn's circle. Kind of court jester—always had a joke, made people laugh. A sort of charm—essential to a successful confidence man. But he was a through-and-through villain, and he could be mean as sin. Then he got older; so did the kid he was using for the game, got too big for the game. Galpin went on the booze and killed somebody—his mean streak. Twelve years hard. Why would it matter if Goldensohn visited him in Reading?'

'It's a loose end.'

Morriss frowned. He looked as if he might be reminding himself how grateful he was to Denton. 'We don't deal in loose ends, Mr Denton. I think you mean it's a possible connection. It'll be taken care of, now I know about it.'

'In due time?'

Morriss nodded. 'We're stretched, as I told you.'

'And I'm not to talk to Galpin.'

'I'm terribly sorry. No, you're not.' That was final, his tone said.

'May I visit the prison?'

'I can't keep you from looking at a prison. That's the warden's business. What are you getting at?'

'Galpin's visitors.'

Morriss studied his pencil. He looked at the clock. 'I can give you a letter to the warden asking for all cooperation, short of your talking to any prisoner. It's unusual, but I'll do it.' He might be endangering his own arse, he meant.

'That's more than I was going to ask for, Superintendent.'

'Let's say it's for Donnie Munro.'

The morning's mail was laid out next to his armchair. There was the usual stuff, none of it welcome, and a cheap envelope with an address near University College. Inside was a note from Miss Heckham saying that she'd had a reply to her letter to Guyenne et Sarmonteux Frères (enclosed), which she'd taken the liberty to translate as follows:

> *Dear Mademoiselle,*
> *I have been instructed by the directors to inform you that they have no knowledge of the writer Balzac, nor do they know of any myths or legends about the said Balzac and any antecedent member of this distinguished family. We would caution you that any implication to the contrary could be cause for legal action.*
> *With all cordiality, Francois Rémy, Secretary to the Board.*

He waved the letter at Atkins, who had come up the stairs. 'The French never heard of Balzac.'

'Neither did I. Is this important?'

'Having to do with H. James's missing box.'

Atkins waved that away. 'Look here, I came up to ask you— you want to see the films I made at James's tea party? Tomorrow's the day if you do. Two in the p.m., behind the Alhambra. First look before we do what's called edit them.'

He so clearly wanted Denton to say yes that that was what he said.

Denton looked back at Miss Heckham's note. There was a PS. 'They are so typically French in their *hauteur*. I may be doing better with Marie-Célimène's wedding. I'm on the track of a newspaper notice! More tomorrow (I hope).'

Denton went upstairs and stared at the paper on which he had now an entire page scribbled over with notes that started *The Monster.* After a while, he turned the page over and wrote, *The child—their child. Grows up. Doesn't know man is the father? Mother incites him to confront father, now old man, with gun. Father lets himself be shot down. Then mob lynch mother and son.*

A bit lurid, when he thought about it. *Good.* Right up Lang's alley.

The motion-picture offices on Charing Cross Road were in an undistinguished, deeply drab building whose outside gave nothing away. Inside, young men in very dark suits and shiny hair whizzed about as if they'd been launched from guns and had wheels instead of feet. Denton had expected the exotic, maybe the scientific; instead, he got commercial frenzy.

'Is it always like this?'

'Day and night. Second floor.' Atkins indicated a lift.

'I'd rather walk.'

'No you wouldn't. Knock you down as soon as look at you, this lot.'

The viewing room—a sign on the door said that was what it was—might have done for a Rotherhithe penny theatre: mismatched chairs in not entirely regular rows, a white cloth screen, a smell of chemicals and damp. Atkins went to the back to make sure his films were ready, then stood by an electric switch.

'Any time,' a bored voice said from the rear. The lights went out.

A machine began to clatter behind them as Atkins made his way among the chairs. He threw himself into the one next to Denton, said, 'I confess I'm a bit nervous.'

The screen became bright white, then black, then flickered with what looked like fireflies. Abruptly, Denton saw himself coming out of a black-and-white, apparently pasteboard mock-up of Lamb House.

'No titles yet,' Atkins whispered, as if there were other people who might object. 'Put those in later. We shot you leaving first, remember? Title—"The End of a Perfect Day".'

'Perfect day, my arse.' Denton watched himself leave Lamb House three times. He looked as if he'd been fitted up with mechanical limbs. It was horrible.

'Well, that'll do,' Atkins said. 'Not bad at all.'

Suddenly Denton was arriving at Lamb House. The door opened. Henry James appeared. Without a title to identify him, he might have been a butler, probably a drunken or demented one, because he never stopped grinning.

'Brilliant,' Atkins said.

They had had to do the arrival three times. Each was more excruciating than the one before. Denton found himself putting his fingers over his eyes.

'Hard to choose among those,' Atkins said.

'I'll say!'

Without transition, he and James were coming out into the garden. James was holding a book as if he meant to thump Denton with it. He raised it over his head. He might have been in the midst of a speech at Hyde Park Corner.

'Nice. Nice. The book was an inspiration,' Atkins muttered. 'This part will have the title "The Two Authors Discuss Modern Literature".'

'Atkins, dear God...!'

'You got to remember the audience, General. They don't know any authors. What are they going to think you talked about, girls?'

To Denton's relief, his image disappeared.

'Title—"At the Garden Party".'

This was when Atkins and the camera had been off in the trees. A lot of jerky movement was shown, people with some sort of nervous condition bobbing back and forth across a lawn like marionettes, men and women, all of it meaningless, nothing much happening. The camera seemed fascinated with them; it went on and on, swinging from side to side and back to take it all in—the rear of Lamb House, chairs, a window with the crippled woman visible, more chairs, a maid with a tray, more figures with St Vitus's dance, flower beds, a man eating with a fork and staring at the camera.

'I can take that to the bank,' Atkins said. 'Even better than I'd hoped. A real sense of the *bone tone*. I only wish I'd got them to play croquet.'

And then far across the garden, Henry James was seemingly alone, playing with Nicco. He threw a ball. Nicco chased it, fell over himself, got the ball, raced back. James applauded.

'What's this going to be called?' Denton said. '"A Boy and His Dog"?'

'I was thinking of "The Great Man at Play", or possibly "The New Dog". Nice human touch. Makes him real. There was other people there, but they were behind a tree. He didn't know I was cranking. You get the best stuff that way, people don't know they're being filmed. Real.'

The screen turned dazzling white. The voice behind asked if they wanted to see it again; Denton said in rather strong terms that he didn't; Atkins said he didn't need to see it again just now.

Atkins bumped his way through the chairs and turned on the lights. One of the shiny-haired young men was leaning against the back wall. He said, 'Bloody marvellous. I'm sure we'll take a couple dozen prints at least for the British Isles, Atkie, plus it'll be corking in France and Germany, they love artistic stuff there. And two Americans in it, it's sure as shit for the US. Stop by L.D.'s office and work it out, will you?' And he launched himself through the door and sped away on his wheels.

Atkins was grinning. 'Well!' he said. He somewhat dramatically mopped his face with a pocket handkerchief. 'I was that worried it'd be a dud.' He blew his nose. 'What do you think, General?'

'I think there's something wrong with either my eyes or his.'

He spent the night with Janet, including another dull supper with her and Walter, which she pronounced absolutely fine. 'You're growing on him,' she said.

Very slowly, he thought.

In bed, post-coital, he said, 'I don't understand the moving pictures.'

'You don't like the theatre much, either. You like reality.'

'That's what Atkins sees in his pictures—reality! As if he's going to show people the *real* thing. In jerky black-and-white.'

'Well, you think you give people the real thing in black-and-white on a page.' She was lying mostly on top of him, her legs still spread over his; her head was beside his on his pillow. 'I rather like reality without the trimmings. This sort of reality, anyway.'

He thought about that and decided it was a kind of compliment. He said, 'I'm thinking of going up to Reading tomorrow.'

'Reading, good God. Speaking of reality.'

'I thought I'd send my book proposal off to Lang and then take the day off.'

Janet hoisted herself up on her elbows. 'Are we going to engage in this reality again?'

'You expect a lot of an ageing man.'

'Take it as a compliment.' She got off him, pulled on a somewhat ratty cotton nightgown and went out, came back a couple of minutes later and said, as she was pulling the nightgown over her head, 'Ageing indeed. We're all ageing, Denton.'

He held out his hands and pulled her to him.

Miss Heckham came so early next morning that he was still at Janet's, and Alfred, returned to duty but nervous, was sent through the gardens to summon him. Finding Denton at breakfast in somebody else's house was apparently too much for him; his accent got so thick that Denton couldn't understand what was wanted. With his breakfast still unfinished, he went to his own house and asked Atkins, who jerked a thumb upwards. 'The University College female.'

'Good God, it's barely eight!'

'Alfred mucked it up, did he? Didn't get the message right? I'll flay him alive.'

Denton, muttering, 'Now, now,' went up and found Miss Heckham in his armchair with a cup of tea. She jumped up, but he told her to sit still.

'I'm terribly sorry it's so early, but I absolutely *must* do some work for somebody else today. A scholar!'

'Ah. Well, in that case...' Meaning, *Get on with it.*

'I've found Joshua Hardaker!' She grinned. She was tremendously pleased with herself.

'Joshua.'

'Yes, it was only "J. Hardaker" in my source, but I asked one of our faculty, a specialist in names and places and things, and he said that Hardaker's a Yorkshire name. Well, that didn't help just then, but I went down to the BL and flailed about a bit and finally asked a librarian for help. They're all alike down there; they don't like women and they think they're there to keep people from using the books, but I said that I was doing research for a published author, and I said *he* so he'd know you were male, and he began to help me out and then got all caught up in the hunt. He also turned out to be *not*— well, you know—he seemed to warm to me as a female.' She tittered. 'He knew to look in something called *Eminent Men of the Day*, which has had oodles of editions, so we had to go through them by the score, but we found a Hardaker—who was from Yorkshire, actually—an industrialist, metals and so on, in fact built one of the first cast-steel outfits, if it matters. Well, on we slogged, and there in a later edition was Simon Hardaker, who'd inherited from the first one we found, so I could see where the Sarmonteux had got the money to go into the *parfumerie,* couldn't I. It was the reverse of the *dot*, don't you think? Not an impoverished European marrying a wealthy American girl, but an impoverished European girl marrying a wealthy English boy! I suppose the Sarmonteux were willing to sell off a daughter for a good price.' She frowned. 'I'm rather a socialist, don't you see.'

'You've done very well.'

'There's more! My librarian—I shan't say "friend", but he was really being rather nice by then; in fact, there may be something going on there…well, that's personal. He said he thought it wouldn't have been beyond the arrogance of a big industrialist to put a notice of his son's marriage to a French aristocrat in the newspapers, and that's where it was! Not in a *French* one, but an *English* one. More than one, in fact! There was ever so small a bit in the *Times,* only the sort they run down the left-hand edge with no story, but—oh, I should say that at this point I had to go down into a *cellar* and deal with old newspapers that were wrapped in brown paper that was *filthy*! But there it was, in the *Leeds Astonisher* or whatever they called it back then—I've it written down somewhere—Mlle Sarmonteux de Guyenne and Simon Hardaker of Ilkley! *Ilkley!* It's near Leeds, as it turns out. The works are actually in Bradford, but the family manse is in Ilkley—I'll wager they started out in Bradford, living right in the works to keep an eye out that the workers were being sweated for good value, but once they'd made a pile they headed for the country! And I have the address!' She waved a paper. She waited. 'I'd hoped that as it took me an entire day and is *not* in my area of specialisation, you might see your way to pay a bit more.'

Denton was smiling. 'Usually we pay more for special knowledge, not the lack of it.'

'Well, I mean—I worked so hard! And I am competent! I know how to do research, Mr Denton, and that isn't a skill that many people have!'

He laughed. 'Don't get your dander up. You did a fine job. Of course I'll pay.' He did so, realised he had rather spoiled her mood, knew there was nothing he could do about it.

When she had gone, he carried the piece of paper with him up to his bedroom and immediately wrote to 'The Hardaker Family' at the Ilkley address. He repeated the tale, now nearly true, that he was an author doing research on the youth of famous men and sketched the Balzac Marie-Célimène story, pointed out that Marie-Célimène seemed then to have married Joshua Hardaker. Did they know anything of the Balzac legend? Did they have memories of Marie-Célimène herself?

For a moment, he had a fantasy of the Hardakers' having staged the James burglary to recover Grandmama's Balzac mementos, but he got over it. He scrawled 'Yours most sincerely' and his name and scrabbled about for an envelope.

Then he remembered that he hadn't finished his breakfast, but when he got to Janet's she was gone and the remains of his breakfast had been taken away.

He made himself coffee on his spirit burner and filched some bread and jam from the downstairs cupboard; and then, perhaps to make the lie about writing a book less untrue, he wrote a proposal for a short book (he emphasised its shortness) about the early peccadilloes of famous authors and artists. For example, Balzac. And Poe, he thought, there had to be a good story about Poe, who had been practically a cradle-robber. Then he wrote a proposal for *The Monster,* and when he had written out a fair copy of both, he gave them to Atkins, who sent Alfred to the postbox with the letter to the Harakers and went himself for a commissionaire to hand-carry the proposals down to Denton's publishers.

Then Denton started off for HM Prison at Reading, a journey that took him again through the disliked Paddington— twice—and yielded as much as if he had stayed at home and played with the dogs. The warden was too important to see him; the deputy warden was too convinced of his own worth to make him any concessions; a letter from a superintendent at Scotland

Yard meant less than one from any member of the prison board might have. Denton could not be allowed to see the visitors' book; he could not see any recent entries in any prisoner's file; he could not talk to the guards on any wing.

Reading was a model of a modern prison (built 1844) and had the highest standards. Unspoken was perhaps a need to shake the reputation it had had ever since Oscar Wilde had written *The Ballad of Reading Gaol*, which had used to be its correct name and was what most people still called it.

'So Ginger Goldensohn makes two trips to Reading Gaol in the months before the James burglary. What does it mean?' Denton was sprawling in his own armchair, his feet on a hassock. The windows were open to coax some of the summer night indoors in hopes it would be cooler.

'It means you can't trust a drunken coachman. Probably can't trust him sober, for the matter of that.' Atkins was leaning against the window frame, looking down into the lamp-lit street. Both had sherry.

'But let's say the coachman is all Sir Garnet.'

'Oh, well, for the sake of argument, then. So Ginger goes to see his old pal in chokey. Old man, lonely. Relive old times. Bit of goosing.'

'Twice in a couple of months?'

'Why not? Nothing to do, lost his pedestal—said so himself, didn't he?—so he goes to get some flattery. Take a cake, some dirty mags, ciggies, lag would fawn like a dog.'

Denton stared at his boots. 'I think Ginger went up to Reading to talk to Galpin about the James bust.'

'You're making it up, Colonel! That's what you *want* it to of been, but wanting don't make it so.' Atkins sipped his sherry. 'Lot of activity at the Lamb tonight. Fellow just came out, drunker than they ought to allow in a proper public house. I shall have a word with Sam next time I'm in.' He shifted his weight and looked at Denton. 'But let's play your game: Goldensohn goes to Reading, has a confab with What's-His-Name, and, what—he tells the pal he wants to rob Henry James while he's away in America? Doesn't make sense.'

'No, the other way around.'

'The lag wants Goldensohn to rob Henry James? Whatever for? Furnish his drawing room in Reading Gaol?'

'It's all about the box. The Balzac stuff. I told you.'

'You told me James could be embarrassed, full stop. The lag wants to embarrass H. James? Far-fetched, Major.'

'Embarrass him, blackmail him, worry him. I don't see any other way to understand the burglary except as a cover for taking the box. Yes, there would have been money if they'd fenced the stolen goods, and maybe not a bad sum, especially if Wragge had managed to jack up the insurance offer. But they didn't! It was as if the loot was secondary. Unimportant. The loot may in fact have been important to Wragge, not the anarchists.'

Atkins grunted. 'The wrong kind of copper might make a nice living, setting up burglaries and then dealing with the insurance fellows.'

'But that's nothing to do with Goldensohn. Goldensohn goes to Reading; Galpin says, "I've got a job I want somebody to do." Goldensohn goes home, looks around. He settles for some reason on a bunch of anarchists. Maybe they're cheap. Or maybe nobody else wanted to go all the way to Rye. But why are the anarchists willing? They aren't smash-and-grab artists.'

'All right, I'll be a good chap and say, "The automatic pistols."'

'Damned hard guns to get for free. Guns are difficult enough to get in England, now there's licensing. And these are special guns—powerful, fast-firing, fast-reloading. Miles beyond what the police have. Maybe they didn't really want to do the burglary much at all, and so they thought of something outlandish as payment—"Bring us a box of Mauser automatics." Or maybe they saw it as a chance to pull a special job. Assassinate somebody with a barrage. Anyway, yes, they wanted the Mausers.'

'Which Goldensohn just happened to have in his attic.'

'No, which somebody would have to get. From the German factory, maybe, as the guns were all in a series, suggesting a factory box of them.'

'The old man trots off to Germany?'

'No, but…I don't see Goldensohn getting involved. It was never his way. No, I see Ginger going back to Galpin—that's the second visit—to say, "All right, these are the lads, but you got to get them Mauser pistols."'

'Loony. Nobody'd take the risk, not to mention the cost and the bother.'

'It's personal. It's like a huge joke—like putting a po on the top of a church steeple. Enormous effort, but people do it. A joke on Henry James. Bring the great man low.'

'You have a candidate?'

'Not yet.'

Atkins stared at the street. 'So if the old man keeps his fingers out of the pie, how does he deal with the anarchists? Through Wragge?'

'More likely his bodyguard. Who's gone missing. I suspect it was he who told the anarchists that Goldensohn had turned stag. Either he's doing a hell of a job of hiding, or they did him when they did Goldensohn. They're ruthless enough.'

'Ruthless enough to do Wragge, too?'

'Wragge was already dead before Goldensohn shopped them. I'm afraid that really was the wives.'

'No offence, Captain, but I believe you've built a house of cards on a foundation of sand. And the sandy part is, why does an old lag in Reading Gaol want the eminent author's house burglarised? He probably never heard of Henry James, let alone this Balzac!'

'He's just a go-between, too.'

'For who?'

'Well, if I knew that, I wouldn't be sitting here jawing, would I? It's why I wanted to see the Reading visitors' book.

I'll lay you three to one that Galpin had another visitor not long before Goldensohn, and that he had that same visitor after Ginger went to see him the second time. But as I couldn't see the visitors' book, it's time I gave that to the police.' Denton looked gloomy. 'Except they won't tell me what they find.'

'Bribery,' Atkins said.

'Bribe Guillam or Morriss? You're crazy.'

'Not Inspector Guillam! Somebody at Reading Gaol! Prison guards, worst-paid servants of the Crown in Britain. Worse even than the army, and I can tell you that's bad enough. You hungry?'

They talked about sausage and eggs, sausage and bread, fried tomatoes and sausage. Denton guessed there was a sausage somewhere downstairs, jokingly suggested sausage and spaghetti. Atkins, who looked upon Italian food as a plot to weaken British resolve, made a face. Denton said, 'Sausage *and* eggs *and* bread. You fry up eggs for yourself; hand one up to me uncooked. I'll cook spaghetti for one on my gas ring while you do the others, toss in the egg and some cheese and maybe some breadcrumbs. And gammon or bacon, got any crumbs of that? You don't have to watch me eat if you can't bear it.'

'Those Italian visits of yours are corrupting you, Major. Another good man gone.' He started downstairs. 'I'm getting Rupert off to the veterinary surgeon day after tomorrow. Because he's in pain, remember?'

'Or so said Walter. Our medical expert.'

'More things under heaven and earth than you dream about, Colonel.'

They ate in companionable silence, the subject of James and Goldensohn and Reading Gaol talked out. For now.

The next afternoon, he got an envelope from Geddys, the art dealer. In it was a printed circular, unfortunately for Denton in German. It was a list, one item circled by Geddys having only the recognisable name *Honoré de Balzac* featured on a separate line; Denton saw 'Balzac' several more times in the short paragraph below.

He snatched up a hat and headed for University College, tracked down Miss Heckham with the help of the porter. She was displeased to see him but said that of course she read German; German was the language of scholarship. She grudged him enough time to look at the piece of paper.

'It's a kind of catalogue. Oh, I see, it's page five. An auction catalogue. The circled items—oh, it's Balzac stuff, all of it. Oh, Heaven—an unpublished *conte*! And letters from Balzac to— they're to Marie-Célimène!' She looked at Denton. 'Did you know about this?'

'Some of it. There should be a box, too—any mention of a box? Made in Florence?'

She shook her head.

He held out his hand for the notice. 'Where's the auction?'

'It doesn't say. You need the other pages. Are you going to *buy* an unpublished Balzac?' Her eyes looked hot behind her glasses. The scholar's avarice.

He offered to pay her, and she said with a good degree of frost that payment was hardly necessary. As that was also Denton's view, he left it at that and headed for Geddys's shop.

'Didn't take you long,' Geddys said with a malicious smile. Denton was reminded of Miss Neville. Did the twisted body twist the sensibility within?

Denton said, 'I wouldn't have come at all if you'd given me the whole list or whatever it is. You sent me one page.'

Geddys fumbled around in a drawer and pulled out some pages and held them out.

'I don't read German, Geddys.'

'Of course you don't! The wonder is you read English.' Geddys looked at the pages. 'Turin, Italy. What day's the twenty-fourth? Friday, I think. Next Friday.'

'Next Friday! Why the hell didn't you give me some warning?'

'One thing I particularly like about you, Denton, is your capacity for gratitude. I sent you the damned page as soon as I got it. The auction house didn't send it direct to me; I'm not a big enough customer. It got sent on by a friend in the business. And he didn't send it until I mentioned the Balzac stuff as something I was interested in.'

'Next Friday, good God.' Denton sighed. He'd have to tell Henry James; maybe James would go. He said, 'How much do you think that stuff will sell for?'

Geddys looked at the pages. 'Estimated sale price on the *novelette* is two to three thousand francs—a hundred pounds or so. The letters, a third to a half of that.'

'There wasn't any mention of other letters? They'd be in French. Not from Balzac, but... How about a box? Made in Florence.'

Geddys looked through the papers again. 'No other letters. Here's the box, though. It's on a different page. 'Box, Florentine, eighteenth century.' Fifty to a hundred and fifty, not much. More my kind of stuff.' He turned his head up to Denton. 'You going to Turin?'

'God, no. Why the hell are they selling these things in Italy?'

'Convenient spot to get to from all over Europe.' Geddys picked up a tiny bronze thing, maybe a gold weight, looked at it, blew invisible dust off it. 'This Balzac stuff stolen?'

'Maybe. You think there's time to stop the sale?'

'A word of advice, although you never listen to me. If you try to stop the sale, they'll withdraw the items and you'll lose sight of them.'

'The police can deal with that.'

Geddys laughed. 'The Italian police? Anyway, you'd have to prove ownership. Can you prove ownership to an Italian magistrate?'

Denton had had dealings with an Italian magistrate. Still worse, James would never admit in public that he was the owner. The letters to him, the letters from the man to whom he'd played 'coquette', as he'd put it, were the proof of James's ownership, also the things he feared being made public. They didn't seem to be in the sale; they were no doubt being held, probably by whoever had stolen the box and its contents, as a weapon if James should make a move.

'I need to send a telegram,' Denton said.

'Golden Square.' Geddys pointed over his shoulder with his thumb. 'East side, next to the school. Post office.' As Denton started out, he said, 'You might buy something, or at least say thank you.'

'Thank you, Mr Geddys.'

He sent a telegram to James to tell him about the sale, the date and place, then walked home. He left his coat and hat in his own house and went through the gardens to Janet's. Coming in through the back of the house, he was surprised to hear the rumble of a heavy male voice, then a lighter laugh, also male. Then both voices laughed, and he could hear Janet saying something. He went to the front of the house and to the sitting-room, where she kept her piano.

'Guillam!' he said. 'Don't get up.'

Guillam was smiling and looking rested and at ease on the little sofa. Walter was sitting next to him in a hard chair, as if he wanted to be close but not close enough to touch. Janet was sitting behind a tea wagon that was so loaded with food that he guessed that Mrs Cohan had baked that morning. Janet began to fill a cup for him without asking. Guillam said, 'I decided to bite the bullet and simply come by. Mrs Striker's nice enough not to mind.'

'The wonder is that Mrs Striker was home early from work.' She handed up Denton's cup and saucer. 'Try the things with the black seeds on them; something of Leah's.'

'Damned good!' Walter said.

'Don't swear, dear.'

'I was being positive. Anyway, Denton swears. Why is "damned" swearing? It's in the Bible.'

Guillam laughed. Again, the laughter was open and easy. 'That's where all the swear words are, lad. That's where we get them from.'

'Is this like ladies not looking when their dogs are doing it?'

'Very much.' Janet offered more tea to Guillam with a lifted eyebrow; he held out his cup. Guillam and Walter talked together; the subject seemed to Denton to be police court and what truth was, but he was distracted by Janet. She murmured that Guillam forbade discussion of the Wragge case because of Teddy—Mrs Wragge's solicitor and Janet's boss. 'I feel a little left out,' she whispered. 'They're like lifelong chums.' She nodded at Walter and the policeman.

Guillam was turned sideways on the sofa, one leg thrown over the other, an arm along the sofa back and his head tilted as he smiled and laughed. Walter looked bright-eyed, even—the word had never fit before—happy. What did they see in each other?

He thought of Walter's use of 'pain' and 'safe'. Did they see pain in each other? Did they see safety?

'I have to go,' Guillam said. Walter said that no, he mustn't, but Guillam said that he had work in Stoke Newington; he'd be working until midnight as it was. He smiled at Walter. 'Don't become a policeman, lad.'

'Oh, no, sir. I'm going to be a horse-leech. Unless I'm a motion-picture maker.'

Denton walked Guillam back to his own house. He asked if there was anything new; Guillam scowled. Whatever lightness, cheer he had shown at Janet's, he had shucked off. 'I can't talk about it.'

'Same old Guillam. All right, maybe I can tell you something.' Denton shooed Alfred out of the way and stood with one hand on the inner knob of his front door, telling Guillam about Goldensohn's coachman and his own trip to Reading. 'The deputy warden wouldn't give me his used truss, but he'll give you whatever you ask for.'

'How many times do I have to tell you to keep that big nose out of police business?'

'Tell the super of Central CID; he's the one who gave me the letter to the warden. The point is, Guillam, there could be something there.'

'What?'

Denton didn't feel like spelling it all out; it seemed very thin when he thought about it from Guillam's point of view. 'All I'm saying is that if Goldensohn went there to talk to a convict, maybe that had something to do with the James burglary.'

'Denton, the James burglary has sunk to the bottom of my pile. He's got his goods back. I'm running as fast as I can with all the other crimes in Islington. I don't have the time to go to Reading and I don't have a tec I can take off of something else to do it. They're supposed to send me a new DC; if he shows up, maybe I'll send him to get his feet wet. Don't push me.'

Guillam waited for some reaction, got only a shrug, finally shook his head and said he had to go.

Denton went upstairs and started through his mail. He heard a ring at the door, got to the top of his stairs in time to see Alfred racing for the door. He thought it would be Guillam, something forgotten, but it was a telegram from James. He gave Alfred a coin for the telegraph boy (actually a man in his forties) and tore it open:

DO NOTHING STOP COMING LONDON AT
ONCE STOP MEET ME REFORM CLUB HALF
NINE STOP JAMES

Denton was led up two flights of stairs and then along a surprisingly unfurnished-looking corridor that might have served some sort of dormitory—worn carpet, a single small table with a lamp, both looking as if they'd known a better life elsewhere. The porter knocked at a door and James opened it, didn't smile but simply stood aside. Outside, a summery evening was blowing up, dry so far, leaves swaying, loose bits of paper skittering over the pavements and rising into the air. Denton could feel it as soon as he entered the room, an open window letting the air in, puffing the curtains.

James looked scrubbed and just shaved, odd for that time of night; his face was pink, his jaws shiny. He said almost nothing except to offer brandy and coffee. Denton took both and withdrew to the most comfortable chair he could see. The room was not, as he had expected, Lamb House in miniature. It was by comparison monastic, the furnishings in the club's economical taste, not James's. A few knick-knacks and a drawing of James himself made it only a shade homier. A bed was not to be seen.

James let himself down into a faded chintz chair and passed a hand over his face. He looked like somebody who had given up on life—all of it, even the comforts of dogs and old triumphs. He said, 'I'm so very sorry about what happened between you and Gosse.'

'You apologised for that in Rye.'

'It isn't only apology, it's—oh, dear, one so wants one's friends to like each other! I know that what Gosse said seemed to you, mmm, unwarranted, mmm, excessive...'

'What Gosse said to me was offensive.'

'I know, I know! I do feel so badly about it. Gosse means so well.'

'He doesn't. He wants to rule from his paper throne, handing down moral fiats.'

'He's quite the nicest of men. Truly, Denton, he is a dear, dear friend!'

'You didn't get me here to talk about Gosse, I hope.'

James put his head back and closed his eyes. 'No.' He breathed deeply twice. 'What you told me about the sale of the Balzac papers in Turino had an unhappy coincidence with my receipt of a letter from, from, mmm, *them*.'

Denton thought he knew what James meant but said nothing.

James opened his eyes. 'They want a hundred and fifty pounds.'

'For the letters?'

'That wasn't spelled out. But surely, for that sum...'

'Take the letter to the police, James.'

'No, no.' James's voice was a groan. He was as much frightened as depressed, Denton thought. 'I'm to hand the money over in Paris next week. Better to see the thing through.'

'There is no "through". They'll bleed you. For years.'

'I shall demand the letters. Refuse to pay more.'

Denton laughed, not kindly. 'That's fantasy. The hard reality of blackmail is that if you make the first payment, you're theirs for life.'

'No, no.' James closed his eyes again. 'Don't, Denton. I can't bear much more. If it's money, I shall pay. If I have to, I can come back here to live—sell Lamb House, if I must. I've thought it through.'

Denton snorted with disgust. He wanted to call James a coward but saw at the same time that James was showing a kind of courage, even grace: he was willing to pay for a mistake, a rare virtue. Denton said, 'I thought you might want to go to Turin for the auction.'

'Dear God, no.'

'Or maybe you'd want me to go.'

'No, no! You mustn't think of such a thing. It would call attention. Give people reason to think...'

James had passed beyond common sense, Denton thought. He tried to bring him back by saying, 'You'll be committing a crime, you know—concealing evidence.'

'I don't have any evidence.'

'Your knowledge is the evidence. Or so the police will say. Their view will be that if you had told them, they'd have caught the blackmailers.' He hesitated, then decided to tell it all. 'And if they catch the blackmailers, they'll catch the brain behind the killing of the four policemen in Clemence Street.'

'That had nothing to do with the intrusion at Lamb House!'

'I didn't use to think so. Now I believe that it had everything to do with it. And your Florentine box was the object of the intrusion. James, the police want blood for blood; they won't be nice to you.'

James stared at him and then shook his head. He stood, walked to a window, still shaking his head. After a silence, he said, 'The police will never know.'

'I'm afraid they will. I'm going to tell them in the morning.'

'You swore you wouldn't!'

'I said I'd respect your privacy until it meant breaking the law. Concealing evidence is breaking the law.'

'You can't!'

'I'm sorry, James.'

'It isn't honourable! It... You're supposed to be a gentleman.' James's nostrils flared; his face was dark with blood. 'Perhaps Gosse was right about you.' He was working himself up to a tantrum. 'You *villain*! I entrusted you with my reputation; I asked for your help, and you've done nothing, *nothing* but cause me trouble with the police. The police! Dear God—do you think a man like me has to do with the *police*? You had best leave.'

'Of course.' Denton got up. Not unkindly, he said, 'What are you going to do? My advice is—'

'I shall be well gone without any more advice from you. I had intended to go to Paris in a week, but I shall leave at once. Tomorrow!'

Denton picked up his glass, drained the last drop of brandy, put it down. 'There's no boat train until morning now. Scotland Yard keep detectives at Calais and Boulogne; they'll meet you there, thanks to the telegraph.'

'I shall be on French soil! They'll have no authority.'

'You're not on French soil until you've been through the *douane* and the control. The detectives would probably come out on the pilot boat, anyway. That's how they got Wragge's other wife.' James looked frantic, cornered. Denton said, 'If you take the ferry from Harwich to the Hoek, you'll be all right. You can get down to Paris from there. I'd try to get to Harwich tonight, though, if I were you.' He looked for his hat, found it on a chair. 'Or you could go with me to see Inspector Guillam in the morning and tell him everything.'

James's face was partly shadowed. He looked saddened now but determined, his anger and fright purged. 'Please go.'

Denton picked up his hat. 'I'll put off seeing Guillam until mid-morning.'

He found his way back through the bleak corridors and down to the more welcoming lobby, then walked through bright, sometimes festive West End streets. Somebody was giving a ball, the Season nearing its end; Denton moved among pretty young people in front of a brilliantly lit house, carriages and one motorcar standing along its kerb, more in a row halfway around St James's Square. There was a lot of laughter, the slamming of carriage doors.

He walked home, thinking about James, whom he found he pitied now. He thought too about Turin and the auction, thinking he should go, then that there was no point in going: he couldn't afford the Balzac papers, and what good would the empty box be? The papers wouldn't register any fingerprints, even if the thieves had handled them. The box, on the other hand, might. But wood didn't take fingerprints well. But the box was gilded, so it might. But the gilt was worn...

He was back to thinking about James when he turned in at his own gate. No Alfred this late to meet him at the front door; he let himself in, went quietly up the stairs, but he heard a muffled yip from Rupert or his son, and thirty seconds later Atkins appeared, a mashie in his hand.

'Thought you might be a drug-maddened anarchist.'

'Golf?'

'Oh.' He looked at the club as if he'd never seen it before. 'Pal gave it to me. Owed me two bob, gave me this.'

'One of the dogs made himself useful, anyway.'

'Bill.'

Denton had supper with Janet and Walter, the boy now fairly easy to be with. Afterwards, he told Janet about James and the blackmailer. 'D'you have any interest in going to Turin?' he said.

'Are you still on about that? What possible good could it do?'

'They might have somebody there. Watching.'

'Somebody there to kill you, like as not. Are you going?'

'I'm thinking about it.'

'Is James paying?'

'James has enough on his mind.'

She was exasperated with him but shook her head and seemed to get over it. But she wouldn't, couldn't go to Turin even if she wanted to: Teddy was pushing several cases forward and needed her. 'Anyway, I'm getting to the end of my first year as an articled solicitor's clerk—that sounds so Dickensian—and Teddy says I have to start thinking about how to make my case to the Board. There's the problem of my past. I shall have to get some extra-special endorsements. Munro, I think, would give me one.'

'He's not in much condition for it.'

'He's out of danger, surely.'

Denton shrugged.

'And Guillam. He was quite nice when he was here, And a couple of my teachers from University College. I'm boring you.'

He shook his head. 'You're so busy, and I'm not doing anything. Maybe that's why I'll go to Turin.' He held out his hand. 'Bed?'

'Only if I can bring my books.'

He groaned.

CHAPTER

14

A letter from Yorkshire came with the third mail of the day. The paper was heavy, laid, beautifully not quite white. At the top, 'Moor View' was embossed. Hand-written below it were the date and a more complete address, and then a message:

> *My dear Mr Denton,*
>
> *My brother has asked me to reply to your recent letter concerning the writer Balzac and our maternal grand-mother. The story you have heard is true! I have heard it again and again from the lips of* grand-maman *Marie-Célimène herself. It is very* Romantic *and quite* tragic, *although we console ourselves that if it had not been for the strict views of my grandmother's father, we would now be French! You as a writer would know far better than I what it must have cost the young Balzac to give up one of the products of his creative imagination, one of his* chil-dren, *if I may say so, but* grand-maman *insisted that he had, and that until her marriage it constituted the dearest possession of her young womanhood!*
>
> *We do not, alas, have the letters or Mr Balzac's unpublished story. Upon her betrothal to my grandfa-ther, Marie-Célimène's father insisted that the papers all*

be burned, and he stood by while the poor girl put one page after another to the flames and stirred the ashes until nought remained! However, she was a young woman of spirit (and a trifle naughty, I think), for, as she loved to recount, what she had burned were letters from other suitors whom her father had imposed upon her, as well as a literary production of her own at a young age. The fruits of Mr Balzac's labour (and of his love, if I may so say) were secretly given to a young nephew of hers, himself intensely Romantic and devoted to the story of her own lost amour. I shall not mention his name, for he is gone now, but I shall say that, so far as the family know, the papers have disappeared, for they were not among his effects. We had hoped to recover them to return them to their rightful owner (I mean my grandmother), who was then still living, but they were not to be found. It is my own belief that they were stolen by a servant who, knowing nothing of their value, sentimental or pecuniary, subsequently threw them away.

You asked in your kind letter if the condition and existence of the papers were known outside our family. I have no way of knowing what the recipient of the papers—I mean my dear grandmother's nephew—may have told or revealed. The Romantic story and its aftermath were of course matters of history within the family and so were discussed, although my brother felt and feels that no family of importance should be too liberal with its secrets. It is enough, and perhaps too much, that the myth of the young woman to whom Balzac gave his heart still persists, as your letter avows. I do know that my beloved grandmother often told the story herself, and on some occasions to listeners who were perhaps not its proper hearers. We have had to caution certain servants on the matter.

My brother wishes me to say that, while we have no wish to impede your work as an author, we must ask

that the name of our family, and indeed of my grand-
mother before marriage, be honoured as beyond the pale
of public awareness. He wishes me to say that any intru-
sion on our reputation would be cause to seek the aid of
our solicitor, although I know that such you would never
presume to commit!

If I am able to be of any further help to you, do let
me say as a lover of literature that you have only to put pen
to paper, and I shall reply.

Your most obdt, etc.,

Hypatia (Hardaker) Fitznaughten

Denton went down to Atkins's quarters. 'Are you working
for me or the motion pictures today?'

'Thought I might take the machine up to Aldwych and
Kingsway, which they aren't yet but are beginning to show
promise. Britain on the move—London ever building—all that.
Alfred's on duty, for what that's worth.'

'Where is he?'

'Made himself a lair out of the old pantry. Him and the
beetles. You want me today?'

Denton was carrying the letter in his hand. He tapped an
edge against a fingernail. 'What are the chances of getting still
photos from the stuff you shot at James's? You know, like cabinet
photos, *cartes de visite*, whatever they are.'

'Portraits? Quality'd be way off.'

'But recognisable?'

'Well, you and H. James will look like yourselves, o' course.
You want your own pic, is that it?'

'God, no.' He flourished the letter. 'There's a family in Yorkshire
has had an elderly woman telling the tale of the Balzac story and his
letters to all comers. I thought they might recognise somebody.'

'To do what? You think James's thieves were at his party?'

'It's a long tale, but it could be that the inside man on James's
burglary heard about the Balzac stuff up north.'

'Bit of a reach, innit?'

'Requires a very long arm. But somebody knew something, else they wouldn't have taken the damned box!' Denton blew out an exasperated breath. 'It won't hurt to send some photos up. Can we get pictures or can't we?'

Atkins shrugged. 'Let's have a look.'

Denton let Atkins drive. Finding a place to leave the vehicle in Charing Cross Road was impossible; Atkins finally threaded a needle with the motor-car and left it two streets away between a dray and a carriage, and they walked to the film offices. Atkins seemed to know everybody now; he nodded at the brisk young men, called most by their first names. 'Friendly business, films.'

Atkins wanted somebody named Maurice, who wasn't to be found until he thought to look in the room where they'd watched the film. 'Last place I'd expect to find you,' he said. Maurice, who was fat and slow, looked disgusted. 'I spend all day of every day of every bloody week in the year in here. Whatcha want?'

Atkins told him. Maurice objected. Atkins pleaded. Denton handed over a coin. Maurice went off to 'the vault' and Denton fidgeted. He ought to be telling Guillam about James's blackmail. When Maurice came back, he was carrying a reel the size of a wheel of cheese, 'Atkins Cinemantics 2 Fam Authors' written on a tag.

'Skip the early part, Maurice; what we want's the garden party.'

'Garden party, what the bloody hell do I know from garden parties?'

Eventually, a machine began to whir and tick, the lights went off, and Denton had to sit again through his multiple farewells and arrivals, the awful stroll in the garden. Then the shots with the other guests came up. He had to ask to see some of it again; there was a lot of backing-up of film, with curses as musical accompaniment from Maurice. Denton selected frames with Mr and Mrs Graham, the Lamb House tenants while James had been in America; Benson, simply because he had been bad-tempered; all of the young men; three older men who seemed to have given him equivocal answers. He picked out a couple of other faces for no better reason than that they were very clear. 'It's hopeless,' he said.

'Cripes, don't let Maurice hear you say that; he'll go into fits.'

Denton asked for 'stills', as Maurice called them, of those frames. He'd pay, of course. That seemed to cheer Maurice up. 'Want 'em enlarged?'

'What I want is the faces. Can you make them the size of— what? Like three inches by three inches, just the faces?'

'Mister, I can do anything if the pay is good.'

They drove back to Lamb's Conduit Street; Denton moved into the driver's seat and went up to Stoke Newington. Guillam, however, wasn't there. 'Gone off on a case to Mile End Road, sir. Going to be a bit of time, I expect.'

Denton said he'd telephone, thought of going home but wondered what was on Mile End Road. He'd been on Mile End Road himself recently—what for?

'Judas Priest.' Ginger Goldensohn's house was on Mile End Road, although Denton kept thinking of it as Whitechapel High Street. He scrambled into the motor-car and drove south and east. Two constables and several onlookers were standing by the gate where he had dealt with the coachman, and the gate was open.

Denton left the car in a side street and ran back, to be stopped by a constable at the beginning of Goldensohn's drive. 'Police business, sir. No admittance.'

'I have a message for Inspector Guillam.'

'Can't let you in, sir. Might be I could pass the word if you'll give me your name.'

Denton did so; the constable muttered to another constable, and he walked back and talked to somebody at the rear corner of the house. Then Denton was left to wait on the pavement until, far back towards the coach house, Guillam appeared. He looked about, found Denton, stared at him, then waved him in and disappeared again.

'Sorry to make you wait,' the constable said. He was at least fifty, placid, probably what an American cop whom Denton had known called a 'pigeon-cop', good only for chasing the birds away from statues.

'Now what?' was Guillam's greeting.

'I could say the same for you. What're you doing at Goldensohn's at this late date?'

Guillam made a face. 'Next-door neighbour reported a dust-up in the coach house, thought it was mayhem at the least. Turned out to be the carriage horses banging on the stalls. Close to kicked the stall down, one of them—they're big buggers. No water, no feed. And no coachman.'

'No mayhem?'

'Nah. Looks like he's scarpered, left the horses to take care of themselves, the sorry bastard. Like to have him in a cell and try it on him for a few days. Well, we'll find him.'

'What's it got to do with you? A couple of hungry horses don't get an inspector out.'

Guillam eyed him. He had lit a cigarette, now looked at it and sucked on it and blew out smoke. 'What is it you came all this way to tell me?'

'I came all this way because you're at Goldensohn's.'

'I thought that would be it—you and that big nose of yours. Who told you I was here?'

'The station sergeant at Stoke Newington said you were in Mile End Road. The rest was guesses.'

Guillam shook his head. 'So that was a lie about having something to tell me?'

'No. Henry James got a letter demanding a hundred and fifty pounds. Presumably for the embarrassing stuff that was in the box I told you about. Remember? I *did* tell you!'

'I remember.' Guillam sounded detached, maybe simply tired. He stepped on his cigarette, immediately took out the box and offered Denton one. 'Why isn't he telling me this himself?'

'I saw him last night. He said he was off to Paris. That's where he's supposed to make the payment.'

'Christ. Does he know what he's doing?'

'He seemed to.'

'A hundred and fifty quid's a lot of stiff. And that's the first payment? What the hell was in it, a picture of him having a knee-trembler with the Queen?'

'Potential embarrassment.'

'Well, he's for it now, the stupid old fart. I'll have him picked up in Calais. Goosens!' His bellow echoed in the brick-paved area between the stables and the house. The constable who had carried Denton's message came at a run. Guillam scribbled in a page of his notebook. 'What's the nearest railway station?'

'Bethnal Green Junction, sir. Hop, skip and a jump.'

'All right, hop up there and send this, marked urgent.' Guillam handed over money. 'Off you go.' He looked back at Denton. 'Your Henry James is a stupid twat. If we don't get to him in time and the French police do, they'll rake him over the coals. Both ends of blackmail are a crime over there.'

Denton thought of James in a cell, James in an interrogation room. James was perhaps the most sophisticated man he knew, but he would be a babe in arms in that setting. Guillam said, 'You should have stopped him.' Denton agreed but said nothing. Guillam finished his cigarette and tossed it away. 'Come on.'

'Where?'

'I'll show you what brought an inspector here.'

He led the way past the open door to the stable, where Denton could just see a big horse tearing at wisps of hay. 'What happens to the horses?'

'We've called some damned do-good society.' Guillam led him to a separate building, also brick, with two doorways, like a fire house, each a dozen feet wide. The farther door was open; two men in white smocks were working on an ancient vehicle of some kind. When Denton got close enough, he saw it was a closed carriage of a type that had disappeared in the seventies or earlier, black, shabby, small, with shafts for a single horse.

'A funny old carriage.'

'You bet it is. It's what those two harpies used to get Wragge's body up to Stoke Newington. The Gold woman knew about it, of course; she grew up here. My guess is she came during the day, paid the coachman whatever blood money he asked for to drive it.'

'This is fact?'

'H Div tecs interviewed up and down her street right after we found the body. Nothing, but I had them expand the search—this was before Clemence Street—and there was a woman a street away who said she'd seen a hearse. Just standing by the kerb, middle of the night. A hearse? Well, look at this thing.' He pointed at the carriage, which had an elongated body with a single tiny window. It was dead black and dusty. 'She said it might have been some sort of pantechnicon, but it looked to her like a hearse. Made her wonder who'd died.'

'You think Ruth Gold went to Ginger to get it?'

'Ginger would have dumped Wragge's body in the acid at somebody's works, or put him under the macadam at a building site. Ruth Gold has the brass to've gone to the coachman herself. I s'pose he helped get Wragge's body from the house to the carriage, but I wonder if that thing would hold the two women and Wragge and the coachman on the box. It's long, but it's narrow. All behind one horse? Maybe. That big one's a thumper. Pull a 'bus all by his lonesome, he looks. Anyway, that's neither here nor there right now. They're going over it for blood and fingerprints.'

'And if you find prints, you've got the women for conspiracy to conceal evidence.'

'At the least. Meaning I'll have evidence that will force the prosecutor to toughen the charges.' He turned on Denton. 'Satisfied?'

'I think the whole business with the women stinks.'

'Right. I'm fussing about two women who may have killed a bent cop, and now I've got to fuss about a goddam author who doesn't know his arse from an axe-handle, and meanwhile four cops are dead and others are in hospital, and we still don't know where those automatics came from or why. Anybody tried to kill you yet?'

'No. You hoping?'

Guillam grunted. 'I've put out a bulletin on the coachman. I'll put him in the room with a rozzer'll knock the truth out of him one-two-three, and then I'll have the women, at least. James I'll get in Calais, and from him we'll get the blackmailer. But I want it to fall together, and it won't.'

'Anybody gone to Reading yet?'

'Let it go, will you? We're up to our arses.' He walked over to one of the men who were searching the carriage. 'Anything?'

'Dirt on the floor. No fingerprints anywhere—wiped down like it was the parlour sideboard. Jackie found an old penny under the seat cushion, little cheer there.'

'Shit.'

'Live in hope, die in despair.'

Guillam gave the man an angry look and led Denton out to the gate. Denton said, 'I thought your people had been all over Goldensohn's after he was killed.'

'They were. They listed two carriages, no details. We didn't twig when we got the report about the "hearse", either—didn't see the connection.' He bit his lower lip with his front teeth and spat. 'If I don't get evidence to convict those women, I swear I'll leave the force!'

Driving home, Denton wondered if he should tell Teddy Mercer about the carriage, then knew he couldn't. Anyway, so far there was no proof it was the right one.

CHAPTER 15

He detrained in almost the centre of Turin, walking into a cityscape of arcaded streets and graceful old buildings, cafés common on the shaded pavements. He liked Turin on sight, its grace, its practicality, its lack of famous sights. It was a fine place, he quickly found, simply to be.

He had used his Baedeker to put himself up at a second-class hotel 'in the Italian style' called the Tre Corone; he wasn't sure what the Italian style was, but he liked it. Two seasons in Naples had given him a fairly fluent Italian and, apparently, a southern accent that made the Turinese smile. He had allowed himself a day and a night to recover from the train trip, although he found that he had arrived in good shape, thanks to the *wagon-lit,* and so instead of sleeping he walked.

He dawdled in shops and cafés. He bought a brooch for Janet and a bright-coloured pullover, also in the Italian style, for Walter. He ate too much at a *trattoria* and later in a restaurant, having in the second birds the size of sparrows on a spit. In the evening he, who rarely went to the theatre in London, went to one and understood only a fraction of what he heard.

On his second day, he went to the auction room in the Grand Hotel de Europe and looked over the items stolen from Henry James.

The Balzac letters and *novelette* had been given pride of place with a seventeenth-century diamond necklace and a Persian sword. Kept from damage by a glass case, the papers looked mundane enough: crabbed writing that he found hard to read on paper that had got long since dog-eared. Maybe Marie-Célimène had read them over and over. But what, really, was there to see? Nothing of either Henry James or the thieves, certainly.

He bought a catalogue in English (five francs, a hefty enough price) and saw that the provenance of the Balzac material was listed only as 'private party'. That apparently covered thieves as well as antiquarians.

He had to search for the Florentine box, which had been exiled to a corner farthest from the auctioneer's desk with some chipped pottery and half a dozen rusty muskets. It might once have been quite handsome; now, the gilt was faded and worn, and the lock, he could see, had been scratched, almost certainly in opening it to get at the contents. The catalogue made no connection between it and Balzac.

He toured the entire sale, was chatted at by an attendant who offered to show him anything in which he was particularly interested. He registered as a bidder, meaning he gave a rather slick young man his name and his bank and got in return a piece of white card with a number.

Number nineteen.

'You begin at two o'clock?' he said in Italian.

'Promptly, *signore.*' Said again with the northern amusement at the southern accent.

When he came back at a little after half past one, an ante-room was crowded, and in the sale room the entire front row of chairs and the centre of the second were already occupied, all by men who didn't look as if they had enough money to buy anything that was being offered. Was this part of the auction mystique? Did serious buyers disguise themselves? When other, better-dressed men came in, however, and the front-row men started to drift away, he realised that they had been place-holders. The real buyers looked as if they could afford whatever they liked; Denton thought they were probably staying in the hotel, the city's priciest, too.

He took a chair on an aisle five rows back. The place was going to be filled, he realised; the would-be buyers came in a rush just before two, as if there were no point in sitting down a moment too soon. Many of them seemed to know each other. A few women were sprinkled through the crowd. Denton studied them all, female and male, looking for any sign that one of the thieves or a murderous anarchist (in fact the same person?) might be there, but nobody except a tall, fair woman met his eye. She met it more than once. He wondered if she had a pistol or a grenade in her purse, or if, even less likely, she thought he looked young and virile and amorous.

On the dot of two o'clock, the auctioneer took his place, made a few remarks, told one joke and said he would sell 'the items of greatest importance', with a gesture at the cases directly in front of him, at four-thirty. He banged his gavel once and asked who would give him three hundred francs for this lovely copy of a Roman Venus? The Venus, half-sized, maybe cast rather than carved—Denton knew nothing about it—was being carried by two men in boiler suits, who hefted it to shoulder height and then strained to keep it there. The Venus went for a hundred and ninety francs.

This was the pattern of the auction: a request for a bid at the upper edge of what the auctioneer hoped to get, then an opening bid of half that or sometimes a good deal less, and then a very quick climb towards the real price. The auctioneer moved fast, sometimes too fast for Denton's Italian, even more so when he chose to work in German or French; the prices, most of all, escaped him, not least because he was trying to translate francs into pounds at twenty-five to one. While the auctioneer registered bids with the quickness of a machine, two other men in well-tailored suits stood below his podium, their eyes ranging over the crowd as if they, too, were looking for criminals; each time they saw a bid, they spoke but did not yell. It was all so tasteful, so mannerly, that it would almost have been possible to forget that they were talking about money.

At four-thirty, the Persian sword and its jewelled scabbard went for nine thousand and seven hundred francs. At four-thirty-seven, the Balzac love letters went for five thousand six hundred francs. Four minutes later, the Balzac story went for an even fifteen thousand. There was a spatter of applause, but it was overwhelmed by what greeted the sale of the necklace at eighty-four thousand, six hundred.

After that, there was a slow decline to the run-of-the-mill and the third-rate. Men began to drift away from the front row. By seven, only a hard core remained, Denton among them. He watched eighteenth-century porcelains go by, Greek amphorae (or their copies), slightly damaged tapestries, ormolu clocks, brass lamps, horse pistols, books. When the Florentine box came up, he almost missed it.

'One hundred and fifty?' the auctioneer said. 'One hundred and fifty? One hundred?'

Only then did Denton realise what the now weary man in the boiler suit was holding against his chest. He wasn't holding it high enough for Denton to see anything but a corner. Unthinkingly, Denton said, 'Hey!'

'One hundred francs! Thank you, sir.'

Denton opened his mouth to say he hadn't bid, but the slick young man was already standing next to him, peering at his number.

'Sold! One hundred francs.'

Christ, that's four pounds! Geddys had said that from the sound of it, he wouldn't give the box house room. Maybe five shillings.

Denton had seen somebody else take an item back to the auctioneer and get waved aside to the slick young man. It had worked, because the item had come up again later as 'sold earlier with a crack we had missed'. Could he claim a crack? The box was in his lap now. It seemed well made, heavy. He tried to open it, but it stuck. He tried again, failed, thought he knew what had happened: the lock had been jimmied but not broken, and when the things had been taken out and it had been closed, it had locked again.

Could he claim that he hadn't known it was locked? He looked around for the slick young man.

Then he thought, *If the thieves took the stuff out and closed it and it locked, then the only fingerprints inside are theirs and Henry James's.*

'This should have been sold hours ago,' he heard the auctioneer say. He looked up. The two boiler suits were holding up between them a length of fabric. It was glowing ivory, undoubtedly silk, with flowers worked on it in some sort of sewing—embroidery? It reminded him of Janet's at-home gowns. The colours were remarkable, the hand work unimaginable. There was enough of it there to make her a gown, he thought.

'A thousand francs? A thousand? Five hundred. Do I hear five hundred? Ladies and gentlemen, this is outrageous. This is seventeenth-century embroidered silk! Two hundred and fifty?'

But the fabric buyers, if there had been any, had fled. Denton wanted revenge for paying so much for the box. He said in English, 'Twenty-five.'

The auctioneer looked at him. He opened his mouth, probably to say something caustic, but said instead in Italian, 'That is more than I had, sir. I have twenty-five. Do I hear a hundred? A hundred? Fifty?' His voice faded. Somebody tittered. The gavel banged. 'Sold.' He looked down at Denton. 'To the English gentleman. *Quite* a good buy, sir.'

Denton went to the cashier's, a desk by the door, and paid up. The silk was brought to him in a clean but old white sack, as if it were somebody's laundry. He peeked inside to make sure it was the right thing. Even the glance was stunning. It was extraordinary stuff.

What if she hates it?

Then he'd sell it to Geddys.

It was almost eight. He had already checked out of his hotel, taken his one bag to the station. His train left at eleven. He would sleep, if he could, as far as the customs at Modane, then really sleep until somewhere beyond Lyon and the morning. He ate in a *trattoria* near the station and, for only a small tip, was allowed on the train early. By the time it began to glide out of Turin, he was lying in his upper berth with the curtains drawn on the busy corridor, drowsy and unaccountably pleased with himself. The trip, which had seemed so foolish, had not been a complete waste of time.

If Janet liked the fabric.

He awoke in the Mont Cenis tunnel. Was it the change in the train's rhythm? Or the flash of the oil lamps at intervals on the tunnel's walls? Or...?

He had been dreaming about the cat again. The cat was lost, but he could hear it. He searched for it, had to get into some sort of theatre for which he didn't have a ticket, and then the cat gave a terrible yowl and he woke.

It had been a sound. Not a dream sound, a real sound. Odd, because all sorts of sounds had reached him at the beginning as other travellers had settled down. Footsteps, muffled voices, the thud of a bag being dropped. But this sound... He knew that sound, if only he could remember it. It was the sound of, of...

The sound of somebody feeling a blade in his chest.

He came fully awake and sat upright; banged his head on the low wooden ceiling. Surely that had been a dream, that sound. A dream brought on by the murder of Goldensohn, maybe, or the dream about the cat.

Or not a dream. Maybe it had been somebody being stabbed.

He pulled himself to the far end of the berth and began to feel in the rack for his toilet kit. He wanted a weapon. The razor was the only thing he had. No guns allowed in Italy; maybe he'd been a fool not to risk one. But use it, and he'd be culpable. No...

Something changed. The slightest of movements in the curtain that separated him from the corridor. Was anybody in the berth below him? He didn't think so. The porter had said that the train was not full, in case he wanted to change berths to a lower. Now somebody was standing just there outside the curtain—just there where his chest would have been if he'd still been asleep.

A light moved past the window: another lamp on the tunnel wall.

Denton watched two fingers appear where the curtain divided in the middle. They felt down to the bed, then began to inch along it. More of the hand appeared. It was like watching a snake creep up on its prey.

The curtain lifted. The back of a head rose under it. Now the hand was guided by sight; if there had been more light, the man would have seen that that end of the bed was empty.

The other hand appeared. With a long blade like an elongated triangle.

Denton launched himself with a roar and fell on the man's head and back, feeling with his right hand for the other's. He heard a snarl and a scuffle of feet on the corridor floor. The man tried to rear back. Denton caught his right wrist and wriggled his own left hand under the other's left arm, trying to lift and turn him so that he could put his own hand against the back of the man's neck and so immobilise him, but Denton was above and kneeling and he couldn't make the lift, and the curtain was caught between him and the other. He twisted, and they both fell out into the corridor, the tough fabric of the curtain ripping with a sound like a saw going through wood.

Denton swung himself to his left and so landed on the man and on his own left arm; he felt a shock to the shoulder, then pain in the hand. He kept his grip. The man's right wrist was still in his own right hand, and he banged the hand and the knife on the floor.

'*Cosa succede?*' somebody called.

'*Eh—che bruttezza...*'

Denton rolled on his back and now could slip his hand behind the other man's neck and begin to push the head down. The man growled, then screamed, and Denton rolled them both back and pushed the head against the floor and got up on the man's back and rump as if he were going to sodomise him, and he shouted, '*Aiute me! Aiute me! Assassino! Assassino con coltello!*'

He couldn't see people, but he could hear them. Curtains were whipping back; feet were hitting the corridor floor; a woman was screaming. Denton saw a pair of feet approach;

apparently the newcomer saw the knife, and even though he was wearing slippers, he put a foot down on the knife hand and began calling for the porter.

Then people were all around them, two trying to haul Denton off, Denton saying he needed the police, the man was an assassin, he was going to kill him. Then the weight on the knife hand made the attacker let the knife go, and Denton got his right arm under the other's and then on his neck, and then he could really apply pressure.

Then a man screamed.

'*Il portiere e morto! Dio, dio, il sangue! Ah...!*' There was a sound of retching. He had found the porter in a pool of his own blood.

Two people helping, Denton got the attacker to his feet and pushed his head against the hard edge of the upper berth. Somebody else was moaning. A kind of chaos followed, then gradual calm as a porter was brought in from another car, and then a conductor. Denton's assailant was taken from him—a youngish man with a black moustache, some sort of dark uniform. In a heavy accent, the young man said that he was a policeman, but nobody believed him.

Denton went to where people had gathered around the door of the porter's little compartment. He was lying back on the bench, blood all over his shirt and waistcoat and the floor. He was dead.

'They took me off the train in Modane and held me for a day. You'd think I was the criminal.' Denton was home with Atkins, still exasperated. 'Everything was going blue blazes until then.'

'Cripes, and we thought you'd be safer over there.'

'The assassin was another anarchist. Told the Italian cops all about it—proud of himself. Cops were sure I must also be some sort of crook until they sent half a dozen telegrams back and forth to Scotland Yard. You feeling all right, Atkins?'

'Why wouldn't I feel all right?'

'You seem a little—not all here. Thinking about something else?' Denton studied Atkins's face, which seemed unusually solemn. He remembered that Atkins was to have taken his dog to the veterinarian's. 'How's Rupert?'

'Oh.' Atkins shrugged, looked away. 'Nothing to be done, the vet says. He says...' Atkins's mouth tightened. 'Maybe a year.' He shrugged. 'He gave me some pills. Rupert seems to be a little sprightlier.' He shrugged again. 'Too old and too far gone, the vet surgeon said. Wouldn't risk him in the ether.' He pressed his mouth tightly closed, then blew out air. 'At any rate, you ain't hurt?'

Denton put a hand on Atkins's shoulder, but the small man moved away. 'I'm sorry.' When Atkins said nothing, Denton took the hand back, became too bright and cheerful. 'No, I wasn't hurt, but the would-be killer was carrying a photo of me. Guess where it came from?'

Atkins looked horrified. 'Not my motion pictures!'

'No, but it was taken at James's garden party. The cops showed it to me—there's my mug, with a corner of James's goddam house in it!'

'I thought you were going to tell me that Maurice is an anarchist.'

'What I'm telling you is that somebody at that party took my photo and then passed it to a man who meant to put a shiv between my ribs! You should have seen the job he did on the porter—right up into the heart, one stab, that was it. I heard the poor bastard, a sort of groan and he was done. How's things in the house behind?'

Atkins seemed to become a little distant. 'Capital, couldn't be better.'

'Mrs Striker all right?'

'Better than. I heard her piano off and on of an evening.'

Denton started to go through the mail. 'Whoever spotted me at the auction, I never saw him. I don't think it was the one who tried to kill me. Hell's bells, they're a bad lot! Anything from Inspector Guillam?'

'You think I'm his con-fee-dant? He's never forgiven me for whacking him on the napper that time.' This had been years before.

Denton threw the mail into his armchair. 'I got the Florentine box.'

'Whatever for?'

'Four pounds. My mistake. Auctions are a mare's nest, especially in another language. My own fault.'

'So where is it?'

'The box? I dropped it at Scotland Yard on the way home. Slight chance there are fingerprints in it.'

'Oh yes—of some dago clerk..' There was a kind of desperation, not much humour in his voice.

Denton grimaced. 'You get those photos from Maurice yet?'

'Maurice said yesterday, then he said tomorrow, but tomorrow's Sunday. Monday, then.'

Denton started to say something more about Rupert but suppressed it. He carried his bag up to his bedroom, stripped and put on one of his comical rowing suits—flannel knee breeches, knee socks, short-sleeved flannel shirt with no collar—but left off the Eton cap, then went up to the attics and tormented himself for an hour. After he'd shot his parlour pistols and held his old Navy Colt at arm's length for five minutes, he came down again and lay in hot water for half an hour.

Denton finished the accumulated mail, then sat down at his desk and tried to make notes about James's burglary, the Clemence Street massacre and Wragge's death. He tried to do it in three columns, but things kept migrating from column to column. He tried drawing lines that showed connections, but he got what looked like a bicycle wheel with several hubs and too many spokes.

He wrote *To be done* at the top of a new sheet of paper.

Then *Get photos and mail to Yorkshire.*

He looked at that and wrote, *Get results of fingerprints in box*, added *if any.*

He thought about that, looked at his list, added, *Did Wragge leave a list of people fingerprinted after burglary?* He had to believe that such a list existed. Superintendent Morriss certainly had believed in it when Denton had given him the box that morning. Morriss had objected that if the box had come from James's burglary, then it should go to Guillam. Denton had persuaded him that Clemence Street was an outgrowth of the James burglary, the Mauser pistols the link, therefore a fingerprint in the box might tell them who had funnelled the pistols to the anarchists.

'It's far-fetched,' Morriss had said. 'If it wasn't you, I'd tell you flat no.'

'But it is me. And it needs to be done quickly.'

Morriss had frowned at him. 'It's a good thing you're not one of my coppers.' He had sighed. 'We'll do the best we can.' He had put the box on his desk. 'I think you'd better make a statement.'

'I just finished making statements to the Italians!'

Morriss had sent for a stenographer. Denton had made a statement about buying the box to return it to Henry James.

Now he looked at his own list and thought how feeble it was. If the Yorkshire Hardakers didn't recognise any of the photos from the garden party, or (more likely?) if they refused to look at them, that line was finished. If there were no fingerprints in the box, or if there were but they couldn't be matched to any of the fingerprints Wragge and his detectives had taken right after the burglary, then that possibility was finished, too. And that, so far as Denton could see, would be the end of it, except for James's blackmailer, and that would be between James and the police when he came back to England. If he did.

Denton pushed out his lips and wrinkled his nose, as if the list were giving off a smell. 'It stinks,' he said aloud. What had he missed? He thought it through but found nothing, then wrote it all out as a kind of story. A fairly long story, by the time he was finished. It was well after lunch by then; Atkins had sent Alfred up with a tray from the Lamb, and Denton had picked at it while he wrote his notes.

He read over what he had written. Nothing struck him.

When he was sure Janet would be home from the office, he started for her house, remembered when he was in the garden that he had bought the piece of embroidered silk for her, stopped, wondered if he should give it to her after all. Or should he have it wrapped? Or...? They didn't give each other gifts. She might be angry. Still, he went back and got it as well as the brooch he'd bought before the wonderful silk had even been thought of. Now, the brooch seemed tawdry. He left it on his desk, wondering what to do with it.

It seemed ridiculous, handing a woman a sack of cloth, but that was what he did, after he'd kissed her, the sack still in one hand. 'Something I bought,' he said, as if he were sorry he'd done so. 'Just something.'

She took the sack, frowned because she didn't like surprises, opened it as if she thought there might be a snake inside. The frown deepened. She put a hand in, apparently felt the fabric, then sat in a chair and began to draw the silk out, first by inches, then feet, then a yard. It spilled over her lap and down to her feet, the lustre of the silk almost a glow in the late sunlight. She stroked the embroidery and then looked up at him. He was astonished to see that tears were running down her cheeks—she who never wept.

'Janet ...!'

She shook her head and held out a hand. He took it, felt a grip as if she were drowning. Then she gathered the silk and the sack and ran from the room.

He heard her going down the stairs to the Cohans'. Leah Cohan was her seamstress as well as her housekeeper and cook. Denton waited, paced, opened a book, closed it, turned at her footstep and felt her put an arm around his neck.

'It's magnificent,' she said. 'Too good for the likes of me.'

'Nothing's—'

'We're going to see if Leah can make something without cutting it. Denton, where did you ever find such stuff?'

Then he told her about the auction and the box and the silk, and, eventually, the attempt to kill him.

'I'm quite sorry somebody tried to kill you. Was it bad?'

'Every time I go out without a gun, I need one.'

He took her to supper at a favourite Italian grocery-restaurant in Clerkenwell. They were eating greens with garlic and anchovies; she was dipping bread in a bowl of golden olive oil with black pepper and herbs, grinning at him and licking her fingers, when she said, 'Are you done with detecting now?'

'If there's nothing in that damned box, I'm stuck, if that's what you mean.'

She watched a platter of small fish go by. 'They have mullets tonight.'

'Atkins seems to have got himself into the dumps since I left.'

She sighed. 'Atkins and I had words about the dogs. I got impatient with him, and the poor man burst into tears. He told you that Rupert's been given a year?'

Denton nodded.

'I went to see the veterinary surgeon. It's less than a year, actually. But I did find that he's willing to try the new ether mask for dogs on the young one so as to neuter him—the operation's very quick; he thinks he needs to be under only a couple of minutes. I told Atkins I'd pay, but I'm in his bad books, anyway.'

Denton said, 'I suppose he thought he could just keep postponing it.'

'Whereas the truth is, we'd be so much better off if you were all clipped at birth.'

'That would end the human race, Janet.'

'A side benefit.' She grinned. 'Except that I wouldn't get gifts of eighteenth-century silk, would I?'

He spent the night in her bed. About two, he met Walter in the dark at the door of the WC. Walter said, 'Hello, sir,' and Denton said, 'Hello, Walter.' If they'd been wearing hats, they'd have tipped them.

Lying beside her next morning, Janet still asleep, he smiled at the memory. He wondered if people who liked Janet would always dislike him. His thoughts wandered to James—had he paid the blackmail money yet?—then to Guillam and Wragge and photographs and fingerprints, and then she woke and he persuaded her that she could both make love and go to early church, and he went home and stared at more pieces of paper for a while.

Atkins brought back thirteen photographs from the motion-picture factory. They were clear enough, some quite good, but Denton wondered why he'd included some of the people and ruled out others. Still, they were better than nothing. He took them to his solicitor and asked him to agree to a draft of a letter that Denton had written for him.

'Hardly legal prose,' Brudenell said with a smile. 'It's so very clear, Denton.'

'I just want something that will convince a rich family they ought to help me out.' He handed over the letter from Hypatia Hardaker Fitznaughten about the Balzac tale.

Brudenell read it, still smiling. 'Grandfather made the money, her brother's now running the works, she's widowed and come home to live with him. Fitznaughten is probably one of those good but poor county names, glad to marry the daughter of an industrialist. One's relieved she never tried to write books— the prose style, I mean. Yes, of course, I'll lend my legal weight to your appeal, but that's a thick stack of photographs. They will look like physical work to her, and she's been raised to think that physical work is what other creatures do.'

'I want them to go express delivery.'

'It's your money. Even though you've asked her to, you know, she won't telephone you with a reply.'

'Why ever not?'

Brudenell smiled. 'It isn't done. We shall include a prepaid express envelope and hope she will use it.'

Denton walked from Brudenell's chambers in Gray's Inn down to the Embankment and so to Scotland Yard. Morriss was in a meeting, but not for long; Denton waited. When Morriss came in, he was with two other men, both seeming important (older, heavier, louder). Morriss pointed them at his door, murmured to Denton that they had found six good fingerprints in the Florentine box, five of them Henry James's, the other unknown. 'Probably somebody unknown between James's place and wherever you picked the thing up. Sorry.' He started for his office.

'They're sure?'

'Don't ask stupid questions.' Morriss looked harried. 'Sorry. See for yourself.' He pointed at an accordion file on another desk.

The file was mostly empty. It contained the fingerprint technician's report and a list over Wragge's signature of people whose fingerprints had been taken. In fact, probably several detectives in both Rye and London, and not Wragge himself, had gathered them right after James's burglary.

Denton looked down the list. Everybody he could remember from the garden party was there, and a good many more, from Gammon the gardener to the two discharged housemaids to somebody with '(plumber)' after his name. The Grahams were there; the authors—Wells, Conrad, Benson, the lesser lights—were there; James's young men were there, Clara Neville along with her brother. So far as Denton could tell, all the people whose photographs had been sent off to Yorkshire were there.

It was a dead end.

The technician had ticked off the names with a pencil as he worked. The marks made a little winter forest of rather faint lines, like dead twigs through which the names could be seen. For 'Mr Ronald and Mrs Graham', for example, there were two ticks. And so on for other couples—

He almost missed it, but caught it the third time through: there was no tick on Clara Neville's name. The mark on the name below came up and looked as if it was meant for hers, but it wasn't

Did it matter? She was crippled. But...

Denton took the list as if he were entitled to do so and walked out of the office. It was something he had learned in the army: in camp, always have a piece of paper with you; you get many fewer questions.

'Fingerprint Office?' he said to a porter.

'Up one and turn left top of the stairs, fourth or fifth along, sir. There's a sign.'

The Fingerprint Office door was massive hardwood, panelled; the sign was small, brass, freshly polished and probably as new as the Fingerprint Office itself. Denton opened the door and flourished the paper. Two youngish men were sitting at facing desks with strong electric lights suspended over them from the ceiling. The rest of the room was filing cabinets.

'Got a moment to give a bit of advice?'

They looked like tired bookends. Both were holding magnifiers; both had head on hand. Denton approached the less hostile-looking one. 'This list,' he said.

The man groaned. 'I spent all day yesterday on that. On a Sunday!'

'And Superintendent Morriss is grateful.' He thought he'd get the super's name in before one of them asked who he was. He held out the list. 'There's a name on it that wasn't checked off.'

'I know there was. Why the hell can't they get the paperwork right?'

'I thought maybe you'd forgotten to check it.'

'You did, did you? We try not to make stupid mistakes. That's a woman, right? Named...'

'Neville.'

'Right. All right, there's one file named Neville. There aren't two files named Neville. The one file is a man, and his fingerprints don't match the print that we were checking. The bloody list is wrong. There is no Miss Neville.'

'Well, there is a Miss Clara Neville on the list.'

'*But not in our files!* I don't give a farthing whether she's on somebody's list. *There's no fingerprint file.* If there's no file, there's no set of prints for me to compare to.'

'I see. Good. Thanks very much—just checking...' He got out.

On his way back to the CID super's office, he thought about Clara Neville. Was it worth chasing around, trying to find a missing set of prints that were probably somewhere in Wragge's case files by mistake? Worth annoying the police, probably riling Guillam? But if it was all he had left, however unlikely...

He replaced the list in the accordion file. He asked the secretary if he might call the Stoke Newington station on the telephone. The secretary seemed to think that would be all right.

'Inspector Guillam, please.'

'Out, sir.'

'Who's this?'

'DS Todmore, sir. Who'm I speaking to?'

'I'm in Superintendent Morriss's office at the Yard. Look here, we're checking a list that the late Inspector Wragge put together, names of people who'd been fingerprinted in connection with the James burglary in Rye, and we've got a name on the list for which we don't have the prints. I'm trying to find out what's happened here. Are the prints somewhere in Wragge's case files, maybe?'

'I wouldn't think. We've pretty well been through those and put them the way Mr Guillam wants.'

'Well, they have to be somewhere.'

'I wouldn't know about that, sir.'

'Where's Guillam?'

'Robbery in Canonbury, sir. I can leave a message, if you want. Who shall I say it is?'

'Tell Guillam to call Denton. As soon as he can.' He rang off before he could be asked to give a police rank. He sat, chewing a thumbnail, hoped that Morriss would have to pop out of his office for something, was disappointed,

'Superintendent Morriss in there for the morning, is he?'

'Looks like it, sir. If I was you, I'd leave a message. They're having lunch brought in.'

'Oh, God.'

Denton waved at a cab along Whitehall and had himself taken home, in hopes that Guillam would telephone and he'd be there to answer.

He was—four hours later.

'Guillam?'

'I've already said so. What d'you want? And what are you doing calling from Morriss's office?'

'Wragge made a list of everybody whose fingerprints he or his detectives had taken after the James burglary. Now Morriss has sent a print to the Fingerprint Office, and a set of prints from Wragge's list is missing.'

'What the hell is Morriss doing in one of my cases?'

'Don't get your dander up, Guillam. It's my doing.'

'It would be.'

'Anyway, it could have to do with Clemence Street, too.'

'Only if it's off one of the guns. Well?'

'It's from that box I told you about.'

'You and your goddam box! What the hell are you taking up my time for with a box?'

'I told you, it was stolen—'

'Would you believe I don't give a fart?' Guillam was shouting.

'Guillam, if there's a set of fingerprints that didn't make it to the Fingerprint Office, it *is* your business. They were Wragge's responsibility. You've taken over his cases.'

'I had nothing to do with any bloody fingerprints.'

'But N Division did.'

'We don't have any fingerprints! I'd have seen them, and I haven't done. It's a clerical error.'

'Or the prints never got taken.'

'And they're not going to be! We're too bloody busy. The James business is closed. Except for this crap you told me about blackmail. I'm just waiting to get James in an interrogation room!'

'Guillam, look. All I need is to know who took the fingerprints.'

'Oh, that's all? And then you'll pester the poor bugger until he confesses he did a sloppy job, is that it? Then where are we?'

'I won't pester anybody! I just want to know if the prints were actually taken. That's all—yes or no.'

There was a silence, then, 'Morriss knows about this?'

'He does.'

'So you've got my nuts in the mangle. Thank you very much.'

'It isn't like that.'

'It is like that! Inspector Guillam wants to get assigned back to the Yard; the super at the Yard can bring him back if he likes; the great Denton has the super's ear! What choice do I have! You're a fucking shark. All right, give me the name.'

'Clara Neville.'

'Somebody'll telephone you. It won't be me!'

It was evening before the call came, and the man on the other end was so angry that Denton had trouble understanding him. Guillam had apparently flayed him alive as a substitute for Denton.

'DS Hopkins. About this Neville woman.'

'Oh, yes. Right. You calling about the fingerprints?'

'I'm calling because Inspector Guillam ordered me to.'

'About the fingerprinting.' The man didn't speak. Denton said, 'Did you fingerprint her?'

'I was told to take the prints of a Mr Neville and Miss Neville.'

'Here in London, then.' Again, the man didn't speak. 'It was here in London?'

'Where else?'

'Well?'

'I have my notebook. July the eleventh. "Went to Burgoyne Hotel, Bayswater, to take statements and fingerprints of Mr Raphael Neville and Miss C. Neville. Only Mr Neville present; Miss Neville ill. Chronic case. Bed-ridden." Then I summarised Mr Neville's testimony, which is not your business. Now I'm back to my notes. "Took Mr N's fingerprints." End of notes.'

'So you never took her fingerprints.'

'She was crippled! Palsied, I remember him saying that. Hands shook too bad to take the print, something like that. But it would've been useless; what'd she have to do with a burglary? I remember telling him I'd be back.'

'But you weren't.'

The man was silent for several seconds. Finally he said, 'That's that, then.' And he rang off.

Shit.

Denton called down to Atkins, got a mumble from his sitting room.

'The motion picture of the garden party.'

'What about it?'

'Did you get any shots of Miss Neville?'

'Who's Miss Neville?'

'Crippled woman. In an invalid's chair. Sat by a window.'

'Might have done. Hardly the sort of thing they'd want on the screen, though.'

Denton went down. 'I think I may want a print of her.' He went on through to the garden and to Janet's house. Walter was in his room when Denton called to him; he appeared, scowling, book in hand.

'Walter, remember Miss Neville? The—'

'Of course I do. The lady in the chair with wheels on it.'

'Do you remember you got her a book?'

'Of course I do. Part of my mind may be missing, Mr Denton, but I'm not an idiot.'

'Could you find the book again?'

'It's in Rye.'

'If we went to Rye, could you find it again?'

'Of course I could.' *You idiot.*

When Janet came home, Denton kissed her and said, 'Walter and I are going to Rye tomorrow.'

She fell into the sofa and threw her arms out. 'Oh, good! I've been neglecting him and I'm worn to a frazzle and Teddy's loading more work on me.' She blew air upward to get some hair off her forehead. 'What in the world are you going to Rye for? Actually, I don't care. Make sure Walter takes his earplugs. Is James back? Then you're going while he's away, so it's something skulduggerish.

Lucky you. I thought the law might be fun or at least interesting, but it's simply *work*.' She shrugged. 'It's no good you thinking you'll spend the night. I've stacks of work to get through.'

He went over and kissed her.

She smiled, but the smile was mere reflex. She was thinking about her work, he knew.

It was raining next morning in London and still raining in Rye at eleven. The sky, grey and lavender, seemed low enough to touch with an umbrella tip, pressing down on the village and its hill, smudging the church steeple and the higher houses. Towards the horizon, the land and the sky became the same colour and disappeared into each other, and the train, chuffing away from them, seemed to be abandoning them to a grey wetness on which the sun would never rise again.

Walter had said nothing for the whole journey, perhaps because of his earplugs. Denton had read several newspapers and had found the real reason that Guillam had been so angry yesterday:

Police Inspector's Widow Pleads Guilty.
Unintentional Manslaughter—'Afraid for My Life'.
A History of Beatings and Adultery.

After the sort of lead paragraph that was required when a once-hot story had gone cold, it said, 'The accused woman's attorney has announced that he will place a guilty plea today in magistrates' court in the case of Ruth Gold, bigamous "wife" of the late Detective Inspector Arthur Wragge. Mrs Gold will also take full responsibility for hiding Wragge's body, it has been announced. She has made a statement that she "snatched up a souvenir policeman's billy when her husband began to beat her, and lost all memory of the event until she was standing over her husband's body".' Her solicitor has provided police and the magistrate with photographs of bruises to Mrs Gold's face and "elsewhere on her person".'

Ruth Gold had apparently taken the whole load of blame, then, letting Mrs Wragge off completely: 'Mrs Gold has stated that she hid Detective Inspector Wragge's body in a closet for a day, and next night dropped it out a window into a waiting barrow, then trundled it through the darkened streets to a closed carriage that she had arranged to be waiting, though the coachman was ignorant of what she had intended.' Ruth Gold was described as a 'large, strong woman fully capable of moving a man's body'.

Denton smiled at the last line of the article: 'It is believed that the Public Prosecutor will accept the plea.'

Indeed.

And Guillam had threatened to resign.

Now, walking up the hill in Rye, he heard Walter say, his earplugs removed, 'I want to see that little dog at Mr James's again.'

'You can, of course. But there's something I want you to do, too, remember.' Walter plodded ahead, his cuffs already wet from the downpour despite the umbrella and a mac. 'I'd like you to get that book you took to Miss Neville.'

'All right. Are we stealing it?'

'We're borrowing it. I'll leave a note for Mr James.'

'Does he know?'

'Not yet.'

'That's stealing.'

They splashed on, getting wetter. When they were nearing Lamb House, Walter said, 'Janet is being cruel about Rupert and Bill. I think it is wrong of her, and I like her and I don't want her to be wrong about anything.'

'Janet isn't cruel, Walter.'

'She wants them to take the young dog's nuts off. Mr Atkins said he couldn't, it was cruel, and she said he must. That's cruel.'

'They're going to give him ether.'

'It's a new thing, which they've used on humans for fifty years and they still lose patients, but for dogs it's new and it'll be cruel if Bill dies of it.'

One of the maids, name forgotten, opened the door for them. Denton thought that normally she'd have kept them outside, but the rain was too daunting. Maybe she hadn't had a ruling on rain yet from Mrs Esmond. She let them in but stood between them and the rest of the house and said, 'Mr James isn't here, sir. Is there something?'

'I came to see Mrs Esmond, actually. My name is Denton.'

'I remember you, sir. From before.' She held out her arms for their wet macs as Denton thrust the umbrella into a stand. 'In the breakfast room, if you please. The house is part shut up. Tea or coffee?'

'Walter? Tea? Two teas. Thank you.'

She went away and Denton nodded at Walter, who disappeared. When Mrs Esmond came up from below, Walter was back, reading the book he had filched. Denton saw the large, pasted-in photographs, knew it was the right one. He whispered, 'Don't touch the photographs.'

Mrs Esmond was no friendlier than before. 'I thought we were done with questioning, sir.'

'We are, Mrs Esmond, only a matter of nailing things down. I wanted to make sure that the two maids who were here—the ones who went off in the motor-car and were discharged—had in fact started their service here.'

'If you mean did I teach them their business, I did, but I'm afraid I did a poor job when it came to their judgement or their morals.'

'So they couldn't have been in service someplace else first— Yorkshire, for example?'

'Yorkshire! Whyever would a girl from Rye want to go to *Yorkshire*? Of course not! They weren't yet sixteen when they started with me. And look at all the good it did!'

'All right. And the guests who stayed here overnight—a lot of them were at the garden party—did they jog your memory at all? Anything new?'

'My memory don't need *jogging*, thank you very much, sir. No. I hardly saw them, all *I* had to do downstairs. The guests are not my business, sir.'

'You remember Miss Clara Neville?'

'Mr Neville's sister, yes, a sad case, if I may say so.'

'Did she ever stay at Lamb House?'

'She couldn't manage the stairs. She visited sometimes afternoons but stayed down in the town—at the inn by the church, I believe.'

'But *Mr* Neville stayed in Lamb House.'

'He was in and out. He was very good to his sister, sometimes stayed in the village to be with her. When he wasn't working with Mr James on his book.' She seemed to be trying to keep her voice neutral.

'That's also true of the other young men who have visited here—MacCarthy, Reeves, I forget the others...? Did they also stay at Lamb House?'

'I think some of them, sir. Unless it was before my time, and I've been here more than ten years.'

'Mr James is in Paris now, I believe.'

'It's where I forward his mail, yes.'

'Do you have an address for him there?'

'Only that *poste restante*.' Her accent was no better than Denton's would have been.

He asked her another question or two and let her go, his last words 'Please tell Mr James when he returns that I've borrowed a book.' She only sniffed and left the room.

Walter carried the book under his mac so it wouldn't get wet. 'Why are we stealing?' he said as they walked down to the station.

'Borrowing.'

'They teach us not to make excuses like that.'

'They're absolutely right.'

'This page.' Denton laid the open book in front of Morriss. It was the photograph of the country house that had reminded him of New Scotland Yard. Walter had said that Miss Neville 'never turned the page from that one, like she didn't care'.

'Talcum powder will dirty the book.'

'I'll take the grief for that. She had this open in front of her for a long time; at one point, I know, she rested her fingers on it. The photograph should have taken fingerprints pretty well, shouldn't it?'

Morriss looked sceptical. 'We're not very good yet at picking up prints that aren't made with something like paint or grease.' He put a sheet of onion skin on the photograph and closed the book. 'Give them a day or two.'

Denton had to give them three. Then Morriss telephoned and said, 'It's a match.'

By then, Denton had been to Yorkshire and back.

The train journey to Leeds took five hours, with more time tacked on at the end to get to Ilkley. Denton had got an express envelope hand-carried to him from his solicitor's, in it a reply to the request that the Hardakers look at the photographs from the garden party. It was neither welcoming nor helpful, distinctly chillier than the first letter:

> My dear Sir Francis Brudenell,
> It was with some consternation that my brother opened your package to find *thirteen* photographs of perfect strangers. He has asked me to inform you that none of these faces is known to him (nor to me), and that he is an industrialist with many burdens, to which he does not need to have added the encroachment upon his *valuable* time by requests to look at *portraits.*
> We do hope that this will be the end of this matter, which began not unpleasantly, but has ended *distressingly.*
> Yours,
> Hypatia (Hardaker) Fitznaughten

Rumbling towards her through Bedfordshire, Denton mused that she didn't know the half of it: he was about to present her with still another 'portrait'. Atkins had prised a print of Clara Neville out of Maurice with the help of several shillings. The print was not superb, not even particularly good, but it was recognisable.

Denton liked trains, although not in the doses he'd been getting lately. He had laid railway track; he had honchoed a railway crew; he had hunted buffalo to feed railway workers. He wondered how different it had been in England in those days. Not so very, he thought, although most of his workmen had been Poles and Italians and Chinese, not the case in England, he supposed. Or had they brought in coolies from India? That was how, he had read, they had built their railed folly across East Africa. Capital took its cheap labour where it could be found.

He stretched his legs at a couple of stations, read Mrs Wharton's *House of Mirth* because she was one of James's newer friends (but hadn't shown up at the garden party, thank God— one more face to worry about). He had a surprisingly good lunch in the station buffet at Leeds, then got on a local train and puffed out to Ilkley. Beyond its industrial blight, Yorkshire spread out like a muted but gorgeous backdrop, hills and crags and then the vast spread of moor that gave the Hardakers' house its name.

In fact, Moor View was less a house than an architectural exclamation point. It proclaimed the family's tight grip on its world, announcing with medieval turrets and Renaissance arches and Romanesque doorways that it had seized all of the past as well as the present—such is money—and made it its own. There was a resemblance, mostly in tone, to Ginger Goldensohn's house. Moor View also looked to him uncomfortable—and it was, as he found when he got inside. Even on a wet summer day, it was icy, and water ran from its eaves like melting glaciers.

He was shown into a room in which Mr Naismith could have played basketball with the entire Young Men's Christian Association and had plenty of room left over for wives and children. An enormous fireplace, perhaps pilfered from a real castle, took up one end; it had an actual but small fire burning in it. Denton thought he smelled peat, a nice touch.

When Hypatia Fitznaughten came in, she did so with a kind of dramatic posture that suggested she was going to stop in the doorway, put one hand over her heart and declare that he must be her long-lost Uncle Stanley. However, she swept right on in, rather impressive in a corseted day gown that gave her a dreadnought bosom and hips like battlements. Ecru lace cascaded down to a pelvic V. Greying hair massed around her head like a corona. 'Mr Denton!' She sounded shocked. 'I sent your solicitor a *letter.*'

In the flesh, she had a Yorkshire accent that knocked the stuffing out of her manner. Denton thought she was a good study for somebody—not James, maybe Wells. *The Industrialist's Daughter.* He wondered what Janet would have made of her.

'I apologise for disturbing you again, Mrs Fitznaughten.'

'You're not disturbing *me*, Mr Denton, and fortunately my brother is at the works, as he always is at this time of day. But I only just sent a letter to the lawyer, and, and—here you are!' She laughed. The laugh was completely out of place, rather girlish.

'Here I am, indeed.' Denton smiled what he hoped was a charming, shy smile and which he suspected looked like a set of false teeth glimpsed through a screen of Spanish moss. 'I've got one more photo I'd like to ask you to look at, if you would.'

She frowned, did something with her eyes. Seen close up, she looked to be half a dozen years younger than he, more or less well preserved but with reddened vessels in her cheeks, probably the climate and not alcohol. Her posture said she was a lady; the laugh said she wasn't quite sure what she was; the eyes said that she'd learned the hard way to be sceptical. Then he thought he could guess what Janet would have thought: a woman who had traded life for the jiggery-pokery of marriage, and now the husband had died and she was living on her brother's bounty. And where was life?

'As long as you're here...' She made a small gesture towards a sofa some yards from the fire. He sat; she sat a few feet away. He handed over the photograph of Clara Neville.

She looked at it, tilted her head, held it farther away, then raised it so it caught the murky light from a window. 'Oh,' she said, as if the photograph confirmed something she'd known was coming.

'You recognise the face, ma'am?'

She put her hands and the photograph in her generous lap. 'What is it you want, Mr Denton?'

'I'm trying to identify people who might have known the story of Balzac and your grandmother. As I told you in my letter.'

'Ah, Balzac. But why not ask the people themselves? Why...' She held up the picture. 'Portraits?'

'I had a large group of people to, mmm, winnow down.'

'You are really writing a book?'

'Beginning the process, yes.'

Her eyes narrowed. He thought that if her brother were here, he'd show Denton the door, and she was thinking the same thing. Her next question, however, surprised him. It came with the inappropriate laugh. 'Are you a policeman, Mr Denton? You seem to me to act like a policeman. I've never met an author before, but you don't seem like one to me.' Another laugh. 'I don't know that I've ever met a policeman, either. Are you?'

'I'm not a policeman, for sure, ma'am. And I am an author—half a dozen books, starting with—'

She waved a hand. 'My brother looked you up.' Laughter. 'Or had you looked up.' She waved a waggish finger at him. 'Your methods been't nowt t' do with authoring.' Her imitation of Yorkshire speech was meant to soften what she said; she laughed after saying it. Sobering abruptly, she said, 'You do understand that my brother feels *very strongly* that our name is not to be... abused.' She tittered. 'There's something called "poetic licence". I hope you don't have one.'

He made a standard author's speech about integrity, responsibility, respect for sources. 'All I really want to know is the identity of this young woman. You do know who she is, don't you?'

She gave him more of her scepticism. Was she also amused? Or—*flirting?* 'She's named Mary Ann Gledhill. She was with us for three years, caring for my dear grandmother—the recipient of the attentions of Mr Balzac, you know.'

Caring for an old woman? From her invalid's chair? He said, 'You're sure?'

'The hair is quite different, but I know the face. I saw it for three years!'

'There's some kind of crippling disease...'

'In the family. You know, then. But not Mary Ann, fortunately for us. She was quite a treasure. *Grand-maman* was devoted to her. But the illness is terrible: the mother and two of her sisters suffered it, whatever it is. Mrs Gledhill in fact has since passed away.'

'But not Mary Ann.'

'Not at all.' She arched her eyebrows. 'I believe I would have heard if she had.'

'How long ago was she here?'

'Oh, let me see—she left, it must be...four years ago.'

'So, it could be that your grandmother told her the story of Balzac.' *And it could be that a family disease has struck her since she left.*

She tittered again. 'I'm sure she did! Probably over and over.' She gave another surprisingly hearty laugh. She put the photograph on the sofa halfway between them as if to announce that she was done with that and wanted to move on to more interesting things. 'My brother found that you wrote a book that was *anti-religious*, Mr Denton.'

'My last one? I think of it as very religious, in fact.'

'My brother is devout.'

And never wrong, Denton thought. The brother wouldn't have read the book himself; he would have said he didn't have the time. The brother, of course, was the real author of the letters to Denton and his solicitor; she had simply done the writing and the underlining. What a life! He said, 'I write what I believe, and I stand by it, ma'am.'

'Oh.' This seemed to sadden her. 'Oh, I see.' And with that, the interview was over.

She stood; he stood; she said things that Denton had heard before about how interesting writing must be, how much she wished she had taken up writing herself, of course to write *good*, *moral* things, and by that time they were at the door and the maid was holding his hat and his mac. Denton hurried through his thanks and his goodbyes, and by then she was glad to see him go. Whatever interest had been in her eyes earlier had been withdrawn: the shadow of her pious brother was too dark and too heavy.

Seven hours later, he was back in London.

He came in by King's Cross station and walked down to his house, found that Janet was still working and Atkins was out. He washed, changed, strolled down through Soho to the Glasshouse Street entrance of the Café Royal and into its ground-floor Domino Room. There was the usual noise: forks and plates and glasses and talk, talk, talk; the gold caryatids looked down from their green and gold pillars like superior eavesdroppers. Denton walked among the tables but didn't see the man he wanted, so hunted out a waiter called Louis but really named Luigi.

'*Signore*, a table?'

'Yes, but I'm looking for Mr Harris.'

'Not in tonight. Very busy. Putting out a double issue.' Harris was a magazine editor. Clearly, he had been confiding in Louis.

Denton took out a card and wrote on it, 'Must see you—urgent!' He handed it to Louis with a coin. 'Make sure he gets it if he comes in later.'

'*Senza dubito.* Give my best to the lady, please.' Denton was a frequent visitor, though not so frequent as Harris; Janet came with him often enough to be remembered. He ate the usual—the chicken pie with hard-boiled eggs, odd but inexplicably satisfying—and walked home and went to bed alone.

Harris turned up before nine the next morning, frightening Alfred and surprising Denton. 'I thought you didn't get out of bed until noon, Harris.'

'Up to my arse, stroking *The Housemaid's Knee.*' Denton was to understand that this was a women's magazine, probably the same one he referred to as *Female Troubles* and *The Monthlies Monthly.* Harris had been with it for an unusually long time, for him.

'Louis said you were busy. A double issue?'

Harris, who wouldn't pause to sit down, nodded. 'I think of it as having twins. My brain is being rotted by childbirth, nursing and painful menstruation. I don't know how women do it. If the letters we get are any sign, it's all they think about. I'm turning into a woman myself. What is it you want from me?'

'How to find Violet Hunt.'

'Well, don't go looking in Wells's bed; they've had a row. Her new young man. I think they've gone off somewhere together.'

'Where?'

Harris shrugged. 'Hunt keeps a flat in Chelsea, but I heard something about her not being there. Is this important?'

'Would I ask if it wasn't?'

'All right, I'll ask around. When do you want this? Yesterday? You aren't after *la* Hunt for yourself, are you? I'd advise against it. No? Good. I understand you had a fight with Gosse.'

'Nobody could have a *fight* with Gosse.'

'My informants tell me he means to call you "the greatest insult to modern English prose" in the next *Review*. You must really have put your finger up a painful place. I'd be happy to give you space in the *Wet Nappy* if you want to respond, but it's really not the right venue. I have to go.'

Denton walked him to the door, waving Alfred away. 'The sooner the better, Harris.'

'I know, I know...' Harris stepped outside, stood on the step. 'If you hear of a particularly virile mag that's looking for an editor, let me know. Something like *Dumb Bells and Big Johnsons*.' He tipped his hat and started off. 'Ah, the lit'ry life, the lit'ry life...'

The next morning was the one when he got Morriss's telephone call about the fingerprint. 'It's a match.' Morriss had barely said who he was; Denton spent two seconds trying to figure out a match of what, then said, 'The fingerprint!'

'In the box, yes. Got the report from the Fingerprint Office. Luck was on our side, for once; he or she had some red stuff on the finger, maybe rouge. We need to talk.'

'Mmm.' Denton was thinking about how much he would be telling Morriss if they talked. Even after they'd rung off, the question persisted. In fact, there was no good reason he couldn't tell everything—Mary Ann Gledhill, the crippling condition that hadn't been there and now apparently was. And a brother whose name wasn't Gledhill. As hers didn't seem to be Neville. Unless there'd been a marriage? But then they wouldn't be brother and sister... But there was the problem of the letters with which James was being blackmailed. He'd got over being irritated with James, was back to being sorry for him. And he'd made a kind of promise, after all.

He puttered about, filling time, then dressed to go out. He was still there when a commissionaire came to the door with a message that Alfred brought to him on a salver, walking carefully as if it were a goblet of the precious blood.

'It won't break, Alfred. It's paper—forget the tray after this.'

'Mr Atkins says—'

'Mr Atkins is always right. Still, I don't need the tray.'

He tore open the envelope. A curt message from Harris was inside, scribbled on a card: 'Paris. Hotel Prince de Galles. Best I can do.'

Violet Hunt's address. And therefore Raphael Neville's. Well, nothing he could do about them right then. It was too late for the morning boat train.

He saw Morriss a little after eleven at New Scotland Yard. Morriss surprised him by having Guillam there, as well. Denton said, 'Am I here because you're admitting there's a connection among Wragge, Clemence Street and Henry James?'

'Who said there is?' Guillam growled.

'Well, I did. And you wouldn't be here if the superintendent didn't think something of the sort.'

Morriss waved a hand. 'We'll be the judges of all that, Denton. Tell us what you know All this about the fingerprint and Reading Gaol and the rest.'

'What I know.' Denton sighed. 'Well, I know from you that the Fingerprint Office got a match for a print inside a box that had belonged to Henry James. It should have been a match for a set of prints taken by one of the N Division detectives from a woman named Clara Neville, but in fact he never took them.'

Guillam said to Morriss, low-keyed but not apologetic, 'She's crippled with some kind of palsy. The day the tec went to finger-print her, she was too sick to see him. Then it just got lost in the crush after Wragge's murder, then Clemence Street. Anyway, they didn't lift enough prints in James's house that were worth a damn to matter.'

'You've had a talk with the detective? A serious talk?'

'I read him the riot act, if that's what you mean.'

Morriss nodded. 'Send me something about it. If he was negligent, it's got to go in his file. If it was only overwork...' He looked at Denton and nodded.

'I'd met the woman, the one whose fingerprints he didn't get—Clara Neville. I'd seen her at Henry James's, sitting with a book in her hands. I borrowed the book from James's library and brought it to you, Superintendent, and you sent it to the Fingerprint Office. They say the prints they lifted from the book match the one they found in the stolen box. *That's* what I *know*.'

Guillam had his notebook out. 'Where do I find her?'

'I don't know.' Denton was being disingenuous; the detective who'd failed to get her fingerprints had said she and her brother were staying at the Burgoyne Hotel in Bayswater. Weeks ago. 'Try your files.'

Guillam nodded, head down. Morriss said, 'All right, that's what you know. Now we know it, and we'll act on it. We're very grateful, Denton. Beyond that, what do you *think*?'

'Oh, I think the Neville woman's connected with the burglary. How else could it be? The box was one of the things stolen.'

'The one thing,' Guillam said, 'that James didn't put on the list, and the one thing that wasn't with the rest of the loot in Deptford. You said it has "sentimental" value for James...'

He turned to Morriss. 'That's what he told me.' Back to Denton. 'You go all the way to Italy to buy this bloody box. An effort for a friend? He couldn't go himself?' Before Denton could answer, Guillam said, 'No, because he's too busy paying ransom to a blackmailer he didn't bother to tell the police about!' He looked back at Morriss. 'I sent you a report, sir.'

Morriss nodded. Denton was impressed: they were both moving faster than he'd expected. He said, 'I told you what I knew, Guillam.'

'But never quite soon enough.'

Morriss shook his head at Guillam and shifted forward to say to Denton, 'We missed Mr James at Calais, but the Paris police have located him. Fortunately, the French keep better track of hotel registers than we do. They've questioned him but got nothing.' Morriss seemed to be studying his blotter. 'James is a distinguished visitor, quite well known in Paris, apparently, a lot of friends in various places. They've got a watch on him, but nothing's happening.'

Denton said, 'I think the blackmailer's playing with him.'

'What's this got to do with the crippled woman and the fingerprint, do you think?'

'Well, the print makes it look as if she's in it, doesn't it?'

'Is she the blackmailer?'

'That seems a long reach. She goes around with a man who's supposed to be her brother. She's in an invalid chair; he kind of plays nursemaid.'

'Maybe the brother, then?'

Guillam scowled. 'That doesn't explain her prints inside the box.'

Morriss tipped his head. 'A real villain might get his sister to take things out of a box so that his prints wouldn't be in it. Mmm? If push comes to shove, who's going to prosecute a crippled woman on that evidence?'

Denton scratched his chin and shifted his bulk in his chair. He was thinking of telling them about his visit to Yorkshire, but at the same time he was warning himself that what he had learned there was thin. And it was his own. 'Clara Neville' might really be named Mary Ann Gledhill, but they might both actually have a third name; and even if she hadn't been crippled with degenerative palsy four years ago, she could be now. So he said only, 'At least the fingerprint is evidence. The rest of it's just speculation.'

Guillam laughed. 'That's a change! Usually I'm the one says that.' He closed his notebook with a little slap. 'I'll get on to locating the Neville woman and her brother.'

'He's an author. First book is out. I don't know the publisher.'

'Under his own name?'

'As far as I know.'

Denton was getting ready to go. Morriss said, 'How does this play into Clemence Street?'

Guillam ran through the possible connections with Goldensohn and Wragge. He all but shouted, 'If, if...! *If* Goldensohn commissioned James's burglary; *if* somebody else did it to get the stuff to blackmail James...!'

'Did you send somebody to Reading prison to see if Goldensohn had been there?'

'I did not! I can't shake somebody free for a whole day yet! I telegraphed the warden and I got back the answer that I'll have to have a warrant. I can't get a warrant because I don't have any evidence! I could go before the magistrate and say that the famous Denton, the fiction-writer and gentleman detective, has a hunch, but somehow I don't think he'd take that as evidence.'

'That's enough of that!' Morriss's jaw was out, his face hard. 'You're not to take that tone here.'

Denton smiled. 'It's kind of a joke between us, Superintendent. I don't take it to heart.'

'Well, I do. All right, Mr Denton, I gather you have theories about all this but you can't glue them together with proof. Am I right? In your view, there's somebody out there above and beyond the bunch who did the burglary and also did the shooting and killed Goldensohn—that much, at least, we think we know—but somebody else. A crippled woman? I don't think so. And Goldensohn was in it somehow? Yes, them killing him could seem to speak to that, that and him knowing enough about Clemence Street to put us there to capture the villains, as we thought we'd do. But then it stops, doesn't it? It stops at Goldensohn and it stops at the anarchists.'

'Wragge,' Denton said.

'Wragge was killed by his wife; she's confessed, nothing to do with the other.' Guillam sounded absolutely sure of himself.

'But how does the box get from James's house in Rye to Italy with a woman's fingerprint inside it?' Then, before either could venture an answer or, likelier, an objection, Denton said, almost to himself, 'Wragge.'

Guillam, 'You lost me.'

'Wragge gives her the box.'

'Wragge! For Cripe's sake, why? Who's Wragge to a woman in an invalid chair?'

Denton was pursuing a galloping idea but jerked himself back and said, 'I don't know. Just a thought. Forget I said it.' He changed the subject to Munro, now being moved to a nursing home. Morriss made motions towards getting rid of them; Guillam made motions towards leaving.

'I'll follow up this crippled woman, shall I?' Guillam said.

Morriss, standing now, said, 'You have the files; have a look. If you find her, let me know. We'll certainly want to question her, but you can have first go. Today, if you can.'

'I'll telephone it in, then I'm off to the Angel. If we can do it today, we will.' Guillam glanced at Denton. 'But I wouldn't get my hopes up.'

They walked out together, both men silent until they neared the outer doors. Then Denton said, 'Munro's really better?'

'They're talking about getting him on his feet.' Guillam stopped. 'Look, I was rough on you back there. Overdoing it for the super, maybe. My apologies.'

'I get a little tired of "gentleman detective".'

'Yeah, well, I get tired of theories. Anyway, I've got six new cases up in Islington, none making it big in the gutter press but important all the same. The James thing is over. I was riled when you told me about the blackmail, but the French say nothing's going on. The super nixed me sending a tec over to talk to him— same old crap, not enough men, plus James is a public figure, juries are always sympathetic with somebody being blackmailed, let's go after real villains. I suppose he's right.' Guillam ran a hand through his black hair.

'No rest for the weary.'

'That's the truth.'

'You satisfied with Ruth Gold's plea?'

Guillam made a sound of disgust.

'Did she say what she'd done with the billy she killed him with?'

'Threw it into one of the New River reservoirs, but she can't remember which one. She *says*. Of course we won't go looking for it now.'

Denton said, 'What about Mrs Wragge?'

'Released.' He headed for the underground. Denton said to his back, 'You going to stay in the Met?'

Guillam stopped, turned back, his pocked face locked into a scowl. 'I'm thinking about it.'

Denton let him go, then waved down a cab and jumped in. 'Ever hear of a hotel called the Burgoyne?' he said to the driver.

The man was old, stooped, missing a lot of teeth. 'Up Bayswater, o'course, the Burgoyne. Not what yous'd call the Savoy.'

'Take me there.'

They trotted west, then north, Denton staring dully at Kensington Gardens as they skirted them. In a street behind Moscow Road, the driver pulled up at what seemed to be two houses thrown into one, BURGOYNE splayed across one under the eaves, the U threatening to leave the other letters. The interior, too, seemed to have started out as a private house with a very small entry, but that look gave up in a labyrinth of interrupted cornices and new walls and doors that looked as if they'd been made from tea-box wood. Denton passed a couple of dispirited rubber plants and found reception, which was only a counter put across a doorway.

'Yes, sir!' The man seemed much too sprightly. 'Room?'

'I'm looking for one of the residents.'

'And which one would that be?'

'Mr Neville.'

'Oh.' Inadvertently, the man glanced at a rack of pigeon-holes behind him. 'We did have the Nevilles, but they moved out. They travel.'

'Where to?'

'Oh, they don't tell me, do they.'

'Miss Neville is a crippled lady.'

'Unfortunate, terrible thing, so young. Terrible at any age, ha! Yes.'

'Do you forward their mail?'

'Oh, I couldn't say.'

'Couldn't or won't?'

'Shouldn't, is the fact of it.'

'I need an address.'

'Awfully sorry.'

'Half a crown. A crown. Ten shillings.'

The man had been shaking his head, then smiling, then saying, 'Oh, no,' but ten shillings caught his attention. He said in an oddly innocent way, as if he were a kid doubting his good luck, 'You mean it?'

Denton felt around and made up the amount from several pockets. The clerk, who may well have been the owner, said, 'I've never done this before.' The idea seemed to tickle him. He looked at something under the counter, turned a page, wrote on a slip of paper that he traded for the ten shillings. 'My, my.' He grinned. 'Have a good day.'

Going down the front steps, Denton looked at the paper. 'Care of Sponn, 374 Pentonville Road.'

He got into the same cab. 'Lamb's Conduit Street. Know where it is?'

The old man sighed. 'I know where everything is, mate.'

At his own front gate, Denton told him to wait again, rushed into his house, frightened Alfred, shouted for Atkins and ran upstairs to get his revolver.

'What's up?' Atkins shouted.

'We're going out. I need your help.' He appeared with the revolver in his hand.

'Oh, murder, off again. Right—let me get my hat...'

In the cab, Atkins said, 'This is serious?'

'Maybe.'

The ride was a short one; as they neared Pentonville Road, Atkins said, 'If you'd warned me, I could have brought the camera.'

'Not a chance.'

The house they wanted was austere and stark and astonishingly clean. Even the bricks looked as if they had been scrubbed. The glass in the windows, even on a grey day, seemed to enlarge the light as it threw it back. The railings were newly leaded, the door most unfashionably taken down to the wood and varnished.

'Not your typical Pentonville terrace house,' Atkins said.

'Rooms, you think?'

'Flats, more like. Nothing on the windowsills.' Indeed, the sparkling windows had nothing perched outside them—no plants, no cups, no leftover chips in greasy newspaper.

Several cards had been tacked in a neat row on a board nailed to the wall of the shallow doorway. None of them said 'Sponn'. Denton twisted an iron bell crank, heard the ring inside like a firebell's clang. He was reaching for the crank again when the door jerked open, and a woman as austere as the house—grey and black from head to foot, face the colour of wheat paste—said, 'What is it?' She brought with her the smell of carbolic.

Denton raised his hat. 'I'm looking for Sponn.'

'What for? I don't like strangers coming in.'

So it was her house, he thought. She must have been a formidable landlady. He said, 'My name is Denton.' He held out a card, which said nothing more than his name; it had seemed ridiculous to put 'author' on it. 'This is my associate, Mr Atkins.'

'I run a Christian house. I don't want layabouts or casuals here. Nothing's available, anyway.'

'Sponn?'

She folded her arms over her black silk front. 'Why?'

'It's a matter of money.'

'You a creditor? She's a week behind in her rent—my claims come first!'

So it was like that—*she*, not *they*, and out of money. 'No, ma'am, it's the other way round.'

'What other…? You mean you owe her?'

Denton produced some money. 'How much does she owe you, ma'am? Four shillings? There's two and six—three—four…' He smiled. 'I have some good news for her in that line.'

'What, she's come into something? She was saying she expected something. Putting me off, I thought. But there's this week, too—pay in advance, I always insist on that—if I didn't have a Christian heart, I'd have put her out…'

Denton handed over another four shillings. 'May I see her?'

'Well.' She eyed him and then unfolded her arms. 'No need to stand in the doorway for all the neighbourhood to see.' She turned away but left the door open. Denton pushed in, Atkins right behind.

'Two rear,' the woman said. She pointed up a narrow but immaculate enclosed staircase. Everything Denton could see was immaculate. The central hall they stood in had no furniture, and only a sisal mat on the floor, but everything looked as if it were still wet from scrubbing.

Denton went to the stairs and put a hand on the newel post, but stopped to ask her, 'Does she have only the one door?'

'Front and back. It's one of the first-class flats.' As Denton reached the third stair tread, he heard her say, 'No more than ten minutes! This is a Christian house!'

The same sisal matting lay on the stair tread, held in place by worn iron rods with traces of brass plating. Denton went on the soles of his feet; Atkins must have seen and done the same, because there was almost no sound. On the second floor, Denton stopped at the head of the stairs, stepped a little aside to make room for Atkins, and pointed down the corridor that ran along the side of the house. These had been bedrooms once, he was sure; now, there was a card tacked to a door on their left and, farther down, two more doors, the farthest at the very back of the house and facing a narrow stair that had once been for servants.

Denton pointed with a finger and thumb like a gun. He tapped Atkins, who nodded and set off down the sisal-padded corridor. He stopped opposite the farthest door, looked back, got a nod from Denton. Then Denton went to the middle door and knocked.

A voice said something from inside. Female, not welcoming.

'Telegram,' Denton said, roughening his own voice.

Footsteps rushed towards him. He heard the sound of a bolt, then the turning of a key, and the door was pulled open with force because it was warped and it wanted to stick. She swayed back, pulling at the door, then swung into the opening and looked at him and recognised him. She was standing straight with her head up; too late, she twisted herself into the attitudes he had seen in the invalid's chair, but she knew it was too late and she tried to slam the door, but his weight was already against it.

She didn't scream. She cursed, a very masculine curse: 'God*dam* you!'

Denton pushed on the heavy door, which scraped the floor and didn't want to open any more than it had for her, but he went through and saw her skirts already disappearing through another doorway. That door slammed; he heard her running feet.

He didn't hurry. He wanted, in fact, to give her a little time.

Then more footsteps and the sound of a lock and then a kind of yelp when she opened the door, Atkins's voice a rumble, and then that door's slamming.

Denton opened the inner door, the door to her bedroom, and stood in the doorway and saw her. She had her shoulder against the far door still, her face flushed, a coat over one arm and a pale brown envelope in her other hand. He said, 'I'll take them, Miss Gledhill.' The name shocked her. He held out his hand.

Her eyes flicked from side to side and found no way out.

'Give them to me.' He took a step towards her. 'It's over.'

She put the envelope behind her and leaned back against the door.

'I don't want to take it away from you by force. But I can.'

'They're my, my—p-papers! They're personal!'

'They're letters that belong to Henry James. Come on...' Denton was standing in front of her now, close enough to reach around and put his hand over hers behind her back. Close enough to have kissed her, he thought. Always the male advantage— height, weight, strength. He moved his hand down hers and wrapped it around the smooth, cool feel of the flat packet, which was not really an envelope but an oiled silk wallet of the sort tobacco was kept in. He backed away. When he opened the wallet with two fingers and looked in, she said, 'No!' in a kind of groan.

Denton saw '*Mon très cher Henry*' at the top of the first page, and a date in the seventies. He closed the wallet and put it into an inner pocket of his suit jacket. She moaned.

'Come on. We need to talk.' He stood in the doorway, pointing into her sitting room, which was as austere as everything else in the house. Less clean, because of her, he supposed. There were three chairs, a sort of desk that was really a wash stand with the arms knocked off, a cast-iron fireplace about as big as a wine crate that couldn't ever have done much against a London winter. 'Sit down.'

'I won't.'

'The police are about an hour behind me, Miss Gledhill. They'll be a lot worse than I will.' He raised his voice. 'Atkins! Come to the other door!' He put his back to the fireplace as if it might give him some warmth for what was going to be a very cold deed. Atkins came in and took a position by the bedroom door so that she was pretty well boxed in. 'Sit, Miss Gledhill, you might as well.'

'You've stolen my property.'

'Don't make me laugh. Where's "Raphael"? Not his real name, is it? Nor Neville. And not your brother. What—lover? Husband?'

She sat down in a brown velvet rocker that was much worn. She put her head back and the chair rocked, and he was reminded of the invalid chair. He said, 'Where's your wheeled chair?'

'I don't need it here.'

'But kept in case you have to fool James again?'

She looked away.

'Why? *Why?*'

'Because I hated him!' She sat up suddenly and the chair came too far forward and struck her back. 'Because he's a dirty-minded old man who can't keep his hands off Charlie— Rafe—and because he treated me like shit! He felt *so* sorry for me, but he left me in that damned chair for hours while he took Charlie off and petted him and felt him up and played with his hair! Because he took him away from me!'

'He was helping—Charlie?—to write his book.'

'Helping Charlie! Who do you think wrote the book? *I* wrote the book! I did! Me! And I wasn't good enough for the great Mr James even to speak to! He deserved what he got. He humiliated me, he made me *dirt*; well, I humiliated him and he's living like dirt now!'

'In Paris.'

'In Paris! In a hole of the kind he didn't know existed! And that I've spent years in.'

'And Charlie's in Paris.'

She looked away.

'With Violet Hunt.'

She wailed and put her head down, both hands over her eyes. The seat of the rocker was low; she seemed to embody *brought low*. He was reminded of a theatre poster, a play called *Divorce*, a woman weeping like that. Well, grief could be real or theatrical. He said, 'Has he left you for good?'

She raised her head and then dropped her forehead on the heels of her hands, her elbows on her knees. He heard her muffled voice say, 'I don't know.'

'Why did Charlie do it? He didn't want to get back at James, did he? For being petted and touched and all that?'

She gave him a kind of half-smile. 'Charlie loves to be loved.' She shook her head. 'He did it for the money. We were going to bleed the old man.'

'And there was the money from the auction. And then the swag from the burglary.' She didn't move. Denton looked at Atkins, who shook his head and looked down at his feet. Denton said, 'Did Wragge give you the box with the letters in it?'

Her head moved, maybe a nod.

'Were you the third woman Mrs Wragge and Ruth Gold hated so?'

She looked up, her eyes as shiny as the windows but her lips smiling a little. 'They needn't have bothered. I was going to chuck him as soon as it was over.' She laughed. 'Glad to be rid of him.'

'One of them killed him, you know.'

'Not my doing.'

Denton glanced at Atkins again. 'Was that Charlie's idea—you and Wragge?'

'Wragge was the one in the middle. He knew me and he knew Charlie, though not the two of us together, and he knew the ones that did the thieving, but we and them never knew each other. That was Charlie's idea, sure.'

'To put you with another man.'

She lay back in the chair again. 'It wasn't the first time.' She put the back of one hand against her forehead as if the light hurt her eyes. 'Charlie and me work the detective dodge all over—Germany, France, Switzerland, the north of Italy. Some gent loves me up, I take him to a room, get him into the bed, Charlie crashes in and makes threats and all. They always pay.'

'This time Wragge paid. With his life. Charlie's a confidence man?'

'One of the best.'

'That's how he made the contact in Reading Gaol. Well?'

'If you say so.' She seemed listless now.

The Past Master

'A prisoner there had run a con with a boy—that was Charlie? No? Yes?' Denton took out a cigarette box. She held out a hand and he gave her one, lit both cigarettes. She said, 'The old woman doesn't allow smoking.' She drew in deeply.

'So Charlie went to Reading and said he had a job he wanted done—you two had already worked it out—but he didn't want to be seen in it. I suspect he didn't know that class of criminal, anyway. Did he?'

She blew smoke out of the side of her mouth. 'Always kept himself clean, Charlie.' She flicked ash on the bare floor.

'So the man in Reading sent a message to Ginger Goldensohn—did you know Goldensohn?'

She shook her head. Her eyes were closed, her head back again.

'And he got the anarchists, who agreed to do it for a share of the swag and the Mauser pistols. Where did you get those?'

She shook her head again. 'They did. Pals in Germany. They just needed them brought into the country.'

'That was you and Charlie. In your steamer trunk? Or in the seat of your invalid chair? I'm sure it was something of yours, not Charlie's. Mmm? Well?' But she said nothing. 'So they staged the burglary and Wragge gave you the box, which was all you really wanted. And then everything went to hell.'

She flicked more ash. 'And then everything went to hell. Stupid bint murdered Wragge, so we lost the deal with the insurer for the loot. Then the shootings. We'd no idea that was going to happen. I knew what anarchists are, but I thought they were a joke—throwing bombs with a thing like a string sticking out and sparks coming off. We had *nothing* to do with that!'

'Except for bringing in the pistols.'

She put her head back, eyes closed, drew in smoke. He thought that when she closed her eyes, she was avoiding looking at a difficult truth. He said, 'You heard about the Balzac papers from the old woman when you took care of her.'

She flicked ash. 'She was good to me, that old woman. More than I can say for Mr Godly-Goodly Hardaker, with his wandering hands. She taught me French; she taught me to walk

327

like a lady; she actually taught me English—good English, so I didn't sound like a Yorkshire pudding.'

'But the letters you blackmailed James with—she can't have known about those.'

'The ones you just stole from me, you mean? No. She told me about the box. The box had been hers; she'd kept the Balzac stuff in it. She could describe every scratch and dent on it. That box *was* her lover. I saw it at James's. I couldn't believe it. At first, I thought it was just another box. Then I looked at it some more and I knew what it was. And when I looked inside and found the letters to James, I knew how he'd got them— payment for service.'

'You got into James's study.'

'They left me alone for hours! Of course I got into the study.'

'Why didn't you steal the letters then?'

'Because I didn't know but what the old poof read them over every night and got off on them. Charlie was afraid we'd get caught.' She flicked ash. 'Bit of a coward, Charlie. I'd have taken them and be damned, but he wouldn't, so we cooked up the scheme. And it'd have worked but for Wragge's women and those stupid anarchist buggers.'

'And Violet Hunt.'

She flushed.

'She took Charlie out of the game, didn't she?'

'He didn't know what he was doing.'

'He does now.'

'Shut up about it.'

'Is he coming back? He got the money from the auction, didn't he? He's getting the blackmail money, isn't he? He's left you here with nothing—you haven't paid the rent in—'

'Shut it, shut it!' She jumped to her feet, the rocker swaying and almost tipping behind her. 'Shut up!'

'He's left you.'

'He wouldn't, not for her! She's old! But...' She started to weep again. 'It wasn't her. It was *this*!' She held her hand close to his face. It had a slight tremor that he'd missed until then. 'I'm getting it. You know about me so you know about *it*. I thought it had skipped me.' She tried to laugh. 'All the time I've spent in that bloody invalid's chair! Curled up like a corkscrew. *Well, that's what's really going to happen to me!*'

'And Charlie knows.'

The energy went out of her. 'And Charlie knows.' She used a toe to grind some of the ashes into the worn carpet. 'What are you going to do with me?'

'Take you to a woman solicitor I know.'

'I won't go to prison!'

'You will if you don't do as she says. If you sit here, the police will show up—in about thirty minutes, I'd say—and they'll arrest you. If you turn yourself in through a solicitor, you'll get a better deal.'

'What about Charlie?' Which was to say, she still loved him.

'I'll deal with Charlie. You take care of yourself. Don't you take responsibility for it—especially the pistols. As it is, it can be made to look as if you're guilty only of receiving stolen goods— the box, which is of so little value it's likely not a felony—and the rest is down to Wragge and Goldensohn and Charlie.'

'I won't turn on Charlie!'

'He'd turn on you, and you know it. We'd better be going.'

He held out her coat, which she'd dropped on the floor at the beginning. Atkins murmured that she'd need a hat and glided into the bedroom. She said, 'How'd you get on to me?'

'Something a boy said.'

'That dummy you brought to James's party? What'd he say about me?'

'He said you weren't in pain but you were very unhappy.'

'Well, he was right about that. I should have been nicer to him. But I couldn't think about him. I'd only just started to show the palsy, and Charlie'd seen it only that morning. I knew he'd leave me then. He didn't know it, but I knew it. And there he was, out in the gardens, kissing arse with Lady This and Sir That, and I thought, they're all going to live and I'm going to have *this*! If I'd had an anarchist's bomb, I'd have pitched it right into the middle of them!'

Buttoning her coat, she said, 'What difference does it make? Any of it? I know what's going to become of me.' She held up the only faintly trembling hand.

Atkins held up a hat. She put it on and they went down through the house, watched for the last few of the stairs by the woman in grey and black.

'We're just going out,' Denton said. 'We'll be back when we've been to the bank.'

They went out to Pentonville Road and Atkins hailed a cab.

He spent ten minutes telling Teddy Mercer the woman's story, Teddy looking dubious, but after that she took the woman into her office and closed the door.

'Teddy's very strong on women who've been victimised by men,' Janet said. 'It guarantees a steady flow of clients.'

'She's going to have to talk her into turning herself in.'

'Will she try to run off, the woman?'

'If she gets a chance. She's like a street cat.'

'You going to hang about to watch her?'

Denton shook his head. 'I need to be on the evening boat train. Back the second day, I hope.'

'More James?'

'The last.'

She was standing quite close to him. They were alone in the outer office, Atkins gone home to throw things into a bag for Denton. She put a hand on his lapel. 'I never am quite sure whether you're a very good man or a slightly peculiar one. You never let up.'

'I promised James I'd help him.'

'Mmm, the man-to-man promise.' She kissed him. 'Well, don't get yourself shot this time.'

A few minutes later, Teddy came out of the office. 'Is this woman going to do a bunk if I let her?'

'Probably.'

Teddy turned to Janet. 'Get somebody to help me take her to the police station. I don't want her scampering off while I'm paying the cabbie. Fanny Holzer, she's strong as an ox, assaulted a policeman, and she's only two streets away.' As Janet began to pin a hat on, Teddy said to Denton, 'Who's the detective on the James burglary?'

'Inspector named Guillam, N Division. Janet knows him.'

'All right, we'll take her up there. Where, the Angel? Stoke Newington! Good God. All right, Janet, when you come back, close the office; you'll come with us.' She looked again at Denton. 'How bad a man is Charlie?'

'Bad enough.'

She grunted. 'You're all "bad enough". Will he be coming back to England?'

'That's what I'm going to take care of next.'

'It would be best if you could. I can make up a tale for her, but if he's on the scene, it'll all come out. As it is, if it's only stealing that box, she won't need a barrister and I can plead her guilty in magistrates' court and she'll get a fine. *If* the police will swallow it. You'll help with that? It will be the first time you've been of much use around here.'

'What about Mrs Wragge?'

'Wragge's going to live with a daughter. I'm trying to get her late husband's pension for her, the filthy swine. There's some doubt about it—"blotted his copybook" was actually said to me. So as to deny a woman that hasn't any other income in the world.' She stamped away. 'Bad enough, indeed...'

Denton waited until Janet came back with a huge woman in a grimy dress. They went into Teddy's office and then Janet came out. She said, 'You'd better go.'

'I don't want to, now I have to.'

Her face was grave. 'If you see Henry James, thank him for asking me to his party. It was courageous of him, considering who his friends are.' She was silent for a fraction of a second. 'Walter, too.' She smiled. 'Not to mention Atkins.'

He came out of the Gare du Nord into sunlight so pale he cast only a thin blur of shadow. Overhead, the sky was dove-grey but bright. He thought it would rain, something thin and probably rather pleasant.

He got into a horse cab and, by saying *'Poste restante'* several times in an atrocious accent, got something across, and they jogged off by what he supposed was a deliberately tortuous route to the central post office. He had his usual struggle with French coins, almost gave away ten francs for one, finally got it sorted out and went into the overworked glories of the Paris Poste Centrale.

Again, *'poste restante'* got him, by several misunderstood directions, to a marble counter where two clerks were busily handing over the morning's mail to two lines of travellers. Denton himself usually used Thomas Cook's because they spoke English. The two clerks, he thought after listening to them for a few minutes, spoke German as well as English. And French.

He found himself what he thought was an unobtrusive alcove from which he could watch the window, but after half an hour a man in a uniform with something that Denton thought meant Postal Security embroidered on his collar spoke to him in French.

'I'm waiting for somebody,' Denton said in English, and smiled.

'Ah, you are Ang-*lish*.'

'American.'

'Ah! You meet someone?'

'A friend. He is staying in Paris.'

'Ah, bon. You have papers?'

Denton did have papers, the stuff with which he'd travelled to Turin, snatched up as he ran for the boat train. They more than satisfied the officer, especially when he came to the line for 'occupation' and saw 'author'. *'Auteur? Comme notre écrivain.'* He mimicked writing with a hand. 'You are a wry-*teur*. Of *romans*! *Mais, quel honneur, monsieur. Bienvenue à la poste française.'*

Henry James marched in a few minutes before eleven. He looked exactly as he might have in London—broad hat, dark jacket, lighter trousers, a slightly fashionable checked waistcoat, boots and spats—and not at all as if he were living in a Parisian fleabag. He walked directly to the *poste restante* counter, the line now gone, where the young men seemed to know him; several letters were handed over, and he turned and started away, glancing through the envelopes as he walked, looking up every second or two to see where he was going. That was how he saw Denton.

'Good morning,' Denton said.

'I told you not to come here!'

Denton took James's arm. 'It's all over.' He steered him towards the enormous doors. 'I have the letters.'

'But you can't have!'

Denton led him outside, where a very thin drizzle was not so much coming down as hovering in the air, hardly a rain at all. He took the oiled pouch from a pocket and handed it over. 'They're the real thing, I think.'

James took shelter against a Beaux Arts façade and opened the packet. He looked down at the things in his hands, slowly separating pages with a fingernail. He cleared his throat and blinked. 'I thought I'd never draw a free breath again.'

'I need some food. Somewhere *déclassé* that serves omelettes and fried potatoes and beer.' He took James's arm again. 'I shall a tale unfold.' They began to walk, rain or no rain.

James mentioned a club where he had guest privileges, then a restaurant, but Denton insisted on a place where he would be comfortable. They found it down a side street beyond the Comédie. Denton settled at an outdoor table under an awning that kept off the drizzle; James followed but, perhaps reminded of the hole where he'd been forced to stay for more than a week, said that he'd been sleeping in a bed that had insects. 'Actual insects!' He shook his head. 'I didn't think such things happened to people like us.'

Denton didn't say that James should have been in the war, that probably his brothers knew all about lice and fleas. Instead, he said, 'After I eat, we're going to see your blackmailer.'

'Shall I have to pay more?'

Denton laughed. 'No, it'll be the other way 'round.' Then, as he ate *omelette jambon* and *frites* and they both drank Belgian beer, he told James everything. He didn't try to dramatise the naming of the blackmailers but made it simply part of the fabric of the story. It took as long as the omelette did, and when he was done and was wiping his slightly greasy moustache with a napkin, he said, 'Shall we go?'

'I... I'm not at all sure I want to.'

'I'd rather you were there, to make the point that he can't come running to you later with some excuse. But if you can't face him, then you can't.'

'It isn't *facing* him, it's... Did I tell you the story of the cat, or I did I dream it?'

'You told me.' He didn't say that it had given him, round-about, the idea for a new book. But it did suggest what James might fear doing to Neville.

'I shall simply have to hold myself aloof. Where are we going?'

'A hotel called the Prince de Galles.' He mangled the pronunciation, but all James said was 'Ah, on the Île. We can walk.'

The drizzle had started again, but shafts of pale sunlight nonetheless fell on wet rooftops and patches of pavement, shining like fresh gilt. They walked almost in silence, James indicating their route with his furled umbrella, across the Pont Neuf and then to the Place Dauphine. The hotel was a narrow building at right angles to the more recent, and far bigger, Palais de Justice.

'It's quite small,' James said, seeming to hesitate as he looked at it.

'Ever stayed there?'

James shook his head. 'One's friends do.'

Denton strode in, established that the monocled and musta-chioed man behind a tiny counter spoke English, and asked if Miss Hunt was in. James flinched at the name.

'I have not seen Miss Hunt yet today, monsieur.'

'Then she's in. Good. We'll go up. What number?'

'That, I am afraid, monsieur, would be—'

'Miss Hunt is a noted author. I am a noted author. My friend is the most noted author in England, Mr Henry James. It's ridiculous to think we're going up for something improper.'

'I will send a *garçon,* monsieur.'

'And I'll be right behind him!' Denton didn't want 'Charlie' running off.

The clerk started to protest, but James said something in rapid French, quite a paragraph of it, some of it sounding to Denton like a scolding, then turned and pushed Denton gently with a finger and made for a highly decorated lift whose brass gates looked like the entrance to a bank vault. A *garçon* of about sixty came hurrying after them and squeezed into the lift first so he could usher them in with a wave.

'One has to understand the French mentality,' James said.

The aged boy knocked on Violet Hunt's door; when a maid opened it, allowing a glimpse beyond her of a gaunt woman in a lot of apricot-coloured wrapper, the *garçon* stepped back and said something, of which Denton caught only *messieurs,* and a woman's somewhat furry voice said from inside, 'Henry, good God.'

James stepped back; Denton stepped forward. He had a sense of a lot of scent and hair not yet brushed, and then beyond the maid and the woman he saw 'Raphael Neville', now Charlie, just getting out of an armchair. He was wearing a silk robe and he had a huge smile and was opening his arms to say *'Maître!'*

Denton moved into the room, registering that it was a sitting room and not a bedroom and that dirty dishes were piled on a serving cart. He said, 'Miss Hunt, my name is Denton; you know James. Would you leave the three of us alone for a few minutes, please?'

'Oh, but...' She looked at Charlie. She looked at James. She was either very acute or very subservient, and Denton thought the former. 'As you like.'

She crossed in front of him, saying something in French to the maid. Charlie was coming the other way, trying to throw his arms around James, but James was turning away. Denton caught Charlie's raised left arm and used it to push him back and into his chair.

The door closed on Violet Hunt—her bedroom, Denton thought.

'How dare you,' Charlie said, as if he'd learned the line for a play.

'Jam it, Charlie, it's over. James has the letters; Mary Ann's on remand by now.'

A sick expression passed across Charlie's face like a tiny cloud and became a smile.

James, now standing at a window, half turned and said, 'How could you? How could you?'

Charlie tried again to get out of his chair. 'Henry, let me explain. It was all a—'

James turned his back. Denton pushed Charlie into the chair again and, looming over him, said, 'We've come for the money. A hundred and fifty pounds in English notes.'

'That's ridiculous. I don't know what all this is about! What money?'

Denton put his huge hand on the young man's chin and closed his thumb and fingers around the lower jaw, then lifted the head until Charlie couldn't help but look at him. 'I said it's over, Charlie! I want the money in thirty seconds or I'll beat in that pretty face of yours. Thirty seconds!' It was like his taking the letters from Mary Ann Gledhill—weight, height, strength; utterly unfair, essential.

He stared into frightened eyes, then let go and grabbed the collar of Charlie's dressing gown and pulled him to his feet. 'Get it.'

'It isn't here—it's in my room...'

'Then let's go.' Denton caught his left wrist and put it behind the young man's back and marched him to the door and out into the corridor. 'Where?'

'You're hurting me.'

'Prison guard's tactic. Get used to it.'

Charlie pointed, and they walked past one door and then stopped at a second, the last on the floor. Denton let him go so that he could open the door. Inside was a small, disordered room. Rubbing his wrist, Charlie crossed to a highboy that looked to be an authentic old piece; he hesitated in front of it as if trying to decide which drawer to open. He reached for one of the narrower upper drawers with the hand Denton had twisted and raised his right hand to reach in.

Denton jumped across the space between them and slammed the drawer shut. Charlie yelped. Denton opened the drawer and felt around with his left hand, his eyes and his right hand busy with Charlie. He found round, cold metal, took it out. 'Guns aren't your style, Charlie. You'd only hurt yourself.'

It was a cheap Belgian .22. Denton dropped it into a side pocket. 'Where's the money?'

'You broke my hand.'

'I don't think so. The money, Charlie. The money or your face.'

One-handed, Charlie took out a Russian-leather three-fold wallet from the drawer. Denton looked inside. There was a good deal more than a hundred and fifty pounds, most of it in Swiss francs. He said, 'Count out one fifty. In English notes. You get to keep the rest. What is it, the money from the auction?'

'Take it.'

'And share the guilt for profiting from theft? No thanks.' Denton took the English pounds and fished out a folded paper that was behind the Swiss money. He didn't need French to decipher the numeral 5 and '*lettres*' and 'Balzac', then the numeral 1 and '*conte*' (something to do with account? recount?) and 'Balzac' again. It was the receipt for the auction sales, marked with some sort of stamp and a scrawled word and signature. *Vendu à M. Francis Hogenbaum* was written near the bottom, with two signatures, one of them probably decipherable as Hogenbaum. 'You have a lot of aliases, Charlie. All right, let's go back.'

'You've got what you came for.'

'You don't know what we came for, Charlie. Put your left hand behind your back so I don't have to do it for you. It'll hurt less.'

He frogmarched Charlie back to Violet Hunt's sitting room. James was still standing by a window with his back to the room, but Denton thought that the scent had been renewed; Violet Hunt had come in briefly, probably to ask what was going on. Denton wondered what James had told her. He let go of Charlie, who rubbed his wrist and said to James's back, 'Henry, *please*. This has gone too far. It was simply a jape of Clara's that got out of—'

Denton turned him back. 'It wasn't Clara and there was no jape. Here's the deal: you're never going to show your face in England again. Got that? If you do, you're going down for the illegal importation of five Mauser automatic pistols that caused the deaths of four policemen and the wounding of others. Do you understand what that means? Do you know what it means if you're arrested and taken into an interrogation room? Don't have any illusions about how nice the English cops are when they've got somebody who caused the death of other coppers. They'll get a confession, Charlie. You may not live through it, but they'll get a confession. So my advice is, don't ever come back to England.'

'It wasn't me! It was Mary Ann. She hid them and—'

'Tell that to a sailor on a horse. Mary Ann has already told them that you brought the Mausers in, in the false bottom of a steamer trunk. Anyway, as you know, Mary Ann is a very sick woman. You know how sick, and what of. You think that anybody is going to believe you instead of her?'

Denton took a step away and leaned his buttocks on the back of a soft chair. 'I'll make sure that photographs of you go to the Special Branch tecs in Calais and Boulogne and to all the customs and port officers. Police all over the country will coop-erate—because of the guns, understand? Maybe you'll want to stay out of Germany, too; we'll send photos there. They're upset about the theft of the pistols. They don't like anarchists, and you supplied weapons to anarchists. You may want to stay out of France and Italy, too. We'll send some photos and tell them about the con games you and Mary Ann worked.' Denton took out his box of cigarettes. 'You might try South America. Or somewhere like Siam.' He took out a cigarette. 'You're cooked, Charlie.'

Charlie gave him a gorgeous smile. 'I don't believe you! You're just trying to bully me!'

'Believe what you like. But I'll do what I said.' He lit the cigarette. 'James, you have anything to add?'

James's head moved side to side and was still.

'Then we're done here.'

Denton went to the door, and James turned from the window and started out. Charlie cried, 'I can explain!' and reached out, but James went past him and through the doorway, and Denton followed.

The evening ferry pulled out of Calais under a low sky already almost black. James insisted that they go to the stern deck, initially crowded, then more and more almost private as people fled to the bar and the restaurant. The wake churned behind them, almost white, and now far away the lights of Calais and the French coast looked like little dots of warmth in a remarkably cold universe.

'I always try to see departure from this vantage,' James said. His voice was low and rather husky. He kept his hands in the pockets of his light overcoat and looked not at Denton but at what they were leaving behind. 'Things dwindling in size. Lights growing dimmer and then going out. One inevitably begins to think in sentimental clichés. "Last things", as the old words have it.' Without a change in tone or rhythm, he went on, 'I shall write no more fiction.'

Denton started to protest.

'No.' James took a hand from his coat pocket. It was too dark for Denton to see, but James fumbled with something lighter-coloured than the rail or his hands. *The letters,* Denton thought.

James leaned his forearms on the rail and looked at the distant lights. A scrap of white sailed away into the wake, then another. 'I knew my last novel was to *be* the last. I've said what I could say, as well as I could say it.' His chuckle was sardonic. More bits of paper dropped behind them. 'The reading public told me by their abstentions that I had best give it up, as well. No, I intend now to finish my book about America, then perhaps embark—I am infused with nautical metaphor this evening—on a *mémoire* of my youth, in which I find still some things of perhaps more popular interest. But long fiction, except some revision of older works—that is past.' He tore a strip of paper more vigorously, tore the strip into bits and scattered them all at once.

'I feel great sadness about Raphael. "Charlie"' Dear heaven! I know—I think I know—what you believe you saw when he was at my garden party. I "fussed" over him, did I not? I made an old fool of myself, did I not? What you probably believe is…' More paper flew behind them. 'I know what they say about me. They say I'm an old pederast, or some more vulgar term that they use. Do they not? But they're wrong. You're wrong.' He tore another strip from a letter, ripped it into bits. 'I have loved a number of people, most of them men, but I have never "consummated"—horrible word—what I felt. I have never been intimate with any creature, male or female. I have a horror of it. It seems to me not a consummation but a doom. Love, the pursuit of perfection, is in what one doesn't allow to happen, not what one believes, for one's own physical gratification, must happen.' He opened his fingers; paper sailed away.

Denton started to say that James had it all wrong, but he saw that this was not meant to be a discussion, nor was it a confession. It was an explanation, given without apology.

'I have long believed,' James said, 'that the finest behaviour comes from self-abnegation, from self-denial, from loss, not from "consummation." Physical pleasure is a cheap achievement, surely—it dignifies nothing, gives nothing value, shines no light on our inner selves. It is the *not* having that enriches, that brightens—indeed, dazzles.

'I decided long ago, and it was a *decision*, not a discovery or an accident or a revelation; I decided that it was only by denying myself in that sphere that I should be able to create great art. You may laugh; I am sure that many people would laugh. But—I don't mean to suggest that I was like some superstitious Calabrian at a roadside shrine, hanging up a silver image of a leg in hopes of buying back a broken femur from the Almighty—it was meant to be something *fine,* an ultimate and lifelong and *secret* sacrifice. From it, because of it, with its aid came my books. You see, I knew even at the beginning that if I forsook physical love then I should lose love itself, and *that* was the sacrifice. The other person, the loved one, would always drop away when it was clear what I wouldn't do.' Did he smile in the darkness? 'And they always did.'

A whole handful of paper fluttered into the wake. James had been tearing it as he talked, perhaps unaware he was doing so. Denton thought that James's notion of sacrifice probably came from deeper roots than art, but surely it was true that self-sacrifice was a kind of ultimate gauge in James's books, as violence was in Denton's. *Both very American,* and he grinned into the darkness.

'You will say,' James murmured as he let a few more scraps go, 'that it has not been worth it. I say that it has. I stand by my work as being worth its cost. Although the world will say not, will say the opposite, will say I have gone unread as well as unloved and I'm only a rather ridiculous old auntie who has friendships with young men.' He opened his fingers to let the last of the letters go. 'Young men who then betray him.' With a sideways gesture, he tossed the oilskin wallet after the letters. *'Fin!'*

He turned and took Denton's arm. 'Now let us, as they say in nautical terminology, "go below." More invitation to sentimental cliché.' He started for the door that led into the ship. In the shadow near it, a couple were kissing, oblivious to them. 'We shall both go below soon enough, I sooner than you, I think. Where there will be no concern with either books or love. Or anything else, so far as I can determine.' He chuckled, pulled at Denton's arm. 'Come.'

They went down into the ship.